CHANGING TIMES

A Ragley Story 1963–64

Jack Sheffield

CORGI BOOKS

TRANSWORLD PUBLISHERS
61–63 Uxbridge Road, London W5 5SA
www.penguin.co.uk

Transworld is part of the Penguin Random House group of companies
whose addresses can be found at global.penguinrandomhouse.com

Penguin
Random House
UK

First published in Great Britain in 2019 by Bantam Press
an imprint of Transworld Publishers
Corgi edition published 2020

A CIP catalogue record for this book
is available from the British Library.

ISBN
9780552174046

Typeset in 10.34/14.14pt Zapf Calligraphic 801 BT by Jouve (UK), Milton Keynes.
Printed and bound in Great Britain by Clays Ltd, Elcograf S.p.A.

Penguin Random House is committed to a sustainable
future for our business, our readers and our planet. This book
is made from Forest Stewardship Council® certified paper.

1 3 5 7 9 10 8 6 4 2

In memory of Tricia, a very dear friend

Contents

Acknowledgements		ix
Map		xi
Prologue		1

1	The Keeper of Secrets	3
2	Painting Rainbows	19
3	Days of Youth	34
4	From Ragley with Love	51
5	The Beatles Concert	65
6	The End of the World	83
7	The Single-Parent Nativity	100
8	A Time to Forget	116
9	The Butterfly Effect	136
10	Reaping the Whirlwind	151
11	Sweet Valentine	169

12	A Sign of Peace	187
13	The Road to Reconciliation	204
14	Difficult Decisions	222
15	The Initiation of Miss Nobbs	239
16	New Beginnings	256
17	A World Without Love	271
18	Fond Farewells	286
19	The Importance of Being Lily	304
20	Changing Times	318
	Epilogue	333

Acknowledgements

Thanks to Penguin Random House and, in particular, my editor, Molly Crawford. It was my previous editor, Bella Bosworth, who came up with the idea of a series of prequels to the *Teacher* novels and Molly has continued this work with discipline and unflagging support. Sincere thanks for bringing this novel to publication, supported by the excellent team at Transworld including Larry Finlay, Bill Scott-Kerr, Jo Williamson, Hannah Bright, Brenda Updegraff, Vivien Thompson and fellow 'Old Roundhegian' Martin Myers.

Special thanks as always go to my hard-working literary agent and long-time friend Philip Patterson of Marjacq Scripts for his encouragement, good humour and the regular updates on the state of England cricket.

I am also grateful to all those who assisted in the research for this novel – in particular: Clive Barnett, Canon Emeritus of Salisbury Cathedral, HMI (retired), member of MCC, lyricist *Smike* the musical and Fulham

FC supporter, Emsworth, Hampshire; Helen Carr, primary-school teacher and literary critic, Harrogate, Yorkshire; David Collard, business director, Francophile, agrarianist and folk musician, West Chiltington, West Sussex; Tony Greenan, Yorkshire's finest headteacher (now retired), Huddersfield, Yorkshire; Ian Haffenden, ex-Royal Pioneer Corps and custodian of Sainsbury's, Alton, Hampshire; John Kirby, ex-policeman, expert calligrapher and Sunderland supporter, Pity Me, County Durham; Roy Linley, Lead Architect, Strategy and Technology, Unilever Global IT Innovation (now retired) and Leeds United supporter, Leeds, Yorkshire; Susan Maddison, retired teacher, social historian and expert cake-maker, Harrogate, Yorkshire; Elke Pollock, German translator and gardening enthusiast, Medstead, Hampshire; John Roberts, retired railway civil engineer and film historian, York; Bob Rogers, Canon Emeritus of York and Liverpool supporter, Malton, North Yorkshire; Nikki Bloomer, dynamic events manager at Waterstones MK; the excellent Kirstie and the team at Waterstones, York; and all the staff at Waterstones, Alton, including the terrific manager Sam, Scottish travel expert Fiona and Simon (now sadly retired).

Finally, sincere thanks to my wife, Elisabeth, without whose help the *Teacher* series of novels would never have been written.

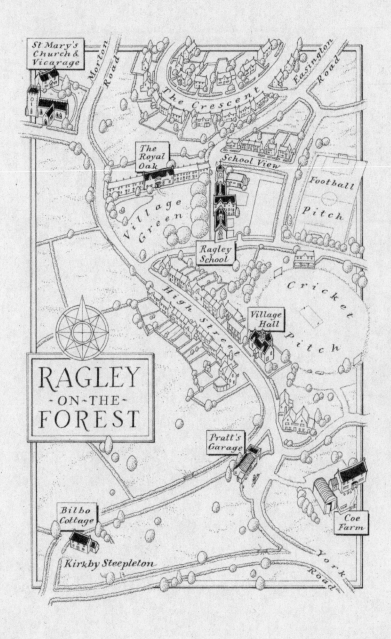

Prologue

Destiny . . . one life.

No one knows what the future might bring. In changing times there are always choices to be made. We each set out on our own journey not knowing how it will end. There may be a chance meeting or a turn in the road. The path we choose can be influenced by the kind thoughts of a friend or the harsh words of a rival. Or it could be a conversation we are not meant to hear . . . a deep secret from the past.

So it was on an August morning in 1963 when a tall, fair-haired teenager parked his bicycle outside the General Stores & Newsagent in Ragley village High Street in North Yorkshire.

It was the day of a meeting that changed his life for ever.

The bell above the door jingled and a seventeen-year-old girl appeared carrying a cardboard box full of groceries. She was tall and slim with long auburn hair and her T-shirt, hanging loosely over her tight blue jeans, proclaimed 'Peace Not War'.

As she stepped out of the shop, her black-framed spectacles, reminiscent of Buddy Holly, slipped down her nose. She released her hold on the box with her left hand to push them back into place. In the same moment the box tipped forward and a bag of onions fell out and rolled gently down the forecourt towards the pavement. The boy swooped swiftly, gathered them up, stepped towards her and placed them back in the box.

'Shall I carry that for you?'

The girl looked up, curiosity in her hazel eyes. 'Thanks, but my dad's car is just across the road.'

'I haven't seen you before.'

'No, we've just moved here. We live up the Morton road.'

'So will you be going to Easington School?' The words tumbled out.

She nodded. 'Yes, I'll be in the upper sixth from next week.'

'So will I,' said the boy.

'Anyway, my dad's waving, so must go.'

'My name's Freddie . . . Freddie Briggs.'

The girl answered with cool appraisal. 'I'm Rose . . . Rose McConnell,' and she set off towards her father's Austin 1100.

'Maybe I'll see you at school then,' added Freddie a little lamely.

She glanced over her shoulder.

'Perhaps,' she said . . . and smiled.

Chapter One

The Keeper of Secrets

It was Tuesday, 3 September 1963 and John Pruett rang the bell to begin another year at Ragley-on-the-Forest Church of England Primary School in North Yorkshire. He tied the bell rope to the metal cleat on the wall and walked to the ancient oak door that led to the playground. A kindly fifty-year-old with thinning hair, this was his eighteenth year as headteacher of the village school.

Groups of children, sunburned following their six-week summer holiday, were playing an assortment of games. Girls were bouncing tennis balls against the wall and boys were kicking an old leather football on the field. Ten-year-old Racquel Smith was teaching nine-year-old Anita Swithenbank how to do a cat's cradle with intricate movements of loops of string. Racquel's brother, eight-year-old Duggie, was peering through the metal railings that topped the school wall. He was staring up at the avenue of horse chestnut trees and dreaming of playing conkers.

John nodded knowingly at the boundless energy of the

children before him. The adventure of life stretched ahead of them and in their world of innocence they believed they would live for ever.

He blew a whistle and shouted, 'Line up smartly, boys and girls.'

Seventy children ran across the tarmac playground towards the school entrance porch and stared expectantly at their three teachers, who were standing side by side on the stone steps. The children in Class 3, the nine- and ten-year-olds, knew what to do and formed a straight line in front of John.

The deputy headteacher, Lily Feather, smiled at the children in Class 2, the seven- and eight-year-olds, who had begun to form a straggly line next to her. An attractive thirty-eight-year-old with dark brown, wavy hair, Lily loved her work and was an excellent teacher. 'Well done, everyone,' she said.

John glanced across at her and, for a moment, felt a familiar ache of sadness. He had been in love with Lily ever since he had first met her, but he knew there was no hope of his feelings being returned. It was a secret that could never be revealed.

Lily had arrived at Ragley School in 1952 and, after an eventful first year, had married Tom Feather, the local police sergeant. Tom had since progressed to the rank of inspector and they lived in the nearby village of Kirkby Steepleton. Lily was respected in Ragley and generally regarded as the school's problem-solver. However, her personal life was another matter. She looked above the heads of the children in front of her and sighed as she reflected on her life. These last eleven years had been a time of hope and healing. She smoothed her cotton print dress, which emphasized her slim figure, and smiled at the eager faces turned towards her. Another school year beckoned.

The Class 1 teacher was thirty-one-year-old Anne Grainger and the five- and six-year-olds gathered round her like baby chicks clamouring for attention. A tall, slim brunette, Anne had married local woodcarver John Grainger. After ten years of matrimony the early excitement had faded. His regular comment that they had never been *blessed with children* had become tiresome. As far as Anne was concerned, she had found contentment in her work and with the children in her care. With a gentle smile, she held the hands of the two youngest children and led the way up the entrance steps and into school.

The academic year 1963/64 had begun.

In the office the school secretary, Vera Evans, was sitting at her tidy desk and typing a letter on her Imperial typewriter. Late-summer sunshine slanted in through the high arched windows and she paused to watch the children hurrying into school. A tall, elegant forty-one-year-old, she felt that time had passed her by, as over the years the office clock with its faded Roman numerals had measured the heartbeats of her life.

When Vera wasn't in school her days were filled with the local church, the Women's Institute and the twice weekly cross-stitch club in the village hall. She lived in the vicarage in the grounds of St Mary's Church with her younger brother, the Revd Joseph Evans, a rather nervous but well-meaning man who relied entirely on his sister. So

Vera had decided long ago that she would never marry and there would be no children. Her organized life provided sufficient contentment and she was committed to helping others who were less fortunate than herself.

In fact, one of them was about to knock on her door.

'Come in,' murmured Vera, looking up from her typing.

Thirty-year-old Ruby Smith put down her mop and enamel bucket in the entrance hall and walked into the office. Her ample figure filled her brown overall and wavy chestnut hair framed her rosy cheeks.

'Scuse me, Miss Evans.'

Vera didn't like to be disturbed, but she always had sympathy for the school's hard-working assistant caretaker. 'Yes, what is it, Ruby?'

Ruby sighed deeply. 'Ah don't know if ah'm comin' or goin'.'

'And why is that?' asked Vera evenly.

'Well, Mrs Ollerenshaw's 'avin' a tea party that's jus' f'girls.'

'Yes?'

'An' she's invited my Racquel.'

'That sounds like a lovely idea.'

'But 'er daughter, Janet, 'as got measles – or so Mr Grinchley in t'chemist shop 'as been sayin'.'

'Yes, I know,' said Vera, who was aware of every child's illness in the school, as was Herbert Grinchley, village pharmacist and renowned purveyor of local gossip.

'But there's no rhyme nor reason to it,' continued Ruby. 'It doesn't mek no sense.'

As always Vera ignored the double negative. 'It's because

Mrs Ollerenshaw believes it could be helpful for girls to catch rubella – or German measles as we know it – and particularly while they are young.'

Ruby looked puzzled. 'An' why is that?'

'Because rubella can affect unborn babies in the womb if contracted during pregnancy.'

Ruby looked aghast. 'Oh 'eck. Thank you, Miss Evans, ah didn't know that . . . an' me wi' three daughters.'

'Well, we can all learn something new,' said Vera as she returned to her typing.

Ruby paused in the doorway before leaving. 'But not you, Miss Evans, 'cause my mother sez you know ever'thin',' and she hurried out.

Vera stared at the closed door. *No . . . not everything*, she thought.

It was clear to her that something was troubling Ragley's deputy headteacher. Lily had been her friend for many years, but on occasions there were awkward silences. Vera was determined to discover what it might be. After all, it was her Christian duty.

But that would keep for another day. There was work to do, and she swept the carriage return once more and returned to the satisfying *ker-ching* of her typewriter.

At 10.30 the bell rang for morning playtime and Lily was on playground duty. She collected her cup of tea from Vera, opened the entrance door and stepped out under the archway of Yorkshire stone. Above her head the date 1878 had been carved in the lintel. She headed for the welcome shade of the horse chestnut trees that bordered the school wall, which was topped with high wrought-iron railings decorated with fleurs-de-lis. Around her, children were playing in the September sunshine.

She sipped her tea and watched Anita Swithenbank and Racquel Smith winding a long skipping rope while Susan Derwood skipped lightly in and out. Together they chanted:

> *Rosy apple, lemon, pear,*
> *Bunch of roses she shall wear,*
> *Gold and silver by her side,*
> *I know who will be her bride.*

Lily smiled as she remembered the familiar skipping rhymes that had echoed around Ragley School over the years.

There was a reassuring rhythm to the seasons in her life as a village schoolteacher. She enjoyed the autumn term with its Harvest Festival, the village bonfire and the anticipation of Christmas. The spring term heralded cold weather and children playing in the snow, followed by spring flowers and the celebration of Easter. With the summer term came the warmer days, maypole dancing, school visits and sports days. As she walked down the cobbled drive she breathed in the clear Yorkshire air and leaned on the school gate, knowing she had found contentment in her work. It was a job she loved and she smiled as she took in the scene around her.

On the village green she saw sixty-six-year-old Doris Clutterbuck sitting on the bench under the weeping willow tree and feeding the ducks on the pond. She often sat there these days since she had sold her Tea Rooms to local entrepreneur Aloysius Pratt. To Doris's surprise, his daughter, Nora, had transformed it into a thriving and popular Coffee Shop.

Coffee . . . thought Doris. *Those Americans have a lot to answer for.*

Next to the green, in the centre of a row of cottages with pantile roofs and tall, rickety chimney pots, stood the white-fronted public house, The Royal Oak. The twenty-five-year-old barmaid, Sheila Bradshaw, appeared in a new skimpy dress to wipe the wooden tables on the forecourt and she gave Lily a friendly wave. When she tottered back inside on her high heels, Doris gave a frown and wondered why standards of dress were slipping.

On the other side of the village green, at the top of the High Street, Lily caught sight of twenty-eight-year-old Felicity Miles-Humphreys, the voluble producer of the Ragley Amateur Dramatic Society. She was dashing out of the Post Office clutching the hand of her frail three-year-old son, Rupert, and hurrying up the Morton road to watch *Andy Pandy*, their favourite television programme. Meanwhile, around her, the villagers were getting on with their daily lives.

Lily sighed and reflected on this quiet corner of North Yorkshire where she had carved out her new life. For many years she had been the keeper of secrets and the time was coming when all must be revealed. Ten school years had passed since she had arrived and the world around her had changed.

For this was 1963. A new teenage generation had emerged who were free from conscription and wanted to express their individuality. They were playing Cliff

Richard records on their Dansette record players and marching from the Atomic Weapons Research Establishment at Aldermaston in Berkshire to London to 'Ban the Bomb'.

In the newspapers, Mandy Rice-Davies had shocked the nation with her part in the Profumo scandal and the police were searching for Ronald Biggs following the Great Train Robbery that August. Martin Luther King had delivered his 'I have a dream' speech and Kim Philby had been named as the 'Third Man' in the Burgess and Maclean spy ring. Meanwhile, doctors were prescribing the new Sabin polio vaccine to be taken with a lump of sugar.

It was an age of dramatic change, but in the quiet village of Ragley-on-the-Forest the talk was of the forthcoming Harvest Festival, the advantages of rotary clothes-dryers and why the barmaid, Sheila Bradshaw, had started wearing short skirts.

During lunch break in the staff-room Vera was boiling a kettle of water on the single electric ring when John Pruett walked in.

'Tea, Mr Pruett?' she asked. She had always believed it was right and proper to address the headteacher in this way.

'Yes, please, Vera,' said John. 'It's been a busy morning.'

'So it has,' agreed Vera as she spooned loose-leaf tea into the pot. It seemed a good moment to commence her investigation.

'How is Lily?' she asked. 'I thought she looked a little *distracted*.'

John had no idea that Vera was fishing for information. The machinations of the female mind had always been beyond his grasp. 'Fine, I think. I thought she sang beautifully in morning assembly.'

You would, thought Vera. She had been aware of John's feelings for Lily for many years. 'I just thought she wasn't quite herself . . . clearly preoccupied with something.'

'Really?'

Vera knew she shouldn't have bothered. It was clear that the headteacher was unaware of the subtle nuances of his female colleagues. *After all*, she thought, *he's just a man*.

Shortly before afternoon school, Anne Grainger was preparing her classroom for a chalk-and-pastel art lesson when Lily walked in.

'Need a hand?' she asked.

Anne grinned. 'Yes, please.' She pointed to an old wallpaper samples book. 'Can you tear out a few more sheets?' The reverse side of the heavy-duty paper was ideal for children's drawings and paintings.

'So, how's your John these days?' asked Lily.

Anne was quiet for a moment, seeking out the right words to describe her husband. Finally she said, 'The same.'

Anne had been appointed to a full-time post at Ragley in 1954 after her marriage to John Grainger. Following a brief honeymoon, she had begun to realize that married life was not the same as a carefree courtship. John was a tall, handsome woodcarver who produced oak furniture that was made to last many lifetimes. He took a pride in his work and had developed an interest in DIY. In consequence, Anne lived in a house filled with off-cuts of timber and with sawdust in every crack and crevice. She soon learned that John liked *routine* and expected a cooked meal to be on the table every evening when he returned from work; he would presumably have demanded that Anne warm his slippers on a cold night had he owned a pair.

'Why not come round for a meal with us?' asked Lily. 'It would be good to catch up.'

Anne smiled. 'Thanks. I'll mention it to John.'

He will say no, thought Lily and continued to put a sheet of paper on each desk.

Anne decided to change the subject. 'How are your brothers?'

'George writes every week from Northern Ireland. He's a sergeant now and enjoys army life.'

'And what about Freddie?' asked Anne. 'I've heard great things about his rugby up at Easington. I saw his photograph in the *Herald*. You must be very proud.'

'Yes, I am. He's captain this year. We were all thrilled at the news. I'm just hoping it doesn't distract him from his A-levels.'

'He'll be fine,' said Anne. 'A lovely young man.'

Lily nodded, but for a moment her mind was elsewhere.

Three miles away at Easington School the second sitting for school dinner was well under way and hundreds of pupils filled the dining hall. The noise of scraping chairs and the clatter of plates was almost drowned out by the chatter of excited voices as friends were reunited after the long holiday.

Freddie Briggs had collected his tray and joined the queue. A blond, athletic seventeen-year-old, he was one of the tallest boys in the sixth form. He was served with Spam fritters, chips and beans, plus jam roly-poly pudding and purple custard. Finally, he picked up a tumbler of water and looked around for his best friend, Sam Grundy. It was then that he spotted a familiar face. Rose McConnell was sitting at one of the dining tables . . . and she was alone.

He carried his tray over to her and paused hesitantly. 'Hello again.'

Rose looked up, surprised. 'Oh, it's you.'

'How's the onions?'

Rose recalled their first meeting outside the General Stores in Ragley village. 'Fine thanks, they survived.'

'Can I sit down?'

Rose looked around at the empty seats. 'I'd be glad of the company.'

Freddie studied her for a moment. She was wearing her bookish spectacles and her dark auburn hair had been tied back in a severe ponytail.

'So how's your first day?' he asked.

'Everything's different to my last school.' She looked around at the heaving mass of pupils sharing their news on neighbouring tables. 'And I don't know anybody yet.'

Freddie took a sip of water and gave her a level stare. 'Well, you know *me*.'

Rose considered this for a moment. 'I meant *female* friends . . . ones I can talk to.'

Freddie didn't respond and began to tuck into his meal.

Rose hoped he wasn't offended. 'We moved here because my dad got a job in York in the summer.'

Freddie looked up. 'Where did you come from?'

'Doncaster. My dad works for the railway.' Rose studied him with new interest and put down her knife and fork. 'So what about you? Have you always lived here?'

'Pretty well. We moved here eleven years ago from Buckinghamshire. It was when my sister, Lily, got a teaching job at Ragley School.'

'I wish I had a sister . . . or even a brother,' said Rose. 'There's just me.'

Freddie grinned. 'I've got a brother as well. George is in the army.'

'What A-levels are you doing?' asked Rose.

'English, French and German. How about you?'

'English, History and Art.' Rose had finished her meal and stacked the plates on her tray. 'Anyway, I need to get on,' she said. 'I've got an art tutorial.'

Freddie glanced up at Rose. 'I've got PE, then double English.'

Rose took a sheet of paper from her satchel and studied it. 'English . . . with Mr Morris?'

'Yes,' said Freddie, nodding with enthusiasm.

'What's he like?'

'He's great. You'll enjoy his lessons. He's also our rugby coach.'

Rose appeared unimpressed. 'I'm more into hockey.'

'Well, see you later then,' said Freddie, a little too eagerly.

Rose gave him a measured look. 'Maybe,' she said and picked up her satchel.

*

It was afternoon break and Vera had prepared refreshments in the staff-room when Lily walked in.

Vera smiled. 'How are you, Lily?'

'Fine, thank you, Vera. A busy first day.'

'Would you like a cup of tea?'

Lily sat down in one of the comfortable armchairs. 'Love one, thank you.'

'By the way,' said Vera as she poured the tea carefully through a strainer, 'choir practice tomorrow evening. Will you be able to make it?'

Lily was a mezzo-soprano and added much to what was, in Vera's opinion, a rather mixed bag of a church choir.

'Yes, I'll be there and I'm coming in with Millicent. I thanked her for the beautiful hassock in memory of my mother.'

'It is rather special, isn't it? She's been doing it on and off for a few years.'

Millicent Merryweather was a dear friend of Vera's and a member of the Ragley cross-stitch club. She was also a neighbour of Lily's and lived in Bilbo Cottage in the nearby village of Kirkby Steepleton. As a regular churchgoer, she used one of the padded kneelers, or hassocks, when she prayed. It seemed an appropriate way to remember Florence Briggs.

'It's a really thoughtful gift,' said Lily.

'Yes, I miss your mother,' said Vera quietly. 'A lovely lady.'

Lily pursed her lips and said nothing. Her reminiscences were very different.

It had come as a great shock when Lily's mother,

Florence, was killed in the terrible London train disaster of 1957. Her sister had moved to Ramsgate and, on the evening of 4 December, following a pre-Christmas visit, Florence was one of ninety people killed when two trains collided and a bridge collapsed. The villagers of Kirkby Steepleton and Ragley mourned and Joseph Evans had conducted the funeral service.

Lily and her husband, Tom, had decided to continue living in Laurel Cottage, which they had shared with Florence since their marriage. They wanted Freddie, a twelve-year-old at that time, to retain some stability in his life by completing his secondary education at Easington School and then, hopefully, moving on to university. At first it had been hard for Lily, given the memories of her difficult relationship with her mother, but Freddie's needs were greater. As the years passed by it appeared to be the right decision.

'So ... you seem a little *preoccupied*, Lily,' said Vera as she picked up the tea strainer and poured more tea. 'Can I help in any way?'

Lily stared down at her cup and saucer. 'That's kind, Vera, but I'm fine.'

'Well, I'm here if you need a listening ear.'

Lily looked up and gave a hesitant smile. She knew Vera was fishing for information, but she also knew the time wasn't yet right for her secret to be revealed.

The bell rang for the end of school and Mrs Violet Fawnswater arrived in Anne's classroom to collect her five-year-old son, Tobias.

'Hello, darling, have you been a good boy?'

After a brief moment to collect his thoughts, Tobias replied, 'Yes, Mummy.'

While Mrs Fawnswater went out to the cloakroom to collect her son's coat, Tobias looked up at Anne. 'Saying something nice is being polite, isn't it, Miss? Even if you don't mean it?'

Before Anne could answer, Mrs Fawnswater hurried back in. 'Now, let me give you a hug.'

The ever-practical Tobias gave his mother a considered look. 'I'd rather have a KitKat,' he said with sincerity.

She bent down to button up his coat. 'I do love you, darling.'

'Thanks, Mummy, I love me too.'

Mrs Fawnswater, blushing slightly, looked up at Anne. 'Well, I always taught him to be honest.'

'And polite,' added Anne with a smile.

It was six o'clock and in the pretty village of Kirkby Steepleton, Inspector Tom Feather arrived home in his police car and pulled on to the driveway of Laurel Cottage. Over six feet tall and with broad shoulders, he was a formidable presence in his uniform. A year away from his fortieth birthday, his wavy black hair was showing the first hint of grey.

'I'm home,' he shouted from the hallway.

'In the kitchen,' replied Lily.

'I'll get changed,' and he went upstairs to take off his uniform.

Freddie was helping prepare supper.

Lily looked up at him, her eyes full of pride in this young man. 'Thanks for your help,' she said.

He grinned. His mind was elsewhere.

When Tom came back down, Lily was frying sausages and Freddie was chopping onions. Tom gave Lily a peck on the cheek and smiled. 'So how did the first day go?'

'Fine, thanks. Apart from most of the children having forgotten how to write, it's been a successful day. What about you?'

There was only so much Tom could divulge about his work. 'Usual,' he said. 'A few arrests for shoplifting in Northallerton.'

Freddie looked up from his chopping board. The onions were making his eyes smart and he wiped away a tear. 'Anyone I might know?' he asked.

'No,' said Tom. He went to stand beside Freddie. They were the same height now. 'Watch out, Freddie,' he said, patting him on the shoulder. 'Even tough rugby players shed a tear when chopping onions.'

'Lean back from the chopping board,' advised Lily. 'Tom's right. Onions do make you cry.'

Freddie thought back to his first meeting with Rose McConnell outside the General Stores.

'Not always,' he murmured and gave a secret smile.

Chapter Two

Painting Rainbows

'Look, Mam, a rainbow!' shouted an excited Duggie Smith. It was Friday, 20 September and there had been a sudden brief, heavy shower. A rainbow lit up the primrose-blue sky.

Ruby Smith glanced out of the window from the chaos of her kitchen. Preparing breakfast for her five children was always a chore. The eldest, twelve-year-old Andy, had already left to catch the school bus to Easington and was soaked to the skin by the time he reached Ragley High Street.

Ruby scraped out the last of the porridge and put it in a bowl for Duggie. 'Yes, luv, an' there'll be a pot o' gold at t'end of it.'

'A pot o' gold?' asked Duggie, suddenly interested.

'So they say,' said Ruby. 'That's where y'find buried treasure.'

Duggie's eyes were wide. '*Buried treasure*?'

'Yes,' said Ruby, 'at t'end of a rainbow. Now, come an' sit down an' eat y'breakfast.'

Her youngest child, one-year-old Natasha, had crawled under the kitchen table and was collecting stray lumps of porridge from the floor and licking her chubby fingers. Ruby scooped her up and wiped the child's pink cheeks with a grubby tea towel.

Meanwhile, Racquel, a competent ten-year-old and the image of her mother, was helping her three-year-old sister, Sharon, to eat a final spoonful of porridge. 'Mam, we did rainbows in our weather project when ah were in Mrs Feather's class. She said y'can't find t'end of a rainbow 'cause it's like tryin' t'walk to t'end of yer own shadow.'

Ruby was impressed. Racquel worked hard at school. She looked down at Duggie and shook her head. 'Y'see what y'learn if y'listen to y'teacher? Now, come an' wash yer 'ands before y'go t'school.'

But Duggie had other things on his mind – playing conkers with his friend, Chris Wojciechowski, climbing trees ... and now there was something else that had caught his imagination: *buried treasure*.

In John Pruett's classroom the children were sitting in four rows behind desks with sloping lids, each with an inkwell, chanting their tables in loud voices as they did every morning. This was followed by copying a poem in their best cursive handwriting, using dip-in pens and blotting paper. Writing in black ink could be a messy business, as nine-year-old Norman Barraclough soon discovered. His fingers were stained with ink but they would have to be clean before he went home to help his father, the Ragley and Morton fishmonger.

John Pruett firmly believed in the Three 'Rs' and

learning by rote. A one-way pedagogy was the rock on which he based his teaching. The result was that the children were uninspired and subdued ... but they knew their tables.

In contrast, the children in Class 2 were full of awe and wonder. Lily had collected a list of 'rainbow words' on the blackboard and was now using a prism to break sunlight into the colours of the spectrum. She explained that water droplets acted like tiny prisms, resulting in the colours we see in a rainbow. She was so pleased with the children's responses.

'It's like magic, Miss,' said eight-year-old Stevie Cole-clough.

Lily smiled. 'It is, Stevie, it really is.'

Meanwhile, in Anne's class four five-year-olds were playing on an off-cut of carpet near the home corner. Margery Flathers and Jane Grantham were dressing two dolls, while Tobias Fawnswater and Clint Ramsbottom were connecting pieces of Lego.

Margery looked at Clint. 'Would y'like t'play with one of our dolls?'

'Yes, please,' said Clint.

'What about you, Toby?' asked Jane.

Tobias paused in his Lego building and frowned, unsure where this was leading.

'Well *you* can choose,' said Jane. Her mother had told her it was important to share, but she had responded by saying that boys were *different*.

'Yes,' said Margery, a little more forcefully. 'Which one would y'like?'

Tobias nodded thoughtfully and came to a decision.

'The one that does the dishes and the ironing and cleans my shoes.'

Margery studied her classmate phlegmatically and reached a conclusion. 'Play wi' y'Lego, Toby.'

It was the end of assembly and ten-year-old Colin Appleyard had recited the school prayer in a calm, solemn voice:

> *Dear Lord*
> *This is our school, let peace dwell here,*
> *Let the room be full of contentment,*
> *Let love abide here, love of one another,*
> *Love of life itself, and love of God.*
> *Amen.*

'Very good, Colin, and well done, boys and girls,' said the Revd Joseph Evans, who came into the school each week to take assembly and read Bible stories with the children, 'for when we pray we speak to God.'

Six-year-old Trevor Poskitt put up his hand.

Joseph was encouraged by the little boy's enthusiasm. 'Yes, Trevor. What would you like to say?'

'It's my mam, sir,' said Trevor.

'And what about your mother?' asked Joseph in a soft, reassuring voice.

'She talks t'God.'

'That's wonderful,' said Joseph. 'And when does she speak to God?'

'When we need more money, sir.'

It was at times like this that Joseph wished he could be a librarian.

On the High Street, Ruby Smith pushed little Natasha in her pram towards the forecourt of the General Stores. She parked it next to two metal plaques screwed to the wall advertising 'WILLS'S CUT GOLDEN BAR TOBACCO' and 'TIZER THE APPETIZER'.

Forty-six-year-old Prudence Golightly, the diminutive shopkeeper, smiled as the bell rang over the door and Ruby walked in carrying her youngest child.

'Good morning, Ruby, and how's little Natasha?'

'Teethin' summat rotten, Miss Golightly.'

'Oh dear,' said Prudence, 'and she looks so bonny with her rosy cheeks.'

'M'mam's bought 'er this teethin' ring an' that 'elps.'

Natasha was chomping vigorously on a pink plastic ring and drooling.

'And how is your mother?'

Fifty-year-old Agnes Bancroft lived with Ruby and her family in their council house at 7 School View and gave her daughter unstinting support in difficult times.

'She's fine, thank you. She were watching t'*Woodentops* on telly wi' Natasha afore she left t'mek them fancy chocolates in York.'

Agnes had worked in the Rowntree's factory for many years.

'A hard-working lady,' said Prudence. 'Yes, *Watch with Mother* is really popular. When the shop is quiet I let Jeremy watch it.'

Ruby looked up at the large and beautifully dressed teddy bear that was the village shopkeeper's pride and joy. He was sitting on his usual shelf above the counter, beneath two advertisements for Hudson's Soap and Carter's Little Liver Pills. Dressed in a checked shirt and black trousers, the name 'Jeremy' was neatly stitched in royal blue cotton on the pocket of his white apron.

It was well known in the village that Jeremy had been named after Prudence's late fiancé, a young fighter pilot who had been killed in the Battle of Britain in 1940.

Such was Jeremy's status as the constant companion to Prudence, Ruby considered it perfectly normal for the village shopkeeper to sit her teddy bear in front of the television.

'So, what's it to be, Ruby?'

'Jus' some washin' powder an' a loaf, please.'

Ruby rummaged in her purse and put a few coins on the counter.

'And what's Ronnie doing these days?' asked Prudence.

Ronnie Smith, Ruby's unemployed, bone-idle husband, spent most of his time in The Royal Oak and the betting shop. When Ruby had left the house that morning he was sitting up in bed smoking a Wills's Woodbine and reading the *Sporting Life*.

'T'usual,' said Ruby forlornly.

'Oh dear,' replied Prudence with feeling.

It was after school dinner when Lily walked into the staff-room. Vera was preparing a pot of tea and John Pruett was engrossed in a newspaper.

'You look happy,' remarked Vera. She thought it was a change to see Lily so animated.

'It's been a terrific morning,' said Lily, bright with enthusiasm. 'The children were excited about the rainbow. It proved a great opportunity for language development.'

John glanced up from his *Times Educational Supplement*. 'Rainbows . . . Yes, they're fascinating.'

'Wonderful colours,' said Vera as she poured milk from a third of a pint bottle into a china jug.

'It's simply a spectrum of light,' explained John. 'It appears in the sky when sunlight is refracted through raindrops or other drops of moisture in the Earth's atmosphere.'

As Vera poured the tea she and Lily nodded knowingly and shared a conspiratorial smile.

John put down his paper and looked at Lily. 'By the way, how's your brother George? Is he still in Ireland?'

'Yes,' said Lily. 'He seems to enjoy his life and writes long letters to me.'

Thirty-year-old George Briggs had remained in the army following his National Service.

'I saw him in his uniform the last time he was on leave,' said Vera. 'A fine young man.'

John Pruett had been in the Royal Engineers during the Second World War and always showed an interest in military matters. 'I read there was some concern that the Catholics were being marginalized because the Protestants have a two thirds majority.'

Lily nodded. 'George said he thought there might be trouble on the horizon, particularly as only rate-payers have the right to vote.'

'But that seems perfectly sensible,' said Vera.

'Except if you own a property in more than one ward,' said John. 'Then you can vote more than once.'

'Up to six times apparently,' said Lily.

Vera sipped her tea. 'Yes, I can see why that would be a problem.'

Lily nodded. 'Also, in his last letter George mentioned police harassment against Catholics.'

'Well, let's pray they can resolve it soon,' said the ever-trusting Vera.

'Hope so,' said Lily. 'I wouldn't want George to be in the middle of a conflict.'

Lily gave a deep sigh and Vera picked up her Harvest Festival notice, while John merely looked thoughtful.

Meanwhile, on the High Street thirty-year-old Muriel Tonks, the curvaceous wife of a local farmer and mother of seven-year-old Henry, walked into Diane's Hair Salon.

Diane Wigglesworth smiled at her regular customer, who always enjoyed sharing a bit of gossip.

''Ow are you, Muriel?' she asked as she lit up a cigarette.

'Fair t'middlin',' replied Muriel. 'A few ups an' downs.' She settled on the chair in front of the large mirror.

'What's it t'be?' asked Diane.

Muriel studied the cut-out magazine pictures that were taped around the frame of the mirror. 'Usual,' she decided. 'A 'lizabeth Taylor.'

'Comin' up,' said Diane, as she reached for her box of rollers. 'So 'ow's 'Arold?'

'T'same. Face like a wet weekend.'

Diane nodded knowingly. 'Men,' she said with feeling and began to brush Muriel's hair. 'So . . . any news?'

Muriel pondered before answering. 'Ah los' m'charm bracelet again yesterday. Must 'ave dropped off somewhere. Mebbe when ah were walkin' t'dog. It were t'one 'Arold bought when we were on 'oneymoon in Cornwall.'

'Worth much?'

'Not really. Jus' a nice chain wi' one o' them Cornish imps on it, bit like a leprechaun. Ah lost it a year ago an' then ah found it again. It were down t'back o' t'sofa. 'Arold were thrilled. Said it's s'pposed t'bring us luck.'

'An' did it?'

Muriel smiled. 'It did. T'day after 'e fell off a ladder an' broke 'is leg.'

'Flippin' 'eck!' exclaimed Diane. 'An' why were that lucky?'

''Cause 'e couldn't milk cows no more.'

'So what did y'do?'

'We 'ad to advertise in the *'Erald.*'

'Did y'get any replies?'

'Jus' the one,' said Muriel.

Diane paused and looked in the mirror. 'So . . . what's 'e like then?'

Muriel was smiling. 'Tall, dark an' 'andsome.'

'Oh yes.' Diane stopped brushing, keen to hear more.

'Ah tek 'im a flask o' tea ev'ry mornin'.'

Diane nodded knowingly. 'What's 'e like at milkin'?'

'Dunno, but 'e sez 'e 'as a tattoo on 'is bum.'

'On 'is bum?' Diane stared in the mirror. 'What's it like?'

''Is bum or 'is tattoo?'

'Well, *both* ah s'ppose.'

The two women shared a secret smile. 'Ah'll tell you nex' time ah'm in.'

In Class 2 Lily was preparing the tables for an afternoon painting lesson when Anne called in.

'Snap!' said Anne with a grin when she saw the vivid collection of poster colours and powder paint. 'It's got to be "Rainbows".'

Lily smiled as she studied the collection of bristle brushes and hoped they would last another year. 'This morning certainly captured the imagination.' She nodded towards the blackboard and the list of rainbow words.

'Impressive,' said Anne, then looked at the battered paint pots. 'Mixing indigo should be fun.'

During afternoon break Anne and Lily were in the staff-room and John was on duty.

'Did you see that John was following the rainbow theme?' asked Anne.

'No, what's he doing – poems or painting?'

'Actually a poem, the one by William Wordsworth.'

'"The Rainbow",' said Lily. 'Yes, we had to learn it off by heart at school. "The child is the father of the man" and all that.'

'The children were copying it out in their best hand-writing.'

'Oh well, John *is* keen on handwriting,' said Lily.

Obsessive, thought Anne, but didn't want to say it out loud.

They sat back and Lily smiled.

'What is it?' asked Anne.

'Just thinking of that D. H. Lawrence novel, *The Rainbow*. Did you read it?'

Anne grinned. 'Yes, under the covers when I was a teenager. Banned because it was sexually explicit . . . so I *had* to read it.'

'I suppose it seems tame these days,' mused Lily.

Anne shook her head sadly. 'Depends who you married,' she murmured.

There was a silence while the two women thought of their respective husbands.

Finally, Lily decided to change the subject. 'We ought to be thinking of the music for Harvest Festival.'

Half an hour after the bell had rung for the end of school, Lily was collecting her coat from the cloakroom area between the school office and the staff-room.

John Pruett was sitting at his desk. 'You look in a hurry,' he said.

Lily smiled. 'Tom doesn't surprise me very often, but we're going to the cinema tonight.'

John was interested. He would have loved to go to the cinema with his dynamic and attractive colleague. 'What are you going to see?' he asked wistfully.

Lily rummaged in her shoulder bag and held up a copy of the *Easington Herald & Pioneer*. '*Cleopatra* with Elizabeth Taylor and Richard Burton. It's supposed to be spectacular.'

'So I heard,' said John.

'You ought to go, John. Here, you can keep this. Read the reviews.'

He took the newspaper from her and scanned the films page.

'Rome's conquest of Egypt is a dramatic story,' he said. 'I always felt a little sad for Cleopatra and her attempt to manipulate Julius Caesar and Mark Antony in order to save her empire.'

Lily was in too much of a hurry to discuss the politics of Ancient Egypt. 'Anyway, must go. Bye, John,' and she skipped out of the office.

John sat at his desk and spread out the newspaper before him. The final line of the review read: *'This three-some is one of the most famous and gloriously powerful love triangles ever to be captured on film.'*

He looked out of the window as Lily started up her smart almond-green Morris Minor 1000 Traveller, a recent gift from Tom Feather. As she drove away, John sighed and thought of another love triangle.

Outside school Duggie Smith and Chris Wojciechowski were playing conkers.

'My mam says there's a pot o' gold at t'end of a rainbow,' confided Duggie.

Chris stared down at the shattered remains of the conker at his feet. Suddenly his face lit up. 'Ah know where t'end of it was. Ah saw it this morning from m'bedroom window. It were clear as day.'

'Flippin' 'eck!' exclaimed Duggie. 'Let's go,' and the two intrepid explorers ran off to the woods beyond the Ragley cricket field.

It was Chris who spotted the little plastic leprechaun amidst the detritus of fallen leaves. 'Hey, Duggie, look what I've found.' He picked up a bracelet on which hung the tiny figure. 'What is it?'

Duggie's eyes were like saucers. 'Dunno, but it mus' be t'treasure 'cause it's at t'end of a rainbow.'

'What shall we do, Duggie?'

Duggie took out his penknife and opened the blade. 'We can dig an 'ole wi' this an' bury it.'

Chris nodded. Understanding dawned. ''Cause that's what y'do wi' treasure.' He had an empty blue cone of a paper bag. It was all that remained of the two ounces of aniseed balls he had bought that morning on the way to school. 'We can put it in this.'

As the two excited boys ran home, they waved to Mrs Muriel Tonks, who was walking Max, her cocker spaniel. Muriel had a smile on her face when she waved back. She was thinking of their handsome cowman . . . and a certain tattoo.

In the vicarage Joseph Evans switched on the television set. It was *Ready Steady Go!* with Keith Fordyce, who was about to introduce Acker Bilk. As Vera walked in she heard the lively disc jockey invite the viewers to find out 'what's swinging this weekend'.

'Oh dear,' said Vera. 'What a dreadful use of English. Please switch over, Joseph. It's almost six twenty-five.'

'Six twenty-five?'

'Yes, Joseph, *Gardening Club*.'

Vera settled down in her favourite chair, while Percy Thrower discussed the merits of Michaelmas daisies, heleniums, sedums and red-hot pokers.

'I think I'll check on my home-made wine,' said Joseph

a little forlornly. He left Vera engrossed in late-autumn colour in the flower garden.

'I quite like Acker Bilk,' he murmured to himself.

It was late evening and in Laurel Cottage Tom and Lily were hanging up their coats in the entrance hall.

'Thanks, Tom – a wonderful film.'

Tom smiled. 'Burton and Taylor are really special, aren't they? Great chemistry between them . . . a bit like us.'

Lily stretched up and kissed him on the cheek.

'Coffee?' he asked.

'Yes, please,' said Lily.

Freddie was still busy with his homework at the kitchen table when Tom walked in and began to fill the kettle. 'Fancy a hot drink?'

'Thanks,' murmured Freddie, clearly engrossed in a French translation.

Tom left a mug of coffee on the table for Freddie and carried two more into the lounge. He closed the door quietly.

Lily sipped her coffee thoughtfully and wondered why Tom was so quiet.

'What is it?' she asked.

'Just thinking.' He nodded towards the kitchen. 'Are you going to say something?'

There was a long silence until finally Lily replied in a hushed whisper, 'Not now. He's got his A-levels. You can see how hard he's working.'

Tom shook his head. 'You said that two years ago when it was his O-levels.'

'It's difficult. There never seems to be a right time. Maybe next year.'

'So next summer?' asked Tom.

There was another long pause. She stared out of the window, where a crescent moon hung in an indigo sky.

Finally she said, 'Yes, next summer.' Her thoughts were drifting now on an ebbing tide of fear. There would be a time to reveal the truth and she could not foresee the outcome.

A day that had begun with painting rainbows was ending under dark clouds in a firmament of uncertainty.

Chapter Three

Days of Youth

'I think Freddie has a girlfriend,' said Lily as she stared out of the leaded bedroom window of Laurel Cottage.

It was a pale autumn morning on Friday, 4 October and a grey dawn light covered the land. The season was changing and fallen leaves covered the fields like scattered souls. In the garden beneath her, robins were claiming their territory and the bounty of wild fruit filled the hedgerows. However, for Lily, the wonders of this early autumn morning were not uppermost in her mind.

Tom was non-committal. 'Oh yes?'

He was aware there had been a few girls in Freddie's life over the past couple of years, but had never interfered.

'I was in the chemist's shop and Mr Grinchley mentioned it.'

'Yes, he doesn't miss much,' murmured Tom as he got out of bed.

'He said they had been seen going into the Coffee Shop in Ragley.'

Tom stretched. A busy day lay ahead.

'And when they came out they were holding hands.'

'It must be love,' said Tom with a smile as he headed for the bathroom.

Lily continued to gaze out of the window. Affairs of the heart could be complicated, as she knew only too well.

At 7 School View Ruby was also looking out of her kitchen window and thinking of the day ahead. With five children to feed and her husband still in bed, it was the usual hectic start to the morning.

The school caretaker, fifty-seven-year-old Edna Trott, was unable to do most of the work owing to an arthritic condition, which meant that many of the cleaning duties fell to Ruby. There was talk that Edna might retire soon and Ruby would take over. According to Mr Grinchley, who appeared to know everyone's business, it would be a blessing for all concerned.

Meanwhile, on the radio, Alan Freeman was playing the popular new song by Brian Poole and the Tremeloes, 'Do You Love Me' Ruby gave a wry smile as she scraped a piece of blackened toast and wondered about her life. Those youthful days were long gone, and now poverty and hard work were taking their toll.

When John Pruett walked into the school office, Vera was turning the handle of the Banda machine and producing neat foolscap copies of a Harvest Festival notice for the children to take home. The church service was in two days' time and this was a final reminder.

'Good morning, Vera,' said John.

'Good morning, Mr Pruett,' replied Vera without looking up.

John could see Vera was in concentration mode and sat quietly at his desk to check the morning's post. Vera had placed it in a neat pile alongside a note indicating which letters were important. Her efficiency was remarkable and he knew he would be lost without her.

Vera had the process of producing duplicated letters down to a fine art and she regarded the machine as a wonder of the modern age. The master sheet could be typed, drawn or written upon and the second sheet was covered with a layer of wax that resembled carbon paper. She had filled the machine with duplicating fluid consisting of an equal mix of isopropanol and methanol, hence the slightly addictive odour enjoyed by all the staff. Finally, she had attached the master sheet to the revolving drum and was turning the handle in a metronomic fashion while quietly humming the tune of Elgar's 'Nimrod' from his *Enigma Variations*. Along with Johann Pachelbel's 'Canon in D Major', it was perfect for such a repetitive task and for forgetting the worries of the world.

Vera took a copy to the window and held it up. 'Perfect!' she said without a hint of modesty. She approved of the aniline purple text, particularly as mauve and purple were her favourite colours. Also, yesterday evening she had watched the *Horse of the Year Show* on television featuring her favourite commentator, Dorian Williams. So Vera was in a contented mood, with perhaps one predictable exception. Her brother, Joseph, had left preparations for one of the most important church events of the year a little late.

In Vera's opinion, he was spending far too much time on his dreadful home-made wine.

At 11.45 a.m. Ruby was in the school hall setting out the dining tables when Mrs Emily Poskitt walked in to collect her six-year-old son, Trevor, for his visit to the dentist.

"Ello, Ruby, 'ow's things wi' you?'

'Middlin',' replied Ruby without conviction.

'Ah've jus' seen your Ronnie at t'bus stop.'

Ruby shook her head. "E'll be goin' int'York to t'bookies.'

Emily nodded knowingly. 'Ah guessed as much.'

Ruby sighed. Her cheeks were flushed with the effort of lifting the heavy tables and chairs. 'This mornin' when 'e went out 'e said he'd be back in two shakes of a cow's tail.'

Lamb's tail, thought Emily, but didn't correct her friend. 'Anyway ah'm 'ere for our Trevor. Ah'm tekkin' 'im to t'torture chamber.'

The torture chamber was the local name for the dentist in Easington, who made Sweeney Todd look like a choirboy.

'Good luck, Emily,' said Ruby with feeling.

Lily was expecting Mrs Poskitt, so she had Trevor standing by the classroom door. 'Here's Trevor, Mrs Poskitt. He's worked hard this morning. We're learning about pounds, shillings and pence.'

Mrs Poskitt was a Yorkshirewoman who told it as it was. 'Ah'm not tryin' t'teach you y'job, Mrs Feather, but t'best way t'teach our Trevor 'bout money is t'borrow some off 'im.' With that she strode off leaving a smiling Lily behind her.

At lunchtime Anne Grainger and Lily were discussing television programmes. Ragley School was the proud owner of a television set with a grainy black-and-white picture. It was a monster and, with its huge cabinet, was moved around with great effort on its tubular legs and squeaky castors. John Pruett would boast frequently that he had been using television programmes for schools since 1957, even though it was Lily and Anne who had done the persuading.

This morning his class had watched the BBC programme *Indoors and Out: Man and His Home*, while Lily and Anne were keen for their children to end the afternoon with the ITV programme *Story Box*. It featured a nature-study theme and both Lily and Anne agreed it added variety to the curriculum.

They were discussing this when Mrs Fawnswater walked in to deliver a recorder for her son Tobias. Anne Grainger's recorder group practised each Friday lunchtime.

'Please could you give this to Tobias, Mrs Grainger?' asked Mrs Fawnswater, slightly out of breath.

'Of course,' said Anne.

Mrs Fawnswater fumbled in her pocket. 'And if he does well, could you give him these?' She held out a packet of Rowntree's Tooty Frooties. 'It's so important to encourage him.'

Lily stepped in. 'Perhaps *you* could ask him after school how he's got on and give them to him yourself?' She delivered this request with a straight face and absolute aplomb.

Mrs Fawnswater looked a little crestfallen and stared at the packet of sweets. 'They're his favourite. In fact, these days he doesn't want to eat anything unless it's been advertised on television.'

She wandered off and Lily murmured, 'The power of advertising.'

Anne raised her eyebrows and grinned. 'Go to work on an egg,' she said as she hurried off for recorder practice.

At the end of school, John Pruett was in the office. Ruby had finished her cleaning and the school was silent apart from the ticking of the ancient clock and the scurrying of tiny mice in the distant dark corners of the hall.

John unlocked the bottom drawer of his desk and took out the large, leather-bound school logbook. Then he opened it to the next clean page, filled his fountain pen with ink and wrote the date. It was a ritual he completed most evenings, but particularly at the end of a week. The whole history of the school was there and, as he was writing, it occurred to him that he was merely the custodian of the village school until someone came to take his place. He wondered who that might be.

Perhaps Lily, he thought.

He looked out of the window at his car. It was a 1946 Ford Anglia, a black two-door saloon, and, although he polished it frequently, it was definitely showing its age.

There had been a time when he had hoped that he and Lily could drive to Fountains Abbey for a picnic, or to Scarborough for a fish-and-chip supper, but that was never to be. He sighed and returned to the events of the past week.

After school, Lily called in at the General Stores. As she approached the counter, Mrs Fawnswater was being served. She paid sixpence for a *TV Times*. The front cover featured Roger Moore as *The Saint* alongside a vivacious Jackie Collins.

Violet Fawnswater had her mother with her, a very short and decidedly plump lady, and she was holding Tobias by his hand.

Suddenly Tobias asked, 'Were you ever a baby, Mummy?'

Violet was keen to demonstrate in front of Ragley's deputy headteacher that she was both caring and sympathetic, a modern sixties mother. She crouched down and gave her son a benevolent smile. 'Yes, darling, once *I* was in Grandma's tummy.'

Tobias considered this for a moment and stared at his corpulent grandmother. 'So is that why Grandma's tummy is like that?'

Mrs Fawnswater gritted her teeth and hurried out with Tobias and her mother in tow.

'Oh dear,' said Prudence. 'Out of the mouths of babes . . .'

Lily smiled. 'Prudence, I just need something quick and easy for Freddie's tea before he goes out.'

Prudence took a tin from the shelf behind her. 'How about this? Heinz Macaroni in Cheese Sauce. That should do the job.'

'Excellent.' Lily put a shilling on the counter. Prudence rang the till and gave Lily a ha'penny change. 'Must rush,' said Lily. 'Tom's dropping him off in York on his way to a police training meeting.'

As she walked out she almost bumped into Stan Coe, the local pig farmer. Like his pigs, Stan wallowed in his own filth. The stench of decay that hung over him resembled his damp, putrid sties.

'Excuse me, please,' said Lily sharply as he blocked her

way. He was developing a large paunch following his regular intake of best bitter at the Pig & Ferret.

'Y'still a bit uppity then, Mrs Teacher,' sneered Stan.

Lily recoiled from this offensive man with his rank smell and fetid breath.

'Stay away from me!' she warned in a voice that brooked no argument, then she hurried to her car.

'Proper little Goody Two-Shoes,' Stan called after her.

As she drove home she recalled that day, ten years ago, when Stan in a drunken state had attempted to molest her. She had never revealed the details to Tom, fearful of what he might do and the impact on his job.

By the time she arrived home she had managed to control her fury.

In one of the large new bungalows on the Morton road, Rose McConnell was eating a hasty meal.

'So who's this boy you're meeting?' asked her father.

Brian McConnell was a tall, athletic forty-two-year-old. He had moved from Doncaster to take up a new appointment as senior manager in the York Carriageworks with a brief to progress the development and construction of new rolling stock. A shrewd man, he was aware that the steam era was drawing to a close, particularly after the Beeching cuts, while new diesel engines were being developed.

'Freddie Briggs,' said Rose, blushing slightly as she finished off her beans on toast. 'He's in my English class.'

Mary McConnell smiled at her husband. 'He's also captain of the rugby team, Brian. You've seen his photograph in the *Herald*.' Mary, tall and slim, appeared to be an older version of her daughter.

Brian nodded appreciatively. As a young man and before he moved to Doncaster he had lived in Grassington in the Yorkshire Dales and played for Upper Wharfedale Rugby Union Club.

'Sounds a good lad,' he said.

'You need to leave now,' said Mary, glancing up at the clock, 'and then collect Rose at ten thirty.'

Brian had grown used to being his daughter's chauffeur over the years, mainly to hockey and netball matches.

'Fine,' he said. 'Shall we go?'

As they walked out to the car he thought Rose was wearing a little too much make-up, but he had learned to hold his tongue. Soon they were driving down the A19 towards York and the Odeon Cinema.

Meanwhile, in the vicarage, the Revd Joseph Evans had struggled with his Harvest sermon and sought refuge in one of the outbuildings, where he was rummaging through a jumble of bottles of home-made wine. Labels written in his spidery handwriting included 'Pea Pod Supreme', 'Rosehip Revelation' and 'Strawberry Sensation'. Joseph was far from modest when naming his wine.

It was unfortunate the results had the distinctive bouquet of paint stripper. No one doubted his generosity, as his clerical colleagues were all too aware when he gave them a complimentary bottle. They would smile, offer thanks and pour the contents down the sink when they returned home.

In contrast, Vera was in her beautifully organized pantry. She had switched on the radio, tuned it to the BBC Home Service and was listening to Max Bruch's Violin

Concerto No. 1 in G Minor. In her disciplined world she was content. She checked the contents of the shelves, which were filled with neat, serried rows of large Kilner jars containing a variety of fruit, the results of a labour of love from her bountiful garden.

She selected a jar of apricots in order to prepare one of her specialities, a Harvest Festival cake. Then, on her ancient scales, she weighed cherries, sultanas and prunes. After putting the mixture into a large bowl she poured in cider and left it to soak overnight. Finally, she put away her scales and the set of brass imperial weights and cleaned the worktop until it was spotless.

The grandfather clock in the spacious hallway chimed eight o'clock and Vera decided to seek out Joseph. She had promised to check his sermon before they settled down to watch one of her favourite television programmes. It was *Dr Finlay's Casebook*, with the perceptive Bill Simpson as the inquisitive doctor. However, when she opened the back door and peered in the direction of the outbuildings, she heard the distant clinking of bottles. She frowned, retired to the lounge and settled to watch another medical drama set in the Scottish town of Tannochbrae during the late 1920s.

In the back row of the cinema, Freddie was facing a dilemma. He wanted to put his arm around Rose's shoulders but didn't wish to appear too eager. Also, he wasn't sure what the response might be.

It was clear Rose was enjoying the film, *The Great Escape*, which turned out to be both entertaining and tense, with moments of high drama. Steve McQueen, as a daredevil

American captain, along with the measured and thoughtful Richard Attenborough, playing the part of a British squadron leader, were leading a group of Allied soldiers in an escape attempt from a German POW camp.

However, Freddie had other things on his mind. He was an intelligent young man and had decided that on a first date a non-tactile approach was advisable. Meanwhile, Rose was wondering why her tall, handsome partner was so shy.

After the film they had twenty minutes to wait before Rose's father arrived, so they called into a coffee bar close by. On the jukebox the Beatles were singing 'Love Me Do' and they ordered two frothy coffees. Rose insisted on paying for hers.

'What are you doing over the weekend?' asked Freddie.

'Joy Popplewell asked me if I'd like to go to watch your rugby match.'

'Sam's girlfriend?'

It was well known that Sam Grundy and Joy were now an 'item'.

'Yes, so I might see you there.'

'We're playing Leeds Grammar School, so it will be a tough match.'

The conversation ebbed and flowed and they felt content in each other's company.

'My mum and dad go to church,' said Rose. 'It's the Harvest Festival on Sunday.'

'I know,' replied Freddie. 'My sister's in the choir.'

'I'll be going with them,' said Rose.

Ten thirty arrived too quickly, and they hurried out and stood under the canopy in front of the cinema. Brian

McConnell pulled up by the kerb, leaned across and opened the passenger-side door. He didn't want to get out and witness the possibility of a goodnight kiss.

'I've enjoyed tonight,' ventured Freddie tentatively.

'So have I,' said Rose with a smile.

'Maybe see you tomorrow,' he said.

'Do you need a lift?' called Brian from the car.

'No thanks, Mr McConnell, I'm fine.'

As they pulled away from the kerb Rose turned and waved.

Fifteen minutes later Tom Feather arrived in Lily's car to pick up Freddie and they drove off past Micklegate Bar and the railway station, then out of the city.

'Good film?' asked Tom.

'Excellent,' said Freddie.

'What's Rose like?'

'OK,' answered Freddie.

Tom smiled and they drove home in silence, each with his own thoughts.

On Saturday evening Freddie made an unexpected announcement: 'I'd like to go to the Harvest Festival tomorrow.'

Tom looked up in surprise. Freddie wasn't a regular visitor to St Mary's.

Lily was delighted. 'That's good, but we'll have to leave in time for the choir practice. There's usually a quick rehearsal before the service.'

'That's fine,' said Freddie. He looked at Tom. 'I was wondering if I could borrow a pair of black shoes? Mine have had it.' Both Tom and Freddie wore size ten and Tom

45

had four pairs, all with toe caps polished to a military shine.

Tom was curious, but simply said, 'I'll dig out a pair and put them outside your bedroom door.'

Freddie smiled. 'Thanks, Tom.'

'It's always good to smarten yourself up for church,' said Tom. He clearly approved that the generally untidy Freddie was making an effort.

However, Freddie had other things on his mind. Rose hadn't come to the afternoon rugby match, but he knew where she would be tomorrow.

It was Sunday morning, the day of the Harvest Festival, and Vera walked from the vicarage across the gravelled courtyard to St Mary's Church. Alone in this quiet sanctuary she felt in a haven of peace. As she approached the altar, morning sun filtered through the stained glass of the East window and refracted light lit up the ancient walls in amber and gold.

She had prepared a basket of flowers to add to the wonderful display prepared by the Flower Committee and she placed it on a stone shelf, and stood back to admire it.

'Perfect,' said a voice from the doorway of the vestry. It was Joseph, who had come into church to prepare the readings from the ancient Bible and mark the pages with long silk ribbons.

'Thank you,' said Vera. 'They do look pretty, don't they?'

Joseph walked towards her. 'Just like my sister.' His eyes were full of pride.

She looked at her brother, a tall, skeletal man with a Roman nose and a loose clerical collar around his neck. There was a crease of worry across his forehead.

'Don't concern yourself, Joseph,' she said. 'The Harvest Festival is always a wonderful village occasion. All will be well.'

Joseph stood behind the brass lectern. It was decorated with an eagle and on its outstretched wings rested the Bible. He opened it to Deuteronomy, chapter twenty-four, verse nineteen, and read out loud, 'When you reap your harvest in your field . . .'

'. . . and forget a sheaf in the field . . .' continued Vera quietly. For, on occasions, that is how she felt. The one that was left behind.

'Freddie's up early,' remarked Lily.

'That's good,' said Tom as he got out of bed and headed for the bathroom. When he stepped out on to the landing he got a surprise. Freddie emerged from his bedroom dressed in his Sunday best – grey suit, white shirt, striped school tie with its two shades of blue and Tom's spare pair of shiny black shoes. He had even combed his long wavy hair into the semblance of a parting.

Tom stared into the bathroom mirror, lathered his chin with his badger-hair bristle brush and began to shave. As he splashed his cut-throat razor in the soapy water he paused and smiled at his reflection.

He's either discovered religion or he's in love, he thought.

Meanwhile, in St Mary's Church, Anne Grainger was arranging the children in order of height in the choir stalls. Behind them the rows were empty; they would be filled with the adult members of the choir after they had processed up the aisle at the start of the service.

In the vestry, Joseph opened the old wardrobe and donned his white surplice and cope, a full-length garment that covered his shiny black shoes. Around his neck he draped a stole stitched with intricate gold crosses. It was a special day and he smiled in anticipation. Archibald Pike led his well-rehearsed team of bell-ringers as they announced to the folk of Ragley that the Harvest Festival service was soon to start.

Joseph walked out to check the altar. He was ready to begin.

As Tom drove up the Morton road it seemed as though the whole village was on the move. All paths appeared to lead to the church.

There was a special quality to the light at this time of day, a golden hue. October mists were slowly clearing over the plain of York. In the hedgerows goldfinches pecked at the ripe seeds, while wisps of wood smoke hovered above the pantile roofs of Ragley village.

'A perfect morning for the Harvest Festival,' said Lily, but it seemed that Freddie had other things on his mind.

Tom and Freddie decided to enjoy the open air for a while longer. They left Lily clutching her hymn book and choir robe. The tranquillity of St Mary's church-yard touched the souls of all who entered. As Lily walked slowly up the gravel path she knew she always found peace here. It was a safe haven away from the problem that troubled her at the core of her soul. Around her the silk of spiders laced the hedgerow, while above her head a pair of beady-eyed rooks spiralled the clock tower.

Vera was standing at the entrance to the church, elegant as always in a lavender dress and a royal blue jacket.

'Good morning, Lily,' she said. She studied her friend carefully. 'Is everything all right?'

Lily sighed. Vera was always perceptive.

Rose McConnell had arrived with her parents and they were enjoying a conversation with Freddie and Tom in the churchyard.

'It's Freddie,' said Lily. 'I've not seen him like this before. He's met a girl and seems particularly keen.'

Freddie and Rose were exchanging smiles.

Vera linked arms with Lily. 'Let's go and sing, shall we?'

They walked into church together. 'And we can remember Ecclesiastes, chapter twelve, verse one,' Vera added.

'Ecclesiastes?'

'Yes,' she said. 'Remember now thy Creator in the days of thy youth.'

Lily was silent.

It turned out to be a memorable Harvest Festival. Joseph was relieved and Vera sighed in contentment. The church looked its best. In front of the altar was a display of produce, including fruit, home-baked plaited bread and sheaves of barley.

Elsie Crapper on the organ led the choir into a rousing rendition of 'We plough the fields and scatter the good seed on the land' and the congregation sang lustily. At the close of the service Joseph announced that God's bounty would be distributed tomorrow to those in greatest need.

Then, with a final flourish, he blessed the congregation with the sign of the cross.

Afterwards, Vera stood outside church and watched as friends gathered. It was a happy, colourful scene. Albert Jenkins, the erudite school governor and a dear friend of Joseph and Vera, came to stand beside her. He followed her gaze.

A few yards away, Mary McConnell, in a smart russet tweed suit, was in relaxed conversation with Lily. Tom Feather and Brian McConnell were chatting about rugby, while Freddie and Rose, some distance away, were in their private cocoon.

Albert nodded towards the young couple and smiled. 'Now all the youth of England are on fire.' Albert loved his Shakespeare. '*Henry V*, Act 2,' he added with a grin.

'Very true,' said Vera quietly, but, deep down, she knew *her* days of youth were behind her.

Chapter Four

From Ragley with Love

It was early afternoon on Friday, 25 October and Vera was tidying her desk. She picked up her coat and handbag, left school and walked under the avenue of horse chestnut trees towards the village green. The cool breeze scattered fallen leaves at her feet and the branches above her swayed with the rhythm of the wind. In the hedgerows teardrop cobwebs shivered and the red hips of dog roses were a reminder that the dark days of winter were approaching.

Vera tightened her knitted scarf and strode out purposefully towards the village green. It was then that she saw him. He was hunched under the weeping willow tree, wearing a distinctive long overcoat in the style of an Australian sheep farmer. She recognized him at once. Hedley Verity Bickerstaff had always dressed in a flamboyant manner. However, Vera could see that today there was a problem.

Hedley was a soul in torment.

She approached him cautiously. 'Hedley, whatever is the matter?'

He looked up, pushed his long flaxen hair from his eyes and stared back at Vera with haunted eyes.

'Life,' he said simply.

He leaned back against the tree and stared up at the branches and the gunmetal sky. Approaching his thirtieth birthday and over six feet tall, he had a foppish appearance. Frail, with a skinny frame, he looked as if a strong wind would blow him over.

Vera had known him for many years, ever since he had attended the Lawnswood Preparatory School for Young Gentlemen in Thirkby. After passing his accountancy examinations he had received an invitation from his brother, Alan, to join the Easington accountancy firm of Bickerstaff, Crapper and Pugh. With a talent for music and art he had often sought out the views of Vera. She had recognized his obvious creative talent and over the years they had become friends.

'Come with me,' she said decisively and took his arm. 'Let's go back to the vicarage and you can tell me about it.'

He nodded, wiped away a tear and together they walked up the Morton road towards a meeting Vera would never forget.

Anne Grainger had enjoyed a busy afternoon with her five- and six-year-olds and finished the day by paraphrasing the story of *Charlotte's Web*. The children's novel by the American author Elwyn Brooks White was one of Anne's favourites, and the boys and girls were fascinated by the story of Wilbur the pig and his friendship with a spider named Charlotte.

The concept of love was central to the novel and Anne asked the children what they thought it might be. The responses were memorable to the extent that Anne was suddenly reminded why teaching was, for her, the best job in the world.

Tobias Fawnswater was the first to raise his hand. 'I know what love is, Miss. It's when Mummy kisses me to sleep every night.'

Margery Flathers spoke with the innocence of a five-year-old. 'My big sister must love me 'cause she gives me 'er old clothes and then 'as t'go out wi' Mummy t'buy new ones.'

Anne smiled as the discussion gathered momentum.

Jane Grantham, a neat and tidy little girl, put up her hand. 'My mummy always gives my daddy the biggest pork chop so I think that's what love is.'

The tall, athletic six-year-old Janet Ollerenshaw surprised Anne when she suddenly said, 'I think it's to do with *kissing*, Miss. My mum and dad used to kiss a lot and now they just talk . . . so love is probably that.'

Clint Ramsbottom, the son of Deke the singing cowboy, finished off the discussion rather well. 'When my dad comes 'ome all mucky, Miss, my mam says 'e still looks like John Wayne . . . even when 'e looks like our bulldog.'

Anne helped each child to copy their sentence in their writing books and took a few of the best ones into the staff-room to share with Lily.

*

After having a cup of tea with Anne, Lily had the evening meal on her mind as she left school. Up the Morton road the same thought was occupying Violet Fawnswater.

Less than 10 per cent of the population owned a telephone, but Violet was one of the privileged few. She had read in a magazine about a special telephone recipe service if you dialled ASK8071. It had become popular among many thousands of callers. So Violet spent the afternoon creating the perfect shrimp cocktail followed by beef bourguignon. She found peace in her culinary expertise. It gave her contentment and was also a diversion from thinking about her husband. He had continued to deny he was having an affair with his secretary at the chocolate factory, but Violet knew better.

Preparing an evening meal was far from the mind of Vera Evans, however. She was in the vicarage kitchen adding boiling water to a pot of tea leaves. Hedley's long coat was hanging in the hallway and now, leaning against the worktop in his cream linen jacket and bright orange cravat, he appeared more relaxed.

'Two sugars, I recall,' said Vera.

Hedley forced a wan smile. 'You remembered.'

'Of course,' replied Vera. 'How could I forget?'

They had drunk a lot of tea together on one particular afternoon two years ago. Following a church event, Hedley had watched television with Vera. It had been her favourite black-and-white film, *Brief Encounter*. She knew this sensitive young man would appreciate the final evocative scene, filmed in Lancashire's Carnforth Station in 1945. In the story, the actress Celia Johnson, playing a suburban housewife, had found a fleeting love with

Trevor Howard, but after a brief affair they parted and returned to their previous lives. When the film ended, Hedley had considered the difference between infatuation and true love. He was unaware that Vera had experienced the same thoughts.

Now, two years later, Vera asked quietly, 'So, Hedley, what do you want to do with your life?'

There was a long silence. 'I want to be an artist and perhaps one day open a gallery in London.'

'That's a wonderful ambition,' said Vera, 'but what about all the training you've done to be an accountant?'

The haunted look reappeared. 'I hate it.'

Vera stared at this introspective young man. 'I can understand that.' It was clear his work was crushing his creative aspirations.

'Also, it's embarrassing being named after a Yorkshire cricketer.'

'But it's a wonderful name,' Vera reassured him, 'so distinctive.'

'I suppose so . . . but I'm hopeless at cricket.'

Arthur Bickerstaff had named his newborn son on the day Hedley Verity, the legendary Yorkshire left-arm spin bowler, had bowled out Australia. When Arthur had died on the beaches of Dunkirk his wife, Iris, had bought a large detached house in Ragley village for £515. So Hedley had enjoyed a privileged upbringing, during which he had developed a passion for art that had become overwhelming.

'You may not be a cricketer, Hedley, but your paintings are outstanding. Your recent work in oils merits an exhibition.'

To Vera's surprise, Hedley came close and held her hand. 'Vera, I have to say this . . . You are the only person who understands me.'

Vera did not remove her hand. His touch awakened feelings she had not experienced before. 'I simply want to help. You have a special talent and should fulfil your ambitions. An opportunity must be taken when it arises.' She looked up into the eyes of this troubled young man. 'One life, Hedley. Follow your heart.'

'I shall, Vera,' he said quietly.

Hedley knew in that moment that he longed to embrace this elegant, attractive woman. He put his hands on her shoulders. There was a pause as they looked into each other's eyes. Then Hedley stroked her face gently. For a moment Vera froze at the intimate gesture, but his long, delicate fingers became balm to her troubled thoughts. Then came the moment. One that was destined to be seared into the mind of the Ragley School secretary.

Hedley leaned forward and kissed her gently.

Vera found she could not resist.

Then he collected his coat and walked away.

For Vera, the memory of that single stolen kiss was an anthem to her soul and would live with her for ever.

It was early evening and in Laurel Cottage Lily was looking at a photograph on the mantelpiece. It was of her parents, Arthur and Florence Briggs, on their wedding day in 1924. She missed her father, but felt differently about her mother. It had been the iron-willed Florence who had determined a life for Lily that, on occasions, felt like a millstone of memories. The enormity of the problem that she carried around with her was almost too heavy to bear.

She had needed to find a few moments alone in the front room after glancing at the title of Freddie's English homework. It was from Shakespeare's *Henry IV, Part 1*, Act IV, scene 5: ' "Let life be short, else shame will be too long" – discuss'.

Unaware of Lily's dilemma, Freddie was busy at the kitchen table, hurrying to complete as much as he could before he caught the bus into York to meet Rose McConnell. It was their second visit to the cinema and, in the sixth form, they were gradually being recognized as 'a couple'. For Freddie it was a special experience. He felt relaxed in her presence and he wondered what it would be like to kiss her.

At 6.15 p.m. Ruby's mother, Agnes, had arrived home from the chocolate factory. As usual on a Friday evening she put a large brown paper bag on the kitchen table.

'There y'are, Ruby luv,' she said, 'y'weekend treat.'

Agnes always collected the so-called 'waste' products from the factory: namely, the chocolate bars that were misshapen and couldn't be sold to the general public.

'Oooh, Mam, m'favourites!' exclaimed an ebullient Ruby. 'KitKats an' Aeros.'

'Well, enjoy 'em,' said Agnes. She took off her coat and looked around. 'So where's laughin' boy?'

'Dunno, Mam, 'e's been out all day.'

'Well, one thing's f'certain, 'e won't 'ave been lookin' for a job.' Agnes popped her head around the door to the sitting room. The children were eating doorstep sandwiches in front of the television as they watched *Ready Steady Go!* on ITV. Keith Fordyce was introducing Joe Brown and the Bruvvers, followed by Billy J. Kramer and the Dakotas. Racquel was singing along contentedly while nursing a sleeping Natasha on the battered sofa.

Ruby made a pot of tea and the two women sat at the kitchen table.

'Bit o' gossip goin' round t'fact'ry,' said Agnes.

'What's that then?' asked Ruby.

'It's that posh new manager, Mr Fawnswater. 'E fancies 'imself summat rotten does that one. Flash suit an' a big quiff like Billy Fury. God's gift t'women, so 'e reckons.'

'So what's 'e up to?'

'Only gives 'is secret'ry a Dairy Box ev'ry Friday, an' that's not all so they say.'

'Bloomin' 'eck!' said Ruby as she bit into a KitKat.

'In t'packagin' department they say she's on t'pill an' by all accounts they're 'avin' sexual conjugations.'

The pill had become available to the public in 1961 and, according to Mr Grinchley in the village Pharmacy, a whole new world of carefree sex had opened up and there was no stopping it. It was widely agreed the older generation did not approve of the new sexual freedom.

Agnes was on a roll. 'An' she's only twenty, a reight tarty piece an' allus 'as *three* buttons on 'er blouse undone.'

'Three?' mumbled Ruby through a mouthful of chocolate.

'Yes, an' she sez in t'staff canteen that when she opens t'box o' chocolates 'e allus 'as an Almond Crispy Cluster and she picks a Nougat de Montelimar 'cause she sez it sounds posh.'

Ruby shook her head. 'Gimme a Coffee Cream any day.'

'Y'spot on there, luv,' said Agnes. 'No accountin' f'taste.'

Freddie and Rose were in the back row of the Odeon Cinema in York and enjoying *From Russia with Love*. There had been great excitement when, earlier in the month, the latest Bond film had been released. It was proving to be another blockbuster. Based on the fifth James Bond novel written by Ian Fleming, it was Sean Connery's second outing in the role of the MI6 agent.

As the title song, composed by Lionel Bart and sung by Matt Munro, echoed around the theatre, Freddie decided to make his move. With great care he moved closer to Rose and slowly put his arm around her shoulders. She responded by leaning her head against his chest.

Freddie felt content and together they watched Daniela Bianchi, the former Miss Universe runner-up, fall for James Bond's charms, while Robert Shaw was wonderfully menacing as the villain. It was only later in the film that Freddie decided he could wait no longer and he kissed her gently. To his surprise, Rose responded eagerly. By the time Lotte Lenya as the Russian agent Rosa Klebb attacked our hero with a poison-tipped knife in her shoe, they were in a world of their own and Anglo-Russian relations were far from their minds.

In the vicarage, Vera pondered her meeting with the young artist. It was one she would always remember. As a spinster she had dedicated her life to her brother, the church and Ragley School. There had been no relationships, no amorous feelings . . . and no passionate kisses.

Today had been different and she reflected on the experience. She had allowed a young man to kiss her and for a few brief moments had understood the meaning of real devotion.

As she stood beneath the giant elms in the churchyard a barn owl, like a ghost of the night, swooped by, searching for its midnight prey. She shivered. The evening breeze was cool as a blade. Above her were a myriad stars and a gibbous moon cast a pallid light on the vicarage walls.

'That's the problem with *time*,' Vera murmured to herself. 'It's not our friend.'

Finally she went inside and, when she slept, it was a night of disturbed dreams.

On Saturday morning Lily gave Freddie a lift into Ragley village to do a few hours' work in the Hardware Emporium. Timothy Pratt needed help, as his empire was expanding and the demand for his new range of dome-headed screws was increasing. The strong and willing Freddie was the ideal part-time Saturday assistant.

Lily had grown to love the drive from Kirkby Steepleton. A gauze of mist drifted slowly across the distant land towards the hazy purple rim of the Hambleton hills, where a golden thread of light appeared. The last field of barley had been harvested and in the hedgerows wrens were chirping out their shrill warnings. As they drove up Ragley High Street the first rays of an autumnal sun lit up the borders of chrysanthemums, bronze, amber and scarlet, outside the village hall.

Lily pulled up outside Nora's Coffee Shop. 'I've got some shopping to do, so I'll catch up with you later.'

'Fine, thanks for the lift,' said Freddie and got out of the car. Before he closed the passenger door he leaned back in. There was a mischievous glint in his eyes. 'Maybe next year when I've finished my driving lessons and passed my test I'll be able to borrow your car.'

'Or you could save up to buy one of your own,' retorted Lily with a smile. *Just like Tom did on the day he proposed to me*, she thought.

'By the way, Tom said he would pick you up later to take you to your rugby game. Maybe you can have lunch with him.'

Freddie waved and walked confidently into the Hardware Emporium. Lily noticed that he was looking particularly pleased with himself.

In Nora's Coffee Shop two sixteen-year-olds, Lizzie Buttershaw and Veronica Collins, were enjoying a frothy coffee and discussing an issue that had begun to dominate the music scene; namely, who was more popular – Cliff Richard or the Beatles?

Lizzie had spent sixpence on her *Boyfriend* magazine and was reading an article about her heart-throb. Cliff Richard was celebrating his fifth year in show business. The magazine reported that after leaving school he had worked as a filing clerk for Atlas Lamps. Then, after joining a skiffle group, in 1958 he made a record, 'Move It', and it sold half a million copies.

"E's got an American sports car that does a 'undred an' seventy miles an 'our,' said Lizzie.

The Beatles' 'She Loves You' was playing on the jukebox and Veronica was singing along. 'Yes, but jus' listen t'that, Lizzie. They're fantastic. Ah mus' say, ah thought 'Summer 'Oliday' were great wi' Cliff an' t'Shadows, but now ah'm in love.'

'In love? Who with?'

'Paul McCartney, o' course. Who else?'

Lily had called into the General Stores & Newsagent. The shop was silent for a change and there were no other customers as she approached the counter.

'Good morning, Lily,' said a smiling Prudence. It was always 'Mrs Feather' when there were children or parents around.

'Good morning, Prudence,' replied Lily, 'and good morning, Jeremy.'

They both looked up. Today the bear was in an autumnal ensemble, with brown cord trousers, an oatmeal shirt and a green corduroy waistcoat.

'We're doing a little gardening later,' explained Prudence.

Lily nodded in acknowledgement. She was aware that Jeremy, like Prudence, was a keen gardener. 'Just a loaf, please,' she said, 'and four pounds of potatoes.'

'Are you working in school this morning?' asked Prudence as she weighed out the King Edwards.

'No, I brought Freddie in. He's got a Saturday morning job with Timothy in the Hardware Emporium. He's saving up for driving lessons.'

'Your brother is a fine young man. You must be very proud.'

Lily gave a shy smile and filled her shopping bag. 'I'll take a newspaper as well, please.'

Next to this week's copy of the *Radio Times*, with its front cover of the handsome Richard Chamberlain as Dr Kildare, were all the daily newspapers. Recently the news had been dominated by Harold Macmillan's resignation as prime minister and his replacement, Alex Douglas-Home. However, at that moment, the shop bell rang and a stream of new customers arrived. Lily thanked Prudence, looked at her wristwatch and decided to take a break in Nora's Coffee Shop.

She was sitting at a corner table when Nora served her.

'There's y'coffee, Mrs Feather,' said Nora, 'an' a cwumpet.' The twenty-five-year-old had always had trouble with the letter 'R'.

The Coffee Shop was empty apart from a few teenagers, including two sixteen-year-olds, Arnie Icklethwaite and his new girlfriend. They were holding hands. Nora looked across at them wistfully.

'What is it, Nora?' asked Lily. 'You look sad.'

'Jus' wemembewin',' murmured Nora. 'I 'ad a boyfwiend once.'

'Who was that?'

'My Fwank,' said Nora. There was a faraway look in her eyes. ''E were lovely. We used t'go t'Easington market an' 'e bought me a bwacelet.'

'That was a kind thing to do,' said Lily.

'An' 'e took me t'meet 'is mother an' she gave me owange juice an' Witz Cwackers an' we used t'listen t'Buddy 'Olly.'

Lily nodded. 'He was a wonderful singer and that terrible plane crash was so sad. I remember buying "Raining in My Heart".'

Nora's eyes were wide. 'Oooh, my favouwite.'

The bell above the door rang and another customer walked in. Nora gave the table a cursory wipe with her tea towel and picked up the ashtray, as she knew Lily was a non-smoker.

'So what happened, Nora?'

'Well, ah loved 'im but 'e found someone else t'love.'

Lily looked at the youthful Nora as she hurried away and thought how love could be an unpredictable companion.

In the vicarage, Joseph was puzzled. Vera seemed distant. There was clearly something on her mind.

'How are you, Vera?' he asked.

'Fine,' said Vera, but she didn't look up from her *Be-Ro Home Recipes* book. She had decided to make a custard tart and had just rolled out the shortcrust pastry and lined a seven-inch sandwich cake tin.

'I'm going into church,' said Joseph. 'I have a wedding this afternoon.'

'Good,' replied Vera without conviction.

Joseph shook his head and recalled Oscar Wilde as he walked out. He murmured to himself, 'Women are meant to be loved, not to be understood.'

The radio in the kitchen was burbling away when Brian Hyland's 1962 hit single 'Sealed with a Kiss' was played. Vera stared out of the window and gave the hint of a smile, but her eyes were soft with sorrow.

Chapter Five

The Beatles Concert

It was an iron-grey morning on Friday, 1 November and a reluctant light spread across the land. The weather had changed and a long winter was in store.

In Laurel Cottage Lily and Freddie were eating a hasty breakfast. Tom was in the hallway unbuttoning his uniform having returned home after a long stint of night duty. He pulled an envelope from his pocket as he walked into the kitchen. 'I've got the tickets,' he said. There were four and he gave them to Freddie. 'I was in Leeds so I called in and bought them.'

'Brilliant!' said Freddie. 'I'll pay you back.'

'No need,' said Tom with a grin. 'Save your money for driving lessons. The tickets for you and Rose are on me, but Sam and his girlfriend will need to settle up for the other two.'

'Thanks, Tom.' Freddie was excited. He knew Rose would be thrilled to travel into Leeds on Sunday to see the Beatles. They were her favourite group.

Lily looked at Freddie with new eyes. He had changed from a boy into a man in the blink of an eye.

When Lily arrived at school, John Pruett was in the entrance hall talking to John Grainger. Anne's husband looked distinctly dishevelled. He hadn't shaved and his thick cord trousers were stained with wood glue.

Anne was in the staff-room when Lily went to hang up her coat and scarf. 'He's volunteered to be in charge of the firework display on Bonfire Night,' she explained.

'That's good,' said Lily with an encouraging smile.

Anne sighed. 'Well, it will keep him occupied, I suppose.' There was a hint of sadness in her voice. Living with her woodcarver husband had become a life of monotony.

'Let's set up for the orchestra,' suggested Lily suddenly. 'It will give them a chance to shine in assembly.'

Anne thought 'orchestra' sounded rather grand as a description of the multifarious group of children who had expressed an interest in playing an instrument. Anne's recorder group was to the fore, with a supporting cast playing Indian bells, tambourines, triangles and a wooden glockenspiel. The children loved it and Anne found contentment in their enthusiasm. Also, deep down, she knew Lily was trying to cheer her up.

Three miles away in Easington School, Freddie and Rose were sitting at adjoining desks in preparation for their A-level double English lesson. When Mr Charles Morris walked into the classroom all conversation ceased immediately. He removed his spectacles and surveyed the thirty pupils before him.

'Before we study the poetry of Percy Shelley, I want you to remember that it's important to read widely and not simply focus on the set texts.' He stepped up to the raised teacher's desk, put down a paperback novel and wrote *Catch 22* on the blackboard. 'This is one of the most significant novels of our time.' He noticed Sam Grundy lower his eyes. His star rugby fly half was clearly not familiar with the Joseph Heller classic. 'So, has anyone read it?'

A dozen pupils raised their hands, including Rose and Freddie.

'Rose,' he asked, 'what did you make of it?'

Freddie turned to admire her profile.

Rose tapped her long, slender fingers on the desk top and removed her spectacles as she considered her reply. 'Well, I was puzzled by the chronology.'

'That's understandable,' Mr Morris said, encouraged by the considered response. 'Heller uses third person omniscient narration, so events are described from the points of view of a variety of characters. These are often out of sequence, so it can be difficult to follow the plot.'

The discussion gathered momentum until finally he came to Freddie.

'Now, Freddie, you usually give us some interesting insights. What's your view?'

Freddie pondered a moment. 'Well, I liked the fact it was set in the war, sir. My brother-in-law fought, but never speaks of it. I've often asked him, but it's a closed book.'

Charles Morris nodded in acknowledgement. 'I'm sure he will have his reasons.' He had always appreciated Freddie's thoughtful honesty.

'I liked the character Captain Yossarian, sir,' continued

Freddie. 'The only way out of flying bombing missions was for him to declare himself insane. It was crazy to continue flying into danger, so if he refused it meant he was sane, but that meant he had to carry on. He couldn't win.'

Charles smiled. Winning was everything to the earnest young man before him. Under the school badge on his navy blue blazer he sported his school colours for rugby and cricket. Charles had recommended Freddie, along with Sam Grundy, to take part in the trials for the Yorkshire Schools rugby union team. As captain of the Easington school team, Freddie's determination to give his all in every game marked him out as a leader. When he spoke, others listened.

Mr Morris held up the novel. 'In fact, Heller himself flew sixty bombing missions, so he knew this subject well. He used this satirical novel to present a paradoxical problem in which a resolution to a dilemma cannot be solved; hence the catch.'

Freddie leaned back in his chair and sighed. Life seemed to be full of paradoxes. He had grown to care deeply for Rose, but the words were not there to express his feelings. Also, the more he tried to help his sister, the more likely she was to sink into quiet reflection. It was as if there was a problem she could not solve and would not share. He wondered what it might be.

Back in Ragley, Joseph Evans had just finished a Bible studies lesson with John Pruett's class as the bell rang for morning break.

The twins Luke and Scott Walmsley were clearly impressed by Joseph's words of wisdom. He considered the two nine-year-olds, who were completely dissimilar in every way. They were non-identical dizygotic, or fraternal, twins who also had different personalities. Luke was polite, thoughtful and neat, whereas Scott was careless and loud.

'Thank you, Mr Evans,' said Luke.

'That were a good story,' added Scott, 'bout doin' good an' sharin' an' suchlike.'

'We're goin' to 'elp our 'Enry when we get 'ome, sir,' said Luke.

'Henry?' asked Joseph. He was unaware they had a brother.

'M'mam sez 'e's depressed,' explained Scott forcefully. '*Really* depressed.'

'Depressed? Oh dear! Why is that?'

''E's on 'is own all day,' said Luke.

'Prob'ly gets lonely,' added Scott.

Joseph delved further. 'How *old* is Henry?'

'Three, sir,' replied the twins in unison.

'Only three,' said Joseph in surprise. 'But I thought your mother went out to work.'

'Yes, sir, she does,' confirmed Luke.

'That's why 'e gets fed up,' said Scott, ''cause 'e's no one t'talk to.'

Joseph was concerned. Suddenly this was a serious matter.

'We try t'cheer 'im up,' continued Luke. 'We give 'im cucumber.'

'An' bananas,' added Scott.

'Well, that sounds very healthy,' said Joseph, keen to bring this conversation to an end. He glanced at his watch. 'Time to go out to play now, boys.'

They rushed off and Joseph hurried to the staff-room. Vera was on her own preparing a pot of tea.

'Tea, Joseph?' she offered.

'Yes, please.'

'How did your lesson go?'

'Er, fine, thanks,' said Joseph, clearly preoccupied.

Vera stirred the tea leaves in the boiling water and replaced the lid on the pot. 'What was your theme?'

'Do not forget to do good and to share with others,' recited a distracted Joseph.

'Hebrews, chapter thirteen, verse sixteen,' murmured Vera without looking up from pouring the tea.

'I need to have a word with John about the Walmsley twins.'

'Really?'

'We may need to contact Social Services. Apparently they have a little brother who is left alone.'

'A brother?'

'Yes, Henry, three years old, clearly neglected . . . and he's depressed.'

Vera held out the sugar bowl. 'Sugar, Joseph?'

Joseph was surprised. 'But you know I don't take sugar.'

'I think you need some *sweet* tea this morning.'

'Whatever for?'

'And I wouldn't mention Henry to our headmaster.'

'Why not?'

'Because Henry is a *hamster*!'

'Oh . . . I see,' mumbled Joseph as realization dawned.

Vera stared out of the window and smiled. 'Never mind, Joseph, we all stumble in many ways. James, chapter three, verse two.'

Joseph sat down and added two heaped spoonfuls of sugar to his tea. It was the first time in his life that he had had empathy with a hamster.

It was Saturday morning and Mary McConnell had prepared scrambled eggs on toast for Rose and herself, while Brian had gone into York Railway Station for a morning meeting.

'It's ready,' shouted Mary.

Rose was working at the table in the dining room and she closed her History textbook and a summary of the Franco-Prussian War. It was a subject she enjoyed.

'Thanks, Mother,' she said.

They sat down together in the kitchen and Mary studied her daughter. 'How's it going?' she asked.

'Fine,' said Rose, 'but there's something happening next week. We've been asked to make cakes for a school party, so I thought I might make a Victoria sponge.'

'I'll get everything you need,' offered Mary. 'I'm going shopping later. We'll do what we did last year in Domestic Science and put all the ingredients in the old Christmas biscuit tin. The eggs will need packing carefully.'

'Thanks, Mum.'

Mary always made sure her daughter received every encouragement and Rose had gained top marks in her O-level Domestic Science examination. It was a subject in which she had excelled.

For a few moments they ate in silence, each with her own thoughts.

'Pity there isn't an A-level in Domestic Science,' remarked Mary. 'You would have passed easily.'

'Maybe ... but the time needed for the practical part of the course would have made my three A-levels impossible.'

Mary nodded. 'And you could do with another apron. I could make one for you.'

Rose gave a whimsical smile. 'Perhaps in a brighter colour.'

At her previous school in Doncaster, Rose had made a pinafore and hat in the sewing class. This had been a compulsory forerunner to the Domestic Science lessons. The material had been provided by the school and resembled old army surplus.

Mary enjoyed these conversations with her daughter. Rose seemed to have grown up so quickly and she knew her almost better than Rose knew herself. 'Do you think you might continue with cookery after sixth form? There's a good course at the college in Bingley and another at the Ilkley College of Housecraft. You could become a Domestic Science teacher.'

Rose shook her head. 'Not sure.'

In the background the radio was on with the volume turned low. Gerry and the Pacemakers were singing their number-one hit record 'You'll Never Walk Alone'. Rose smiled. It was one of Freddie's favourite songs.

'You would need to complete an application form,' said Mary.

Rose considered this. 'I'm still keen to be a teacher.'

'That's wonderful, darling.'

Rose put down her knife and fork. 'The thing is ... I'm enjoying *English*.'

Mary nodded. 'And your marks are excellent.'

'So that's another possibility.'

Mary was keen for her daughter to focus. 'Where would you apply?'

Rose replied with confidence, 'Probably Leeds University. That would be my first choice. Maybe Sheffield after that.'

Mary was quietly pleased. *Far enough for the break from home . . . but close enough to visit.* 'Well, anything you need, just say and your father and I will do everything we can to help.'

'Thanks, Mum.' Rose got up to return to the dining room.

'Are you looking forward to the Beatles?'

'Can't wait,' said Rose. Her cheeks flushed. She had bought their first number-one record 'From Me to You' back in April and had played it so often even her father knew the words. 'Sam Grundy's driving us there in his mother's car.'

Mary considered this. 'Well, make sure he doesn't drink.'

'Don't worry, Sam and Freddie are very sensible.'

Mary was aware of Rose's developing relationship with Freddie Briggs. 'So . . . has Freddie any plans for his future?'

'Yes, he wants to read Languages at university.' Rose walked out of the kitchen.

A thought occurred to Mary. 'And where will *he* be applying?'

'Leeds,' called out Rose from the next room.

I should have guessed, thought Mary.

*

Lily was deep in thought as she and Freddie drove on the back road from Kirkby Steepleton. Beyond the hedgerows, mist shrouded the silent fields like a cloak of secrets.

It was clear to Lily that Freddie was besotted with Rose. They seemed to go everywhere together and she hoped it would not affect his future. Freddie had switched on the car radio and was humming along to the Searchers singing 'Sweets for My Sweet'. A busy day was in store. After a morning assisting Timothy Pratt in the Hardware Emporium, he had arranged to meet Rose in the Coffee Shop. From there Sam Grundy had offered to drive him to Easington for the afternoon rugby game. Then, tomorrow, it was on to Leeds and the Beatles concert. Another evening with Rose beckoned and he felt content in his world.

Lily glanced at the fuel gauge and pulled up next to the single pump on the forecourt of Victor Pratt's garage.

Victor ambled out wiping his greasy, oil-smeared hands on his filthy overalls. ''Ello, Mrs Feather. What's it to be?'

'Four gallons, please, Victor.'

Petrol was five shillings per gallon and Lily took a pound note from her purse. 'And how are you?'

There was always something amiss with Ragley's local mechanic and this morning was no exception.

'M'back's killin' me.' Victor was a martyr to his ailments.

'Oh dear,' said Lily. 'Perhaps you ought to visit Doctor Davenport.'

'Thank you kindly, Mrs Feather, but m'dad gave me some goose grease. 'E sez it never fails.'

Lily had her doubts, but had learned not to contradict the old-fashioned remedies supported by the locals. She drove into Ragley under a leaden sky and the torn rags of cirrus clouds. As she pulled up on the High Street, the first harsh frosts heralded the coming of winter and the smell of wood smoke hung in the air. The villagers had put on their warmest coats before setting off for Prudence Golightly's General Stores and the welcome smell of freshly baked bread.

After Freddie had gone into the Hardware Emporium, Lily decided she would call into school, so she walked up the High Street towards the village green. William Braithwaite was outside the Post Office, leaning his considerable bulk against the door of the red telephone box. William, known locally as 'Billy Two-Sheds', was president of the Ragley Shed Society.

'Good morning, Mr Braithwaite,' said Lily.

'G'mornin', Mrs Feather,' replied Billy. 'Ah'm jus' waitin' f'our Petunia t'ring.' It was his weekly call from his sister in Skegness. She rang the Ragley public telephone box at exactly nine o'clock each Saturday. It was a regular routine and villagers tended to avoid using the telephone at that time.

He glanced anxiously at his wristwatch. 'Y'weren't wantin' t'use t'telephone ah 'ope?'

Lily smiled. 'No thank you. I'm just calling in to school.'

At that moment the phone began to ring and William squeezed through the door.

In The Royal Oak, Ruby Smith had finished her morning's cleaning. It was a cash-in-hand job and Sheila Bradshaw gave her a brown envelope.

''Ere's y'wages, Ruby,' she said.

Sheila was a friendly young woman who worked hard and always gave the regulars in the taproom a good view of what was generally regarded as the finest cleavage in Yorkshire. She was confident in the knowledge that no one would dare to 'try it on'. Don, her giant of a husband, was an ex-wrestler who had appeared at Bridlington Spa under the name of 'The Silent Assassin'.

'Thanks, Sheila,' said Ruby. 'Ah'm grateful.' Ruby knew she would now be able to go to the village Pharmacy to buy a small bottle of Delrosa rosehip syrup for half a crown. She knew it contained Vitamin C and she wanted her children to have strong bones and healthy teeth.

'How's your Ronnie?' asked Sheila.

'Same as usual,' said Ruby. 'Daft as a brush. 'E's feedin' 'is pigeons. Thinks more o' them than 'e does of 'is fam'ly.'

'Ah'm sorry, Ruby,' said Sheila. 'Y'deserve better.'

'Mebbe so, but 'e's given me five wonderful children. So ah'm blessed.'

Ruby left for the council estate, where her mother, Agnes, was childminding. Meanwhile Sheila stared after her and wondered if *she* would ever be blessed.

Ronnie Smith was in his shed feeding his pigeons and humming Elvis Presley's 'It's Now or Never'. Ronnie still regarded himself as a 'Rocker', a Teddy boy stuck in his own time warp. He had continued to preserve his fifties rock-and-roll image with drainpipe trousers and Brylcreemed hairstyle, greasy and combed into a duck's tail.

As he fed his pigeons, Ronnie dreamed of owning a motorbike, ideally a Triumph or a Norton 650, but he couldn't afford it. He had seen girls in leather jackets riding pillion on motorbikes, blonde hair flying in the wind as they roared down the A19 towards York.

'A bike gives you *respect*,' he said out loud, with absolute conviction.

However, the pigeons took no notice . . . rather like his mother-in-law.

After finishing his work in the Hardware Emporium, Freddie met Rose in Nora's Coffee Shop. Blasting out on the jukebox was the Beatles 'From Me to You'.

'I'd like to buy the LP,' said Rose as Nora arrived at their table with two coffees. She had heard the conversation.

'Wose . . . ah go t'Woolwo'th's f'my weco'ds.'

'Woolworth's?' queried Rose. She knew Nora was the local aficionado of pop records.

'Yes, ah buy them Embassy weco'ds for 'alf pwice.'

'Yes, Nora, but they're *cover* versions. I prefer the real thing.'

Nora gave an enigmatic smile. 'Two fwothy coffees,' she said and returned to the counter.

I wonder if I'll ever meet the real thing, she wondered . . . because, of course, in her thoughts she could pronounce the letter 'R'.

'We could go into York one night next week after school,' suggested Freddie.

'Maybe,' said Rose doubtfully. 'My mother wouldn't be pleased. She thinks we're seeing too much of each other and it's affecting my homework.'

Freddie smiled. 'My big sister says the same.'

They relaxed with their coffee in their private space, in which life was an adventure and no one else existed.

*

On Sunday morning Lily was in the choir stalls of St Mary's prior to the Holy Communion service. Outside on the Morton road Tom was leaning against his Ford Zephyr patrol car when Albert Jenkins arrived in his three-piece suit, complete with watch chain. Albert was a prominent member of the local council and a valued friend to Tom and Lily.

'How's it going, Tom? Don't see much of you these days.'

'Stuck in an office in Northallerton, Albert,' said Tom. 'Nothing special these days, just kids on motorbikes. I've got Sergeant Dewhirst dealing with it.'

Tom was in charge of five rural sections, each one with a sergeant. One of them was his old colleague, Harry Dewhirst, now based in Easington. Thirty-two-year-old Harry rode a powerful BSA C15 motorcycle and drove a boxy Morris LD van known as a 'Black Maria'. As a second-row rugby forward, he was a formidable presence when he toured the local villages.

'I heard he collared Stan Coe last week for driving under the influence,' said Albert with a knowing look. There was history between Tom and Stan.

'Let's hope he's learned his lesson,' said Tom.

'I saw his black eye,' added Albert with a grin.

'Walked into a door, so it was reported,' said Tom with a straight face.

The church bells began to chime out. Archibald Pike was putting his bell-ringers through their paces.

'Shall we go in?' suggested Tom.

'Where's Freddie?' asked Albert as they walked up the gravel path.

'Doing his homework.'

'That's good,' said Albert.

'With his girlfriend,' added Tom with feeling.

Albert kept his thoughts to himself as they reached the church door and Aloysius Pratt issued them each with a hymn book.

It was early evening when Sam parked in Leeds city centre. The four of them were oblivious to the biting wind. It was a happy, carefree time and they walked with the freedom of sixties teenagers up Briggate to a pub that Sam knew well. The road was busy with traffic, but no longer did the familiar tramcars run up and down this popular shopping street. They had gone for scrap a few years ago and many had been sad to see their departure. City centres were changing.

Freddie and Sam were dressed in the fashion of the day, with roll-neck Aran sweaters, donkey jackets and desert boots. Rose had chosen a grey skinny-rib jumper, grey flannel skirt and brown suede shoes. With her white knitted scarf, a matching woollen hat and a red PVC mac, Freddie thought she looked sensational.

Joy had gone for her pseudo-intellectual Beatnik look, with a black turtleneck sweater, tight jeans, a beret and dark glasses. She had been reading the spontaneous prose of literary iconoclast Jack Kerouac, who had introduced the phrase 'Beat Generation'. Appropriately, her T-shirt proclaimed 'Beat Poets of America'.

The pub was crowded and a dense pall of cigarette smoke hovered over the heads of the drinkers.

'First round on me,' said Sam with a grin. He was aware the money Freddie earned at the Hardware Emporium, with occasional caddying at the local golf course on Sunday mornings, was limited. He slapped a ten shilling note on the bar. Watney's Red Barrel was two shillings a pint. 'Two pints of Red Barrel, please, and two halves in straight glasses,' he said. He knew the barman would not serve women with pint glasses and definitely not glasses with a handle. 'It's just not ladylike,' he had been told on numerous occasions.

With the exception of Freddie, they had all passed their eighteenth birthdays, including Rose a few weeks ago, and were old enough to drink. In any case, the barman didn't question them and only gave them the merest glance. He had no wish to argue with the two tough-looking young men, particularly the blond giant.

On the jukebox, Carole King's 'It Might As Well Rain Until September' was playing. Joy and Rose knew all the words and sang along. A few other Beatles fans were propping up the bar with their copycat, mop-top hairstyles.

At seven o'clock they joined the huge queue outside the Odeon Theatre. Rose was excited. She had been a big fan of the Beatles ever since they had appeared on television a year ago singing 'Love Me Do'. Her father had shouted, 'Switch off that rubbish!', whereas her mother had smiled and said she thought they made a refreshing change.

They took their seats in the dress circle and looked around in wonder. The place was packed. It was a capacity audience of 2,500, with a further 8,000 fans filling the pavements outside. Freddie noticed he and Sam were in a minority. Most of the seats were filled by teenage girls.

It was a relatively quiet start to the concert, but the anticipation was building. While they enjoyed the Vernons

Girls, the Brook Brothers and the Kestrels harmony group, everyone was waiting for John, Paul, George and Ringo.

The girls began to scream loudly as soon as the Beatles appeared. Twenty-seven ear-splitting minutes of screaming followed, with the result that it was impossible to hear the music. Regardless, Rose and Joy joined in and sang the words of 'From Me to You', 'All My Loving', 'Roll Over Beethoven' and 'She Loves You'.

They performed ten songs in all, but it was the last one, 'Twist and Shout', that created pandemonium. Dozens of girls tried to storm the stage and some of the usherettes were crushed in the seething mass. A few fans threw fluffy toy bears on to the stage for John Lennon's son. It took a while for Freddie to lead the way through the throng and out into the cold night air.

The girls were flushed with excitement.

Sam pulled a packet of cigarettes out of his pocket. He had spent three shillings and ten pence from his generous weekly allowance on his favourite brand, twenty Church-man's No. 1 with filter tips. He offered one to Joy, who accepted gladly. Rose refused mainly because she knew Freddie didn't smoke, but she would have liked one.

Together they crossed the Headrow and walked back to the car. Freddie held Rose's hand and smiled down at her.

'Enjoy it?'

'Terrific,' said Rose. She reached up and kissed him tenderly.

As the four of them drove home, Rose thought of the fictional characters she had read about who had fallen hopelessly in love and she wondered if it was happening to her.

Meanwhile, the Beatles were heading south for their next engagement at the Royal Variety Performance in the presence of the Queen Mother and Princess Margaret.

Sam drove via Kirkby Steepleton on the way back to Ragley and pulled up outside Laurel Cottage. The temperature was below zero when Freddie climbed out of the car, but he didn't feel it. He kissed Rose one last time and watched the red rear lights disappear into the darkness.

'He's back,' whispered Lily as she climbed back into bed.

'That's what your mother used to do,' murmured Tom sleepily.

'What do you mean?'

'You must remember,' said Tom. 'When I brought you home she would peep round the curtain.'

'I'm not like her,' retorted Lily.

'Don't be offended,' said Tom soothingly.

Lily rested her head on his chest. 'I'm just concerned about him.'

There was a long silence and the alarm clock ticked on.

Finally Tom said, 'He'll be eighteen next year.'

After a while his breathing became slow and steady and soon he had fallen back into a deep sleep.

Lily stared at the moonlight flickering on the ceiling and said quietly, 'Yes, I know . . . I know.'

Chapter Six

The End of the World

Jeremy Bear was wearing a black armband.

Prudence Golightly stared up at her dearest friend. She had dressed him in charcoal grey trousers, a crisp white shirt and a black tie. He was sitting on his usual shelf above the counter, but on this dreadful morning his head drooped a little. His glass eyes were clouded as he stared down at the trays of fresh bread, rows of tinned peas and stacks of shoe polish. Prudence knew the world would never be the same again. Even the bell above the door sounded funereal as her first customer arrived.

It was Saturday, 23 November and the villagers of Ragley were waking to harsh frosts that heralded the coming of winter. Beneath a leaden sky and the torn rags of racing clouds, the flag on the church tower was at half mast. In the vicarage Vera Evans had searched out her warmest coat, donned her hat and gloves and set off down the Morton road towards the General Stores & Newsagent.

She had found it hard to sleep. The previous evening was one she would never forget. On BBC television there had been a newsflash. As the luminaries of British broadcasting were at a celebratory dinner, it had fallen to an unfamiliar reporter, John Roberts, to read a bulletin: 'We regret to announce that President Kennedy is dead.' The import of the message was clear. He bowed his head and did not look up again.

When Vera approached the counter, Prudence was staring at the front cover of the *Daily Express*. Her eyes were red with tears. Beneath a photo of a smiling John Kennedy and his wife, Jackie, seconds before that fateful moment, the headline read 'KENNEDY ASSASSINATED – a sniper's bullet'. He had been shot once in the back and once in the head.

It was then that Vera did something she had never done before. The usual 'Good mornings' were absent. Instead she walked behind the counter, put her arms around the diminutive village newsagent and gave her a hug. They held this pose for a moment, two souls stretched tight in sorrow.

On this bitter morning, when a gauze of mist covered the frozen land like a cloak of sadness, grief had no words. The news had raced around the globe, while in the quiet backwater of Ragley the villagers dealt with it in different ways.

At 7 School View Ruby and her mother were drinking tea in the kitchen. Andy was delivering newspapers and Racquel was looking after the young ones in the lounge.

'M'plate's playin' up again,' muttered Agnes and she

took out her false teeth and swilled them in the sink. As a twenty-first birthday treat, her father had paid for her to have all her teeth removed and replaced by a gleaming false set.

'It meks a lot o' sense,' he had announced with confidence. 'Saves a load o' trouble wi' t'dentist.'

Each night she would put them in a tumbler of water on her chest of drawers. 'Ah could strangle 'im. Some present that were.'

Ruby had been a child when her grandfather had offered this unusual gift. It was about the time her father, Charlie Bancroft, had run off to live in Birkenhead with a leggy eighteen-year-old who worked in a toffee factory.

Agnes replaced her teeth and sat down again at the kitchen table. She rummaged in her battered handbag, took out a brown envelope and shook her head in disgust. It was her wage packet.

'Eight pound a week,' she grumbled, 'while men get twelve for t'same work.'

'S'not fair!' exclaimed Ruby.

Agnes sighed. 'It's way o' t'world, luv. Allus 'as been.'

'What can y'do, Mam?'

'Well, that Annabella Outhwaite, her wi' red 'air an' that funny 'usband, tried t'speak up on be'alf of all t'girls.'

'What 'appened?'

'It came t'nowt an' she were frightened she'd lose 'er job.'

'Well it's up to us t'fight for equal pay,' said Ruby bravely.

'It'll never 'appen, luv,' said Agnes. 'We're treated diff'rent. Ah recall once askin' for a pint glass o' beer jus' for t'devilment of it. T'barman came over all 'oighty

85

toighty an' said only *men* can order pints and women can drink 'alves an' think 'emselves lucky.'

'Mebbe we can mek things change,' said Ruby.

'Them Suffragettes did it,' said Agnes, 'but they're long gone. It's a man's world an' we 'ave t'mek best of it.'

They supped their tea while the clock on the window ledge ticked on.

Finally Ruby broke the silence. 'Ah bet that nice-lookin' president would o' changed things if he'd lived.'

Agnes stood up to wash the teacups. 'Mebbe 'e would, but f'now we 'ave t'face it – we're jus' secon' class citadels.'

'Y'reight there, Mam.'

Fifty-year-old Annabella Outhwaite was in the local Pharmacy and Herbert Grinchley could see that here was a customer in distress.

'What's t'matter, Annabella? Y'don't look y'self.'

She dabbed her eyes with a lace handkerchief. 'It's my Claude. He needs a pick-me-up. That president getting shot was the last straw. He's gone into his shell and says the world will never be the same again.'

'An' 'e's right,' said Herbert, 'but fortunately ah 'ave jus' the thing.'

Claude Outhwaite was a regular visitor to the Pharmacy and Herbert knew him well. Claude was a local government officer who worked in York's finance department, and with his black toothbrush moustache he would have won a Hitler look-a-like competition. He worked a thirty-eight-hour week, not a minute more or less. His was a life of precision, repetition and timetables. Each year, for one week in August, Claude and Annabella would visit the same bed-and-breakfast in Morecambe. In his neat collar and tie, checked sports jacket and baggy cricket flannels, he would take in the bracing sea air. It was a relatively cheap B&B, as Claude was careful with his money. Under their brass bedstead was a china chamber pot decorated with pictures of Japanese temples. However, it was only ever used when there was a queue outside the communal bathroom.

Herbert placed a jar of Phyllosan on the counter.

'This is what 'e needs,' he said. 'It'll supply 'im wi' essential nutrients, iron an' Vitamin B.'

'Thank you, Herbert,' said Annabella as she took out her purse.

'Tell 'im t'tek two tablets three times a day before meals.'

Annabella nodded. 'Yes, I'll do that.'

'Mebbe *you* would like some, Annabella?' asked Herbert, sensing another sale in the offing. 'It strengthens nerves an' gives you more energy . . . an' *metabolic tone.*'

'Metabolic tone,' mused Annabella. 'Sounds important.'

'Just what y'need in these difficult times,' added Herbert and placed a second jar on the counter.

As Annabella left the shop Herbert gave a self-satisfied smile.

In the General Stores Edna Trott was pondering over a special offer. With a tin of Cadbury's Drinking Chocolate there was an opportunity to win free central heating.

'That would do wonders in winter for m'arthritis, Prudence.'

'I'm sure it would,' agreed Prudence.

'That school boiler will be t'death o' me. One day ah'll 'ave t'pass on m'job t'Ruby.'

'Well, you've trained her well,' said Prudence graciously.

'Growin' old is no fun,' said Edna.

Prudence paused as she opened the till. 'It comes to all of us one day.'

Edna considered this for a moment. 'Ah keep thinking 'bout that Jackie Kennedy. It's a cryin' shame she'll grow old wi'out 'er 'usband.'

'Very true,' said Prudence quietly and she glanced up at Jeremy Bear.

Edna saw the reaction and leaned over the counter and held Prudence's hand. 'We've still got a lot o' livin' t'do, Prudence,' she said gently. 'Let's be thankful f'small mercies.'

Prudence gave a wan smile and squeezed Edna's hand in response.

As she walked away from the counter, the shop bell rang and two excited eight-year-olds ran in. It was Stevie Coleclough and Shane Ramsbottom.

'We've jus' got our pocket money, Miss Golightly,' said Stevie, 'an' ah were tellin' Shane 'bout them new Animal Bars.'

Prudence smiled. 'That's right, Steven, and there's a game on the inside of each wrapper.'

They put their coins on the counter, picked up their bars of milk chocolate with two different animals moulded into the surface and hurried outside.

Life goes on, Prudence thought.

*

It was lunchtime in Nora's Coffee Shop and the jukebox had been switched off. Conversation was conducted in whispers and many sipped their hot drinks in silence. Rose was waiting to meet Freddie when Joy Popplewell appeared and sat down beside her. It was clear she was eager to impart information.

The assassination of the president had shaken everyone, but Joy had other momentous revelations on her mind. She took a magazine out of her shoulder bag and opened it to a well-thumbed page. 'Look at this, Rose.' It was an article entitled 'Nice Girls Don't'.

Retaining one's virginity until marriage was a regular theme at Easington School and had been drummed into the girls by Miss Plumb, the head of girls' games. However, since the pill had become available to the public, a sexual revolution appeared to have begun.

'I've thought about it,' said Rose. 'What about you?'

Joy gave a self-satisfied smile. 'We did it last night. My mum is away for the weekend.'

Rose stared at her friend. 'What was it like?'

'Bit painful the first time, but when we tried again it was fine. A bit quick but Sam reckons we'll get better.'

Rose looked thoughtful. 'I promised my mother I wouldn't.'

Joy looked quizzical. 'She wouldn't know and it's obvious that Freddie's keen.'

'My mother trusts me. We tell each other everything.'

Joy shrugged her shoulders. 'Your choice, Rose, but you're missing out. Most of the girls in the hockey team have done it.'

'When it happens I want it to be right,' said Rose firmly.

'With Freddie?'

Rose shook her head. 'Not sure. He would need to feel the same as me.'

'And doesn't he?'

'We haven't talked about it yet.'

'You will,' said Joy and stood up. 'Must fly. See you later at the game.'

She rushed out, passing Freddie in the doorway. He came over to Rose's table. 'Shall I order coffee and a sandwich?'

Rose smiled. 'Yes, please.'

'Joy was in a hurry.'

In more ways than one, thought Rose.

It was just after half past one and the Easington rugby team had changed into their playing kit and were standing around uncertainly waiting for Mr Morris to appear. Freddie scanned the changing room, looking at the faces of his teammates. Tension and anticipation always mounted as he waited to lead them out for the most important game of the season.

However, today was different. There was none of the usual motivational shouting, no crashing of studded rugby boots on the concrete floor; no beating out a thunderous rhythm in their pre-match warm-up. Instead they stood quietly and waited for their rugby coach to arrive. The forwards rubbed Vaseline on their ears and the backs checked their laces.

To their surprise, Charles Morris walked into the changing room accompanied by the headteacher, Dr James Hinchcliffe.

'Sit down, please, boys. Before we go out, the head wants to speak to you.'

Long wooden benches lined the walls under the rows of coat pegs and the fifteen boys sat down.

Dr Hinchcliffe waited for absolute silence. 'Boys, listen carefully. Following yesterday's news, today is like no other.' His gaze was cool and determined and his words had gravitas. 'When you go out you are representing the ethos of our school. Remember our motto, *Honore debito* – "Duty with honour".'

All eyes were fixed on the headteacher.

'I want you all to line up ten yards infield from the touchline, facing the school building. The Skipdale team will do the same on the other side of the halfway line. You'll be separated by today's referee and touch judges. At the sound of the whistle there will be a one-minute silence. We have a very large crowd today. Don't be distracted by them. Bow your heads. When you hear the whistle again, take your positions for the kick-off.'

Don't be distracted, thought Freddie. Today both Tom and Lily would be watching and Rose too would be there looking on.

'Finally boys,' continued Dr Hinchcliffe in a sonorous voice, 'yesterday's event in America has affected us all.' He paused and scanned the room. 'While this is a dreadful moment in the history of the world, it is important we put that to one side and focus on this important game. The team we face today are like us – *unbeaten*. When you walk out let us show the dignity the occasion demands.' He paused and looked at the young men before him. Many appeared uncertain. 'But when the game begins, play hard, play well . . . and win.'

Dr Hinchcliffe was a great believer in team sports and proud of the record of the school's rugby, cricket, netball and hockey teams. As he walked out to the playing field he turned to his head of English. 'Charles, I hear the Yorkshire selectors are here today.'

The afternoon game against Skipdale Grammar School in the Yorkshire Dales was important. Skipdale always had a formidable first XV with a stand-off tipped not just for Yorkshire but also for England.

Charles nodded towards two men in trilby hats on the far touchline. 'Yes, it promises be a good contest between Sam Grundy and their number ten, Matthew Elliot. They're the two best fly halves in Yorkshire. At the moment Elliot may have the better chance of selection.'

Dr Hinchcliffe smiled. 'But Charles, we have Freddie Briggs at openside wing forward. He'll knock seven bells out of him.'

The minute's silence was destined to be an experience Freddie Briggs would remember for the rest of his life. In years to come people would recall where they were when John F. Kennedy, the thirty-fifth president of the United States, was assassinated before he had completed his third year in office.

It was a poignant scene on that cold, blustery afternoon. The silence was held perfectly by the players and the supporters. It was as if the earth had stopped spinning on its axis. The stillness was absolute. Sixty seconds had never seemed so long. When the referee blew his whistle the two captains broke away from their teams to join him on the halfway line for the coin toss before the game began.

He shook hands with Freddie and Matthew. 'Well done, boys – a fitting tribute. Now let's have a good game and play to my whistle.'

'Can we get on with the game now, please?' asked Matthew a little ungraciously.

Freddie was surprised at his opponent's cocksure approach. He had been taught always to respect the referee.

Meanwhile, in the crowd, after the minute's silence Tom Feather offered Lily his thick scarf and Lily accepted it gratefully. He used his broad frame to protect her from the bitter wind. 'Life goes on,' she said a little wistfully.

'Yes,' replied Tom quietly, 'but the enormity of what has just happened will take a while to sink in.'

Lily looked up into his blue eyes. 'I understand,' she said.

Tom shook his head in sadness. 'I believe it's the end of the world as we know it.'

The match turned out to be close between two excellent sides. Their fitness was extraordinary and the tackling ferocious. With five minutes remaining and the score level at three points each, Freddie tackled Matthew Elliot with the force of an express train. The ball bounced free and was pounced upon by Sam Grundy. After a mazy run, he passed the ball out and the speedy winger scored in the corner. At the final whistle Easington had won and Freddie, battered, bruised and covered in mud, sought out his opposition captain to shake hands. Matthew was limping badly and grudgingly accepted the gesture. He was a poor loser and it was there for all to see.

After Freddie had called for three cheers for the opposition and led the team off the field, there was applause from the Easington supporters. Dr Hinchcliffe suddenly appeared by his side. 'Well played, Briggs. A fine game.'

'Thank you, sir,' said Freddie.

The headmaster walked back to join Charles Morris. 'Briggs had an absolute stormer,' he said. 'Their stand-off didn't get a look-in. Let's hope the selectors were impressed.'

'I'm sure they were,' said Charles. The two men in trilby hats were striding towards them. 'And I think we're about to find out.'

As the boys trooped off towards the changing rooms, Lily could barely contain her delight. 'Wasn't Freddie simply wonderful?'

'Best player on the field,' agreed Tom, 'and a born leader.' He leaned towards her and whispered in her ear, 'Just like you.'

For a brief moment Lily felt bereft, lost in a reservoir of silence. Then she nodded and looked up at Tom. 'We need to talk, don't we?'

However, their reverie was disturbed. The crowd was drifting towards the car park and the McConnells, Brian, Mary and Rose, were next to them.

'You must be pleased,' said Brian. He shook hands with Tom. 'Freddie was terrific.'

'Thanks, Brian,' said Tom. 'Yes, best I've seen him play.'

Rose looked at her mother appealingly. 'Can I invite Freddie back for tea?'

Mary McConnell sought out a reaction from Lily. 'It's fine by me, but you may have plans.'

Lily gathered herself quickly. 'Mary, that's kind, but it's rather short notice for you.'

'We're fine. I've done the weekend shop. There's plenty in and I guess your brother has a good appetite.'

'In that case, thank you, so long as it's no trouble. Shall I collect him later?'

'I can drop him off back at your place,' offered Brian.

'Thanks,' said Tom. 'We'll stay to say well done to Freddie and then head home.'

Freddie and Sam were sitting on a bench in the changing room and stuffing their dirty kit in a duffel bag. Side by side they appeared an odd couple. Freddie was tall and lanky with blond hair, while Sam was physically the opposite. At five feet eight inches tall he appeared short and squat in comparison. However, with shoulders like a lumberjack's, ruddy cheeks and jet black hair with a straight fringe, he cut a striking figure.

As they walked outside Sam said, 'I'm taking Joy to the Odeon tonight. Fancy coming?'

'What's on?'

'*The Birds*,' said Sam. 'It's a Hitchcock film.'

'I've seen the write-ups,' said Freddie. 'Birds start attacking for no reason.'

Joy was walking towards them, her cheeks flushed in the biting wind. 'Bit like the girls' hockey team,' said Sam with a grin.

'I see what you mean,' said Freddie with a knowing look. 'I'll check with Rose.'

Half an hour later Freddie had forsaken thoughts of a Hitchcock evening and was sitting on a sofa in the

McConnells' house sipping tea from a bone china cup. On the coffee table before him Mrs McConnell had pushed the boat out with plates of sausage rolls, chocolate cup cakes and meringues.

'Thanks for this, Mrs McConnell,' he said.

'You're welcome, Freddie.' She strode out to the kitchen to collect a sponge cake. In a black pleated skirt and a poplin blouse, she cut a fine figure and it occurred to Freddie that this is how Rose would look in twenty-five years' time. He smiled at the thought.

After tea he offered to help with the washing-up but this was declined politely. Then Brian and Mary McConnell, following a lengthy conversation in the kitchen, left the two teenagers in the lounge to watch television.

At a quarter past five Freddie and Rose settled down together to watch the first-ever episode of a new science fiction programme, *Doctor Who*. It was a four-part serial that saw the actor William Hartnell take the role of a time-traveller. At the end the Doctor's police call-box hurtled off into another time and space dimension and Freddie held Rose's hand. When *Juke Box Jury* began and the host, David Jacobs, introduced the panel, which included Cilla Black, they kissed. They barely noticed Jack Warner say, 'Evening all' in his role as *Dixon of Dock Green*. It was at that moment that Brian McConnell, recalling his own courting days, tapped gently on the door, opened it a few inches and called out, 'Time to take you home, Freddie.'

Freddie blushed profusely and jumped to his feet. 'Thanks, Mr McConnell,' he said in a flustered voice, and Brian walked out to his car grinning from ear to ear, though his wife was less enthusiastic.

On Sunday morning Freddie was out for his early-morning run. He had built up his training schedule and it was now a ten-mile circuit via Easington market town, Ragley village and back to Kirkby Steepleton. He wanted to be at peak fitness for the Yorkshire trial in early December at Headingley in Leeds. Mr Morris had passed on the news that he had been selected following his outstanding performance in the game against Skipdale.

Last year he had watched *The Loneliness of the Long Distance Runner*, starring Tom Courtenay. The character in the film enjoyed running to escape the harsh reality of his existence. In contrast, Freddie was happy with his life but wanted to be fit enough to play rugby for the Yorkshire Schoolboys XV.

While he was running through Ragley he looked at the school where his sister had worked since he was a small boy. The railings had finally been replaced, having been cut down to help the war effort. The villagers were proud of their school and it had taken many church bazaars and jumble sales to achieve this restoration. Lily had been prominent in this work and he was pleased his sister was such a respected member of the community.

However, there was something that was clearly troubling her and he did not know what it was. He was aware of it from time to time when she was looking at him doing his homework or watching television and he presumed it was that since his parents had died she was the substitute for them.

In the sharp breeze he could hear the sound of branches chafing and the high-pitched keening of the telephone wires. It was a strange tone, almost like the cry of a baby. Suddenly it was drowned out by a skein of geese, honking loudly, flying overhead in arrowhead formation towards St Mary's Church. He gritted his teeth and ran harder.

The Revd Joseph Evans had begun the early morning communion service.

'The Lord giveth and the Lord taketh away,' he said gravely during his sermon. He asked the congregation to pray for the many who had suffered in recent weeks and ended his sermon with his thoughts about John Kennedy. 'He was a man of vision,' he said. 'He said he would put a man on the moon before the end of the decade and one wonders if that will ever happen now.'

It was a sombre congregation that exited the church.

That evening Tom and Lily watched the news on television and went to bed earlier than usual.

'I can see you're troubled,' said Tom quietly.

'Just thinking.'

'I guessed so . . . and not just about events in America – more about Freddie.'

There was a long silence. Lily was gradually coming to terms with the situation regarding Freddie. She was a traveller through time, a dissipated soul seeking salvation.

'I'm not sure what to do or when to do it.'

'There's never a right time,' said Tom. 'You owe it to him to tell the truth.'

Lily looked up at him and felt the strength in this man.

'I know,' she murmured. There was a disconcerting steadiness in his honesty that she knew so well.

'It's for you to decide,' said Tom. He knew Lily's troubled past had caught up with her and the time was approaching when she would have to face the consequences.

'Oh, Tom. It's so difficult.'

She felt that her soul was an empty husk. The choice was no longer ambiguous. Soon it would be time to tell the truth.

'In the new year,' she said. 'When he's eighteen. I'll do it then.'

Tom put his arms around her and stroked her hair tenderly. 'It will be fine. He'll understand.'

'I hope so . . . but how will he cope?'

'He's a resilient young man,' Tom spoke softly.

'It's how to begin,' said Lily. 'How to say it.'

'Just speak from your heart.'

Lily sighed deeply. 'I shall.'

That night Tom stared at the darkened room and sensed that the world as they knew it was over and a new one was about to begin.

Chapter Seven

The Single-Parent Nativity

The first snow of winter had fallen and Lily looked out of the kitchen window on a world of silence. It was Friday, 6 December and the land was covered in a white shroud that muted the sounds of the countryside. Harsh winter weather was about to descend on the high moors of North Yorkshire and a busy day lay ahead. The children were looking forward to the first rehearsal of the Nativity play; also, she had a shirt to iron for Freddie.

Breakfast was a hasty affair in Laurel Cottage. Tom had a meeting in Northallerton and Lily was determined Freddie would look tidier than usual for his school photograph. She was also aware that Dr Hinchcliffe was very keen on school uniform. Boys and girls wore navy blue blazers, a white shirt and a striped blue tie. It was grey trousers for boys and grey skirts for girls, with the formidable Miss Plumb ensuring that the hem was below the knees.

'And take a comb with you,' said Lily.

Freddie gave her a friendly grin. 'Okay, but it won't do any good. My hair seems to have a mind of its own.'

'He's right,' said Tom. 'I can't imagine that blond mop with a side parting.' He looked down. 'Your shoes are a bit of a mess.'

Freddie grinned. 'It's only head and shoulders.'

Lily stood back to assess his appearance. 'Well, do your best. Sadly, we can't do anything about the bruise over your eye.'

Earlier in the week Freddie had enjoyed a fierce rugby trial in Leeds and, along with Sam Grundy, had been selected to play for Yorkshire Schoolboys against Lancashire next year.

He rubbed the lump on his forehead with pride. 'It was worth it.'

'Come on then,' said Tom, 'I'll give you a lift.'

Lily watched them leave and sighed. There was no palliative for the pain of a lie. It was a blemish that would never go away, a stain on her soul. As she stood in the doorway and waved them off, the sense of defeat tainted the sharp morning air.

In the vicarage Vera had propped her *1963 Woman's Own Christmas Annual* on the kitchen windowsill. She considered it three shillings well spent and was perusing the pages listing 'Hundreds of ideas to make and do'. There was an excellent recipe on page 30 for a walnut gâteau and she was about to search for some vanilla essence when Joseph walked in.

'Shall we walk to school together?' he suggested. 'I need to speak to John about arrangements for the Nativity and confirm the date for the Crib Service.'

Vera smiled. She loved this time of year with the anticipation of Christmas.

'Of course, Joseph. Remember to put on your warm scarf. We can't afford you getting a chill with such a busy time coming up.'

Joseph walked out to the hallway and reflected that he was pleased Vera would always be his big sister.

A severe frost had crusted the rutted back road to Ragley village and Lily drove slowly. Beyond the frozen hedgerows the bare forests were like a child's charcoal drawing in a stark monochrome world. A few flakes of snow tapped gently against her windscreen as she pulled on to the forecourt of Victor Pratt's garage.

'Four gallons, please, Victor.'

Victor seemed more animated than usual. 'If y'go in The Royal Oak, Mrs Feather, tek my advice and don't 'ave the prawn cocktail.'

'Oh dear,' said Lily, 'why is that?'

'Ah 'ad one las' time ah were in an' ah felt sick. Ah reckon there were summat fishy abart it.'

I suppose there would be, thought Lily, but said nothing.

'Ah'm sure y'kiddies will be gettin' excited wi' Christmas comin' up.'

'They certainly are, Victor. It's the rehearsal for the Nativity today.'

Victor paused before screwing on the petrol cap. 'That teks m'back. Ah were a sheep three years runnin'. Ah knew that part like back o' me 'and.'

'That's wonderful,' said Lily with a smile as she passed over a pound note and drove off.

As she walked from the school car park, she shivered. There was a cold, spiteful wind that chilled the bones and dampened the spirits. In the entrance porch blue tits were pecking at the foil tops of the bottles of milk to get at the precious head of cream; they flew away as she walked into school.

In the school office Vera was already at her desk, wearing her coat. The wooden casements were rattling and the room was like an icebox.

'Mrs Trott is struggling with the boiler,' explained Vera, her breath steaming into the cold air.

'Oh dear, I hope it doesn't affect the Nativity,' said Lily.

Vera glanced out of the window at the children running around, carefree and undeterred by the harsh weather. 'I think we'll be fine. It seems to be just us who feel the cold.'

'You're right, Vera. These are hardy country children.'

Vera nodded in acknowledgement. 'And, by the way, the piano tuner is here.'

On her way to her classroom, Lily walked across the hall to speak with Monty Tinkler, a delightful, gentle and remarkable man. Monty, in his sixties, was bent over the strings and his silver hair stirred gently with each movement.

'Good morning, Mrs Feather.'

Lily paused in admiration. 'You knew it was me.'

He stood up. 'Not difficult. You have very brisk, distinctive footsteps.'

Monty had been blinded in the Second World War but had returned to a life of music, with his well-tuned ear and perfect pitch.

'How's the piano?' asked Lily. 'Anne will be playing it more than ever in the next few weeks.'

'I've spoken to her. There were a few persistent high and low notes that were a little off key, but it continues to have a beautiful mellow tone.' He played a few bars effortlessly and Lily left him, feeling that even the most difficult setbacks could be overcome.

It was morning break and Anne was on duty in the playground. A few of the older girls had gathered round her to talk about Christmas presents.

'I've asked for a Doctor Who call-box,' said Anita Swithenbank.

Anne could sense her enthusiasm. 'I've seen them advertised on television.'

'And I'd like one of these,' said Susan Derwood. Out of her pocket she took a folded picture of a Sindy doll. It had been launched recently in the UK to great excitement among young girls. Anne read the advertisement. 'Sindy is more than a doll; she's a real personality. The free, swinging, grown-up girl who lives her own life and dresses the way she likes.'

Anne could see why it was popular. There was a hubbub of conversation involving most of the girls until Tobias Fawnswater suddenly appeared.

'I'm asking Santa for a Doctor Kildare stethoscope,' he declared.

'That's wonderful, Toby,' said Anne. 'Do you want to be a doctor when you grow up?'

'No, Miss,' said Toby. 'I just want to listen to people's chests.'

Anne liked Toby. You always got a straight answer.

*

104

Madge Appleyard, mother of ten-year-old Colin, had called into the General Stores. An affable, friendly lady, this morning she looked concerned.

'Good morning, Madge,' said Prudence. 'I was sorry to hear about Colin. Is it chickenpox?'

'Yes, Doctor Davenport has seen him and he's still off school. A pity, because he's Joseph in the Nativity and they're having a rehearsal today.'

'Never mind, he will be fine by the time the Crib Service comes round.'

Madge nodded, but still looked concerned. Colin was her only child. She opened her purse. 'A tin of beans please, Prudence.'

'Large tin of Heinz reduced to elevenpence ha'penny?'

'That's fine,' said Madge. 'And a packet of Coco Pops and one of those new Toffee Crisp bars for Colin. He likes those.'

Prudence filled her shopping bag.

'And I'll take a paper,' added Madge. She picked up a *Daily Express*. 'I see that Christine Keeler has got what she deserved.' The Profumo scandal had run its course. Back in September Christine Keeler had been arrested for perjury and now sentenced to nine months in prison.

Prudence gave an imperceptible nod of agreement and looked up at Jeremy Bear, hoping he hadn't heard about the infamous Miss Keeler. Such stories were not for the ears of the innocent.

Muriel Tonks, meanwhile, had arrived at Diane's Hair Salon for a long-overdue cut and perm.

Diane stubbed out her cigarette. 'What's it to be, Muriel?'

'Ah fancy a change.' Muriel looked up at the display of photographs stuck round the frame of the big mirror. "Ow about a Sophia Loren?'

'Comin' up,' said Diane and moved smoothly into the first item of gossip. 'Ah see that Myra Pottage is gettin' a divorce.'

'That didn't last long,' said Muriel.

'She's only twenty-two. Went off with that decorator what did 'er bedroom ceiling.'

They shared a knowing look in the mirror.

'What's young people comin' to these days?' asked Muriel. 'It's all 'ere t'day, gone t'morrow. Marriage is s'pposed t'be f'life. It's not meant t'be a 'oliday camp.'

Diane smiled. 'Yes, but what about that 'andsome cow-man you were tellin' me about?'

"E's moved on t'pastures new.' Muriel sounded disappointed. 'My 'Arold got better an' we didn't need 'im no more.'

'So did y'see that tattoo on 'is bum?'

'Ah did – twice, once in t'cowshed an' once in our 'allway.'

'Flippin' 'eck, Muriel! You're a sly one.' Diane put down her scissors. 'So, are y'goin' t'tell me?'

'You'll never guess.'

'What was it then?'

'It were a list o' names in tiny writing. All 'is conquests.'

'That's a bit cheeky!' exclaimed Diane.

"E said all 'is bored 'ousewives thought it were funny.'

'And did you?'

Muriel smiled into the mirror. 'Yes . . . twice.'

*

It was ten minutes before lunchtime and Ruby had finished putting out the dining tables. Vera was buttoning up her winter coat in the entrance hall. Lily needed some wire from the Hardware Emporium for the star of Bethlehem and Vera had offered to collect it.

'Hello, Ruby. How are you?'

'Life's a bit 'ectic t'be 'onest, Miss Evans,' said Ruby. 'M'mam's fed up wi' my Ronnie. She were reading t'Riot Act to 'im when ah left. She says 'e won't get off 'is backside.'

'Oh dear,' said Vera. 'I'm sorry to hear that, and your mother is such a hard-working woman.'

'M'mam sez we're jus' secon' class citadels.'

Vera blinked but chose not to correct Ragley's assistant caretaker. 'So where is Ronnie now?'

'Gone t'see 'is turf accountant so 'e sez . . . which is posh f'bookies.'

'I see. Well, good luck, Ruby, and I'm so pleased your Racquel was chosen to be Mary in the Nativity.'

Ruby glowed with pleasure. 'Ah'm so proud, Miss Evans, she's a lovely girl.'

'Takes after her mother,' added Vera and hurried out of school.

Timothy Pratt held the door open for the Ragley secretary as she left his shop. To her disappointment, she bumped into the local funeral director, Septimus Flagstaff.

Septimus was thrilled. Vera was the quintessence of all he desired, whereas Vera noticed that he had become decidedly portly. In his white wing-collar shirt and black waistcoat he looked like a cross between a magpie and a plump penguin.

''Ow are you, Miss Hevans, on this chilly day?'

'Fine, thank you, Mr Flagstaff, and how are you?'

'All is well. Business is booming.' He gestured towards his shiny hearse, 'We haim t'give hevry satisfaction, Miss Hevans.'

Vera visibly winced. In her opinion Septimus was a man of dishonest aitches, unlike Ruby, who simply avoided aitches at the beginning of words.

Septimus took out a shiny silver cigarette case with the intention of impressing Vera. He had recently changed his brand of cigarettes. He now smoked Camels, the American cigarette. It was his belief that you could tell a great deal from the cigarettes a man smoked.

When he offered one to Vera, she recoiled in horror. 'I don't smoke!' she exclaimed with feeling. 'And I'm in rather a hurry. Mrs Feather needs this wire for our Nativity this afternoon.'

'Well, if y'change y'mind these are the ones f'you, Miss Hevans, proper classy cigarettes for t'connoisseur.'

Vera hurried back to school shaking her head.

Deirdre Coe was standing by the bus stop on Ragley High Street when her brother pulled up in his Land Rover. 'Where you off to?' he asked with a scowl.

'Into York t'do some shoppin'.'

'York's goin' to t'dogs,' he growled, 'wi' all them foreigners on t'buses. What's it comin' to?'

'Y'reight there, Stanley,' said Deirdre, her double chin wobbling as she nodded in agreement.

Stan drove off to meet his duck-shooting friends at the Pig & Ferret.

The bus pulled up and Ruby's mother, Agnes, got off after completing her morning shift at the chocolate factory.

'Look what t'cat dragged in,' sneered Deirdre.

There was no love lost between these two women.

'Why don't y'sling yer 'ook,' retorted Agnes. 'Ah 'eard your Stan were throwin' 'is money about in t'Pig an' Ferret by all accounts accordin' t'Tommy Piercy.'

'What's it got t'do wi' you?'

''E's a conman is your Stanley. 'E'd break t'bank at Monte Carlo if y'gave 'im t'chance.'

'Anyway, gerroff 'ome to y'council 'ouse. Ah don't mix wi' the hoi polloi. Ah prefer a better class o' people.'

'So what meks you so grand?'

'Ah'm off t'buy a rotary drier. No more clothes props an' saggin' washin' lines f'me,' Deirdre boasted. 'Eight pounds, nineteen shillings . . . so there!' and she stepped on to the bus.

Over the years Lily and Anne had taken control of the annual Nativity play. John Pruett's stilted version with children reading lines from slips of paper had been discarded. Lily preferred improvisation, with boys and girls using their own language to tell the story. It had proved popular with parents and definitely added to the entertainment value without losing the sincerity of the story.

During morning assembly Joseph had told the story of the Nativity and most of the children had a good idea of the sequence of events that led to the birth of Jesus. When Anne had played the opening chords of 'The First Noel', Joseph had been unaware that Duggie Smith, a recent and not entirely well-informed addition to the school choir, was singing 'The First Oh-Hell!' at the top of his voice.

Inevitably, before morning break there had been the usual questions for Joseph.

'Mr Evans, what's Franky Scents?' asked Norman Barraclough.

'My dad uses Old Spice,' added Stevie Coleclough before the vicar had the chance to reply.

Joseph had been pleased to retire to the staff-room and a welcome cup of camomile tea.

After morning break he was relaxed again and sitting next to John Pruett at the side of the hall. Lily and Anne put the children through their paces. Although a few boys and girls were absent, Lily was determined to have a brisk run-through. Inevitably, it didn't go to plan.

Luke Walmsley proved to be a particularly determined innkeeper. 'There's no room in 'ere,' he announced when Racquel Smith, playing the part of Mary, knocked on his imaginary door.

''Ow come?' asked Racquel.

'Well, we're full – that's why,' replied Luke, not to be outdone.

'That's a poor do,' complained Racquel, shaking her head.

'You'll 'ave t'go somewhere else,' said Luke, pointing towards the school entrance.

Racquel stood her ground. 'Well ah'm 'avin' a baby an' it's comin' reight quick, so ah've been told.'

'Ah see,' pondered the innkeeper. 'Well, ah've got an idea.' He glanced up at Lily, who smiled back encouragingly, pleased Luke was making this up as he went along.

'Y'can go in t'stable if y'like. There's plenty o' dry straw in there an' y'should be warm enough.'

'Thanks,' said Mary. 'It'll 'ave t'do,' she added, grudgingly.

'Anyway,' continued the innkeeper, looking puzzled, 'where's yer 'usband?'

'Joseph's not 'ere.'

''Ow come?'

''E's got chickenpox.'

There were a few titters among the assembled kings and shepherds.

Scott Walmsley, wearing one of his mother's tea towels on his head as Second Shepherd, decided to speak up. 'An' in any case – it's not 'is.'

Joseph Evans looked shocked and John Pruett glanced anxiously at Lily. She returned a fixed smile as she inwardly determined to have a quiet word with Scott.

Meanwhile, Vera, who had been standing by the double doors that led to the entrance hall, gave Lily a thumbs-up and hurried off to make a hot drink.

At afternoon break, John Pruett was on playground duty and a bewildered Joseph had driven home. Lily and Anne were in the staff-room drinking tea while Vera was dabbing tears of laughter from her eyes.

'Well done, both of you,' she said. 'I think that's the first single-parent Nativity I've ever seen.'

'Yes,' agreed Lily with a grin. 'It just needs a little tweaking.'

'And perhaps a stand-in Joseph when we perform in church,' added Anne with a wide-eyed smile.

Vera had brought in some home-made scones as a

treat and the three women relaxed in each other's company and contemplated Christmas on the not-too-distant horizon.

At 7 School View Ruby was in her kitchen, sifting through her mother's Kays catalogue. She wondered if there would ever be a day when she wouldn't have to live on the never-never.

Meanwhile Agnes was dunking an arrowroot biscuit in her tea while her teeth soaked in a tumbler on the draining board.

'Ah'll be working f'pin money 'til ah pop m'clogs, jus' you wait an' see.'

They sipped their tea in silence while Agnes nursed little Natasha and Sharon sat on the threadbare carpet in the front room and stared at the television. *Watch with Mother* had just begun and Sharon appeared to understand the strange language of the Flower Pot Men and chuckled to herself as she chewed on a rusk.

'That Norman Fazackerley's goin' up in t'world, Ruby, you mark my words.'

''Ow come, Mam?' asked Ruby.

'Ah've 'eard 'e's gettin' into radiators.'

'Radiators?'

'Yes, luv, 'cause 'e says central 'eatin' is t'thing of t'future.'

Ruby shook her head. 'Well, ah like m'coal fire.'

'An' ah'll tell y'summat else,' said Agnes. She was on a roll. 'That Violet fancy-pants Fawnswater 'as got one o' them stimulated coal fires.'

'Stimulated?'

'Yes, luv, it works on 'lectric.'

Ruby's eyes were wide. 'Flippin' 'eck, Mam – wonders never cease.'

Agnes poured another cup of tea. 'An' another thing . . . ah saw that Deirdre when ah got off t'bus an' she were shoutin' 'er mouth off as usual.'

'She's allus been mardy 'as that Deirdre Coe,' said Ruby, 'but who wouldn't be, livin' wi' that brother o' 'ers? What were she sayin'?'

'Summat abart a new clothes-dryer.'

'There's nowt wrong wi' a washin' line, Mam.'

'Y'reight there, Ruby. Y'know what they say – y'can't teach a new dog old tricks.'

Racquel ran in from school just as Ruby was leaving to do her cleaning.

"Ow did y'get on, luv, in t'Nativity?'

'It were good, Mam, but ah don't think Mary 'as a ponytail.'

'Well, we can do summat abart that,' said Ruby and gave her a hug.

'We can do yer 'air like Princess Margaret,' suggested Agnes.

"Ow come, Grandma?'

'She were on t'telly wi' a posh frock an' a sparkly necklace an' lovely 'air wi' a cornet on 'er 'ead.'

'An' who's Joseph?' asked Ruby.

"E weren't there, Mam. 'E's got chickenpox.'

'Well, baby Jesus'll need a dad,' said Agnes defiantly.

'Mr Evans said 'is dad were God.'

'Yes, luv,' said Agnes, 'but he'll still need a *proper* dad.'

Racquel nodded. 'What's f'tea, Mam?'

'Y'Gran'll mek you a butty t'be goin' on with. See

y'later,' and Ruby tightened her headscarf and set off to do battle with the school boiler.

Up the Morton road, Violet Fawnswater was alone in her spacious lounge watching television and reflecting on her life. She looked out of the window at the sylvan shadows in the dark world beyond.

She had taken up smoking again and a packet of Player's Anchor filter-tipped cigarettes was on the coffee table beside her. The advertisement had said that, for two shillings and ten pence for twenty, they gave you 'precise moments of calm in a busy day', and that was just what she needed.

That morning Violet had spent £33 on the de luxe version of the Creda Debonair Spin Dryer, which purported 'freedom from drippy, droopy washing'. But it didn't take away the pain of an unfaithful husband.

She thought of her late mother, who had suffered a similar experience. It felt like a visitation from the Ghost of Christmas Past and she shivered. On her mother's final day she had held her daughter's hand and murmured bravely, 'I played the hand I was given,' and Violet understood the significance of her words.

Upstairs in her bedroom, the expensive bottles of scent on her dressing-room table had an appealing fragrance, but they could never disguise the odour of her husband's betrayal.

She had bought one of the new lava lamps and watched the bubbles rise and then fall . . . rather like her life.

It was four o'clock and outside Easington School Freddie and Rose were walking to the bus stop.

'We ought to celebrate you getting on the Yorkshire team,' said Rose.

'And with Sam,' added Freddie.

'So what shall we do tomorrow afternoon after you've finished at the hardware shop?'

'We could go to Marks an' Sparks,' suggested Freddie.

Rose was impressed. This was unexpected. 'Good choice,' she said.

They had been to look at clothes a number of times and Freddie had grown to admire Rose's swift, confident movements as she sifted through a rack of clothing on a hanging rail like an experienced filing clerk. He presumed this was a 'woman thing', as he had seen his sister doing exactly the same when she was looking for a summer dress or a winter coat.

The full moon, like an oculus in the dark sky, cast a cold, eerie light and long shadows stretched before them. They held hands and made footprints in the snow, a matching pair, together in harmony. Freddie couldn't recall being so happy. The dusting of snow made everything look new and clean, a white world laid out just for them, an undiscovered Narnia. A life with Rose by his side stretched out before him and his heart was filled with contentment.

However, the young man would look back on these innocent days with sadness. Destiny can play cruel tricks, and he had no idea his life was about to change.

Chapter Eight

A Time to Forget

Roland Heckingbottom forgot his wife's name. It was the day the Easington Rotary Club Committee invited him to be Father Christmas.

Each year the club erected a little wooden hut in the local marketplace for the duration of the Christmas Fair. The view of the committee was that Roland would be the perfect choice. A rotund, naturally cheerful man with a fluffy white beard, he certainly looked the part. In a red suit and black wellington boots he would be perfect.

Roland was delighted. At the annual dinner in early December, members' wives had been invited. The chairman, Walter Wimpenny, shook his hand and turned to his wife, Ethel. 'And this must be your lovely wife,' he said. He glanced at Roland waiting for the introduction.

'Yes,' said Roland, 'this is . . . this is . . . my wife.'

The name had gone. In that split second his life changed. It had never happened before and he couldn't understand it. He hadn't been drinking and at seventy-two years old he considered himself to be in fine health.

Ethel smiled at the chairman. 'I'm Ethel,' she said quietly.

'Please call me Walter,' he replied, 'and let me buy you a drink.'

Ethel gave her husband a curious look.

That's how it began for Roland and no one understood why.

After the war he had worked in Leeds at the Fifty Shilling Tailors – a chain of shops selling men's clothes. He would sit cross-legged on the floor all day, sewing lapels and buttonholes. He and Ethel moved on to Winchester when he was promoted to deputy manager, but later, when they reached retirement age, they returned to set up home in North Yorkshire. They were childless and content. Ethel joined the Women's Institute and Roland was introduced to the Rotary. They led a simple, happy life together until Roland felt his mind was playing tricks on him.

Suddenly, for Roland, it was a time to forget.

For Lily Feather it was a time to remember.

Routines are fine until life becomes hectic. Friday, 20 December was such a morning. It was the last day of term and Lily was in the corner of the lounge seeking out her Canon 35mm camera. She had recently inserted a roll of Kodak film and there were a few shots left. It had been a present from Tom for her birthday and she wanted to take some photographs of the children's activities on the last school day of 1963. She was also leading morning assembly, so a busy day lay in store.

An antique pine bureau writing desk with a drop-down lid stood in the lounge. It was definitely Lily's domain and hers alone. It had been passed down to her from her father. As Freddie did his homework on the kitchen table and Tom had a secretary and an office in Northallerton, it was a private space for Lily. Behind the lid were lots of little shelves full of envelopes, writing paper and post-cards. Below were two lockable drawers and then a cupboard behind a pair of hinged doors. It was there she found the camera.

As an afterthought, she took a bunch of keys from her jacket pocket and unlocked the right-hand drawer. There was a letter in her handbag that she wanted to add to her collection. She had just closed the drawer when there was a crash from the kitchen.

'Damn!' came a cry. It was unlike Tom ever to use bad language. Lily ran into the kitchen, where Freddie was on his knees helping Tom retrieve the broken shards of a plate.

'Sorry,' said Tom.

'Not to worry,' said Lily. 'These things happen.'

'Anyway,' said Tom, glancing at the kitchen clock, 'must rush. I've a meeting. Come on Freddie, I'll drop you off at school.'

Lily wasn't far behind and she closed the front door. Laurel Cottage was silent again. The clock on the mantel-piece ticked on, the letterbox clattered when the postman delivered mail and a few flakes of sleet tapped against the window panes.

She drove to school through a stark, desolate world. Overnight snow covered the distant hills and the land was held fast in the grip of winter, while the first pre-dawn light flickered across the frozen fields.

On Ragley High Street posters advertising the Easington Christmas Market were displayed everywhere. Lily crunched to a halt in the school car park. Under a wolf-grey sky she hurried into school, completely unaware she had forgotten to lock the drawer of her writing bureau.

It was something she would later regret.

On her way to school Vera had called into the General Stores.

'A dozen mince pies, please, Prudence.'

'For the staff-room, Vera?'

'Yes, I thought it would cheer them up. Everyone has worked so hard and it's the party this afternoon.' Vera glanced up at Ragley's favourite bear. 'And good morning to you, Jeremy.'

'He's looking forward to Christmas and is hoping for a new cardigan,' said Prudence with enthusiasm.

'Well, I must say he looks most impressive this morning.'

Jeremy was dressed in a red shirt and bright blue over-alls. 'We're doing some Christmas stocktaking later,' explained Prudence.

'It's a busy time for you both.'

'It is,' replied Prudence with a wistful smile.

When Lily walked into the school hall it was a hive of activity. Anne Grainger was preparing the music for morning assembly. She was setting out the instruments for her orchestra and a performance of 'Little Donkey' on treble recorders.

'Morning, Lily,' she said. 'Difficult journey?'

'Yes, but fortunately Deke Ramsbottom was out early with his snow plough.'

Ruby Smith and Edna Trott had just finished hanging small gifts of sweets on the Christmas tree, one for each child, wrapped in North Yorkshire County Council tissue paper, blue for boys and pink for girls. The sweets were provided by the caretaking team from their meagre wages.

'Well done, Ruby – a good job,' said Edna as they stood back to admire their work.

'It looks wonderful,' said Lily in appreciation.

'Thank you kindly, Mrs Feather,' replied Edna. 'Ruby's a big 'elp, what wi' my back an' dizzy spells.'

'I'm sure she is,' said Lily, who was well acquainted with the many ailments of the Ragley caretaker.

In the far corner of the school hall John Pruett had recovered the old wooden Christmas postbox from the loft and was preparing it for the children's letters to Father Christmas.

'Well done, ladies,' he said. 'Let's switch on, shall we?'

Strands of coloured bulbs had been wound round the tree.

'Oooh, look at them lights, Ruby!' exclaimed Edna. 'Aren't they lovely?'

'It's all lit up like Blackpool hallucinations,' said Ruby, her rosy cheeks glowing.

'Y'reight there, Ruby,' agreed Edna.

The children were full of excitement and, after registration and morning assembly, they sat down to write their letters to Father Christmas. By morning break John was checking all their writing to ensure there was nothing contentious and smiling at the children's responses – with one exception. He was not entirely happy with Stevie Coleclough, who had written, 'Santa, please make Christmas a good one for old people . . . like Mr Pruett.'

He was intrigued by Anita Swithenbank, who wanted something out of the ordinary. In neat cursive writing under a picture of Santa in his sleigh she had requested, 'Please can I have a signed picture of you because Scott says you're not real.'

Susan Derwood appeared concerned about Santa's waistline. She had written, 'Dear Santa, I'm sorry you are fat. When you come to my house look on the shelf in the kitchen where my mum keeps her diet books. You would like my mum. She is fat as well.' John Pruett decided not to let Mrs Derwood see this letter.

Norman Barraclough was having a twinge of conscience with this admission of guilt: 'Dear Santa, I have been good all year except on Sundays when my cousin, Lucy, comes to visit and I hide for most of the day.'

As John sifted through the collection he smiled. There were the usual requests for the popular toys of the day, including a Ken doll as a friend for Barbie, a Scalextric and an Easy-Bake Oven.

The final letter was written by the phlegmatic Colin Appleyard, who simply asked the direct question, 'Dear Santa, do you get fed up saying Ho-ho-ho?'

It was a typical last afternoon of the autumn term in Ragley village school. The older children arranged chairs in a big circle and blew up balloons, while the little ones crayoned their Christmas cards. They played lots of games, including The Farmer's in His Den, Statues and Musical Chairs, and there was a party tea with crab paste sandwiches and red jelly.

When the children had departed into the darkness, clutching a card, a balloon and a tube of sweets, the staff relaxed in the staff-room.

'Tea and mince pies, everyone,' said Vera.

Finally they said their goodbyes and agreed to meet up at Sunday's Crib Service. John Pruett was always a little sad at this time of the year as he saw Lily drive away. Soon, with a heavy heart, he was driving past the frozen hedgerows beneath the skeletal boughs of sycamore and elm towards the silence of his home to make a meal for one.

That Saturday afternoon all roads led to the Easington Christmas Market, where the local villagers went in search of a yuletide bargain. The sharp, clean air of the high moors had scoured the countryside as Sam Grundy collected Freddie, Rose and Joy. They drove to the local market town and parked in one of the side streets.

The four teenagers gathered next to Terry 'Tatti' Duckworth's hot potato stall. They munched on a hot snack and listened to the local choir singing 'O Come All Ye Faithful' accompanied by the Ragley and Morton Brass Band.

The bright lights of the tall Christmas tree next to the War Memorial shone down on the stalls that bordered the cobbled market square.

'I love Christmas,' said Rose, her eyes bright with excitement.

Freddie put his arm around her shoulders and smiled. Her eyes were hazel, but to Freddie they were flecked with gold. 'Me too,' he said.

Sam and Joy were a few paces away, deep in conversation, and Freddie looked at the two of them as a meeting between two worlds. Sam, with his farmer's strength and roast beef dinners, and Joy, with her pale complexion and the smell of smoke and blacklead. There were days when they took on the appearance of two odd socks and Freddie wondered what would become of them.

His thoughts were shattered by the Easington town crier in his three-cornered hat and ceremonial frock coat ringing his bell and chanting, 'Oyez, Oyez, Oyez!', and they wandered to where a large crowd had gathered round Fast Eddie's stall.

Eddie Ormonroyd presented himself as a Scarborough entrepreneur. He was renowned for buying and selling and was always too quick for the police. Tall and swarthy, with long hair and a flat cap, he regarded himself as God's gift to women.

'Now then, you sexy ladies,' he shouted. "Ow about a bit o' 'ot stuff on a cold winter's night?'

He had certainly grabbed the attention of Muriel Tonks. 'Ah could do wi' a bit o' that,' she yelled.

There was communal laughter.

'Well, ladies, there's only one o' me t'go round, so 'ow about one o' these?' He held up a box with the label 'Earlywarm Electric Blanket'.

'In them posh shops down in Hoxford Street this'll cost

you gettin' on f'ten poun'. But not 'ere, not t'night, ladies. Ah'm not askin' ten, ah'm not askin' five.' He looked directly at Muriel. 'F'one night only, thanks t'this beautiful lady, this 'lectric blanket is goin' f'two poun' fifty.'

'Ah'll 'ave one,' shouted Muriel.

'An' so will I,' called out Emily Poskitt.

'An' ah'll show you 'ow it works,' leered Fast Eddie as his assistant passed out the boxes and collected the cash.

Freddie, Rose, Sam and Joy were enjoying the banter.

'Now then,' bellowed Fast Eddie, 'who wants a Beatles wig? Y'can look like John, Paul, George an' t'other one for a poun'. Who wants one?'

'It's Ringo,' shouted Joy.

'What is?' asked Fast Eddie.

'The other Beatle,' said Joy.

'Thank you, darlin',' said Fast Eddie with a big grin. 'This lovely girl can 'ave one f'ten bob. 'Ave y'got a boyfriend?'

Joy pointed at Sam.

'Pity,' said Fast Eddie.

The four of them wandered off, leaving Fast Eddie selling his goods like hot cakes. Edie Kershaw bought a Remington Rollershave electric shaver for her husband, Alfie, while Deirdre Coe snapped up a Morphy Richards steam/dry iron at a bargain price as a Christmas present for herself.

In the corner of the market square Ruby Smith and her mother, Agnes, were in the queue outside Santa's grotto along with Racquel, Duggie and Sharon, plus Natasha in her pushchair. Andy had gone off with his friends to look at a stall selling Matchbox toy cars.

'Ronnie told me what 'e wanted f'Christmas,' said Agnes.

'What were that, Mam?'

'A Brylcreem dispenser f'nine bob. Ah told 'im t'tek a runnin' jump.'

'Ah'm not s'prised,' said Ruby. She picked up Sharon. 'Now it won't be long afore y'see Santa, and remember t'be p'lite.'

Inside the grotto, Roland was struggling. There was too much to remember.

Tobias Fawnswater was unhappy. 'Santa, last year I asked for a toy train but I think you forgot.'

'Santa can't remember every request, darling,' said Mrs Fawnswater.

Too true, thought Roland.

Each child had told him their name, but a couple of questions later he couldn't bring it to mind. It was so frustrating.

'Perhaps Santa will bring you one this year,' said Mrs Fawnswater, giving Roland a firm nod.

'Yes, I think I've got one in my toy cupboard,' said Santa with what he hoped was a reassuring smile.

An unconvinced Tobias left, shaking his head as he collected his tube of fruit pastilles from sixteen-year-old Lizzie Buttershaw dressed in an elf costume.

The next customer was Mrs Flathers with her daughter, Margery, who had just passed her sixth birthday. The little girl opened up with an unpredictable question.

'Santa, please can you bring a present for my daddy?'

Roland looked up hesitantly at Mrs Flathers, who just shrugged her shoulders.

'Well, I shall have a look in my sack when I get to your house,' he said.

'Thank you, Santa.'

'So, what does your daddy like?'

Margery thought hard. Suddenly her face lit up. 'Cockporn.'

'Pardon?'

'Cockporn, Santa. He loves it.'

Mrs Flathers blushed. 'I think she means *popcorn*, Santa.'

That's a relief, thought Roland.

Finally it was Ruby's turn. The family crowded into the little hut and Ruby lifted Natasha out of her pushchair.

'What a lovely little girl,' said Santa. 'What's her name?'

'Natasha, Santa.'

'She's jus' like a light bulb is our Natasha,' said Racquel.

'A light bulb?'

'Yes, Santa,' explained Racquel, "cause when she smiles she lights up our 'ouse.'

'Isn't that wonderful,' said Roland. 'And what's your name?'

'I'm Racquel.'

'And what would you like for Christmas?'

Racquel answered with confidence. 'Please could ah 'ave a roll o' Sellotape, some coloured pencils an' a sketch pad. Them's easy ones, Santa, but there's a 'ard one.'

'And what's that?' asked a surprised Roland.

Racquel recalled a tearful visit to the cinema to see a Walt Disney classic. 'Can y'mek Bambi's mother come alive again?'

'I'm not sure about that,' mumbled Roland. Train sets and dolls were fine, but resurrection was definitely beyond his job description.

Duggie decided to share a problem. 'Ah'm Duggie, Santa, an' it's a pity you 'ave t'be good f'Christmas 'cause it's 'ard bein' good . . . an' there's summat else.'

'What's that?'

'Can y'*not* give me stuff wi' no batt'ries.'

It was at this point Roland sighed and reckoned he was not cut out for this job.

That evening Ruby and her family sat down to watch *Doctor Who* and the first episode of a new seven-part serial. William Hartnell as the time-travelling doctor was about to do battle with some scary machines known as 'the Daleks'. They trundled around on wheels and seemed keen to annihilate the population of the Earth. Duggie was unimpressed. 'Bet they can't climb upstairs, Mam,' he said in disdain. 'Flash Gordon would've made mincemeat out of 'em.'

On Sunday morning the church bells were ringing and families were hurrying up the Morton road for the Crib Service. The sky was powder blue as Lily walked through the lychgate and up the path to the church entrance.

As she passed through the Norman doorway, bright light illuminated the stained glass in the East window and lit up the Victorian altar rail. The church filled quickly and children wearing tea-towel headdresses and curtain cloaks were rehearsing their lines for the performance of their Nativity play. It was part of the fabric of a Ragley

Christmas. Anne and a group of mothers were dressing shepherds, kings and angels, and Lily went over to help.

Elsie Crapper launched into 'Once in Royal David's City' on the organ and the children performed their timeless story. After completing his role as Fifth Shepherd, Duggie Smith returned to his pew and sat down between Ruby and Agnes. Joseph asked the congregation to take a few quiet moments to pray for a loved one.

Duggie, head bowed and hands together, suddenly started speaking in a loud voice.

'What y'doin'?' whispered Ruby.

'Ah'm prayin'.'

'Who to?'

'T'God.'

'Well shurrup, God's not deaf.'

'Ah know,' said Duggie, 'but m'gran is, an' ah'm prayin' she buys me a Meccano Elektrikit – wi' batt'ries o' course.'

It was mid-morning on Christmas Eve and in Laurel Cottage Lily had taken down her birthday cards from the mantelpiece and replaced them with family Christmas cards. She wiped the dust from the framed wedding photograph of her parents, Florence and Arthur Briggs.

This morning Lily was wearing an old cardigan that her mother had knitted for her. While there were bitter memories of the burden Florence had placed on the shoulders of the young Lily, she felt it was appropriate to wear it in her memory. The pattern of pretty flowers on the sleeves was faded with age now. As she put the birthday cards on a shelf behind the drop-down lid of her bureau, she recalled Freddie as a small boy and how he had always loved to blow out the birthday candles and make a wish. She smiled at the memory.

Those days had gone, but the images were still sharp in her mind.

Meanwhile, on Ragley High Street it was the busiest morning of the year and Vera was in Piercy's butcher's shop collecting her turkey.

'Thank you, Thomas,' she said.

Vera always called the corpulent village butcher 'Thomas'. After all, that was the name he was given when he was christened. She was not in favour of abbreviations. They seemed too flippant and careless. In fact, she did wonder why 'abbreviation' was such a long word.

Vera had spent some time that morning wrapping Joseph's present. Last week she had gone into York and purchased a large and very loud alarm clock. She thought it would improve his timekeeping. When she placed it under the Christmas tree in the corner of the lounge in the vicarage she saw a clumsily wrapped cardboard box, her present from Joseph, and she wondered what it might be.

Joseph had spent the princely sum of £5 on a Queen Anne yellow rose coffee set. He thought it would appeal to Vera's love of delicate crockery and provide more opportunities to drink coffee rather than tea. Wrapping gifts was not his forte, but he had been brought up to believe it is the thought that counts.

In the Coffee Shop the Beatles' Christmas number one, 'I Want to Hold Your Hand', was playing on the bright red-and-chrome jukebox. The teenagers of the village drank their frothy coffee and hummed along.

Nora had taken over Doris Clutterbuck's Tea Rooms in 1957 and transformed them into Nora's Coffee Shop. Her father, Aloysius Pratt, had provided the funds and it had proved a great success. Over the last six years it had become the most popular meeting place in the village, especially among the younger generation. Apart from drinking coffee, they enjoyed listening to the non-stop music.

Nora had worked hard on her Christmas decorations this year. They included a 'kissing ring' hung above the counter in anticipation and no little expectation. She had wrapped the circular frame of an old lampshade with blue, green and silver tinsel and attached a few shiny baubles. A sprig of mistletoe had been added for good measure. She looked across the counter at the young lovers and wished it would be her turn one day.

Meanwhile, outside the Hardware Emporium Nora's brother, Timothy Pratt, was rearranging his window display of cut-out Christmas snowmen with infinite care until they were in perfect alignment. Timothy was a pernickety soul. His father had told him, 'Success is in the detail,' and he had never forgotten.

Back in Laurel Cottage, Freddie was looking for a Christmas card to give to the McConnell family. He had been invited to their home for tea. Tom and Lily had arranged to collect him at eleven o'clock to join them for Midnight Mass at St Mary's Church.

He looked around the lounge. 'Tom, is there a spare

Christmas card anywhere?' he called. 'It's for Rose's mum and dad.'

Tom was sitting at the kitchen table drinking coffee and reading the Christmas *TVTimes*. One of his favourite films, *Tom Brown's Schooldays*, was on on Boxing Day afternoon and he circled it with a pencil.

'Not sure,' he murmured. 'I think I saw Lily putting some cards in her bureau. Maybe have a look there.'

Freddie wasn't sure. The bureau was usually out of bounds . . . but needs must. He opened the drop-down lid and saw a pile of cards, but they were birthday cards. He closed it and tried the left-hand drawer. It was locked. Then he tried the right-hand drawer. To his surprise, it opened.

There were no Christmas cards in there, just stacks of letters wrapped in rubber bands, plus a few trinkets. He was about to close the drawer when something caught his eye. It was the edge of a photograph sticking out of an envelope. Curious, he eased it out a little further. It was a group of six men, farm workers by the look of them, leaning against a fence outside an old barn. Behind them, a harvest field stretched out into the distance.

Then he looked more closely. One of the men appeared to be him . . . or at least someone who looked very much like him. He wondered if he had a distant cousin.

'Any luck?' asked Tom from the kitchen.

Freddie, puzzled, shut the drawer quickly. 'No,' he said. 'None here.'

'Just remembered,' said Tom. 'There are a few spare ones upstairs on our dressing table. Use one of those.'

'Thanks,' said Freddie.

*

131

At seven o'clock Tom drove Freddie to the McConnells' house. 'Enjoy your evening,' he said.

'Thanks,' said Freddie. 'See you later.' He was excited. Spending an evening with the girl of his dreams was his idea of the perfect Christmas Eve.

Brian and Mary McConnell were generous hosts. They had grown to have a high opinion of this polite young man, who clearly cared for their daughter. With this in mind, they left them alone for a while to settle on the sofa in the lounge in front of a crackling log fire and enjoy watching television.

'We'll be back in an hour,' said Brian. He glanced at the screen. 'This programme isn't for us,' he added with a grin. He walked out to the kitchen and left them to the ITV pop programme *Beat City* featuring Gerry and the Pacemakers and Rory Storm and the Hurricanes. It was a lively show but Freddie didn't see much of it. He was in heaven . . . kissing Rose.

At ten o'clock Brian and Mary came into the lounge to watch *The Good Old Days*. The distinguished chairman, Leonard Sachs, introduced a variety of acts including Frankie Vaughan. Freddie was on his best behaviour and Rose ignored her mother's perceptive glances.

The doorbell rang and Tom and Lily arrived. After a welcome glass of mulled wine, they left in two cars and parked outside St Mary's Church, where Archibald Pike and his bell-ringers were calling on the villagers to join together for the special service that heralded Christmas Day.

Snowflakes pattered against the giant door of St Mary's Church as a stream of people walked in. Regardless of the late hour, this was a popular service and soon all the pews were filled. The ledges on the stone pillars had been decorated with holly, bright with red berries, and, on the altar, candles flickered.

Elsie Crapper was playing 'Away in a Manger' and then, at half past eleven, the bells stopped ringing and quiet descended on the congregation. The choir sang 'Once in Royal David's City' and gradually the church was filled with music. It was a special time for Lily. She had grown to love a Yorkshire Christmas and this was one she would never forget.

It was also a poignant time for Roland and Ethel Heckingbottom.

Earlier in the day Roland had knocked on the door of his neighbour, Gabriel Book. He had carefully parcelled up his Santa suit in brown paper and tied it neatly with string.

'Hello, Roland, what a nice surprise,' said Gabriel. 'Come in and have a festive drink.'

'That's kind, Gabriel,' said Roland, 'but I've got a lot on.'

Gabriel looked inquisitively at the parcel.

Roland handed it over. 'I'd like you to to have this,' he said. 'It's my Santa suit. I'm afraid I didn't do a good job in the Rotary grotto. I thought you might like to give it a go.'

'Oh dear,' said Gabriel. 'Look, just come in for a short while and tell me about it.'

Roland sighed. 'Very well.'

It was an hour later that he left. Gabriel had been a good listener. He was sad for his friend. Roland clearly had a problem but he didn't fully understand what could be done about it.

That evening Roland sat down with his wife and held her hand.

'Ethel, I've passed on the Father Christmas outfit to Gabriel. He said he would have a word with the Rotary Committee.'

'Couldn't you do that?'

'I could . . . but I don't want to.'

'Why not?'

'Because I couldn't explain the real reason without feeling embarrassed.'

'I see,' said Ethel.

'I keep forgetting things and it's getting worse.'

'Don't worry. Everything will be fine. Let's have a cup of tea and the last of the mince pies.'

By their fireside they shared the final hours of Christmas Eve.

'Have one of your Christmas cigars,' said Ethel. 'That will cheer you up.' She had bought a drum of twenty-five Castella cigars for £1.17 from the General Stores.

Later that evening Ethel watched anxiously as her husband puffed on his cigar. Something had happened to him and she didn't know what it was. As Roland stared vacantly at the flickering flames, she wondered what the future held for them. It would be twenty years later, long after Roland had passed away, that Ethel heard of a man called Alzheimer and, in her fading years, she began to understand what had happened to her dear husband.

Back in Laurel Cottage, Tom was locking the doors before going upstairs to bed. The dying embers in the fireplace were glowing red and the candles on the mantelpiece were burning low.

A tired Freddie had gone to bed and Tom had prepared two steaming mugs of cocoa. Lily was sitting at her bureau. After Tom went upstairs she was going to put his present under the tree. She had purchased an Ingersoll wristwatch for £3.10 and knew Tom would like it. It was wrapped in red tissue paper and hidden away at the back of one of the drawers.

She took out her keys from her handbag, but to her surprise she noticed the right-hand drawer was already unlocked and wondered when that could have happened. She looked down anxiously at her collection of letters. The most recent one wasn't where she had left it. It was the one with the old photograph.

'Come and sit down,' said Tom, patting the space on the sofa next to him. 'It's been a long day.'

Lily was frowning.

'What's wrong?' he asked.

'Have you been in my bureau by any chance?'

Tom shook his head. 'No, but Freddie was looking for a Christmas card earlier today.'

Lily's face went white.

Chapter Nine

The Butterfly Effect

It was New Year's Eve and, after a heavy snowfall, the land was silent and still. It was the time of the long nights and a bitter wind blew snowflakes against the bedroom window of Laurel Cottage. All seemed calm once again in Lily's life. Christmas week had passed without incident after the concern that Freddie may have come across something that was for her eyes only. The drawer of her bureau was now firmly locked.

While the creatures of the countryside sought refuge, Tom Feather was enjoying a cup of tea in bed and a gentle start to the day. He had a collection of novels in a small cupboard next to the bed. Tom had been a fan of science fiction since he was a boy and was reading Ray Bradbury's 1952 short story 'A Sound of Thunder'. This was his private escapism from a demanding job and he was enjoying Bradbury's concept of time travel. In particular, he was intrigued by the idea that a single butterfly could eventually have a far-reaching effect on future events.

A simple act could change the course of history.

In Laurel Cottage a 'butterfly effect' was about to occur. It had begun quite simply, with an unlocked drawer and a photograph. As he relaxed with his book, Tom was unaware that before the dawn of the new year the lives of Lily and Freddie were going to change.

Lily was in the kitchen stirring a pan of porridge. A warming breakfast for Tom and Freddie was ideal on a freezing morning such as this. She thought back over the past week. Her brother, George, had been granted two days' leave from his duties in Ireland and had arrived on the morning of Christmas Day. It had been a happy family reunion and they had caught up on all his news. They had enjoyed a Christmas dinner together and then settled down in front of the television to watch Cliff Richard and the Shadows perform on *Christmas Swingtime*, followed by a friendly but fiercely competitive game of Monopoly.

Then it was time for cold turkey sandwiches and pickled onions while they listened to a Christmas message from Dr Coggan, the Archbishop of York. Later, they relaxed with a slice of Christmas cake, topped with a sliver of Wensleydale cheese, and a mug of sweet tea while they watched the Dickens' classic *Mr Pickwick*, with Arthur Lowe playing the starring role.

Boxing Day had followed a similar pattern, with the afternoon film *Tom Brown's Schooldays*, while Lily looked through a Sky Tours holiday brochure advertising holidays in the sun in Majorca from £29.

George was helping Freddie as he studied a smart new copy of the *Highway Code*. For his main Christmas present, Tom and Lily had purchased a set of six driving lessons from the British School of Motoring and Freddie was determined to pass first time. He had been out in Lily's car, complete with learner plates and accompanied by Tom, on several occasions and was already a competent driver.

So it was a relaxed foursome in Laurel Cottage that evening as they sipped VP Rich Ruby Wine and watched *Double Your Money*, the game show starring Hughie Green.

George had left the following day amid many hugs from Lily. Tom had given him a lift to the station in York.

The Coffee Shop was busy on the morning of New Year's Eve and Nora Pratt was particularly excited. It was the day of the annual village pantomime. This year it was *Cinderella* and, as always, Nora had the leading role.

Two tall, slim teenagers, Lizzie Buttershaw and Rosie Finn, were at the counter. 'Two coffees please, Nora,' said Lizzie.

'An' two crumpets,' added Rosie.

'Comin' up,' said Nora. 'Are you weady for t'dwess wehea'sal?'

'Lookin' forward to it,' said Lizzie with confidence.

'We're word perfect,' said the smiling, self-assured Rosie.

Nora looked at her reflection in the stainless-steel coffee machine and then at the two teenagers. The first hint of doubt crossed her mind. She was wondering if these two attractive young women were ideally cast alongside her as the Ugly Sisters.

'Here y'are,' she said. 'Two fwothy coffees an' two cwumpets.'

Rose McConnell and Joy Popplewell were sitting at a table near the window.

'Nice scarf, Rose,' said Joy.

'Thanks. I got a postal order for Christmas from my aunt in Fylingdales and bought this. What about you? Get anything nice?'

'Not much,' sighed Joy. 'My mum's got no spare cash. So Christmas was a bit quiet, but we had a nice time watching telly.'

Rose liked Joy. She never complained in spite of her personal circumstances. Joy lived in a two-up, two-down terraced house on the Easington road. There was lino on the floor of the front room, shabby and long past its best. Her father had been killed in the war and since then her mother had tried to relieve her depression with red wine.

It was a tough life for Joy, but she was a hard worker and had done well at school. She loved to read and had a cardboard box under her bed full of books that she had begged or borrowed. The collection included James Joyce's *A Portrait of the Artist as a Young Man*, along with the works of the American Beat poets Lawrence Ferlinghetti and Allen Ginsberg.

The other love of Joy's life was Sam, but she kept this to herself.

She also earned a bit from doing odd jobs around the village, including dog walking and shopping for elderly neighbours. This helped to fund her smoking habit. From the pocket of her anorak she took out a packet of Embassy cigarettes. 'Have one?' she asked.

Rose shook her head. 'Thanks anyway.'

'Come on, live dangerously,' urged Joy with a wide-eyed

smile. She lit up and exhaled with pleasure. 'You get a gift book with these,' she said, holding up the packet. 'A Dansette record player for five thousand coupons,' she added with a grin.

'Another time,' said Rose.

'So, when are you seeing Freddie?'

'Probably tonight at the pantomime, but definitely tomorrow,' said Rose. 'It would be good to do something special on New Year's Day.'

'I agree,' said Joy, 'and I could think of something *really* special.'

They shared a knowing smile ... but on Rose's part there was a hint of uncertainty.

Ruby was in the General Stores. 'Good morning, Ruby,' said Prudence. 'How are you?'

'Fine, thank you, Miss Golightly,' replied Ruby. She had little Sharon with her, clutching her Christmas doll. 'Jus' givin' Sharon a bit o' fresh air. She's been cooped up since Christmas.'

'I know the feeling,' sympathized Prudence. 'Jeremy has barely moved from the television.'

Ruby glanced up at the bear on his shelf. 'Well, he's back now keepin' an eye on things.'

Prudence smiled. 'So what will it be?'

'Jus' a loaf please, Prudence.' Ruby put a shilling on the counter and then stared at the penny change. 'An' mebbe summat from t'penny selection f'Sharon.'

The little girl was pointing at a stick of liquorice. 'Please,' she said.

Prudence smiled and selected the largest stick from the

box. 'And here's a barley sugar as well for being polite. I love children with good manners.'

'Thank you kindly,' said Ruby.

'Are you going to the pantomime, Ruby?'

'Wouldn't miss it for t'world. Our Racquel's one o' t'dancers.'

'A lovely girl,' said Prudence.

Just like her mother, she thought as Ruby walked out to the frozen High Street.

In Laurel Cottage Tom Feather was putting on his warmest coat and scarf. 'Come on, Freddie,' he said. 'Prince Charming's castle awaits.'

Tom and Freddie had been persuaded by Lily to assist with the preparations for the pantomime in the village hall. Lily and Anne had volunteered to help dress the children ready for a variety of over-complicated dance routines. Sadly, these were performed to the continued disappointment of the flamboyant artistic director, Felicity Miles-Humphreys.

Tom and Freddie collected two paintbrushes from the garden shed and a few tins of emulsion paint. On the stage of the village hall a sheet of eight by four hardboard needed to be transformed into a castle on one side and a scullery kitchen on the other.

'An hour's painting should do it, Freddie,' said Tom, 'then maybe a bacon butty in the Coffee Shop.'

Freddie smiled. Maybe Rose would be there.

In their house on the Crescent just off the Easington road, Anne Grainger was watching John putting the final touches to a wooden umbrella stand made from pine boards. She had bought him an electric Black & Decker drill for Christmas and the constant whirring of its motor was giving her a headache.

'Do you fancy coming with me down to the village hall?' she asked.

'What for?' John sounded slightly perturbed at being interrupted.

'I said I would help Lily with preparations for the pantomime. Then maybe we could have a coffee in Nora's.'

John frowned. 'No thanks. I've got to stain this with dark walnut to provide an antique appearance.'

Anne was not impressed. It occurred to her that her love life was also beginning to take on an antique appearance.

Tom and Freddie had completed their painting in time for the afternoon dress rehearsal. However, it was clear to them as they departed that it was not going as Felicity Miles-Humphreys had planned. In every dance routine the front row of children appeared to be completely out of step with the second row.

Felicity's husband, Peter the bank clerk with the unfortunate stutter, was proving to be a frustrating Prince Charming. 'We m-must find the owner of this gl-glass sl-slipper,' he muttered without an ounce of princely confidence.

Felicity sighed. Peter had worked hard to overcome his stutter, but with limited success.

Nora had a selection of popular songs to sing and she was centre stage wearing her famous Alpine leather corset and giving a passionate rendition of an Elvis Presley hit. 'Wetu'n to Sende',' she sang and Felicity frowned again. When Nora followed this with 'Cwying in the Wain', Felicity wondered if she ought to replace Elsie Crapper as musical director.

At seven o' clock, however, the village hall was packed. Ernie Crapper, the encyclopaedia salesman, was collecting the shilling entry fee for adults and sixpence for children, while his wife, Elsie, played the Shirley Bassey hit 'I Who Have Nothing' on the piano. It was intended to get the audience in the mood, but it caused Violet Fawnswater to shed a private tear.

When Timothy Pratt switched on the single spotlight and the curtains parted, the show opened with the children dancing frantically to Chubby Checker's American hit 'Let's Twist Again', which had taken the country by storm. Everyone clapped, even when the over-exuberant Scott Walmsley fell off the stage, to be thrown back on by his mother in the front row.

Muriel Tonks as the Fairy Godmother threatened to steal the show. However, Nora soon asserted her authority with a convincing performance as Cinderella and a tearful rendition of 'The Stwoke of Midnight'.

Even though the football team on the back row were convinced the Ugly Sisters were the best-looking girls on stage, Nora still received her bouquet at the end with a well-deserved cheer. Felicity was pleased that the silver tinsel on Nora's Alpine leather corset had added that certain professional touch and that she had survived another pantomime without any of the audience demanding a refund.

Meanwhile, the villagers of Ragley filed out to see in the new year in The Royal Oak or at a family party.

Tom and Lily drove back to Kirkby Steepleton. Freddie was in the back seat staring out of the window. Above him the sky was scattered with stardust and he was thinking of Rose. A new year was about to begin and he wondered what lay in store for them.

Back in Laurel Cottage, Tom stretched out on the sofa in the lounge, while Freddie sat down in one of the armchairs. Lily went over to her bureau and put the pantomime programme behind the drop-down lid. It sparked a memory for Freddie.

'Lily, I saw a photograph in your bureau.'

Lily stood still. 'Pardon?'

'Yes, sorry, I was looking for a spare card. It was just before Christmas. One of the drawers was unlocked. I noticed there was a man in a photograph that I thought was me.'

'No, it wasn't you, Freddie,' said Lily sharply. She closed the bureau and got up.

Freddie was persistent. 'So, who was it?'

'Why do you ask?'

'Well, have I got a relation that I don't know about? It looked like an old photo.'

'Freddie, these are my private papers. You know that.' Her voice had suddenly become sharp and abrupt.

Freddie didn't like to be spoken to in that way. 'It's not like you to be obtuse.'

'Obtuse?'

'Yes. It seemed a reasonable question – why can't you answer?'

'I'm tired,' said Lily. 'It's been a long day.' She got up and walked out to the kitchen.

Freddie stared at the bureau. Tom was looking thoughtful.

'Tom, is there something I should know? I'm almost frightened to ask.'

Tom shook his head. 'Not for me to say,' he murmured. At the core of his being he did not want to share a lie. He got up and followed Lily into the kitchen while Freddie, confused and unhappy, went upstairs to his bedroom.

Lily was standing at the sink, head bowed in despair. Tom put his arms around her.

'Oh Tom, I feel as though I'm in the eye of the storm.'

'Maybe you are,' said Tom softly, 'but I'm standing beside you.'

She felt the warm moisture of tears on her cheeks and her heart was aching with emptiness.

'Lily . . . I think it's time.'

'But how can I tell him?'

'Shall I come with you?'

Lily took a handkerchief from her sleeve and wiped her eyes. 'No, it needs to come from me.'

'Are you sure?'

Lily pursed her lips and gave a faint nod. 'I'll get the letter.'

'And the photograph,' said Tom. 'He needs to know . . . to understand.'

Lily went to her bureau, unlocked the right-hand drawer

and took out a letter. With a heavy heart she climbed the stairs and tapped gently on Freddie's door.

'Freddie, I'm sorry.'

'What do you want?' he asked.

'Can we talk?'

There was the sound of footsteps and the door opened.

'Come in,' said Freddie and walked back in to sit on his bed.

Lily moved the clothes draped over a chair and sat down. There was a long silence. Finally Freddie spoke. 'What is it?'

Lily clutched the letter. 'I need to explain something to you. It can't wait any longer.'

'Go on.'

Lily passed over the photograph and Freddie looked at it again. The man who looked like him was smiling at the camera. He turned it over. The year '1944' was written on the back in black ink, faded now but still clear and bold.

'The man who looks like you worked on a farm down in Buckinghamshire. It was during the war.'

Freddie was trying to make sense of what he was hearing. 'You mean when you were in the Land Army?'

'Yes. He was kind and gentle and we fell in love.'

Freddie stared at Lily. 'What are you saying?'

'I was only a little older than you are now. We found happiness together in difficult times.'

Freddie looked at the photograph once again. 'With this man? You fell in love with this man? So who is he?'

'Freddie, I couldn't tell you before. It's complicated. Times were different then.'

'You've not answered my question. Who is he?'

'Freddie . . . he's your father.'

Freddie stood up and walked to the far corner of the room. He clenched his fists. He could feel anger boiling up inside. 'My father? This man is my *father*?'

'Yes, Freddie. And I'm your mother.'

Freddie sat down on the bed again. 'But you're my sister . . . always have been . . . my big sister.'

Lily shook her head. 'Florence said I had brought shame on the family and made me promise not to reveal you were born out of wedlock. So you were brought up to believe that Florence was your mother and I was your sister.'

'But why the lie, Lily?'

'I'm so sorry.' There were tears in her eyes.

'So why didn't you marry him? Where is he now?'

Lily covered her face with her hands.

Freddie held up the photograph. 'Was he killed in the war?'

'No, he's alive. He wrote this letter. Each year I've sent him a copy of your school photograph. He always asks how you are, so we write once a year.'

Freddie's mind was racing. 'You let me think my mother had died. I always thought Arthur was my father. My parents are dead.'

'I'm so sorry, Freddie. We were going to tell you when we felt the time was right.'

'So Tom knows? He let me live the lie as well?'

Freddie jumped up, stormed out of the room and ran downstairs. Tom was sitting on the sofa. He was used to dealing with crises in his professional life, but this was different. Freddie looked frantic.

'Tom, what's happening? I always respected you and what you've achieved. You've been my brother-in-law, my friend. Now this.' He held up the photograph. 'Who is this? Lily says this is my father. What's his name?'

Lily had followed Freddie downstairs. She laid the letter on top of the bureau and sat down on her writing chair.

Tom looked up at her. 'Shall I?' he asked quietly.

Lily nodded.

Tom gestured to Freddie to sit next to him. 'Please sit down and I'll try to explain. I know this is a shock, and it isn't the way we would have wanted it.'

Freddie had always responded to Tom's support and his quiet authority. He sat down.

'Freddie, first of all, Lily loves you. Always has, always will. When she was young she had a child. It was an illegitimate child and in those days that was a sin. The world is different now, but Lily's mother forced her to move away and she's cared for you ever since, both as a sister and a mother.'

Tom's words were quiet and persuasive. Freddie appeared calmer now. He put the photograph down on the coffee table and pointed at the black-and-white image. 'Who is he, Tom?'

'His name is Rudolph Krüger.'

'Krüger?'

'Yes, Freddie – your father is German.'

Freddie looked at Tom, appalled. '*German*? We fought a war against them. Tom – *you* fought a war against them.'

'I know,' said Tom. 'It was a terrible time. War takes lives and leaves others in pieces.' He picked up the photograph. 'All these men were German POWs, prisoners of war.'

Freddie looked across the room at Lily. 'But these were the *enemy*. How could you?'

'The war threw us together. We were both young and vulnerable. Rudi was caring and kind.'

'*Rudi?*'

'Yes,' said Lily. 'He's known as Rudi. You met him once when you were a small boy. We had just moved here. You played cricket with him in the garden.'

Freddie shook his head. He had no recollection. 'So where is he now?'

'He went back to start a life in West Germany,' explained Tom. 'He lives in Hamburg. I met him before he left. He told me he wanted you to have what he couldn't give you – a home, stability, a caring family. He seemed to be a good man.'

'I don't know what to say ... or who I am,' said Freddie.

'It wasn't meant to come out this way,' said Tom, 'but then Florence was taken from us and you were only twelve. We considered it again when you were sixteen, but didn't want to disturb your O-levels. Then it was sixth form and so it went on.'

Freddie looked fiercely at Lily. 'You should have told me.'

Tom could see Lily was too distressed to respond. 'Lily wanted to tell you long ago.' There was a pause. 'Freddie ... Lily is your mother.'

Freddie stood up to leave the room. 'Mother? Lily's my *sister*. Always has been.' He stamped upstairs, went into his bedroom and slammed the door.

Lily burst into tears and Tom led her quietly upstairs. 'Let's give him some space. In the morning it will be different.'

When Tom turned on the light he saw his book lying there on his bedside cupboard. He recalled the story of the butterfly effect and the significance was not lost on him.

Small differences can lead to large consequences and unforeseen outcomes.

He held Lily in his arms, but it was many hours before either of them drifted off into a troubled sleep.

In the early hours of New Year's Day Lily awoke. A pallid moon shone down and in the eaves of Laurel Cottage she could hear the sibilant whispering of the wind. She sat up, wrapped her arms around herself, rocked to and fro and prayed for forgiveness.

Freddie looked at his clock. It was 4.00 a.m. He was still fully dressed and he crept quietly downstairs.

There was enough light for him to see the letter on top of Lily's bureau. He picked it up, returned to his room and spent a long time reading it. His thoughts were a watertight compartment, sealed in solitude. He had made up his mind. It was time for the truth.

He sat down at his desk, took out a sheet of paper from a foolscap folder in his satchel and began to write. At first his thoughts were chaotic and confused, but with the act of writing came clarity. Finally, words dripped from his pen with a new-found freedom.

He had stepped back from the precipice and found a sense of purpose. He knew what he had to do.

Chapter Ten

Reaping the Whirlwind

It was the first day of 1964 and winter gripped the cold and hostile land in an iron fist. Outside Laurel Cottage a savage night had passed to reveal a silent world where all sound was absorbed. The village was covered in a fresh fall of snow and the tracks of midnight foxes patterned the pavements of Kirkby Steepleton. Skeletal trees faded in the frigid distance and the sky was an ominous grey with the promise of more snow.

As Tom got out of bed the bitter rhythm of a malevolent wind rattled the window panes. He looked anxiously at a sleeping Lily. Barefoot, he padded across the bedroom and opened the door. The landing was dark and quiet and the door to Freddie's room was closed.

He returned to put on his dressing gown and slippers, then went downstairs to make a cup of tea. It was then that he noticed the front door key was on the doormat beneath the letterbox. His police training kicked in imme-diately. He tried the door handle. It was locked. Then he glanced at the coat stand. Freddie's duffel coat, scarf and bobble hat had gone. He picked up the key, unlocked the door, turned on the porch light and peered outside.

A fresh snowfall had covered his Ford Zephyr patrol car. Footprints headed out from the front door to where Lily's Morris Minor 1000 Traveller should have been.

It had gone.

Tom opened the drawer of the hall table. Lily's car keys were missing. He ran upstairs and opened Freddie's bedroom door. The room was empty.

Lily had woken up and called from the bedroom, 'Tom, what is it?'

Tom rushed back into the bedroom and began to get dressed quickly. 'Freddie's gone.'

'Gone? Gone where?'

'I don't know.'

Lily leaped out of bed and ran to Freddie's bedroom. She turned on the light. The curtains were closed. His bed was unmade. Clothes were scattered on the floor. On his bedside table was an envelope. It was Rudi's letter. She picked it up and scanned the room, hoping there may be a note from Freddie.

There was none.

Tom hurried downstairs. 'I'm going out to look for him.'

'Wait, I'll come,' said Lily.

'No, you stay here. He might ring.'

Lily clutched the banister rail. 'He can't have gone far in this weather.'

Tom shook his head. 'Lily, he's taken your car.'

She ran downstairs. 'What? He hasn't passed his test!'

'He may have gone to Sam's, or maybe to see his

girlfriend.' Tom dragged on his thick police overcoat and kissed her cheek. 'Don't worry. I'll find him. Stay by the phone.'

He rushed out, swept the snow from his windscreen and set off. He felt anxious, driving west, fleeing the dawn light that crested the Hambleton hills and raced across the plain of York. He forced himself to move into professional mode and try to think like Freddie. *Where would he go?*

He drove towards Ragley village, his mind racing.

The cold wind was like a raging fist and blue ice glittered in the morning light.

In the vicarage lounge Vera was addressing an envelope to her Aunt Emily in Chesterfield. As always, she wrote in her neat copperplate, complete with a distinctive Greek letter E. She had just stuck on a stamp when Joseph walked in.

'I have to go out, Vera. Dominic Spottiswood at the residential home passed away in the night and I said I would call in to make arrangements for the funeral.'

'Oh dear,' said Vera and put down her pen. 'A lovely man. His wife, Minnie, will be heartbroken. A wonderful supporter of good causes . . . she used to knit socks for the sailors during the war.'

'According to Septimus it was the "killing cold",' said Joseph sadly. 'It takes the frail and the weak, and Dominic had been very poorly.'

Vera nodded knowingly. 'Yes, Mr Flagstaff would say that, of course. What a shame for their friends at the retirement home. He will be sadly missed.'

The Hartford Home for Retired Gentlefolk was a

caring, secure place for the elderly and Vera and Joseph were regular visitors. Also, in recent years Lily and Anne had taken the school choir there to sing Christmas carols.

Vera got up and followed Joseph to the hallway to make sure he wore a warm scarf and a hat.

'Joseph, there's something else before you go. I was thinking of inviting a few friends round this evening, a sort of new year soirée.'

Joseph beamed. 'Wonderful idea. They could sample my nettle wine. It's almost ready.'

Vera didn't reply. She merely waved off her brother with a forced smile.

Tom rubbed the condensation from his windscreen as he drove towards Ragley village. Around him it seemed as if the land had emptied of wildlife and the creatures of the night had found sanctuary.

He was concerned. This was different.

If he had been on duty there were tried and tested procedures for finding a missing person, but as he passed Victor Pratt's garage he knew he couldn't stop and ask if he had seen Lily's car. It was a confidential matter. There was too much at stake.

He drove slowly up Ragley High Street looking for a familiar almond-green Morris Minor, but there was no sign. Around him pale shafts of sunlight lit up the crystal air with a golden glow. An early-morning dog walker appeared like a wraith in the mist as a reluctant light crept over the frozen earth. He continued up the Morton road. The car wasn't outside Sam Grundy's house, nor was it parked on the McConnells' driveway, so he backtracked on to the road to Easington. On the outskirts he pulled into a lay-by and stared around him. In the stillness he was at a loss where Freddie might have gone. Then he thought back to a conversation he had had with Freddie and in an instant he knew where he was.

He slammed his car into first gear and drove off.

In Laurel Cottage Lily had dressed and was sitting in the lounge by the telephone. It was almost an hour since Tom had left and there had been no word. She thought over the conversation of the previous evening, seeking out any clues . . . but there was nothing.

'Please find him,' she whispered.

She thought of Tom and of her life. With Rudi, happiness had been a brief interlude and love a fleeting companion. With Tom, it had been different and she had known he was the one. Their relationship had been one of fire and ice, steel and silk. She remembered the early days of their marriage, a time of hot summer nights and long walks on winter days, hand in hand across the high frozen moors of North Yorkshire.

Most of all, Tom was calm in a crisis, a steadfast partner. He was eminently suited to his profession, solving other people's problems. But now it was different. It was their problem . . . *her* problem. She had lost her son. The link between them had gone. A chain had been broken.

She stood up, walked to the window and peered out. 'I'm sorry, Freddie,' she murmured. 'Please come home.'

She picked up Rudi's letter and read it again. It was brief, simply a thank you for letting him see what a fine young man Freddie had become. He was clearly proud of his son.

Our son, thought Lily, *my son*.

Suddenly the phone rang and for a moment Lily froze before dashing to the sideboard and snatching up the receiver. 'Is that you, Tom? Have you found him?'

There was silence.

'Lily, whatever is the matter? It's Vera here.'

Lily sank to her knees and wept. When finally she could speak, she said, 'Sorry, Vera. I thought it might be Tom.'

'Lily, please tell me what is wrong.'

There was a long pause until Lily gathered herself and said, 'I can't speak now, Vera,' and put down the phone.

Vera heard the click and a faint buzz as the call terminated. The house was quiet apart from the ticking of the clock in the hallway. She took a deep breath. There was a decision to be made. Lily was obviously in considerable distress. Vera recognized her Christian duty and knew she had to help her friend.

Moments later she had put on her coat, scarf and hat and picked up her car keys from the hall table. As an afterthought, she went back to the kitchen and put six of her home-made fruit scones in a tin. Then she scribbled a note to Joseph simply saying she had gone out, but didn't say where, and hurried out to her car.

She drove carefully down the Morton road, into Ragley village, then turned left at the end of the High Street. On the back road to Kirkby Steepleton a grudging light spread slowly across the distant fields and, as she drove through a land of bare trees and rutted snow, she wondered what might befall her.

She was a little surprised that there were no cars in the driveway of Laurel Cottage.

Freddie shivered. The cold seemed to freeze the breath in his lungs, but it served to ease the problems in his life. It was the lie that hurt the most, a lie that had lasted a lifetime.

After reading Rudi's letter and copying his address in Germany, Freddie had written a message to a man he did not know. When the time was right he would post it. It was then that he knew he needed space to think and time to understand the revelation that had changed his life. He had to get out of the cottage.

When he unlocked the door he saw it was impossible to walk out into a Siberian winter. Grabbing Lily's car keys had been an impulsive action. When he was outside he locked the front door again and put the house key through the letterbox.

The howling wind hid the noise of the engine kicking into life and, as he drove away, he knew where he must go. On this Bank Holiday morning the Ragley cricket field would be deserted and he knew of a quiet, secluded place by the pavilion. Although he was becoming a competent driver, he took extra care as he drove through the darkness. He also knew that as a learner he was breaking the law.

At that moment it didn't matter. He simply had to get away.

Ragley High Street appeared devoid of life. Freddie drove up the track behind the village hall, parked the car out of sight behind the cricket pavilion and sat on a cold bench under the covered porch in his private frozen cocoon. He felt betrayed, humiliated.

As dawn broke over the distant hills his thoughts raced in confusion.

The doorbell of Laurel Cottage rang and Lily rushed to the door. Panic and hope gripped her in equal measure. Her breathing seemed laboured, coming in short gasps as she opened the door. Then she stepped back in surprise. She was hoping for Tom and Freddie, but there stood Vera with a cake tin under her arm and an attempt at a reassuring smile.

'Lily, I'm sorry to arrive unannounced,' she said, 'but I was concerned. You sounded distressed when I called.'

Lily couldn't speak. She simply stared helplessly at her friend.

'Let me come in for a moment,' said Vera, taking the initiative. 'In any case, you need to keep the house warm in this bitter wind.'

She stepped inside and closed the door behind her. 'I've brought some scones,' she said, holding up the cake tin. 'I always find tea and scones can be so calming.'

They went into the kitchen. Lily looked lost, so Vera took over. 'I'll put the kettle on, shall I?'

She knew her way around Lily's kitchen and five minutes later they were settled in the lounge next to a fire that was burning low. Vera put another log on and served tea while Lily kept staring out of the window. Her expression was taut and fearful. The equilibrium of her family life had been disturbed. A stone had been dropped into a pond and she didn't know where the ripples would end.

'So,' said Vera, leaning forward to touch Lily's hand. 'Tell me, my dear – what is troubling you? I'm here to help and anything you choose to tell me will be in confidence.'

Lily sipped her tea thoughtfully, looked up at her friend and confidante and nodded. This was the moment to unburden herself. Like a moth that danced around a candle flame, she had avoided the final conflict and held back from entering the furnace.

Now it was time to share her secret.

The Revd Joseph Evans was also drinking tea. Minnie Spottiswood was grieving. Her three daughters were in attendance and the eldest, Ruth, was slicing a fruit cake while Joseph discussed Dominic's funeral arrangements.

Minnie found it difficult to articulate her thoughts, but Joseph was experienced in dealing with the bereaved.

'The Gospel of St John would be appropriate,' he said, 'chapter 11, verses 25 and 26.' He put down his cup. 'He that believeth in me, though he were dead, yet shall he live. And whosoever liveth and believeth in me shall never die.'

The two younger daughters nodded their approval and Minnie dabbed away another tear.

'He liked Psalm Twenty-three, Mother,' said Ruth quietly. 'Perhaps one of us should read that.'

'A good choice,' agreed Joseph. He was anxious to glean enough information for the eulogy and listened carefully to what the daughters said about how they would like their father to be remembered. Minnie said nothing until he was about to leave, then she looked up tearfully and said quietly, 'Mr Evans, there is something.'

Everyone looked at her.

'My Dominic was different, special you might say. He had his head in the clouds . . . but he could always name the stars.'

There was silence and then it was the turn of the daughters to reach for their handkerchiefs.

When Joseph left he was hoping Vera would be able to transpose his hasty notes into a coherent eulogy as she usually did. However, when he arrived back at the vicarage he was unaware that his sister was dealing with another kind of loss.

Vera had always been a good listener and she recognized the moment when Lily decided to unburden herself.

'It's a long story, Vera,' began Lily with a sigh, 'and it's troubled me for many years.'

'Whatever you wish to tell me remains within these four walls. Lily, I'm your friend, always have been – and sometimes it's good to share a problem.'

Lily nodded. 'It's Freddie.'

'Yes?'

'He's gone missing.'

'Missing?'

'Tom is looking for him now.'

'Oh dear, Lily, I can understand your distress.' Vera stood up from her armchair and sat down next to her friend on the sofa. 'I'm sure Tom will find him.'

'I thought it was him when you rang,' said Lily quietly.

'I understand,' said Vera. 'So why did Freddie leave?'

'Because last night I had to tell him the truth.'

'The truth?'

Lily took a deep breath. 'Let me show you something.'

She took a bunch of keys from her handbag and walked over to her bureau. Then she unlocked one of the drawers, selected an old brown envelope and carefully removed an old, creased black-and-white photograph.

'On my first day at Ragley I travelled here on a bus and wondered what lay in store. I was nervous. Everything was new. However, I carried a photograph with me in my handbag and from time to time I would take it out and look at it and find a measure of happiness.' She handed the photograph to Vera, who studied it carefully. It was a small baby, perhaps a month old.

'It's the first photograph of Freddie,' explained Lily.

Vera looked up. She knew this was a moment of import.

'Vera . . . Freddie is my son.'

I did wonder, thought Vera, but she said nothing. She merely leaned towards Lily and held her hand.

'You see, my mother insisted,' continued Lily quietly.

'What did Florence say?'

'She said I had brought shame on the family – that a child born out of wedlock is a sin. Her solution was to hide the truth and say it was *her* child. She was young enough for this to be accepted.'

Vera nodded. 'Times were different then. Attitudes have started to change.'

'Yes, but back in those days I was too young to stand up to her. I didn't understand the implications or the outcomes. Later I did, of course.'

'And the father?' asked Vera softly.

'That's the problem. He was a prisoner of war, a German, working on the same farm as me.'

'I can see why that made it much more difficult for you.'

'Yes, my mother said it was the worst thing I could have done. Germans were the enemy, but Rudi was simply a young man who had been thrust into a war he didn't understand.'

'Rudi?'

'His name is Rudolph Krüger. He lives in Hamburg. Each year I send him a photograph of Freddie and he writes back to say thank you. In his last letter he sent a photograph of the German workers on the farm. Rudi was one of the men and looked just like Freddie does now.'

'I see,' said Vera. 'Did you love him?'

'Yes, I did. He was a handsome, kind and sensitive man. We were both lonely and we made each other happy for a while at a hard time. After Freddie was born, Florence shut Rudi out of our lives. It seemed to be for the best. Then I trained to be a teacher and the opportunity of a post at Ragley cropped up. I applied and you know the rest.'

'I can understand why you didn't mention Freddie,' said Vera. 'The school governors would not have given you an interview.' She shook her head. 'And that has to be wrong, in view of everything you have done for Ragley School.'

Lily sighed and sipped her tea. 'Freddie saw the photograph of his father and the questions began. Tom and I had been trying to find the right time to tell him, but we waited too long. He found out the truth last night and this morning we discovered he had gone.'

'Gone where?'

'I don't know. Tom is out there trying to find him.'

'Tom is a fine policeman,' said Vera, sounding positive. 'He will know where to look.'

'I can't bear the pain Freddie must be feeling,' said Lily, wiping away a tear.

Vera looked at her and clasped both her hands. 'Lily, my dear friend, thank you for telling me. Have faith and all will be well.'

The two women stood up and hugged each other.

'Let me know when you have any news,' said Vera as she left.

Tom drove slowly down Ragley High Street and stopped by the village hall. He knew that the cricket field had a special significance for Freddie; it was where he had enjoyed many happy times. Unbeknown to Freddie, it was also the place where, back in 1953, Tom had met Rudolph Krüger. Freddie had been playing cricket and Rudi had come to watch him.

He stared at the track that led to the pavilion. There were recent tyre tracks.

Behind the pavilion was a large area of spare ground where families would picnic in the summer. Lily's car was there and Tom pulled up next to it. He walked slowly round to the front of the building and saw Freddie hunched on the bench, staring out at the frozen field.

Tom sat down next to him. 'I thought you might be here,' he said softly. 'It's one of your favourite places.'

Freddie nodded. 'Sorry, Tom. I just had to get out and find somewhere to think.'

'I understand,' said Tom. 'Lily was worried because you had taken her car. We need to let her know you're safe.'

Freddie looked at him, sadness etched on his face. 'You shared the lie, Tom. That hurt.'

'Then let's talk about it.'

'Maybe,' said Freddie.

Tom put his arm around his shoulders. 'You've scored a lot of runs here.'

Freddie gave the hint of a smile and nodded. 'I guess I have.'

'Rudi came back from Germany once when you were small. He saw you play cricket here. I met him then. He was a good man . . . like you.'

'So why did he leave?'

'He wanted you to have a life that he couldn't provide – a loving home, stability, education. He also knew I was in love with your mother.'

Freddie shook his head. 'She'll always be my sister.'

'Either way, Freddie, she loves you and she must be very worried right now. So let me take you home.'

Freddie sighed deeply. His breath steamed in the frozen air.

Tom stood up and began to stamp his feet. 'I'm freezing here. Let's go and get warm.'

Freddie stood up.

'And I'll drive,' added Tom with a smile. 'We'll collect Lily's car later.'

Freddie climbed into Tom's car and they drove up the High Street and stopped outside the telephone box.

'Lily, I've found him. We're on our way home.'

'Oh, thank God!'

The relief was like spring rain, refreshing the earth and healing Lily's soul. She rang Vera immediately to share the news.

'That's wonderful,' said Vera.

'Thanks for your support,' said Lily. 'And, by the way, why did you phone me this morning?'

'Oh, I'm busy preparing for that now. We're having a little get-together here at the vicarage this evening, school staff and friends, the usual. Call in if you wish if things are settled, but I'll understand either way.'

'Thanks, Vera,' said Lily and walked to the window to wait for the return of Tom and Freddie.

At Laurel Cottage it was a morning of silence. Lily was relieved that Freddie was safe, but it was clear he did not want to speak. Neither did he want to be hugged. Lily knew a chasm had opened between them that could not be crossed.

Freddie went up to his room while Tom drove Lily back into Ragley to collect her car. Later they ate lunch together, but little was said and when they had finished Freddie went back to his room.

The phone rang and Lily picked up the receiver. 'Happy New Year, Mrs Feather. It's Rose here. I wondered if I could have a word with Freddie?'

'Of course,' said Lily, 'and a Happy New Year to you and your mum and dad.' She called up the stairs, 'It's for you, Freddie. It's Rose.'

Freddie came down and took the receiver without saying thank you.

'Hi,' he said.

'That new programme starts on telly tonight,' said Rose. 'We said we would watch it together.'

'New programme?'

'Yes, *Top of the Pops*. Should be good.'

'Oh yes, I remember now.'

'You OK?' asked Rose. 'You sound a bit tired.'

'I'm fine.'

'Well, my dad said he would collect you just after six if you like.'

'Thanks. That would be good.'

After he rang off he turned to Tom. 'I'm going round to see Rose tonight and watch television. Her dad said he would pick me up.'

Lily looked up. 'Tom, we've been invited round to the vicarage tonight for drinks and supper with friends. We could drop you off at Rose's, Freddie, and collect you on our way home.'

'No thanks,' said Freddie. 'I'll go with Rose's dad.'

Monday, 6 January, was the first day of the school term and Tom had given Freddie a lift to school. Little had been said during the past few days and Freddie merely gave monosyllabic replies to any of Lily's questions. Tom hoped things would improve in time.

When Lily drove to school a frigid silence hung over the land. Fresh snow covered the fields like an undertaker's shroud and all was still.

'Good morning, Lily. A new term,' said John Pruett with enthusiasm. He beamed and held open the entrance door for her. Lily noticed that on this cold day he was wearing a Fair Isle cardigan under his grey, worsted suit.

'Good morning, John,' she replied, but she seemed to lack her usual vivacity and John wondered if there was a problem.

It was a quiet start to the spring term.

At the end of the school day, Lily was tidying up in her classroom when Vera appeared in the doorway.

'Call in for a cup of tea on your way home. Joseph is at a meeting and won't be back until after five.'

Lily smiled. 'Thank you, Vera. I'll be there around four thirty.'

Vera was at her kitchen window when she heard Lily's car crunch over the frozen gravel outside the vicarage. She opened the door to greet her. 'Come in out of the cold,' she said.

When Lily came into the hallway the subtle aroma of beeswax and lavender made her relax and in the warmth of the kitchen she felt comfortable. It was a relief to speak freely and Vera was determined to help in whatever way she could.

'A quiet day in school,' she said perceptively. 'So how was it?'

'Difficult, Vera, but the children helped to take my mind off it.'

'And how has Freddie been?'

'Quiet and moody, but at least he's not gone off again. He's keeping his thoughts to himself – or, at least, he did until this morning.'

'I see,' said Vera quietly.

'I told him it was an important year for him with A-levels coming up in the summer and his future to consider. I said I would support him in any way I could.'

'What was his response?'

'Fortunately Tom was out in the car or he would have been angry. Freddie said he didn't need any help and that I would always be his *sister*, nothing more, nothing less.'

'He's hurting, Lily. Give him time.'

They chatted until Lily looked at the clock. 'I need to get home and prepare a meal for two hungry men.' She gave a brave smile, put on her hat, coat and scarf, and walked out to her car.

Vera watched her drive away.

'Hosea, chapter eight, verse seven,' she said quietly to herself. 'They have sown the wind, and they shall reap the whirlwind.'

Chapter Eleven

Sweet Valentine

It was Friday, 14 February and the morning was bright and bitterly cold, the dormant trees shivering in the breeze. The land was frozen and the distant fields were empty of life. A monochrome snowscape stretched out to the far horizon and a golden thread of light crested the ridge of the distant hills. The plain of York was still in the grip of winter. As Vera walked past the brittle hedgerows and across the village green, wisps of wood smoke hovered above the pantile roofs. A few snowflakes sprinkled the pavement like north wind confetti and a thin light bathed Ragley School.

Ruby Smith was putting a handful of bacon rind on the school bird table, a residue of Ronnie's fry-up breakfast in bed. Her unemployed, pigeon-fancier husband had complained he had a cold. 'Mornin', Miss Evans,' called Ruby. Her headscarf was knotted tightly under her chin.

'Good morning, Ruby,' replied Vera. 'Are you working with Mrs Trott this morning?'

Ruby shook her head. 'Edna's badly. She asked me t'get y'boiler up an' runnin'.'

'Well, we're all very grateful to you. And how's little Natasha?'

'Eatin' for England, Miss Evans. Ah left 'er with m'mother.'

'How is Agnes?'

'Like spirit o' spring. Ah don't know what ah'd do wi'out 'er.'

Vera pursed her lips. 'And Ronnie?'

Ruby sighed and shook her head. 'M'mother sez 'e's 'ibernatin'.'

'Oh dear,' said Vera.

"E's a lazy so an' so, but when 'e puts 'is mind to it 'e's faster than a bookie's runner.'

Vera seemed perplexed for a moment, but assumed this was a neat summary of Ruby's husband. 'Well, do send my best wishes to Mrs Trott for a speedy recovery.'

'Ah'll do that.' As she turned to walk home Ruby suddenly remembered an interesting piece of news. 'An' guess what, Miss Evans. My Racquel got 'er first Valentine's card this mornin'.'

'Really? Isn't she rather young for that sort of thing?'

'Mebbe so, but they grow up quick these days. Anyway, it were from that Scott Walmsley an' she don't like 'im.'

'Oh, did he sign the card? I thought they were supposed to be anonymous.'

'No, it's 'cause she recognized t'writin' an' 'e can't spell 'er name.'

As Vera walked into school she thought she ought to mention to John Pruett that Scott's spelling was not as it should be.

*

Lily parked her car and walked to the school entrance hall, where the neat and tidy Jane Grantham was clutching a handful of birthday cards.

'It's my birthday, Miss,' said Jane, her eyes bright with excitement.

'That's right,' said Lily, who knew the birthdays of all the children. 'You're six today. Happy birthday, Jane.'

'I brought my cards to show you.'

'Well, let's go into the warm and we'll have a look at them in the classroom.'

'I love my birthday, Miss.'

'And why is that?' asked Lily, keen to give the little girl a chance to express herself.

Jane looked up, her rosy cheeks glowing and neat ribboned pigtails sticking out under her bobble hat. 'Because for one day I'm famous.'

Lily smiled. 'Yes, Jane, you are,' and she took the child's hand as they walked into school.

It was mid-morning and the local refuse wagon trundled down Ragley High Street. Twenty-one-year-old Dave Robinson had obtained his heavy goods vehicle licence and he and his cousin, twenty-year-old Malcolm Robinson, had been newly installed by the council as the local bin men.

The two had been inseparable friends since boyhood and took pride in their work. Dave, a huge man at six feet four inches tall, always looked after the diminutive Malcolm, who was a foot shorter, although built like a Russian weightlifter. Inevitably, they were known in the village as Big Dave and Little Malcolm.

On this bitterly cold morning the intrepid duo, as northern as beef dripping, were going about their usual work, lifting and tipping, then driving on. They worked in silence until they pulled up outside Nora's Coffee Shop for their morning break.

'Ah don't understand women,' said Big Dave.

'Y'reight there, Dave,' agreed Little Malcolm. It was his stock reply to anything Big Dave uttered, as it gave him thinking time. Even so, he was slightly taken aback by this opening confession. 'What got y'thinkin' 'bout women, Dave?'

'That Rita Eckinthorpe from t'fish an' chip shop 'as been starin' at me.'

Little Malcolm reflected on their most recent visit. 'Y'mean 'er wi' a glass eye?'

'That's 'er.'

'Ah thought she were lookin' at me,' said Little Malcolm.

Big Dave considered this before he answered. It occurred to him that his vertically challenged cousin might be too short to be seen by Rita over the high stainless-steel counter. She would only have heard his voice asking for a fish with plenty of batter and a few scraps with his chips.

'Mebbe so, Malc',' said Big Dave.

'Ernie Morgetroyd reckons she's 'ot stuff,' remarked Little Malcolm.

Big Dave switched off the engine. 'D'you think so?'

'Ernie says she's fit as a butcher's dog.' In Little Malcolm's world this was the highest praise that could be conferred on a member of the opposite sex.

'Not sure,' said Big Dave, shaking his head. 'Bit skinny f'me.'

'Ah don't mind 'em skinny,' said Little Malcolm, 'an' it's Friday, so we'll see 'er t'night.'

It was something to ponder as they climbed out, crunched across the frozen forecourt and walked into the warmth of the Coffee Shop.

During morning break Vera was counting the late dinner money. 'All correct, Mr Pruett.'

I would expect nothing less, thought John as he looked up from a selection of old eleven-plus examination papers. 'Well done, Vera,' he said with a smile. It was then that he noted the frown on her face. 'What is it? You look concerned.'

'The new ten pound notes will be issued next week and I'm not keen on the idea. Parents will be bringing them in and asking for change. It disrupts my routine.'

The Bank of England had announced the introduction of a new £10 note, the first since the Second World War.

'I'm sure you'll manage, Vera. You always do.'

Vera locked the cash in her tin money box and shook her head.

John returned to selecting which brain teasers he would give to the children in his class while pondering the fact that it was Valentine's Day and another year had gone by without his receiving a card.

Three miles away in the students' common room in Easington School, Rose was reading her Valentine's card. 'It's lovely, Freddie,' she said, 'particularly the "violets are blue" verse.' She looked again at the envelope. 'But you shouldn't have wasted your money on a stamp.'

'It was meant to be a surprise,' said Freddie, but without enthusiasm.

Rose had noticed that in recent weeks Freddie had seemed preoccupied, almost sullen at times. She put it down to the extra revision papers they were receiving prior to their A-levels, plus his high commitment to his driving lessons and desire to pass first time.

'We ought to do something special tonight and give homework a miss,' she suggested.

'I'll check with Sam,' said Freddie. 'He mentioned going to see *Dr. No* this week.'

Rose gave him a hard stare. 'When you see him, tell him to wake up and send a card to Joy. She told me she was fed up with him this morning.'

Freddie believed Valentine's cards were more important to girls than boys. 'OK,' he replied lamely.

'We *always* go to the cinema, so how about trying out that new Chinese restaurant? It's supposed to be good.'

'We would need Sam to give us a lift,' said Freddie.

'Well, suggest it and make it a foursome. Joy needs cheering up.'

When Rose walked away Freddie contemplated his life. Time with Rose was an escape from the tension at home but, even so, he was finding it difficult to relax with her. His world was in shadow. There was no trace of forgiveness in his heart for Lily. In consequence there was little communication between them and that morning there had been another subdued breakfast at Laurel Cottage before Tom had given him a lift to school. At least with

Tom he could discuss rugby and politics, though never relationships. Lily had become his mother in name only and there was no going back to the life they once had. The sense of betrayal had become his constant companion.

In the far corner of the common room, Joy was sitting alone on the floor. She was aimlessly reading a copy of the first issue of *Jackie*, a new magazine published last month. One of the younger students had left it on the table in front of the noticeboard. It cost sixpence and was advertised for 'go-ahead teens' and featured a cover picture of Cliff Richard plus a 'Free Twin Heart Ring'. She sighed as she flicked through the pages. There were full-colour pin-ups of Elvis, Billy Fury and the Beatles, as well as an article on 'Outfits to make you pretty' that she thought looked dreadful.

She was in a bad mood. Sam hadn't sent her a Valentine's card, although she had gone to a lot of trouble selecting one for him and posting it to ensure he received it yesterday so that it would also act as a reminder and give him time to buy one for her.

As she glanced at the remaining pages of *Jackie* she decided to forego the advice on 'Super perfume tips for a more kissable you' and wasn't in the mood for the 'Dreamy picture love stories'. Instead she tossed the magazine back on the table whence it came and, as the bell rang, she hurried off to her next class.

Big Dave and Little Malcolm were supping mugs of sweet tea and munching giant pork pies at a table in the Coffee Shop. The Dave Clark Five's recent number-one hit, 'Glad All Over', was playing on the jukebox and the usual villagers were swapping stories and enjoying their mid-morning beverages.

Nora was in conversation with a short, portly man wearing a bright red apron that matched his florid cheeks. The words 'Colin's Cakes' were emblazoned across his chest. He delivered cakes and pastries in his little van to shops in the area.

Big Dave looked across at the animated pair. 'Ah see Cream Cake Colin is in. Ah reckon 'e's a nancy boy.'

'Y'reight there, Dave,' agreed Little Malcolm, although he had no idea why the sexual orientation of a man could be linked to the delivery of chocolate eclairs and almond slices. 'Mind you, Dave, ah think 'e's chattin' up Nora.'

'All talk an' no action,' said Big Dave with the utter conviction of a know-it-all bin man.

Meanwhile, Colin was using all his charms to offload a tray of two-day-old, slightly stale rock buns. 'Y'look radiant today, Nora,' he said.

'Thank you,' said Nora.

'An' ah've got y'summat special.'

'Is it a cweam cake?'

'No, better than that,' said Colin, taking an envelope out from his pocket. 'It's a Valentine's card for my prettiest customer.'

'Ooh, what a lovely su'pwise!'

Nora opened it and there was a picture of a pair of colourful iced buns side by side. Inside were the words 'To my little cream puff with love, Colin'.

'That's weally kind,' said Nora.

Colin moved swiftly into entrepreneurial mode. 'An' a

special offer for m'favourite customer. 'Ere's a tray o' rock buns made by my own fair 'and, yours for 'alf price.'

Nora opened the till and paid Colin, unaware that he had charged the full amount.

As he left, the record on the jukebox moved on to the current number one, the Searchers singing 'Needles and Pins', but it failed to prick Cream Cake Colin's conscience.

In John Pruett's classroom you could have heard a pin drop. The children held their breath while John completed writing two eleven-plus practice questions on the blackboard.

The first read: 'A clock is 12 minutes slow, but is gaining 5 seconds per hour. A watch is 20 minutes fast, but is losing 7½ seconds per hour. How many minutes fast will the watch be when the clock shows the right time?'

'And when you've done that I want you to write the answer to this one,' he said.

Question 2 read: 'The road from a town "A" to another town "B" is uphill for the first 2 miles, level for the next 3 miles, and downhill for the last 2 miles. If I can walk at the rate of 4 miles an hour on the level, 5 miles an hour downhill and 3 miles an hour uphill, how long shall I take to go from "A" to "B"?'

John faced the four rows of children and issued a final warning. 'No one leaves until you have completed them correctly.'

Racquel Smith smiled. For her these were easy and she scribbled busily as she worked out each solution. In the next row Scott Walmsley looked uncertain. He wasn't interested in clocks that didn't work, and walking up and down hills seemed pointless if you owned a bicycle. However, of greater concern was the fact that Racquel had ignored him all day and hadn't sent him a Valentine's card.

It was lunchtime in the General Stores and Prudence was serving Muriel Tonks.

'Anything else, Muriel?' asked Prudence.

'Ah'll try some o' that Ski yogurt please, Prudence. Diane in the 'airdresser's says it's good f'slimmin'.'

'Yes,' said Prudence, holding up the little tub. 'It says it's a low-calorie product.' Prudence was also aware that it had become the new fad for local ladies who were watching their figure.

'Ah'll tek five, please.' Muriel picked up a copy of the *Daily Mirror*. 'Ah see that Peter Sellers is marryin' Britt Ekland.'

'Yes, I believe so.'

'Valentine's Day,' said Muriel as she walked out. 'Love is in the air.'

'It always is,' Prudence murmured with a sad smile.

Ruby's mother had called into Tommy Piercy's butcher's shop on her way home from the chocolate factory.

'Pound o' sausages please, Tommy.'

'Finest on God's earth,' said Tommy, snipping off a few links. Tommy was a member of the SAS, the Sausage Appreciation Society, and he knew a good sausage when he saw one.

'That Stan Coe were shoutin' at me from 'is Land Rover when ah got off t'bus.'

Tommy wrapped up the sausages. 'Ah've banned 'im. Told 'im t'tek 'is custom elsewhere.'

Agnes nodded. 'Y'know what they say about Stan Coe – brass but no class.'

'What were 'e sayin'?' asked Tommy as he wrapped the sausages.

'Not worth repeatin',' said Agnes.

'Least said, soonest mended,' agreed Tommy.

'Ah don't let it trouble me,' said Agnes. 'Ah've got my Ruby an' t'gran'kids.'

'Ah'll tell y'summat f'nowt,' said Tommy as Agnes put the sausages in her shopping bag.

'What's that?'

'There's two good things in life, Agnes: a good bed an' a pair o' good shoes. When yer not in one yer in t'other.'

'Y'not as daft as y'look, Tommy,' said Agnes with a sly wink and hurried off to the council estate.

In The Royal Oak, twenty-one-year-old Eddie Brown had ordered a lunchtime drink and Don the barman was pulling a pint of Chestnut beer. His wife, Sheila, was cleaning glasses.

'So what y'doin' these days, Eddie?' asked Don.

Eddie looked up quickly from staring at Sheila's prodigious bosom and low-cut blouse and hoped Don hadn't noticed.

'Ah'm gettin' into telecommunications. That's t'future.'

'Impressive,' said Sheila, but without conviction.

'Ah'm gonna tek some exams at t'Tec' an' then it's onwards an' upwards f'me.'

Eddie was unaware that Don and Sheila considered

him to be as thick as two short planks, but they admired his enthusiasm.

'So what y'doin' now, Eddie?' asked Don.

'Ah'm a sales executive,' he said proudly as he picked up his pint and wandered off into the taproom.

'What's a *sales executive* when it's at 'ome?' said Don.

Sheila smiled. ''E sells vacuum cleaners door-t'door.'

Big Dave and Little Malcolm were nearing the end of their round when they arrived at Stan Coe's farm. The place looked a mess, with litter scattered everywhere. Behind the barn they could hear the grunting of pigs. It was the first time they had made a collection there and they wondered where the bins were.

'Ah'll go round t'back, Malc'. You 'ave a look be'ind t'barn.'

When Malcolm walked around the barn he saw an overflowing corrugated-iron dustbin. It was leaning on the fence that separated the property from the public footpath. Stan was nailing up a large notice that read:

DO NOT HANG SIGNS ON THIS FENCE

Malcolm smiled when he saw it.

Stan looked up and waved a large hammer. 'What y'grinnin' at? Gerron wi' y'work!'

Malcolm frowned but carried on regardless. He didn't want trouble with his customers. He lifted the heavy bin and staggered out to the dustcart.

'Put y'back into it, short-arse!' shouted Stan.

From the far side of the barn Big Dave suddenly

appeared and grabbed Stan by his coat collar, almost lifting him from the ground. 'Who are you callin' short-arse?'

'Ah'll report you!'

Big Dave pinned him against the fence. 'No y'won't.'

'Why won't ah?'

''Cause ah'll be back t'pay you a visit.'

Stan was going red in the face. 'Are you threatenin' me?'

'Call it a friendly warnin' ... but mebbe wi' a bit o' violence.'

'All reight. Y'can put m'down.'

''Aven't y'forgotten summat?'

'What?'

'Sayin' sorry to my cousin.'

''E's y'cousin?' Stan looked puzzled. 'Y'different, then.'

'That's reight, we are. Malcolm's a lot stronger than me an' 'as a short temper.'

Stan looked at the huge shoulders and bulging muscles that filled out Little Malcolm's boiler suit and nodded. 'Ah'm sorry,' he spluttered.

As they drove away Little Malcolm looked up in admiration at his best friend. 'Thanks, Dave.'

Big Dave grinned. 'Think nothin' of it, short-arse.'

Malcolm gave him a friendly punch in the ribs. 'Pull in at t'General Stores, Dave. Ah want t'buy a Valentine's card.'

Big Dave stopped the wagon quickly and stared at Malcolm. 'Y'jokin'! Who for?'

'That Rita in t'fish shop. We'll see 'er t'night.'

'Y'don't need no cards t'get a girl t'go out wi' you. Bag o' crisps an' a Babycham an' y'laughin'.'

But Little Malcolm was not to be deterred. It was Valentine's Day and he wanted to make it special.

At the end of school Lily was saying goodnight to the children in her class. It was already getting dark and a mist had descended.

'Be careful if you have to cross the road, boys and girls. It's foggy outside.'

Chris Wojciechowski raised his hand. 'Miss, ah reckon it's jus' t'clouds. They're tired and they've fallen down.'

There were times when Lily loved her job and this was one such moment.

Anne Grainger was preparing the evening meal of pork chops, mashed potatoes and carrots – a warming feast on a cold night. John was sitting at the kitchen table smoking his pipe. He had spent 1/3d on the February issue of *Do It Yourself* magazine. He turned to page 131 and an article 'Transport your suitcase the easy way'.

'This could catch on,' he said.

Anne was mashing potatoes. 'What might catch on?'

'Wheels for heavy suitcases.' The exploded diagram showed a construction made from tin plate with three-inch-diameter wheels. The rivets looked like parts of a field gun from the Second World War.

'Maybe,' murmured Anne.

'And this is a great idea,' enthused John. 'Someone here has transformed his fireplace into an indoor pool. Now that we've got central heating we could do the same. We could have miniature water lilies and tiny fish swimming around. It would make a talking point for visitors.'

Anne gave him a cold look as she served up the meal. 'We don't have any visitors.'

He turned the pages. 'Then how about a bamboo cocktail bar?' he asked in desperation.

It didn't appear that Anne shared his enthusiasm. She stared through the door that led to the lounge. Ten years ago on the mantelpiece there would have been a pair of Valentine's cards, but not today . . . not any more.

Rita Eckinthorpe looked up from scooping a battered fish and tossing it expertly on to the display cabinet. The bin men had walked in as they did every Friday.

'Fish an' chips twice, please,' said Big Dave, 'an' two tubs o' mushy peas.'

'An' a bag o' scraps, please,' added Little Malcolm. He had put on his cleanest shirt and scrubbed his filthy hands after work.

Rita served them up in her usual speedy way and wrapped them in newspaper. Her glass eye looked straight ahead at Big Dave. 'What's up wi' y'mate?' Her other eye was fixed on Little Malcolm.

Malcolm was giving Rita his best fixed smile. He had been practising in the mirror.

''E's got summat for you,' said Big Dave a little self-consciously.

Rita leaned over the counter and assessed the five-foot-four-inch bin man.

'My name's Malcolm,' he said. 'An' ah've got a card f'you.'

''Ave y'now?' said Rita.

He passed it over and she opened it. 'A Valentine's card. That's lovely.'

Rita had been brought up in a back-to-back in Chapeltown in Leeds where the outside toilets froze in winter. Her appearance was hard and drawn. It was as if life had worn her down, but, on occasions, there were surprises.

'Well ah can see y'fancy y'self as t'dog's bollocks.'

Malcolm smiled. He had never been a student of etymology and the study of words and their meanings ... but he knew when he was on a winner.

'Ah wondered if you'd like t'go to t'pictures?'

'Wi' *you*?'

'Yes, Rita, wi' me.'

She glanced up at Big Dave. 'Not 'im then?'

Big Dave picked up the parcel of fish and chips and stepped back. 'No, not me. It's Malcolm who's askin'.'

Rita considered Malcolm and decided he had something of the look of Charlton Heston in *El Cid* ... only about a foot shorter. 'Okay then, outside t'Odeon, t'morrow night, seven o'clock.' Rita didn't waste words.

When they walked out Little Malcolm felt seven feet tall.

Freddie, Rose, Sam and Joy arrived at the first Chinese restaurant to open in Easington. Wong Yong was one of the many Hong Kong immigrants who had arrived in England and he had spotted an opportunity. He closed his laundry and opened a restaurant and takeaway. The furnishings were meant to represent exotic luxury and the appearance was definitely more Shanghai than Sheffield.

'Hey, Freddie, this is fantastic,' said Rose.

She was wearing a sleek suede jerkin and a narrow

flared skirt. It was the height of fashion and she felt confident as she walked into the subtly lit restaurant. They were shown to a table, then picked up a menu and studied it carefully.

'What's Mushroom Foo Yung?' asked Joy.

'Like an omelette,' said Sam.

'I'll try one of those,' said Joy. 'Good to be adventurous.' She had cheered up after receiving a late Valentine's card from Sam, unaware that Freddie had bought it for him.

Rose chose Sweet and Sour Pork, Sam selected Chicken Curry with Rice, while Freddie played safe and went for the Mixed Grill.

The many dishes that appeared filled the table and they each sampled a little of everything, washing it down with bottled beer. Freddie gradually relaxed as the evening moved on. Rose was animated and pleased that her suggestion had been well received. Conversation ebbed and flowed as the alcohol took away thoughts of examinations and schoolwork. They were enjoying being teenagers in the early sixties. A special synergy between pop music, television and fashion had burst on to the scene and life seemed full of possibilities.

'Did you hear about the Beatles?' asked Rose. 'They were on *The Ed Sullivan Show* in America last week.'

'Seventy-three million people watched it,' said Joy. She had seen the news and the Fab Four had been singing 'I Saw Her Standing There' to American girls, who appeared to scream just as loudly as their English counterparts.

Sam pulled out a packet of King Size Benson & Hedges Special Filter and offered them round. Freddie and Rose declined but Joy accepted one eagerly.

'Top-quality cigarettes,' Sam said with a self-satisfied smile. He believed there were common fags and classy cigarettes. They were the mark of a man. 'After uni' I'll be an entrepreneurial socialist on a thousand a year,' he boasted. Joy looked a little sad for a moment and wondered if she reckoned in his plans.

Soon a pall of cigarette smoke hovered above the table. 'Miss Plumb gave us girls a lecture about the Nineteen Sixty-two Report on Smoking and Health,' warned Rose. 'She said that cigarettes cause cancer.'

'Not with filter tips,' said Sam confidently, puffing a smoke ring above their heads.

At the end of the evening, Sam dropped them off one by one. Outside Laurel Cottage Rose got out with Freddie. He held her in his arms, then lifted a stray tendril of her hair and tucked it tenderly behind her ear. Above them bright stars wheeled in the firmament like celestial guardians watching over their world.

She responded to his touch. 'You're my sweet Valentine,' he said quietly. Then she stretched up on tiptoe and, fingertip soft, her lips brushed his.

It was a moment to be treasured.

Chapter Twelve

A Sign of Peace

It was Friday, 6 March and, while there was still snow on the ground, it no longer held Ragley village in its chilling fastness. In the far distance the Hambleton hills appeared bleak and grey against a wind-driven sky, the light was growing in the east and a rim of living gold separated the earth from the sky. The raucous cries of curlews heralded the hope of a new season as a pale sun bathed the distant moors with light and warmth. Beneath the hard crust of earth new life was stirring. The dark days were becoming a distant memory and spring was just around the corner. It was a new dawn and the world appeared to be holding its breath.

Lily felt a new sense of optimism as she drove out of Kirkby Steepleton. Her relationship with Freddie was still strained, but there had been some happier moments in recent weeks. He had celebrated his eighteenth birthday by passing his driving test at the first attempt and had also played two more winning games for Yorkshire Schoolboys. She had prepared a celebratory tea, but

Freddie had been quiet throughout and, although he thanked Lily for the occasion, it was a subdued response. Even so, she knew it was a journey that began with small steps.

When she arrived at school, Ruby was emptying a bag of breadcrumbs and chopped strips of bacon rind on to the bird table. 'Mornin', Mrs Feather,' she shouted above the bitter wind.

'Good morning, Ruby. How are you?'

'Champion, thank you kindly. Ah thought ah'd give t'birds a treat.'

Lily paused next to Ruby. 'That's very thoughtful.'

Ruby appeared suitably modest, although her cheeks flushed. 'Well, ah try m'best. Mind you, there's no food wasted in our 'ouse. Our Duggie would lick t'pattern off a plate if y'let 'im.'

Lily nodded in acknowledgement, well aware of Duggie's prodigious appetite during school dinners. 'And how is Ronnie?'

Ruby shook her head sadly. ''E's neither use nor ornament is my Ronnie. Sometimes ah don't know whether t'laugh or cry.'

Lily pursed her lips and said nothing. She knew life was a struggle for Ruby.

'Any road, ah mus' get on. Ah've got m'shift t'do at T'Royal Oak.' She pulled her headscarf a little tighter. 'At least that Stan Coe won't be there.'

'Why not?' asked Lily, suddenly taken aback by a shiver of recollection.

''E were up to 'is old tricks, causin' trouble again an' drunk by all accounts.'

'I see,' said Lily, tugging her coat a little tighter around her.

'But Sergeant Dew'irst sorted 'im out. 'E dunt tek no prisoners.'

Lily acknowledged both the anomaly and the double negative. She was well aware that Harry Dewhirst had his own very direct style of keeping the peace.

Ruby frowned. 'Ah wouldn't give 'ouse room t'that Stan. Should be locked up . . . an' 'is sister's no better.'

Lily saw John Pruett appear at the office window. 'Well, must get on, Ruby. Have a good day.'

'Mebbe ah will, but some days are longer than others.'

She hurried down the drive and Lily looked after her, reflecting that Stan Coe was an evil presence that cast a stain on the village in which she had built her new life.

It was just before nine o'clock and John Pruett had been busy writing on the blackboard in his immaculate cursive script. When the children walked into his classroom there was a sheet of paper on each desk, plus a dip-in pen and a sheet of blotting paper. They sat quietly and stared at the neat writing in white chalk that covered the blackboard.

'Right, boys and girls,' he said. 'We're starting the day with two more eleven-plus practice questions. The time limit is ten minutes, not a minute more. You will show me all the working out on your paper and, as soon as you have finished, put down your pens and fold your arms. So – in complete silence – begin.'

The children were used to mental arithmetic and the first question posed few problems. It read: 'A motorist leaves home at 10.15 a.m. and drives at 32 miles per hour. He stops for lunch from noon to 1.45 p.m. and then continues his journey at 30 miles per hour. How many miles has he travelled by 5 p.m.?'

The second concerned logical deduction. It read: 'My best friend is tall and dark. I am nine and he is ten. He is one of these four boys below. Read the following sentences and write down my best friend's name: Harry is younger than me. He is short and dark. Dick is ten. He is a tall boy with fair hair. Tom has dark hair. He is older than me and is a tall boy. Frank is a tall boy with dark hair. He is nine.'

Susan Derwood frowned. She wouldn't dream of having a best friend who was a boy and wondered why there weren't girls' questions in the eleven-plus. Reluctantly, she wrote the name 'Tom', put down her pen and folded her arms. Her answers to the two questions had taken six minutes.

Across the High Street from school, the familiar pattern of village life was going on. In the Pharmacy Herbert Grinchley was persuading Sylvia Icklethwaite, the forty-six-year-old farmer's wife, that Sanatogen was the solution to her lack of energy. 'It's got glycerol-phosphates, so it must be good,' said Herbert with the conviction of an evangelist.

Muriel Tonks, attracted by the photograph of Gina Lollobrigida in the hairdresser's window, had called in to tell Diane Wigglesworth that so-called 'trendy' unmarried couples in London were 'living over t'brush'.

Meanwhile, in the year when only 4 per cent of the population could afford a holiday abroad, Violet Fawnswater was booking two weeks in an upmarket gîte in Brittany.

Outside the General Stores the local coalman, thirty-year-old Fred Kershaw, was delivering his weekly order to Prudence Golightly. As usual his face was covered in coal dust and a cigarette hung from his lips as he heaved a hundredweight sack from his wagon on to his broad shoulders. Fred was a chain smoker, but his sixty-a-day habit did not seem to hamper the immense physical demands of carrying heavy sacks all day. He was also the centre forward for the Ragley Rovers football team, but they had yet to win a game. Ronnie Smith had offered to change their fortunes by becoming their new manager, but Fred did not hold out much hope.

As he worked his way around the village, he thought of his cousins who also worked in the coal industry at Overton Colliery near Wakefield. They had been taken on as apprentices at the age of fifteen and worked long hours down the pit with their battery packs, knee pads and a metal snap tin with a lid to stop the mice eating their dripping sandwiches. It was hard labour, but they knew it was a job for life and they found companionship in their mining community. They were a few of the half a million men who worked in the pits providing coal for the railways, factories and homes. There had been talk of natural gas, oil and nuclear power, but on this cold morning all that was far from Fred's mind and the mug of sweet tea and two digestive biscuits provided by Prudence were always appreciated.

When the bell rang for morning break Anne was on duty and she put on her coat and scarf and ventured out on to the playground. Lily came out to join her, carrying two mugs of hot coffee.

'Thanks, Lily, that's welcome.'

They stood side by side watching the children at play. Tobias Fawnswater was running around pretending to shoot his friends with a twelve-inch wooden ruler.

'I'm getting concerned about him,' said Anne. 'His drawings are full of graphic images of war.'

'Settle him down with a box of Lego,' said Lily reassuringly. 'He'll enjoy that.'

Suddenly little Margery Flathers was tugging at her sleeve. 'Miss, Miss, my daddy has gone away again.'

'And where has he gone, Margery?' asked Anne.

'Into the woods.'

'The woods?'

'Yes, Miss, he goes there to sleep with his boyfriends,' and she ran off having imparted her news.

Lily looked perplexed.

Anne grinned. 'Don't worry – her father's in the army and is away on night exercises.'

Lily smiled and returned to the warmth of the staff-room while Anne watched Tobias throwing pretend hand grenades at a bemused Clint Ramsbottom.

At the end of playtime Anne sat Toby down in the home corner with the gentle task of building with Lego blocks. When she returned later to check on his progress she was impressed with the tall, colourful structure he had produced. It resembled a tower or a castle.

'So what have you built?' she asked.

'It's a weapon to destroy the Earth,' said a cheerful Tobias.

During lunchtime in Easington School, Rose and Joy were in the sixth-form common room reading an article about the Beatles in Joy's *Pop Weekly* magazine. The Beatles had flown back from America and 12,000 fans had packed every vantage point at London Airport to welcome home their idols. The loudspeaker had blared out 'She Loves You' while girls screamed.

'Wish I'd been there,' sighed Joy.

'Same here,' agreed Rose.

'There might be a concert over Easter,' said Joy hopefully.

Rose looked thoughtful. 'I'm away with my parents. It's their annual trip to see my aunt in Scarborough. I'm not keen, but I can't say no. What about you?'

'I'm stuck here with my mum.'

'What about Sam?'

'He mentioned something about going camping.'

Rose considered this. 'Freddie will probably go as well.'

'Sounds fun,' said Joy. 'Pity we can't join them,' she added with a mischievous grin.

The bell for afternoon school rang and they went off to their lessons, each with thoughts of sharing a sleeping bag with their respective boyfriends.

It was Friday evening and at the far end of the council estate it was bath night in the Ramsbottom household. Minnie Ramsbottom had dragged the tin bath from the back yard into the sparsely furnished front room. There were two wooden chairs, a sofa and a sideboard. She had gone through the usual routine of banking up the coal fire for warmth and placing a peg rug on the battered and stained linoleum floor.

'Do we 'ave to, Mam?' pleaded Shane. 'Ah'm clean.' He

spat on his grimy hands, rubbed them on his shorts and held them up for inspection.

'It's not just yer 'ands, Shane, 'it's *all* of you that 'as t'be washed. Y'need t'be more like yer little brother. 'E's allus clean.'

Shane frowned at Clint, who had always avoided muddy puddles and rough games.

'Can ah sit in t'deep end, Mam?' asked Clint plaintively.

A house brick had been propped under one end of the tin bath.

'No, y'can't, luv. Only big boys sit in t'deep end.'

Shane, suitably placated with the knowledge of his status in the bathtime pecking order, stripped off quickly and stepped into the lukewarm water.

'Your turn, Clint,' said Mrs Ramsbottom.

Clint looked dubiously at the swirling grime that surrounded his brother and stepped gingerly into the raised end of the tub and clutched his knees. He knew what was coming next.

'Mind y'feet,' ordered Mrs Ramsbottom. She picked up a kettle from the hearth and, with well-practised accuracy, poured a stream of boiling water into the centre of the bath. The luxury of sudden heat was always a shock to the two boys.

'Shane, close yer eyes while ah wash yer 'air.'

Mrs Ramsbottom picked up her block of Lifebuoy soap and rubbed vigorously. Then she screwed a stiff flannel into a point. 'Now yer mucky ears.'

That night when the two boys slept top to toe on their bed there was no bedding, just a curtain and an old army greatcoat. However, they did not seem to feel the cold.

'Y'feet smell nice,' said Clint.

'Shurrup,' muttered Shane.

'Shane . . . don't y'like 'avin' a bath?'

'No, baths are f'sissies.'

'Ah'm not a sissy,' protested Clint.

'Y'don't play football,' grumbled Shane.

'Ah don't like football.'

'An' y'don't like fightin'.'

'No, ah don't.'

'So what do y'like?'

'Dunno.' It didn't seem to be the right moment to share the fact that he enjoyed dressing Jane Grantham's dolls.

As ice formed on the inside of the window panes, they dropped off to sleep on the one night of the week when they were clean and smelling of soap.

On Saturday morning Freddie had finished his work in Timothy Pratt's Hardware Emporium. He had arranged to meet Sam Grundy in the Coffee Shop before they went to their afternoon rugby match. As he walked in, the number-one record, Cilla Black's 'Anyone Who Had a Heart', was playing on the jukebox. Sam waved to him from a corner table and Freddie bought a coffee and joined him.

'I've got a great idea,' said Sam.

Freddie grinned at his friend. 'Go on.'

'Joy wasn't too keen, but I mentioned it to some of the lads in the rugby team and a few are interested.'

Freddie sipped his coffee. 'In what?'

'Camping,' explained Sam. 'In the Yorkshire Dales during the Easter break. It'll be brilliant. Malham, drinking in the Lister Arms, then on to Stainforth and Kettlewell. All that fresh air and freedom. A break from revision. Just what we need.'

'Maybe,' said Freddie. 'Sounds good.'

'I've got all the gear,' said Sam. 'Tent, groundsheet, Primus stove. My family have been going camping for years.'

Freddie didn't want to dampen Sam's enthusiasm. 'I'll let you know. I have a few things to sort out first, but it sounds like a good plan.'

Sam took out an Ordnance Survey map of the Yorkshire Dales and they pored over it while he described the proposed adventure.

It was about this time that the beginnings of an idea formed in Freddie's mind.

Lily had called in to Ragley to take Freddie to his afternoon rugby game as Tom was on duty. As she parked on the High Street, Stan Coe's Land Rover pulled up beside her. Lily bowed her head to ignore the leering pig farmer.

'When y'gonna get a proper man instead o' that copper?' he shouted from his open window.

Lily turned away. There were memories that could not be erased.

'Think what y'missin',' he added as he drove off.

Lily took a deep breath, gathered herself and walked into the General Stores, where an irritated Deirdre Coe was expressing her feelings. ''Ow much? That's daylight robbery!'

Prudence had weighed out a quarter-pound of Nuttall's Mintoes. They were Deirdre's favourite sweets. Made in Doncaster and known as 'the five-minute mint', they were certainly value for money.

'They're eightpence a quarter,' said Prudence evenly.

'Ah'll tek 'em.' She slapped two threepenny bits and two pennies on the counter, grabbed the bag of sweets and marched out, ignoring Lily.

'Oh dear,' said Prudence. She looked around the shop. It was quiet again. 'Sorry about that.'

Lily smiled. 'As always, you handled it well.'

'So, what's it to be, Lily?'

She looked at her list. 'A packet of Kellogg's Frosties, please, some Brillo soap pads and a bottle of Kia-Ora orange juice.'

'And how's Freddie these days?' asked Prudence. 'I've seen his photograph in the *Herald*. He's quite a sportsman.'

'Since he passed his driving test I don't see much of him.'

'Freedom, Lily,' said Prudence with a smile. 'New horizons.'

'And he was talking about going camping with his friends over Easter.'

'The great outdoors,' said Prudence with a wistful glance at Jeremy Bear. 'Oh to be young again.'

Lily appeared lost in her own world for a moment, then the bell above the door rang. It was Ruby.

''Ello, Mrs Feather, Miss Golightly. Ah've jus' called in for a few bits an' bobs.'

Prudence and Lily gave each other a knowing look.

The spell was broken.

The Royal Oak was always busy on Saturday lunchtimes. Ronnie Smith and Deke Ramsbottom were leaning on the bar in the taproom, supping deeply on their pints of Tetley's bitter.

Deke opened his packet of Smith's crisps, unwound the blue waxed packet of salt and sprinkled it. ''Ave a crisp, Ronnie.'

Ronnie accepted the offer gratefully. He was wondering what Ruby might have prepared for his lunch. Then he took out a comb from his top pocket and pulled it through his long hair. He had changed his hairstyle from a slicked-back DA to a classy Tony Curtis.

'So, y'want t'be manager o' Ragley Rovers?' said Deke. He had become the unofficial chairman of the local team after making four corner flags in his shed.

Ronnie nodded. 'Ah want t'tek Ragley to t'top o' t'league.'

'But we're bottom,' pointed out Deke.

'Ah know, but ah'll be a tracksuit manager jus' like Alf Ramsey.'

Deke looked puzzled. ''Ave y'got a tracksuit?'

'No . . . but my Ruby can knock one up.'

'You'd 'ave t'get in 'er good books,' said Deke dubiously. 'She told my Minnie you were as much use as a chocolate fireguard.'

'Ah can 'andle my Ruby,' said Ronnie defiantly.

Deke supped on his beer thoughtfully. 'Well, ah wouldn't want t'get on t'wrong side of 'er mother. She's gorra right 'ook like Cassius Clay.'

Twenty-two-year-old Clay had defeated Sonny Liston to become world heavyweight champion. The 'Clown Prince' was now known as the 'King of the Ring'.

Ronnie was suddenly deflated. In his household Agnes

ruled the roost. 'Mebbe so, Deke,' he said. "Ow about another pint? It's your round.'

Deke was sure it was Ronnie's, but he put two half crowns on the bar and didn't argue.

It was early on Sunday morning and a pale dawn light was spreading in the eastern sky as Lily looked out of her bedroom window. Around her all was still and Tom slumbered on. She thought of Freddie. She had heard the front door close as he left for his morning run.

Now he was on the Morton road outside St Mary's Church when shafts of bright sunlight lanced down through the scudding clouds. As he glanced up a skein of geese flew towards the bleak, snow-covered moors.

He stopped and leaned on the church wall, breathing hard. Running helped to conquer his troubled thoughts. There had been times when a wild rage had almost consumed him, but he had moved on with his life. There was contentment in his relationship with Rose, while the reliable Tom continued to be a steadfast companion, someone who shared his views about sport and politics, particularly the fact that he wasn't allowed to vote until he was twenty-one.

However, with Lily there had been no respite and a distance remained between them. On impulse he walked through the gateway of the church and his canvas plimsolls crunched on the ice-rimed grass. It was a path he knew well and he had been here many times to seek solace.

There were rows of gravestones, grey and forbidding in the dappled light. Alongside them winter aconites, pale yellow among the dark leaf mould, gave hope of a distant spring. It was a place of peace and sanctuary, and Freddie's beating heart slowed as his body relaxed. He stopped beneath a huge beech tree and sat down on a bench. His breath steamed in the air as he stared at a familiar gravestone.

Carved into the stone were the words:

FLORENCE MARY BRIGGS
1906–1957
In Loving Memory
Beloved Mother & Wife

He spoke the name out loud and felt the whispering presence of the woman he had believed to be his mother. Moments in his young life when he had turned to her for guidance came flooding back. Now there was no one. A father he did not know was far away and the woman who called herself his mother had lost his trust.

As he sat there, Freddie was unaware of approaching footsteps. Joseph Evans was heading for the early-morning eight o'clock service.

'Good morning, Freddie,' he said. 'Out for your morning run again, I see.'

Freddie looked up, startled. 'Oh, it's you, Mr Evans,' and he gave a strained smile. 'Yes, just taking a break.'

Joseph recognized the signs of a troubled soul and decided to ease his way into a conversation.

'May I?' he asked, gesturing towards the bench.

Freddie nodded, but said nothing.

Joseph sat down and placed his Bible and service sheet

beside him. 'I come here sometimes when I need a little peace and quiet.'

Freddie didn't reply. He simply stared at the gravestone and the white petals of snowdrops as they shivered in the breeze.

'I knew Florence,' said Joseph quietly. 'She was a good woman . . . often strict, but fair.'

'Yes,' said Freddie forcefully, 'but she wasn't always truthful.'

Joseph was surprised, but he had learned to be cautious. 'Perhaps that applies to many of us on occasions. I once heard it said that the war could make liars of us all.'

Freddie turned to face him. 'What do you mean?'

'Just that it was such a difficult time and your mother lived through it. People did things they wouldn't normally do because they didn't know how long they were going to live.'

'But how can that justify a lie?'

Joseph was puzzled by the determined young man at his side. He didn't fully understand why Freddie had these thoughts about Florence.

'A mother shouldn't lie to her son.' Freddie was persistent.

Joseph steepled his hands under his chin as if in prayer. 'I should think a mother would do anything to protect her children in wartime.'

Freddie put his head in his hands. *Maybe this is why my mother allowed me to think she was my sister*, he thought.

'Sometimes things aren't what they seem, Freddie, but usually our actions are born out of love.'

Freddie let this sink in. 'I suppose so,' he acknowledged.

Joseph looked at the clock on the church tower. 'I'm sorry, but I must go and prepare the service.' He stood up. 'Not many attend this one,' he added with a smile, 'but each of them has their reasons. They usually find the loving kindness and mercy we all seek.' He picked up his Bible and service sheet. 'And I believe they all leave feeling refreshed.'

Freddie nodded. 'I'm sure they do,' he said. It seemed the right thing to say. He watched the slightly stooped, angular figure of the vicar as he hurried towards the church and thought about what he had said.

The air was clean and cold.

His thoughts were clear.

He shivered.

It was time to move on.

However, there remained a diamond hardness to his resentment and the bitter taste left by the perfect lie that had shaped his life.

With renewed vigour he trotted back to the Morton road and increased his pace as he ran towards Ragley High Street.

Joseph had paused in the church entrance and watched the athletic young man stride away into the distance. On impulse he sketched a cross in the air.

'Peace be with you, my son.'

Albert Jenkins, the forty-one-year-old school governor and churchwarden, was a regular at this service and he arrived moments later as Joseph was still staring after the blond-haired figure disappearing into the distance.

'Good morning, Joseph,' said Albert. 'You look thoughtful. I saw young Freddie Briggs as I arrived.'

Joseph nodded. 'Yes, he was paying his respects to his late mother and discussing a little philosophy.'

'Philosophy?'

'Well, truth and lies, to be precise.'

Albert grinned. '*Magna est veritas et prævalet*,' he recited. Albert loved his Latin.

Joseph gave an enquiring look.

'Great is truth, and it prevails,' clarified Albert.

'And so it does,' agreed Joseph, and they walked side by side into the sanctuary of the silent church.

It was as Freddie ran back towards Kirkby Steepleton that the cold rhythm of his thoughts began to race.

It was the last breath of winter and the first of a new life.

It was time to rekindle the ashes.

It was time to feed the fire.

Chapter Thirteen

The Road to Reconciliation

'Time to go, Freddie,' shouted Tom from the foot of the stairs. It was early morning on Friday, 20 March, the final school day of the spring term.

'Coming,' said Freddie and he pushed his rucksack under his bed. He had begun to pack spare clothes and a few toiletries, plus an old phrase book. A smile flickered across his face as he hurried downstairs. His secret was safe.

As Tom drove out of Kirkby Steepleton the hedgerows were bursting into new life and the bright yellow petals of forsythia gave promise of warmer days ahead. On the distant North Yorkshire moors curlews found shelter in the gorse, while newborn lambs were taking their first hesitant steps. The long winter days of dark nights and log fires were over and the swallows had returned to build their nests. When Freddie arrived outside the gates of Easington School the breeze carried the warm breath of spring. He walked in with the confidence of youth. The Easter holiday beckoned and he had special plans.

In Ragley School Anne Grainger was preparing her classroom for the morning activities and reflecting on a breakfast conversation with her husband.

He had shown her a diagram of a refectory table in oak, plus a detailed cutting list. Worry had creased his forehead. 'I need some three-eighths dowel to join my crossrail to the pedestal,' he had said. Anne knew where she would like to put the crossrail and it wasn't on a pedestal. She looked out of the window and saw a few parents arriving with their children.

Twenty-six-year-old Molly Swithenbank was walking up the drive with her five-year-old daughter, Connie. She needed to tell Anne Grainger that her daughter had an appointment at the hospital. Connie occasionally had trouble breathing and there had been some anxious moments.

The pale-faced little girl looked up at her mother. 'Mummy . . . when was I born?'

Molly crouched down and smiled. 'The thirtieth of March, nineteen fifty-eight.'

Connie's eyes lit up in realization. 'Hey! That's my birthday!'

Molly gave her a hug. 'Yes, you're a big girl now.'

Connie considered this for a moment. 'Yes, Mummy . . . but in my heart I'm still little.'

Molly stared at her daughter in surprise. It was a moment to treasure. She kissed her forehead with the love of a mother and they walked hand in hand into school.

*

It was morning break and Vera had prepared coffee in the staff-room and distributed the end-of-term report cards.

John Pruett gave Lily an enquiring glance. 'Have you any plans over Easter?'

'Probably taking Tom's mother to Fountains Abbey – she loves to go there. He's got a few days off and Freddie is going camping in the Dales. What about you?'

'My sister is coming to visit.' He said this with a despairing finality. His sister made his life a misery with her constant need to spring-clean John's untidy house.

'A bourbon biscuit, Mr Pruett?' offered Vera, holding out the tin. The Ragley secretary usually had a solution for a soul in torment.

Saturday morning dawned bright and clear and in Nora's Coffee Shop the jukebox was on full volume playing 'Little Children' by Billy J. Kramer and the Dakotas, the current number-one record.

The teenage friends Lizzie Buttershaw and Veronica Collins were humming along while they flicked through the pages of *Ready Steady Go!* magazine. On the cover were photographs of Dusty Springfield and George Harrison and inside were souvenir pictures of the Searchers, Brian Poole and the Tremeloes, the Rolling Stones, plus a giant colour photo of the Beatles. The girls were in heaven as they sipped their frothy coffee and shared news of their heart-throb, Billy J. Kramer.

Lizzie sighed as she thought about their current boyfriends. 'So what shall we do 'bout Darrell and Carl? They'll finish up fighting the way things are going.'

Veronica leaned forward so their foreheads were almost touching. 'Thing is, we can never go out as a foursome.'

'Y'spot on there, Ve.' It was a crisis in their young lives. 'An' Darrell says he 'ates Rockers.'

'Carl told me 'e wouldn't be seen dead wi' a Mod.'

Darrell was clean-cut, wore a smart suit, listened to rhythm and blues and owned a Lambretta covered in shiny badges. In contrast, Carl wore a black leather jacket and motorcycle boots and his hero was Marlon Brando in *The Wild One*. On Saturday nights he changed into his brothel-creeper shoes and danced with Veronica to the music of Bo Diddley.

Suddenly they were distracted. Seventeen-year-old Bertie Stubbs, the burly farmer's son, walked in with his handsome and equally rugged farmhand friend. They smiled in the direction of the two girls, ordered coffee and sat down at the next table.

Lizzie gave Veronica a knowing look, 'Jus' thinkin' . . .'

'What?'

'Darrell an' Carl. Why don't we dump 'em? It'll never work.'

Veronica grinned and nodded.

They stared at the two burly newcomers. Both had weather-beaten faces and shoulders like weightlifters.

'Which do y'fancy?' whispered Lizzie.

'Both of 'em,' said Veronica, who wasn't backwards in coming forwards.

Ten minutes later Mods and Rockers were forgotten and a Saturday night barn dance beckoned with rough cider and a cuddle behind the hay bales.

*

It was Sunday evening and Freddie had packed his rucksack and was standing in the hallway when there was a beep of a car horn outside Laurel Cottage.

Lily hurried to say goodbye, but the farewell was brief as Freddie walked down the path towards Sam Grundy, who had borrowed his mother's car. Freddie was staying the night at Sam's house so that they could set off together the following morning.

'Enjoy the Yorkshire Dales,' called out Lily. 'Hope the weather stays fine.'

Sam waved to Lily, but Freddie gave the merest glance in her direction. Lily felt an emptiness in her heart as she watched the car drive away.

After their evening meal she and Tom settled down in front of the television. *Dr Finlay's Casebook* was on later, one of Tom's favourite programmes, and, although Lily missed Freddie's presence, time with Tom was always precious.

Sunday evening television entertainment was also on the minds of the folk of Ragley. Shortly before seven o'clock Vera settled down to watch *Songs of Praise* from St Mary's Church in Taunton on the BBC. In contrast, Ruby never missed Val Parnell's *Sunday Night at the London Palladium* on ITV. This week it starred Freddie and the Dreamers and, as always, the talented host, Bruce Forsyth, was on form with his Beat the Clock game and a staggering jackpot prize of £100.

On Monday morning Freddie was up at the crack of dawn and insistent on an early start. At first Sam was puzzled – until he realized Freddie had no intention of going camping.

'I've got other plans, Sam. Just trust me on this. We'll talk when I get back.'

Sam shook his head. 'I'm a bit disappointed, Freddie, but I guess you have your reasons.'

They drove down the A19 towards York and pulled up outside the railway station.

'Are you sure about this?' asked Sam, but recognized Freddie would not be swayed. They shook hands.

'See you later,' said Freddie. 'Have a great time and don't worry about me. I'm fine. Just something I have to do.'

He walked to the ticket office and bought a ticket for London.

Half an hour later, as the train pulled out of York station, he settled back, stared out of the window and thought of what lay ahead. It had been a reluctant dawn, but as the mist lifted there was promise of a fine day. He took out his German phrase book and scanned the pages. He had not posted his earlier letter to Rudolph Krüger and had considered writing again, but had then decided it would be best not to forewarn him.

It was time to meet his father and discover his history.

Hamburg beckoned.

King's Cross Station was busy, but he found his way on the underground to Liverpool Street Station and boarded the train to Harwich. Two hours later he was at the port where the Harwich–Hamburg ferry was due to depart at three o'clock.

Meanwhile, life in Ragley village carried on its timeless cycle. The General Stores was its usual busy self, with early-morning shoppers and the exchange of gossip.

Elsie Crapper was buying soap powder and Prudence Golightly passed over a large packet of Lux. 'Anything else, Elsie?'

The church organist was always keen to impart the latest news. 'There's a lot going on, according to my Ernie,' she said with enthusiasm. Her husband was an encyclopaedia salesman and regarded himself as something of an expert in virtually *everything*. 'He said the government's building a new town because there's too many people in London.'

'Really,' said Prudence. 'Whereabouts?'

'Somewhere called Milton Keynes in Buckinghamshire.'

'I know it,' said Prudence. 'I had a friend who lived in Bletchley during the war. That's not far away.'

A queue was forming behind Elsie and Prudence was beginning to look anxious. 'So, is that it, Elsie?'

Elsie returned to the last few items on her shopping list. 'Almost, Prudence. Just a tin of beans, please, and a Toffee Crisp for Ernie and my *Tit-Bits*.'

In Harwich Freddie bought a ticket and boarded the ferry along with a heaving mass of people. It was almost full and a long overnight journey was in store. Some of the wealthier passengers had purchased a cabin, but there were many like Freddie who sought out a comfortable bench on the top deck.

With the benefit of his German studies, he found he could follow much of the conversations of those around him. On the next bench a young German couple were recalling a night back in 1960 at Hamburg's Indra Club when they had listened to a live performance by the Beatles. Freddie smiled and thought of Rose. She was unaware of his travel plans and he wondered what she would think when the time was right to reveal all. Rose had become a constant companion, whereas relations with his family had become flawed, an amalgam with a seam of impurity. His youth was lost now, a time of innocence he could barely recall. The memory had been scarred and the time to seek his own destiny had arrived.

Time passed and he bought a sandwich and a bottle of German beer. Then, as darkness fell, he mused on the events that had brought him to this journey. He tried to get comfortable as the ferry rocked beneath a firmament of inky darkness sprinkled with stars. It was a long time before he fell asleep.

The ferry was due to arrive in Hamburg at around seven o'clock the next morning; following a six-hour crossing of the North Sea, there was still a long journey up the River Elbe. Finally, however, they docked at Landungsbrücken, the largest landing place in the Port of Hamburg. As Freddie disembarked a drift of rain freshened the air and dampened the dockside. He stared in wonder. He was here in Hamburg, a German city in the process of rebuilding itself on a grand scale. Around him were the old piers that had been destroyed during the Second World War and ten years ago pontoons had been built. He took out a map of the city and studied it.

A clock tower loomed before him as he made his way to the local station. He bought a ticket on the overground train to Barmbek-Süd, a district of Hamburg rebuilt in the old style after the war. This was where Rudi lived and

Freddie recalled that twenty years ago Tom had been fighting against a German Army that included his father. When the train pulled in to Barmbek-Süd station he picked up his rucksack and began the last leg of his journey. As he walked, he was aware that this was a time of renewal for a city that had been devastated during the war.

Finally he arrived at No. 4 Weizenkamp, an apartment block with lockable postboxes for each apartment. He saw Rudi's name, stepped inside, climbed the stairs and headed for the fourth floor. The name *Krüger* was next to the bell. He pressed and waited. There was no response. He tried again. There was no one in.

A curious neighbour suddenly appeared across the hallway. She was tall and elegant and studied the stranger before her.

He plucked up courage to use his German and asked if Mr Krüger lived here. *'Entschuldigung, wohnt Herr Krüger hier?'*

The lady frowned and asked who he was. *'Und wer sind Sie?'*

'I'm a relation from England,' he said cautiously. *'Ich bin ein Verwandter aus England.'*

The lady's demeanour softened slightly and she replied in excellent English, 'Rudolph is away on business.'

Freddie's shoulders slumped. 'Oh . . . when will he be back?'

'One week, perhaps two. He is a busy man.'

The plan to surprise his father had backfired. He thanked the neighbour. *'Schade. Vielen Dank.'*

She nodded, clearly appreciative of this tall young Englishman trying hard to speak her language. His disappointment was obvious. 'Is there a message?' she asked.

Freddie shook his head sadly. He had many questions but was unsure how to proceed. *'Nein, danke.'*

She watched him descend the stairs and considered his appearance. *Definitely a relation*, she thought.

Freddie slowly made his way back to the station, his hopes dashed. He walked into a kiosk with the word *Imbiss* over the door and bought a sandwich and a cup of hot chocolate. He used his phrase book to look up 'youth hostel' and asked where he could find one to spend the night. The directions provided by the young woman behind the counter were clear and precise.

On Wednesday morning, after a comfortable night in the hostel, Freddie explored Hamburg. He sat down outside the town hall, the *Rathaus*, and watched the busy scene before him, trying to imagine Rudi appearing from the crowds.

It was not to be.

As he was stepping on to the return ferry from Landungsbrücken to Harwich, he wondered about the life he had left behind him.

On Wednesday afternoon Lily was in Ragley village and had loaded up her car with shopping. Finally, after buying some stamps in the Post Office, to her surprise she saw Sam Grundy coming out of the telephone box.

She called out to him. 'Sam, you're back early. I thought you were going for a week.'

Sam looked a little crestfallen.

'Oh, hello Mrs Feather. We came back last night. There was an accident. I was just ringing the hospital in York.'

'An accident? Not Freddie I hope?'

Sam was confused. 'No, Phil Tomlinson. He tripped up at Malham Tarn and broke his wrist. So we drove back.'

'Did Freddie come back with you?'

'Freddie?'

'Yes, is he still in the Dales?'

'But Freddie didn't come with us. I dropped him off at York station early on Monday morning.'

'York station?'

'Yes, I presumed you knew.'

'Where was he going?'

Sam was beginning to feel uncomfortable. 'I don't know, Mrs Feather. He didn't say.'

Lily ran across the road, unlocked the front door of the school and ran into the office. She telephoned Tom.

'I'll come home straight away,' he said.

As she hurried back across the village green to her car, she saw Vera sitting on the bench under the weeping willow tree. She looked up from her *Woman's Own* and the pictures of the Queen's fourth child and third son.

'Lily,' she called out, 'you look concerned.'

She patted the seat beside her.

Lily paused, breathing deeply, and shook her head.

'Please, sit down and tell me.'

'It's Freddie. He's gone. This time it's more serious. I've just discovered he didn't go camping with his friends. He was last seen at York station.'

Vera considered her response and held Lily's hand. 'You must remember he is a young man now and he can be impulsive. But much more than that, he is intelligent. He will have thought this through and is clearly doing something that he feels is important.'

Lily said nothing.

'Where is Rose?' asked Vera.

'In Scarborough with her parents.'

'Perhaps that's a possibility.'

Lily looked up with new hope. 'Maybe,' she said. She glanced at her wristwatch. 'Tom is coming home. I had better get going.'

Vera stood up and gave her a hug. 'Lily, all will be well.'

'Thank you, Vera.'

As she drove home Lily reflected that Vera had a spiritual armour that had protected her through the years. She wished she had the same.

It was Tom who found the note in Freddie's bedroom. It was under his alarm clock on the bedside table. He called out to Lily.

'You read it,' she said nervously.

Tom unfolded the sheet of paper, torn from one of Freddie's notebooks.

Dear Tom and Lily,

If you find this note you will know I didn't go camping.

I wanted to find my father so I'm taking the Harwich ferry to Hamburg.

I will be back before Easter so please don't worry about me.

It's something I have to do.

I'm sorry for the deception but I knew you would not want me to do this.

Freddie

'Well, at least we know what he's doing,' said Tom. 'It's a big step.'

'Hamburg,' said Lily. 'He must have been planning this for some time.'

Tom nodded. 'Tickets, currency, the Easter holiday. It all adds up.'

Lily looked up at him. 'How do you walk away from memories?' she asked quietly. She took the letter from him and stared at the words. 'There never seems to be a forgiving pathway.'

'When he gets home you need to talk to him,' said Tom.

Lily stood by the open door and stared into the distance. Wind-tears streaked her cheeks and she felt the pain of a fractured soul.

Freddie arrived in Harwich early on Thursday morning and caught the train to London, then at King's Cross boarded another for York. Eventually the familiar countryside of Yorkshire appeared and he thought of what he might say to Lily. Perhaps she still thought he was in the Dales with Sam.

Once he had arrived in York, he managed to catch a bus back to Easington, then another on to Ragley. When he arrived at Laurel Cottage he said nothing and Lily asked no questions. In the evening she prepared a meal for Tom, Freddie and herself. As they sat down to eat, you could have cut the tension with a knife.

It was Tom who spoke first. 'We know about Hamburg. We appreciated the note. Even so, it was a concern.'

Freddie looked at Lily. 'He wasn't there.'

'I'm sorry,' said Lily quietly.

'I needed to meet him, to get to know my father.'

Lily took a deep breath. 'I'll help you find him.'

Tom looked at her in surprise, while a new light of realization dawned in Freddie's eyes.

'Thank you,' he said and finished his meal in silence.

Mid-afternoon on Easter Saturday, Rose telephoned Laurel Cottage.

'Hello, Rose,' said Lily. 'Are you home?'

'Hello, Mrs Feather. Yes, we've just got back.'

'Did you enjoy Scarborough?'

'Yes, thank you. I was wondering if Freddie was home.'

'Yes, but I'm afraid he's out with Sam.' Lily wondered if Rose had known Freddie's plans but guessed not.

'Well, could you mention we're going to church tomorrow for the Easter service and maybe I can catch up with him there – if he decides to go.'

Lily gave a wry smile. 'I'm sure he will, Rose.'

It was when Tom and Lily were watching the end of the BBC Saturday night film, *Caribbean Gold*, that Freddie came home. The film had been recommended by Vera during a call from Lily bringing her up to date with the news of Freddie.

Freddie had spent the afternoon with Sam at his home listening to the first broadcast from the pirate station Radio Caroline, which had begun broadcasting from a ship anchored just outside territorial waters off Felixstowe and had caused great excitement. Just after midday they had listened to the Rolling Stones and marvelled at the constant flow of pop music that was suddenly available to them.

*

On Easter Sunday morning Lily rose early and wrote a long letter to Rudi. Later she let Freddie drive her car into Ragley. Tom sat in the passenger seat looking thoughtful and Lily stared at the back of Freddie's head. It had been a traumatic week, but she was pleased they were together on this special day in the Church calendar.

Gradually she relaxed. The journey into Ragley was always good for the soul at this time of year. On the grassy banks clumps of early daffodils shivered in the cold morning sunshine. They parked on the Morton road and walked towards St Mary's Church.

Archibald Pike was leading his team in some complicated bell-ringing and summoning the villagers to their place of worship.

'I'll see you later,' said Lily, collecting her choir robe from the car. She hurried through the lychgate and walked up the gravel path. Around her rose the damp smell of new-mown grass and the wind in the trees made a melancholy sound. There were shadows behind the gravestones and Lily shivered at the thought of times past.

The McConnells had arrived and stopped to talk to Tom, while Freddie and Rose wandered off in their own private world.

'Did you enjoy camping?' asked Rose.

'I didn't go. Perhaps another time. What about you? How was Scarborough?'

'Fine. Good weather. Sea air.' She sighed. 'Except ... you weren't there.'

Freddie wanted to hold her and say how he really felt. 'We could have a day out at the coast,' he suggested eagerly, 'if Lily lets me have her car.'

She looked up at him. 'I'd like that.'

Freddie was distracted. 'Your mother's waving at us.'

'Time to go in, I think.'

They headed for the gate and Freddie was pleased he hadn't needed to say where he had been all week.

Albert Jenkins was on duty as churchwarden, welcoming parents and children as they entered the church. Minnie Ramsbottom was ushering a cheerful Clint and a reluctant Shane through the entrance, followed by her husband, Derek. Albert knew Derek more as Deke the singing cowboy; his rendition of the theme from *High Noon* was legendary.

'Good to see you, Derek,' said Albert in surprise. Deke was an infrequent attendee.

''Ello Albert, well . . . you know me. Ah'm more C *and* E if y'know what ah mean . . . Christmas an' Easter – not a reg'lar.'

'You're always welcome and you too, Minnie, and your fine boys.'

Minnie smiled and gave Shane a final withering glance as they found a pew and sat down.

Beyond the chancel Vera was lighting the tall candles on either side of the altar. The light flickered on the ancient walls and the stained glass in the East window. Tom, Brian and Mary shared a pew, with Freddie and Rose sitting behind.

The choir was on form for a change, with Davinia Grint, the lead soprano, singing 'Christ the Lord is risen today' at the top of her voice. Lily provided a passable descant while thankfully drowning out Gerald Crimpton's nasal problems.

When the time came for the sermon, Lily left the choir stalls and slipped into the pew beside Tom. Joseph took as his theme 'Forgive without punishment' and read Colossians 3:13. Lily sat up and listened carefully while Freddie also gave Joseph his full attention.

Joseph faced his congregation. 'We live in a broken world,' he announced in a strong, sombre voice, 'until we come to our ending in life and love eternal.' All eyes were on him. It was clear he was speaking from the heart.

'Life is a walk of faith and sometimes the road to reconciliation is long.' He looked down at Freddie and recalled their conversation in the churchyard. 'But remember that road begins with one step. In the Gospel of St John, Jesus says to his disciples, "Peace be unto you."'

He raised his arms and gestured to all assembled. 'Easter is a time for rejoicing, so please look around you. We are all friends here. Let us rejoice together at this Eastertide.'

He stepped down from his pulpit and stood in the aisle. It was an unusual moment of informality. 'Please take a moment now to shake hands and extend a sign of friendship to those beside you and those nearby across the pews.'

The congregation began to mingle and peaceful greetings were shared. Tom hugged Lily. 'Happy Easter, Lily,' he said quietly.

'And to you, Tom,' she replied softly.

Albert Jenkins was standing in the pew in front and he turned to shake hands with Tom and Lily.

Suddenly there was a tap on Lily's shoulder. She turned and Rose smiled. 'Happy Easter, Mrs Feather,' she said brightly.

'Thank you, Rose.'

Rose looked up at Freddie and nudged him. 'Go on then.'

Lily steeled herself.

Freddie stared at her. He remembered her words: *I'll help you find him.*

Suddenly he leaned forward and took Lily's hand. He whispered in her ear, 'Happy Easter . . . Lily.'

Lily clasped his hand tightly. He was back in her life.

Chapter Fourteen

Difficult Decisions

'Lily, we need to talk. Something has come up.' It was Tom ringing from his office. 'I'll be home in an hour.'

It was Friday, 3 April and the Easter holiday was almost over.

'Sounds ominous,' said Lily playfully.

'No, nothing to worry about. An *opportunity* you might say . . . but I need to share it with you.'

'Okay, but I'll have to ring John. He was due to pick me up at six thirty. I had that in-service course in York tonight, if you remember.'

'That's why I'm ringing. I'll be home by seven.'

Lily replaced the receiver.

John Pruett could barely hide his disappointment when Lily told him she was unable to join him for the lecture and follow-up workshop in York. An evening with Lily was something to treasure. Instead he was faced with two hours of Professor Dominic Batey discussing the malign effects of the eleven-plus selection process and the problems of rigid streaming in our schools. The learned professor believed that an incoming Labour government would make comprehensive education a reality. So John, as a keen supporter of the eleven-plus, was in for a disheartening night, particularly as his attractive deputy headteacher would not be sitting beside him.

It was after their evening meal that Tom and Lily had the chance to talk. He picked up his briefcase from the hall and they went into the lounge. Freddie remained at the kitchen table to complete some French translation. Tom found a bottle of red wine in the sideboard and poured two glasses. Then he took out a document from his black leather briefcase. 'It's here in the internal police newsletter. I've been so busy I almost missed it.' He sat down in his armchair and placed it on the coffee table.

Lily glanced down at the page. The words 'CHIEF INSPECTOR' were printed in bold type. 'So, you're considering a new job?' she asked, sipping her wine. 'That's exciting.'

'Yes, a great opportunity. If it came off I would be in charge of my own division – the next natural step you might say. I need to give it serious thought and wanted to talk it through with you.'

Lily was curious. 'You've done well here. Does this mean you're not happy in your work?'

Tom sat back and nodded. 'I am, but I really believe I would have a good chance of a job like this. I'm well qualified, have a good record and the authority has a good reputation.'

'The authority? You mean North Yorkshire?'

When Tom had words of import he always considered them before speaking. There was a long pause.

'No, not North Yorkshire.'

'Oh, where then?'

'Lily . . . we would have to move.'

'Move?'

'Yes. It's in Durham.'

Tom stared into her eyes. He knew her so well and saw the first hint of caution.

'Durham? Not a place I know apart from a visit to the cathedral.'

'It's a vibrant part of the north of England. Shipbuilding on the Tyne and the Wear, collieries and major construction work in Darlington.'

'Oh,' said Lily. 'Sounds busy.'

'Durham is a large police authority with a forward-looking chief constable. Working with him would be special. It could be a stepping stone towards becoming a divisional superintendent.'

'Sounds interesting,' said Lily. 'It's just a lot to take in.'

'As I said, it's something I can't ignore. I would be a chief inspector of a division in Durham.' He paused, judging her mood. 'I suppose it had to happen one day – a new post for either you or me.'

Lily cradled her wine glass and sat back on the sofa. 'This is a big decision, Tom, and I love my job at Ragley.'

'I know that.'

'If John decided to retire at some time I would have a good chance of the headship.'

Tom sighed. 'I know that as well, but there are good

schools further north. With your experience they would snap you up. There could be a headship for you sooner rather than later.'

Lily studied his face. There was an eagerness there. 'If you applied when would the interviews be?'

'Probably in the middle of May up in Newton Aycliffe.'

'As soon as that?'

He held up the form. 'I would have to complete my application this weekend in order to meet the deadline. That's why I was keen to talk.'

Practical issues began to form in Lily's mind. 'What about accommodation?'

Tom riffled through the papers on the coffee table. 'I checked this out with a few of the guys I know up there. I'm told there would be the offer of a police house with three bedrooms. Sounds good, by all accounts. Likely to be on the Waldridge road in Chester-le-Street. I've been up there for a couple of meetings in the past. There's lovely countryside to the west.'

Lily smiled and clasped her hands. 'Gosh, all this has come as a bit of a shock.'

Tom stood up and sat beside her on the sofa. 'I wouldn't have brought this home if I didn't think it might be the best for *all* of us. Not just me.'

Lily nodded. 'I understand.' Tom had always been honest and true.

'There is a middle road for now,' he said.

'What do you mean?'

'Well, I could complete the application form and then wait to see if I was invited for interview. Then we could talk again. Don't forget, I may not make the shortlist and, if it got that far, there's no guarantee I would get the job anyway.'

Lily breathed deeply. Her world was spinning once again.

'Yes, let's do that,' she said simply.

Tom moved closer and looked into her eyes. 'There is another reason, of course. We could have a new life up there.'

'A new life?'

He stretched across and rested his hand on hers. His touch was gentle.

'You know what I mean. A fresh start . . . where secrets aren't needed.'

Lily sat back and drank her wine, her mind racing with decisions but with a hint of sorrow.

It was almost half past nine when John Pruett arrived back in Ragley. He was alone again and his home was almost back to its normal untidy state following his sister's spring clean. He poured himself a gin and tonic, slipped off his shoes and switched on the television.

On BBC1 it was the annual *Miss England* competition from the Ritz Ballroom in Manchester. This was a popular event organized by Mecca Dancing and the entrepreneur Eric Morley. It occurred to John that watching England's most beautiful girls parading around in swimming costumes appeared distinctly inappropriate for the headteacher of a Church of England Primary School. However, he watched anyway and celebrated with a second glass when his personal choice, Brenda Blacker from London, was awarded the crown. He took a last look at the shapely winner and decided that she wasn't a patch on Lily Feather.

It was late when he went to bed after watching *The Sky at Night* with Patrick Moore. The quirky and fascinating astronomer had been discussing the problems of celestial navigation that a space traveller might face, whereas the only navigation problem that concerned John was getting up a flight of stairs after a few gin and tonics.

On Saturday morning Freddie borrowed Lily's car and drove into Ragley to do his three-hour shift in the Hardware Emporium. He had made a good impression on the fastidious Timothy Pratt and always left the counter looking neat and tidy.

He smiled at the thought of meeting Rose for lunch in the Coffee Shop, followed by an afternoon playing cricket for Easington School. Freddie had been made captain of the team, the first time a pupil had captained both the rugby and cricket teams. As an attacking batsman and a ferocious fast bowler, he was a formidable all-rounder.

He wound down the window and let the breeze blow his wavy blond hair. Around him the countryside was waking once again. Spring had touched the land with soft fingertips and the sticky buds on the horse chestnut trees were cracking open, while rooks cawed in the high elms. On Ragley High Street primroses brightened the grassy banks and, across the village green, the flower tubs outside The Royal Oak were bright with colour.

Back in Laurel Cottage Lily was sitting at her bureau and reading the letter she had written the previous weekend to Rudolph Krüger. She had wanted to leave it for a few days before posting it so that she could think over what she had said. She had chosen her words carefully and, when she looked at it again, she was happy with the result.

Laurel Cottage, High Street, Kirkby Steepleton, YORK, North Yorkshire.
4th April 1964

Dear Rudi,

You will no doubt be surprised to receive this letter. Much has changed since I last wrote to you with Freddie's school photograph and I had to get in touch.

There is no need to worry. Freddie is well. You would be proud of him. He is working hard at school and is excelling in sport. You may recall all those years ago when you saw him play cricket at six years of age. He is still playing cricket every Saturday and is captain of his team.

Freddie is a tall, good-looking young man and looks just like you. It is this likeness that caused him to discover that his past is not what he has been brought up to believe.

By accident he found the photograph of you and the other prisoners of war taken in 1944 on the farm in Amersham that you sent to me. He immediately recognized your similarity to him and his questions compelled me to tell him the truth of his history and the fact that you are his father.

He is confused and angry, not with anyone but me, it would seem, but I have to accept that. He wants to meet you and so, unbeknown to me, travelled to Hamburg; he found your address on the letter that was with the photograph. He made the journey ten days ago when, according to a neighbour, you were away on business. He introduced himself as a relative from England, which you may already know about.

He desperately wants to meet you. I know that I cannot hide from the past any longer and that I must help him fulfil his wish.

I think the time has come for us to do this together, Rudi. Can you come to England to see Freddie? I hope that you will consider this carefully as it is so important to him.

Don't worry about Tom. He is fully behind me in writing to you. Please get in touch to let me know your thoughts. I understand that this will be difficult for you too. But I hope that it is something you can do for our son.

With kind regards,
Lily

She sealed the envelope and put it in her handbag.

It was shortly after twelve o'clock when Freddie left the Hardware Emporium and walked into the Coffee Shop. Rose was already there and she smiled up at him. On the jukebox the Bachelors were singing their latest hit, 'I Believe'.

He waved. 'Coffee and a sandwich?'

She nodded, her eyes bright with anticipation.

'Two coffees please, Nora, and two ham sandwiches.'

'Ah'll bwing 'em over, Fweddie,' said Nora.

He sat down. 'So, how's things?' he asked.

'Fine, apart from revision every evening. It's getting close now.'

Freddie reached over to hold her hand. 'We'll be in the middle of it next month.'

'Hard to believe it's come round so quickly. Did you know I've got *three* Art exams? Each one lasts three hours. There are two practicals, one with oils, plus a written paper. I'm up to my ears with Italian Renaissance painters.'

'Can't help you with that, I'm afraid. What about History?'

'We've been doing practice essays on the Napoleonic Wars, so it's dates and battles and more dates.'

'Well, English should be fine. It's your best subject.'

Rose gave Freddie a wry smile. 'And yours, of course.'

Freddie shrugged his shoulders.

The coffee arrived and Rose became thoughtful. 'I've been thinking.'

'Go on.'

'How about during these next few weeks we agree to meet just on Saturdays? Some last-minute revision could make all the difference.'

Freddie could see the logic of this, but was unwilling to commit immediately. 'Only Saturdays?' he asked.

'Yes.'

'But I'm in the hardware shop in the mornings and playing cricket during the afternoons.'

'Good, I'll come and watch you and then we can celebrate you scoring runs and taking wickets.'

Freddie nodded in reluctant agreement and they began to eat their sandwiches.

Around them the tables were filling with the lunchtime regulars. The Walmsley twins were eating sausage rolls at a corner table with their mother. The boys were sharing their sixpenny *TV Comic*, featuring *Fireball XL5*, *Popeye* and *The Range Rider*.

On her usual table in the far corner, Wilhemena Hardcastle, the portly, domineering president of the Women's Institute, was sitting with some of her followers. She was holding forth about how she missed the tranquillity of Doris Clutterbuck's Tea Rooms. It was the afternoon of the WI Spring Fair in the village hall and she was rallying support.

Wilhemena was red in the face as she sipped her camomile tea. Unknown to her husband, George, she had spent seventy-five shillings on a Scheerskin Cinch-Waist Corselette. It claimed to have 60 per cent more control and to smoothe away midriff bulges, but it didn't appear to be working. With an attempt to get comfortable and a scathing look at the clientele around her, she proceeded to devour a chocolate eclair.

Rose had finished her sandwich and looked up at Freddie with a new intensity. 'Did you know Sam and Joy have split up?'

Freddie almost knocked over the bottle of tomato sauce. 'No, I didn't.'

Rose frowned. 'I thought you would have known as you're his best friend.'

'It's because I haven't seen him to catch up, but he'll be at the cricket this afternoon.'

'It was Joy who broke up with him.'

'Has she found somebody else?'

'No.' Rose looked concerned. 'I know she really loves him, but she thinks he doesn't feel the same way about her. Between you and me, I think she's hoping he will come to his senses and ask her out again.'

Freddie thought this was unlikely and gave a noncommittal shrug. With regard to affairs of the heart, he decided caution was the best response to his perceptive girlfriend.

Next to the jukebox, Little Malcolm Robinson was sitting at a table with his new girlfriend, Rita Eckinthorpe from the fish-and-chip shop. They were enjoying bacon butties and two large mugs of sweet tea.

Last night they had gone to see the film *Zulu*, starring Michael Caine and Stanley Baker, who in the thrilling battle scenes had faced overwhelming odds at the Battle of Rorke's Drift.

'Ah liked that Michael Caine,' said Rita.

The actor was tall, blond and good-looking, whereas Little Malcolm was short with dark hair and a face like a bull terrier. Even so, Rita, with her glass eye, still believed that in a certain light he had the look of a rugged Charlton Heston.

''E were all right, ah s'ppose,' said Malcolm grudgingly.

'An' ah liked 'is uniform, all red an' smart.'

''E'd 'ave been too 'ot ah reckon. It's sunny in Africa.' Little Malcolm looked into her good eye and said softly, 'Ah think a lot about you, Rita.'

'Do you now?' She fixed him with a glassy stare. She knew when a man was after something.

'Ah was wond'rin' if y'fancied callin' in t'night after you've finished work.'

'Mebbe ah will an' mebbe ah won't.' Rita didn't like to be taken for granted. She looked at the clock. 'Anyway, m'shift starts soon. We better be off.'

Big Dave was sitting outside in the bin wagon and started the engine when he saw his diminutive cousin and his tall, stick-thin girlfriend. He was fed up acting as their chauffeur and decided he would mention to Malcolm that her previous boyfriend had popped his clogs down an open cellar door outside the Rat and Trap pub in Thirkby. There was more to Rita than met the eye.

Later that afternoon the village hall was a hive of activity. Doris Clutterbuck had been invited to judge the best cake competition. The winner was Valerie Flint, the part-time teacher who in the past used to help John Pruett, and Doris wrote on the first prize postcard, 'This cake was obviously made with *love*.'

As always, Vera won the best marmalade competition and Joyce Davenport, the doctor's wife, was awarded an unexpected third prize for her fruit scones. Joyce had never won a prize before and she was so excited that evening that her husband was contemplating giving her something to calm her down.

There were a few mutterings when Deirdre Coe won a second prize for her plate of ginger biscuits, as their regular size suggested they had come straight from a packet.

That apart, it was a successful afternoon and Vera returned to the vicarage and the fragrant scent of hyacinths in her kitchen.

On Monday morning Lily arrived at school for the first day of the summer term and met Ruby in the entrance hall.

'Mornin', Mrs Feather; nit nurse is 'ere.'

'Good morning, Ruby; thanks for letting me know. Is Mrs Trott not here?' Lily was aware that the Ragley caretaker's arthritic condition was worsening.

'No, it were 'er 'usband's birthday party las' night an' they got through a bottle o' gin, so ah've 'eard.'

'Oh dear, so is she unwell?'

'M'mother said she'd drunk 'erself into Bolivia.'

Lily thought that was a long way to go for a hangover, but merely nodded in understanding and hurried into school.

When she walked into the office Vera was at her desk reading a letter from the college in York.

'Good morning, Lily; you will be interested to hear that the college have confirmed the placement of a student here.' She continued to scan the letter. 'And there's a request for your age group.'

'Yes, I remember John agreed we would take one. Who is it?'

'A young lady named Miss Nobbs. It's her final teaching practice. She has an introductory visit on Wednesday the twenty-ninth of this month and then she'll be with us after the spring bank holiday for a few weeks. According to this she is an outstanding student.'

'Excellent,' said Lily. 'Just what we need,' although her mind was elsewhere.

Vera was ever perceptive. 'How are you today?'

Lily sighed. 'Perhaps we can talk later.'

Vera smiled. 'Of course,' and returned to the morning's letters.

Although Lily was preoccupied, throughout the day she threw herself into her work. The *Music and Movement* radio broadcast was always a joy, with the children dancing freely in their bare feet. Likewise, the *Singing Together* programme included sea shanties and traditional folk songs, and John Pruett paused in his spelling test to listen to the sweet sound of Lily singing, 'Oh, soldier, soldier, won't you marry me?'

Meanwhile, the school nurse was busy with her nit comb. A line of apprehensive children queued up in front of her. However, she was a friendly soul who genuinely liked children, unlike some of the fearsome ones of the past. She was a regular visitor, providing routine eye and hearing tests and working alongside the school dentist. Before she left she spoke with John and Lily to confirm a date to administer a polio vaccine.

'We give it to them on a sugar lump these days,' she added with a smile.

At morning break Lily was on duty. She watched a groups of girls skipping.

They chanted in unison:

> *One, two, three, four, five, six, seven,*
> *All good children go to heaven.*
> *A penny on the water, twopence on the sea,*
> *Threepence on the railway and out goes she!*

As she stood there drinking her coffee, Mrs Poskitt arrived with a bottle of medicine for her son, Trevor.

'I'll hand this in to Miss Evans, shall I?' she said to Lily. 'It's for his cough.'

'Yes, please, and I'll make sure he gets it.'

'Thank you, Mrs Feather, much appreciated.' As she walked towards the entrance porch she turned. 'My Trevor's really looking forward to coming up into your class in September. We're lucky to have you.'

Anita Swithenbank was standing alongside. 'She's right, Miss. He'll love being in Class Two.'

When the bell rang for the end of break Lily was left to ponder Tom's decision to apply for the chance of promotion in Durham. She watched the children scamper up the steps and into school.

Leaving Ragley would break her heart.

At lunchtime Vera put on her coat and set off out of school to take the dinner money to the Post Office. Lily was leaning on the wall deep in thought.

'A penny for them, Lily.'

Lily sighed. 'Tom's considering a new job.'

'Promotion?'

'Yes.'

'It had to happen, Lily. He's a very talented policeman.'

'Yes, but it's not here.'

'Ah, I see.'

'It's up in Durham.'

'A beautiful cathedral city,' said Vera softly.

'I've not mentioned it to John.'

'That's wise, especially as he's in one of his taciturn moods at present. He was disappointed you didn't go on the teaching course with him last Friday.'

'That's when Tom broke the news.'

'So how do you feel about it?'

'We haven't made the commitment yet.'

'Are you reluctant?'

'A little.' Lily looked around at the school and the village green. There was fresh growth on the weeping willow tree and new life in the village pond. 'This is my home, my school. It's where my friends are.'

'All good things come to an end, Lily. Maybe this is your time.'

'Perhaps.'

'Tom will want to know you're with him on this.'

'I know.'

'He has always supported you in the past. We both know that.'

When Vera walked across the village green she glanced back as a shaft of sunlight lit up the school with Lily still deep in thought. It was an image she would never forget.

When Tom arrived home that evening he went upstairs to get changed. Lily followed him into the bedroom and sat down. 'So, how did it go?'

'I posted it this morning.'

'I had time to think it through while I was at school today.'

Tom looked anxious. 'And?'

'It's a difficult decision.'

'I wouldn't go ahead without you by my side, you know that.'

'Yes, I do. It's been on my mind most of the day, but I've been a teacher at Ragley for ten years and I know I've served the school well. It would break my heart to leave the children and particularly my friends on the staff, but I'll support you in this, Tom. I know it's important. So that's my decision.'

He smiled and gave her a hug.

'One more thing,' he said quietly.

'I think you need to tell Freddie you've written to his father.'

Other decisions were made that evening.

Joy Popplewell was determined not to ask Sam Grundy to pick up where they left off. Even so, she missed his strong physique and careless extravagance, their relationship of sex and cigarettes. It was tough being a teenager in love.

Little Malcolm Robinson wasn't sure what love was, but he knew he liked Rita and the delicious aroma of fish and chips that always surrounded her. However, his faithful cousin, Big Dave, had warned him off and their brief courtship had ended abruptly. Now Rita's displeasure was manifested each Friday evening when they ordered their fish, chips and mushy peas, but were never offered a free bag of scraps to complete the feast.

Wilhemena Hardcastle also made a significant decision. In the bedroom of their luxury bungalow she removed her expensive corset for the last time and disposed of it surreptitiously. She had decided to wear loose-fitting, expansive clothing that matched her outgoing character. It was important to be true to oneself, she thought, as she donned her voluminous nightgown.

In Laurel Cottage Freddie was in bed and had just turned out his bedside light when there was a tap on the door.

'Freddie, just to let you know I've posted a letter to Rudi.'

He heard Lily's footsteps pad across the landing carpet. *She kept her promise*, he thought.

Chapter Fifteen

The Initiation of Miss Nobbs

The first soft kiss of sunlight caressed the distant hills and the heavy scent of wallflowers was in the air. It was Wednesday, 29 April and almond trees were in blossom as Lily drove to school. An eventful day was in store. The student, Miss Sally Nobbs, was about to make her preliminary visit prior to her teaching practice. The unexpected was just around the corner.

As she drove, Lily cast her mind back to the letter she had posted to Rudi a few weeks ago. There had been no reply.

Rudolph Krüger had been surprised to see a cream envelope in his postbox when he had returned from his business meeting in Frankfurt. Approaching his fortieth birthday, he was still single and had found steady employment with a construction company. A bright visionary, he had lofty ideas of a new neighbourhood emerging to the south-east of Hamburg, in an area devastated by bombing – a vibrant new phoenix rising from the ashes.

He recognized the handwriting on the envelope immediately. After all the years and distance between them, the thought of Lily still made his heart race. There had never been anyone else for him. A few fleeting affairs had come and gone, but nothing lasting or serious. With Lily it had been a love affair that touched his soul; the prisoner of war and the Land Girl working side by side on a farm in Buckinghamshire. He had loved her from the first moment he saw her and he knew that she had felt the same.

Time and circumstances had changed everything. A child, loved by them both, had ultimately driven them apart. Their family was not to be. Rudi had wanted the very best for his son and so had given him up to Florence, Lily's mother, in the firm belief that he would prosper in England and be accepted among his own. Back in post-war Britain, he could never have given the boy the stable home and family life he deserved.

He was grateful to receive a short annual update from Lily on Freddie's progress and to see his school photograph. The resemblance to himself was clear.

Now he had opened her letter with trepidation. The words were a jumble on the page. Freddie wanted to meet him and had visited his apartment. Rudi had heard from his neighbour that a relative from England had called while he was away on business, but the details appeared confused and he had not given it much thought.

Lily wanted Rudi to go to England – but how could he? He recalled the moment eleven years ago when from afar he had watched Freddie playing cricket. He remembered the meeting that had followed, arranged by Lily when

Florence was away from home. It was the last time he had seen his son.

And, of course, there was Tom. How Rudi wished it could have been different.

To go to England now and rake up all these emotions again ... he didn't know whether he had the strength. With deliberate calmness he carefully folded the letter and placed it in the inside pocket of his jacket.

Back in Ragley village, the countryside at this time of year always lifted Lily's spirits as she drove up the High Street and turned right at the village green. She caught sight of a young woman in the shade of a horse chestnut tree puffing on a cigarette. Her bright orange waistcoat, lime green blouse and mustard-coloured bell-bottom trousers clashed horribly with her bright red hair. She was carrying a heavy satchel, a hessian shoulder bag and, incongruously, six shoeboxes tied together with string.

Lily slowed and wound down her window. 'Hello, are you the student?'

The tall, freckle-faced young woman looked startled. 'Yes,' she said, stubbing out her cigarette with the sole of a slip-on sandal. 'I'm Sally Nobbs.'

'Come on in,' said Lily. 'I'm Lily Feather. You're working in my class.'

Lily parked her car and hurried over to help. She picked up the parcel of shoeboxes. 'These look interesting,' she said with a grin.

The newcomer relaxed and smiled. 'Yes, tricky to carry on the bus, but I thought they would capture the imagination of the children – a way of introducing myself.'

'Good idea,' said Lily, 'and welcome to Ragley.'

They left the shoeboxes in the entrance hall and walked into the school office, where Vera was busy sorting the morning mail. She was in a good mood after reading the report that the Queen's baby son was to be named Edward. *A good name*, she thought.

Her peaceful reverie was disturbed when Lily walked in.

'Good morning, Vera. This is Miss Nobbs,' said Lily. 'Sally, let me introduce our school secretary, Miss Evans.'

Vera was rarely lost for words, but she simply stared in astonishment when she saw the newcomer.

'Good morning, Miss Evans,' said Sally, 'pleased to meet you.' She stretched out her arm to shake hands, but her satchel fell off her shoulder and landed on the edge of Vera's desk. The morning mail tumbled on to the floor. 'Oh no!' cried Sally, stooping to retrieve the letters. Then her shoulder bag fell from her other shoulder and its contents scattered over the floor. Vera stooped to collect her precious mail. A packet of Embassy cigarettes, a box of matches and a sticky, half-eaten bar of chocolate had landed on top of the letters.

'Oh, I'm so sorry,' said Sally as she retrieved her belongings and stuffed them back in the bag.

It was at this moment John walked in.

'Good morning, Mr Pruett,' said Vera. She gave a disparaging glance towards Sally. 'Our student has arrived.'

John Pruett was taken aback by the vision before him. A kaleidoscope of uncoordinated colours swam before his eyes. 'Oh yes,' he said hesitantly. 'It's Miss Nobbs, I recall.'

Lily decided to take over. 'I'll get Sally settled in and we'll catch up with you later.'

They hurried out to Lily's classroom.

John Pruett closed the office door. 'That was unexpected.'

Vera took a tissue and removed a few streaks of chocolate from the topmost envelope. 'Yes, somewhat nonconformist,' she replied.

'The college said she was an excellent student,' said John.

'Really?' Unimpressed, Vera returned to her work without another word.

In Lily's classroom, Sally was red-faced. 'Sorry about that. An inauspicious start.'

Lily smiled. 'Never mind, I've planned a good day for us and we're blessed with good weather. I'll start off the day and you can support the children with their reading, writing and mathematics. Then after break I thought you could introduce yourself and get to know the children.'

'Thank you,' said Sally, smiling at last. 'That's what the shoeboxes are for, some simple detective work.'

'Fine, let's see how that goes, then after lunch we're visiting the local churchyard. There are lots of opportunities for history, geography and natural sciences, a project you may wish to follow up on your teaching practice. We can discuss all this at the end of school.'

By morning break Lily had realized that the report on Sally was correct. She was clearly a born teacher and, although unorthodox, she established good relationships with the children, supported their needs with confidence during the morning activities and was receptive to any advice from Lily.

When Sally collected her cup of coffee from Vera, it was clear the school secretary had significant reservations, not least concerning Sally's outlandish appearance. However, the young student owned no conformist clothing. She did not want to mirror the fashion of her parents. She was a product of a new, free-thinking generation released from stagnant conformity.

Sally had recently read the groundbreaking book *Sex and the Single Girl* by Helen Gurley Brown. She loved the author's revolutionary concept of encouraging sex before marriage and had herself enjoyed experiences with a number of men during her college career. At twenty-one years old she regarded herself as a modern sixties woman, so her first encounter with Vera was a clash of contrasting cultures.

A similar clash was taking place at Easington School. The fifth-form girls had been summoned into the school hall by a very determined Miss Plumb.

'It's come to my attention that some of you girls are ignoring the rules concerning school uniform.' Dressed in thick tweed, she stood like a sergeant major inspecting the troops. 'In particular, I'm concerned about the length of your skirts. So, all of you, kneel down now.'

The girls were used to this. When they knelt down the hem of each skirt had to be touching the floor. However, even by leaning forward, half a dozen or more of the girls could not disguise the fact that they had shortened their skirts. Miss Plumb, with a face like thunder, wrote their names in her notebook.

Then came the part they all dreaded.

'Underwear, now, ladies.'

There was a unanimous groan. Lizzie Buttershaw whispered to the girl next to her, 'It's *nineteen sixty-four* for goodness' sake . . . this is *humiliating*.'

It was compulsory to wear voluminous green knickers made from heavy-duty material supported by thick elastic. They were affectionately known to the fifth form as their 'Harvest Thanksgiving Knickers': *all is safely gathered in*!

'Raise your skirts please,' ordered Miss Plumb.

The girls complied.

Lizzie was wearing her brief lacy black knickers.

Miss Plumb frowned and added another name to her notebook. 'Detention, Miss Buttershaw.'

It was eleven o'clock and Miss Nobbs had the attention of all the children in Class 2. They were seated in six groups, a shoebox on each table.

'Now, listen carefully everybody, we're going to be detectives, or perhaps archaeologists who dig up interesting bones or treasure. Each box contains a variety of items that are clues. I want you to spend five minutes checking the contents and write down what you think it tells you about me.'

The boxes contained photographs, old comics, train tickets, certificates and sweet wrappers, and the children were soon engrossed.

'Now, who would like to start?'

It was unusual to see Clint Ramsbottom raise his hand first. 'Y'like Jelly Babies, Miss.'

'Well done, Clint.'

Lily was impressed that Sally had already learned the names of the children.

'An' y'wash y'clothes in Blue Tide,' volunteered Henry Tonks.

'And you've been to Morecambe on the train,' added seven-year-old Pauline Simpson.

'Does it mean that's where my home is?'

Good question, thought Lily.

'No, Miss,' said Pauline, 'because there's lots of receipts in our box for coffee shops in Leeds, so we think you might live there.'

'Or go there to meet your boyfriend,' remarked the mischievous eight-year-old Angela Pickles. There was some laughter.

'Excellent thought,' said Sally. 'Well done.'

The lesson gathered momentum and the children looked disappointed when the bell rang for lunchtime.

'Good work,' said Lily when all the children had left the classroom. 'A really effective opportunity for deductive reasoning. The children loved it.'

At one o'clock Lily gathered her children together on the playground. They were carrying clipboards, Lily had a shoulder bag filled with books about trees and Sally was carrying a bulky carrier bag with rolls of paper and boxes of thick crayons. The children were used to walking in twos across the village green and up the Morton road towards St Mary's Church. They attended many of the church festivals, but today was different. They were detectives. Also, three parents, Muriel Tonks, Minnie Ramsbottom and Ruby Smith, had volunteered to help supervise the children.

'Now boys and girls,' said Lily, 'we shall divide up into the three groups we decided on. My group will be going in Farmer Tonks' field to identify trees; Miss Nobbs's group will be here doing gravestone rubbings; and Miss Evans will be taking her group into church to look at the stained-glass windows. Any questions?'

Muriel Tonks raised her hand with a smile. 'Jus' thought ah'd mention, Mrs Feather, that Mr Tonks 'as put Buttercup in t'field before taking 'er to t'May Day Show in Thirkby. She's 'is prize cow but gentle as can be. Jus' remember t'close t'gate.'

'Yes, thank you, Mrs Tonks,' said Lily. She glanced over to the vicarage in search of Vera, who was due to join them. 'And that goes for the church door as well. We don't want any little birds flying in.'

The children nodded their heads. They knew the rules.

'You ladies can join whichever group you prefer.'

'Ah'd like t'go in church wi' Miss Evans,' said Ruby.

'An' ah better go in our field,' said Muriel.

'Well, ah'm 'appy looking at t'graves,' said Minnie with a smile.

Vera appeared from the vicarage tugging on her cardigan. The children were already in the church waiting patiently by the altar and Ruby had remembered to close the church door. Vera had been preoccupied with her *Radio Times* following the news of the launch last week of BBC2, the UK's third television channel. In anticipation of cultural programmes of quality, she had earmarked a film based on *Resurrection*, a novel by Leo Tolstoy, which was due to be broadcast that evening. In consequence, she had missed Lily's briefing and hurried into the church.

The children stared in awe at the wonderful stained glass while Vera told them about the history of the church from its origins in the Saxon period and the first known reference in the Domesday Book of 1086.

Soon all the children were hard at work. Sally was on her hands and knees round the rear of the church with her group. Chris Wojciechowski and Henry Tonks were alongside her, holding a large sheet of paper against a gravestone, while Duggie Smith rubbed furiously with his crayon and a perfect image appeared as if by magic.

'Ah'm enjoyin' this, Miss,' said Duggie with enthusiasm.

'Miss, what's an archie-ologist?' asked Chris.

'It's an *archaeologist*, Christopher,' said Sally. 'They dig for bones of animals from long ago and sometimes they find buried treasure.'

'We buried some treasure, Miss,' said Duggie.

'Really? What was that?'

'A bracelet. It were in t'woods.'

'It 'ad a funny little man hangin' on it,' added Chris.

'A leprechaun,' explained Duggie.

'I see,' said Sally thoughtfully.

'My mam 'ad one jus' like that,' said Henry. 'M'dad were real upset when she lost it.'

Sally nodded. The penny had dropped. 'Could you find where you buried it?'

'Yes, Miss,' the boys said in unison.

Lily's group had gone into the adjoining field and Muriel Tonks had shut the gate behind them. Soon they were in a copse of trees and hidden from view. Children were collecting leaves and using the information books to identify the wide variety of trees. Meanwhile, Buttercup was on the other side of the field contentedly munching grass under the shade of a beech tree.

In the church, while the children were sitting in the pews and completing their drawings of the figures in the stained-glass windows, Vera had an idea. She whispered in Ruby's ear, 'I have lots of home-made lemonade. I'll put it on the picnic table outside the vicarage with the box of plastic beakers we used for the church fête. I'll tell Miss Nobbs and Mrs Feather. Back soon.'

She opened the ancient door and hurried round the back of the church, where she had a quiet word with Sally. 'Before we return to school there will be some lemonade outside the vicarage.'

Then Vera walked lightly across to Farmer Tonks's field and opened the gate. Finally she found Lily and her group hidden in the trees.

'I thought the children would enjoy some lemonade before we go back,' she said.

'Wonderful idea,' agreed Lily. 'We'll gather our things together.'

As Vera left the edge of the wooded area, Mrs Tonks called after her, 'Don't forget to close the gate, Miss Evans.'

Vera waved in acknowledgement. She had left it open when she entered the field but now she closed it securely after her. Soon she was busy collecting jugs of lemonade from the vicarage kitchen.

Sally looked at her wristwatch. It was around ten minutes since Vera had announced the offer of refreshments. 'Come on, children, collect all your work and we'll go round to the vicarage where Miss Evans has prepared a soft drink.'

It was when Sally was passing the church door that she noticed it was open, so she closed it quickly and hurried after the children.

Outside the vicarage, Vera was pouring the lemonade and the children were sitting in groups discussing their detective work. Lily was especially pleased. It had been a successful educational visit.

A chilly breeze sprang up and Sally noticed Vera was shivering. 'I'll carry on serving the lemonade, Miss Evans, if you want to go in and get a coat.'

Although she didn't approve of this young woman, Vera recognized a Christian gesture. 'That's kind. I left my cardigan in church.'

Sally saw a further opportunity to redeem herself. 'I'll get it for you if you don't mind keeping an eye on my group.'

She walked across the gravelled courtyard then along the winding path to the front of the church. Around her all was silent apart from the wind in the trees. There was no one in sight. Sally was aware of the peace in this special place. She walked under the huge entrance porch and pushed open the heavy oak door on its great iron hinges.

The sight that met her eyes was one she would never forget.

Buttercup the cow was standing there, inside the church, staring at her lugubriously. However, it was Buttercup's rear end that gave Sally greater concern. A powerful jet of urine was splashing against the stone font.

'Oh no!' she exclaimed.

She realized it was up to her to act quickly and do battle with over half a ton of prime beef. Also, it wasn't something she wanted the children to see. Someone must have left the gate open and she felt partly responsible. She and Lily were supposed to be in charge.

With no little trepidation, she gently tapped Buttercup's substantial bottom and to her relief the cow responded and began to lumber back outside at her own pace. After relieving herself, she was in a placid mood and looking forward to returning to her familiar field.

Sally guided Buttercup through the five-barred gate and closed it. Then she hurried back to the church, found Vera's cardigan and joined the others.

Everyone had finished their refreshments. 'Thank you,' said Lily. 'That was a kind thought.' She turned to the children. 'What do we say to Miss Evans, everyone?'

'Thank you, Miss Evans,' they chorused.

'Now, boys and girls, I want you to sit down in your groups and we shall hear what you have discovered this afternoon.'

Sally spoke quietly to Lily. 'Could you excuse me for a moment? I want to thank Vera personally.'

Lily smiled. 'Of course. I'll start off the discussion with the children.'

Sally caught up with Vera, who was returning the jugs and beakers to the vicarage.

'Miss Evans, may I have a word?'

'Of course,' said Vera. 'Come into the kitchen.'

She put down her tray on the worktop. Vera was curious. There was a hint of anxiety about this young woman.

'I'm afraid I have some bad news, Miss Evans.'

'Yes?'

'Mr Tonks's cow found its way into church. I saw it there when I went to collect your cardigan.'

251

'Goodness me – a cow in church! Is it still there?'

'No, I managed to get it back in the field and I've closed the gate. It's back where it belongs.'

'This is dreadful! How could it have happened?'

'I don't know. Mrs Feather was very clear when she told the children to make sure the gate to the field was closed and the church door was shut.'

'Oh . . . I see . . .'

Realization was dawning on Vera.

'I'm afraid that's not all,' continued Sally.

'There's more?'

'Yes. When I walked in the cow was urinating against the side of the font. It will need a thorough clean.'

Vera sat down on a chair. 'Oh no!'

'If you would like me to come back after school, I should be happy to help.'

Vera put her head in her hands. 'Miss Nobbs, I have a confession. It was I who left the church open when I went to tell Mrs Feather's group about the refreshments. I also left open the field gate and only closed it on my return. So it's my fault.'

'There's no harm done if we clean up . . . and no one will know.'

There was a moment's pause as Vera recognized the gesture. 'Thank you, my dear. I'll start cleaning up immediately and I shall always remember your kindness.'

'I must hurry now, Miss Evans. I need to get back to the children.'

As she ran out of the vicarage, Vera stared after her and whispered the words she recalled from Joshua, chapter one, verse nine: 'Be strong and courageous. Do not be afraid; do not be discouraged, for the Lord your God will be with you wherever you go.'

On the way back to school Sally walked beside Muriel Tonks.

'I heard from Henry that you lost a bracelet.'

Muriel was surprised. 'Yes, ah did, m'little leprechaun lucky charm.'

'Well, I think Douglas Smith and Chris Wojciechowski may have come across it in the woods. If you go with them I'm sure they will show you.'

'Well, ah'll go to t'foot of our stairs! That is a turn-up. Thank you.'

At the end of school Lily sat down with Sally and confirmed the projects they would be tackling later in the term. Then Sally called into the office to thank John Pruett and left school. However, she didn't wait to catch the bus into York; instead she walked back up the Morton road.

Vera was in church with a bucket of soapy water and a scrubbing brush.

'Miss Evans, let me have a turn.'

Vera smiled with relief and stood up. *The energy of youth,* she thought as Sally scrubbed the font with renewed vigour.

In the woods, Muriel Tonks had retrieved her bracelet.

'Miss were talking 'bout us being detectives,' said Duggie.

'An' archie-ologists,' added Chris for good measure.

Duggie nodded in agreement. 'That's right – they find things that were lost.'

'Like your leprechaun bracelet,' said Chris with a triumphant smile.

'An' buried treasure is allus at t'end of a rainbow.'

'Well, thank you, boys.'

Muriel was puzzled about why it had been buried in the first place, but assumed that little boys lived in a world of their own. At least they were honest.

'Here's sixpence each for being good boys an' say thank you t'that student-lady when y'see 'er.'

The boys ran off to buy some aniseed balls, then after a hasty tea of fish fingers and chips they intended to settle down to watch television. Colonel Steve Zodiac was due to travel to a distant planet with Robert, his robot friend.

Muriel smiled as she walked home. The bracelet was in her pocket. It had brought her good fortune in more ways than one.

That evening Joseph was in the hallway of the vicarage and about to leave for a prayer meeting, while Vera was in the kitchen reading her Be-Ro recipe book.

'I have a baptism tomorrow morning,' announced Joseph.

Vera thought back to what had happened to the font that day. 'I gave it a bit of a clean-up this afternoon.'

Joseph popped his head round the kitchen door and gave her a beatific smile. 'What a wonderful sister I have. You think of everything.'

Well almost, thought Vera.

*

It was Thursday morning and a cloud of mist lay over the village green as Lily drove into school.

Both Vera and John were in the school office when she walked in.

'I've spoken to Sally about the May Day preparations,' Lily told them, 'and we should be fine for the maypole dancing. Miss Nobbs offered to come and help.'

John looked up, concerned. 'I wasn't too sure about her.'

Before Lily could say anything, Vera interjected. 'An outstanding young woman, Mr Pruett. Definitely one for the future. I was really impressed.'

Both Lily and John looked at Vera in surprise and wondered why her cheeks were flushed.

Chapter Sixteen

New Beginnings

It was Friday, 22 May, a time of renewal and new beginnings. There was excitement and trepidation in Laurel Cottage. Tom's big day had arrived. Earlier in the month an official letter had arrived with a Durham postmark. He had been shortlisted for interview for the post of chief inspector.

He was wearing his best dress uniform and Lily picked up the clothes brush from the hall table and brushed his shoulders. 'You look perfect,' she said with a smile.

The usually calm Tom looked tense. 'Thanks. I'll try hard but, whatever the outcome, we'll decide the next step together.'

'Just do your best.'

He leaned forward and kissed her gently on the forehead. 'I shall.'

Freddie appeared from the kitchen. 'Good luck, Tom.'

They shook hands. 'You too,' said Tom. 'You've worked hard enough, so you should be fine.'

It was the day of his English A-level examination.

Freddie pursed his lips. 'Just hoping for the right questions.'

Tom grinned. 'Likewise.'

Lily watched him drive away and realized that by the end of the day she would know if her life was about to change.

As she drove Freddie to school, she recalled why she loved this corner of England that she called home. The flower candles on the horse chestnut trees gave promise of summer days. A flock of starlings wheeled overhead and in Twenty Acre Field the unripe barley shivered in the gentle breeze. Carpets of bluebells covered the woodland floor and the bleating of lambs could be heard in the meadows. The warmer days had broadened the leaves of a copse of sycamore trees and, beyond the hawthorn hedgerows, cattle were grazing contentedly in the open pasture land. She wound down the window and breathed in the scent of a new day.

In the vicarage, Vera had prepared an appetizing breakfast for Joseph and herself. She had cut a grapefruit in half and then, with great precision, she sectioned the fruit with her curved, serrated grapefruit knife. A glacé cherry on top was the final touch, along with a sprinkling of sugar. Vera always found this a satisfying task and enjoyed the perfect symmetry.

Neatness and harmony, she thought. It reflected the pattern of her life.

She sipped Earl Grey tea from a china cup, opened her *Woman's Own* and admired the charming photograph in her magazine of Princess Margaret with her baby daughter, born at the beginning of the month. Then she stared out of the window at a flock of black-headed gulls speeding purposefully across a pastel blue sky.

Finally, she cleared away, ensured the worktop was spotless and collected her coat from the hallway. Then she crunched across the gravel courtyard where the wild raspberry canes on the Victorian brick walls stretched up to catch the morning sun. As she stepped out on to the Morton road it was good to feel contentment in her world. Above her head the delicate pink petals on the cherry trees swirled in the gentle breeze. 'Romans, chapter fourteen, verse nineteen,' she whispered to herself with a smile. 'Let us therefore follow after the things which make for peace.'

Peace was in short supply at Easington School. Freddie and Rose were feeling anything but calm. They held hands as they walked through the school gates for the start of their A-level examinations. It was their first English paper.

'Please make it all the stuff we've revised,' said Rose.

Freddie offered an encouraging smile. 'We couldn't have done any more.'

Rose stared up at the school building. 'I wish it was all over, rather than just beginning.'

They paused in the entrance to the school hall and took in the scene. The day of judgement had arrived. Sixty desks were arranged in long rows and labelled in alphabetical order. The space between each desk had been carefully measured so there was no opportunity for one student to see another's work.

Freddie squeezed Rose's hand. 'Good luck.'

She returned a nervous glance and made her way to her desk.

From the far side of the hall, Sam Grundy gave an anxious wave. Freddie knew that Sam had written a few Shakespeare quotes on the inside of his shirt cuff. These were desperate times for some of the students, particularly those like Sam who had done little revision, and Freddie hoped he would not be found out and expelled for cheating.

Mr Morris stood at the front of the hall. 'At nine o'clock you will turn over your question papers. There will, of course, be no talking. If there is a problem, raise your hand.'

He glanced up at the clock.

It was time.

The silence was absolute.

He gave a wry smile. 'You may begin.'

In John Pruett's classroom there wasn't a sound. He scanned all the eager young faces before him and wondered what would become of them when they moved on to secondary education in September.

The eleven-plus tests were over and John hoped all his work had paid off. The tests had included maths, writing an essay and both verbal and non-verbal reasoning papers. The verbal reasoning examination tested the child's command of English and the non-verbal reasoning paper, with its puzzles and problem-solving, was intended to give an indication of the child's IQ.

The children were sitting up straight, arms folded, lips

tight shut and glancing through the window at the cloudless sky. They hoped that this morning might be different in some way. Perhaps they might be permitted to use coloured crayons or write a story from their imagination. It was not to be.

'We shall begin with the eleven times table,' announced John. 'All together . . .'

In Easington School the examination room was silent apart from the occasional suppressed cough or the scraping of a chair. Sixty students were deep in concentration. Pens flowed across pages. There were occasional nervous glances up at the clock as time raced by. *Allocate time well*, they had been told. Feel free to write a few brief subheadings to map out the content of each essay, particularly for the final one. Then, if you run out of time, the examiner will know what you planned to write.

Freddie had been advised by Mr Morris to show his knowledge of Shakespeare by including a few relevant quotes. It was when he wrote 'The web of our life is a mingled yarn, good and ill together', from *All's Well That Ends Well*, that he reflected on his own life. He hoped for a happy ending with Rose, but couldn't foresee a resolution with Lily. The hurt of a lie ran too deep.

He looked across the room at Rose. Her head was bowed and her free hand was twirling her hair, a mannerism he knew so well. With a final burst of energy he raced through his concluding essay on King Lear's descent into madness.

It was twelve o'clock and Mr Morris called time. Papers were shuffled together and collected in.

*

At 7 School View Agnes had arrived home from her early-morning shift. Ruby had prepared jam sandwiches and a pot of tea. Agnes put two chocolate Aero bars on the table for their weekly treat.

'Oooh, thanks, Mam.'

Agnes studied her daughter's florid face. 'What's t'matter?'

'Jus' thinkin'. Ah'm in m'thirties now. Time's marchin' on.'

'Ruby, ah'll tell y'summat now . . . best age is the age you are.'

Ruby nodded and smiled.

They were drinking their tea and enjoying their sandwiches when a thought struck Agnes. 'Guess what? Ah saw that Violet Fawnswater when ah got off t'bus. She'd parked 'er new car on the 'igh Street.'

Violet was the proud owner of a gleaming white Rover 2000.

'Oh yes?' mumbled Ruby through a mouthful of jam and bread.

'Ah've allus said, money doesn't bring you 'appiness.'

It occurred to Ruby that it might help, but she decided to agree. 'Yes, Mam.'

'The sun shines on the righteous,' quoted Agnes.

Ruby looked up, puzzled. 'What does that mean, Mam?'

'Well, a lot o' things.'

'What sort o' things?'

Agnes supped her sweet, milky tea and considered this for a moment. 'It means y'grandad is smilin' down at us from 'eaven.'

'Why is 'e smilin', Mam?'

"Cause 'e knows you'll allus look after 'is great-grandkids 'til t'day y'die.'

'Ah will,' said Ruby.

Agnes smiled at her daughter. 'You're a wonderful mother, Ruby, so be proud.'

'Thanks, Mam.'

'You're allus workin', y'never stop. Y'know what they say?'

'What do they say, Mam?'

'A rollin' stone gathers no moths.'

At lunchtime in the staff-room John Pruett was complaining to Vera and Lily about the state of the British Empire and the modern generation.

'Back in nineteen twenty-one our empire covered a third of the world's surface,' he declared.

'Yes, so I recall,' replied a polite but slightly indifferent Vera. 'We had a population of five hundred million.'

'But now we've transferred power.'

'Really?' said Vera, glancing up from pouring tea.

John was on a roll. 'Yes, Jamaica, then Trinidad and Tobago, and last year Nigeria and Kenya. It's slipping through our fingers.'

Vera sighed. 'I imagine the heavy cost of the Second World War made it hard for Britain to maintain such a vast empire.'

'Perhaps so, Vera, but just look at this.' He pointed to his morning newspaper. There was a photograph of violent clashes over the Whitsun weekend on Clacton beach under the headline 'MODS v ROCKERS'.

'I tell you, Vera, it's the beginning of the end.'

'More tea, anyone?' asked Vera.

Lily gave a wan smile and got up to leave. 'No thank you, Vera, things to do. I said I would help Sally prepare her art lesson.' In truth, she was bored with the monologue and began to think it might not be a bad thing to seek a new beginning.

On the High Street the cycle of life continued for the villagers of Ragley. Muriel Tonks had called into the General Stores to buy a Sunblest loaf.

'An' a jar o' Gale's Lemon Curd, please, Prudence,' she said.

'It's fourpence off,' said Prudence, 'a special offer.'

'Ah'll 'ave two,' said Muriel, who always loved a bargain.

In the Coffee Shop the number-one record, 'Juliet' by the Four Pennies, was on the jukebox. It was a gentle ballad and Nora, behind the counter, was swaying to the music and dreaming of stardom.

Diane Wigglesworth, in the hairdresser's, was cutting out a colour photograph of the glamorous pin-up Diana Dors. She stood back to admire the blonde bombshell. If the fifties had been in black and white, the sixties were in Technicolor. She sellotaped it to the collection that bordered the large mirror in the salon and wondered if there might one day be an honest man out there for her.

In The Royal Oak, Pete the Poacher had called in with some rabbits and held them up in triumph as he passed Ronnie Smith, who was propping up the bar. Ronnie was also in a celebratory mood. His favourite team, Leeds United, had been promoted a week ago to the First Division after they had beaten Swansea 3–0 with a promising debut by Terry Cooper and a goal from Irishman Johnny Giles.

Big Dave Robinson was in the taproom with his cousin, Little Malcolm. He was praising the cricketing exploits of the young Geoffrey Boycott, who had given up his job in the Ministry of Pensions to concentrate on cricket.

''E could be good, this lad, Malc'.'

In the recent Roses match with Lancashire, the Yorkshire opening batsman had scored 131 runs in dramatic fashion against the old enemy.

Little Malcolm supped deeply on his pint and gave his usual reply. 'Y'reight there, Dave.'

Meanwhile, in the village Pharmacy, Violet Fawnswater had been persuaded by Herbert Grinchley to purchase a so-called safe and reliable remedy for women's ailments and irregularities. The label on the jar read 'Wise Women take BLANCHARD'S PILLS – as dispensed during the Great War', and Violet had no doubt they would dispel the feelings of anxiety about her husband's lack of attention.

Back in Ragley School, Lily and Sally were busy in the library. Over the years Lily had built up a wonderful collection of books and she was pleased to see Sally updating her card index system.

'Thanks, Sally,' she said with a grateful smile.

'Thought I would get the new stock catalogued,' said Sally.

The latest PTA jumble sale had raised enough to buy a box of twenty new books. Lily believed libraries were the cornerstone of a cultured society. She wanted to immerse the children in stories that excited their imagination and information that answered their many questions. Over the years the Ragley School library had developed thanks to her efforts.

Sally was adding a sticky label with the Dewey Decimal number 821 to the spine of a poetry book. It was at that moment that they heard a shout from the playground and they looked out of the window. The new dinner lady, Mrs Doreen Critchley, a fierce, muscular Yorkshire woman with huge biceps and a loud voice, was telling Shane Ramsbottom to stop demonstrating how far he could spit.

Sylvia Icklethwaite, a farmer's wife and a close friend of Doreen, waved from the other side of the school wall.

She called through the railings. 'How's it goin'?'

'Fine thanks, Sylvia,' said Doreen and wandered over to speak to her. 'They're lovely children, 'part from t'usual suspects.' She nodded towards Shane Ramsbottom, who was looking sullen.

'What d'you think about that student teacher, 'er wi' t'red 'air?' asked Sylvia. 'Ah saw 'er this morning arrivin' at school wi' a boyfriend in 'is flash car.'

Doreen considered this. 'Well, credit where credit's due. Seems a nice young woman t'me.'

Sylvia shook her head. 'She's playing fast an' loose. You mark my words.'

Doreen answered phlegmatically. 'Time will tell, Sylvia, an' don't f'get, you were young once.'

They shared a knowing smile and wandered off.

It was 5.30 p.m. and Lily had finished marking the children's books. The school was empty now and the silence was like an intimate friend. It was a time to gather her thoughts before going home and she wondered what the evening might bring.

She walked into the entrance hall and her footsteps echoed on the woodblock floor. Outside the office was the familiar brass plaque on the door: 'John T. Pruett, Headmaster'. Many years had passed since she had stood here on her first visit to Ragley School. So much had happened since.

She opened the door and walked in. There was Vera's desk, tidy as always. In the corner next to the window, John Pruett's desk stood like a three-dimensional jigsaw with everything in its place. Around her the walls were filled with black-and-white school photographs showing the eager faces of children through the years.

She recalled the first one in which she appeared. It was in 1952 and everyone was smiling at the camera with the exception of Lily. She was smiling at Tom. John had asked the local bobby to take the photograph with his Box Brownie camera following a visit to school. It had been the beginning of a romance – a love that was steadfast and true.

When she drove home the evening sun gilded the land with a golden light and she wondered what destiny might befall her.

It was shortly after six o'clock and Ruby Smith had washed up after the traditional Friday meal of fish, chips and mushy peas and had settled down to watch television with her children. It was one of their favourite programmes, *The Beverly Hillbillies*. In this episode the Clampett family were holding auditions to find a suitable bride for Jed. It occurred to Ruby that this was a good idea, but, of course, with one significant difference. It should be for the selection of *husbands*.

After *Take Your Pick*, featuring Michael Miles with his ten locked boxes and three booby prizes, it was bedtime for everyone with the exception of Racquel. She was allowed to stay up late to watch her latest heart-throb, the handsome cowboy Michael Landon as Little Joe Cartwright in *Bonanza*.

It was after nine o'clock when Lily heard the sound of a car on the driveway. She jumped up, ran into the hallway and opened the front door. The figure of Tom emerged from the darkness. Lily could see his tiredness in the stoop of his shoulders and wondered what news he may have brought.

He hugged her and kissed her on the cheek.

'How did it go?'

Tom took off his coat. 'Let's sit down, shall we?'

Lily hid her anxiety. 'Would you like a cup of tea?'

'Love one.' He loosened his tie and followed Lily into the kitchen. 'Where's Freddie?'

'At the cinema with Rose.'

'How did his A-level go?'

'Fine, I think. Same for Rose. They're out having a well-earned break.'

Tom nodded. 'Good to hear . . . so, we can talk.'

Lily filled the kettle and turned to face him. 'Well?'

He put his hands on her shoulders. 'I've been offered the job.'

'Oh . . . Congratulations. I'm pleased for you.'

Tom looked into her eyes. 'Really?'

'Yes, of course. It's what you wanted and well deserved. You're really good at your work and highly respected. I'm happy for you . . . honestly.'

He kissed her lightly on the cheek and she turned to place two large mugs on the worktop.

There was a brief silence while the kettle boiled. Then Lily shared a teabag and added milk plus two sugars for Tom. They took their hot drinks into the lounge and sat down.

Tom sipped his tea. 'Perfect. Thanks, I was ready for that.' He placed the mug on the coffee table and leaned back on the sofa. 'I have the weekend to think about it, so we can take our time and make the decision together.'

Lily pushed a tendril of hair behind her ear and smiled at this true and honest man. 'I appreciate that, Tom. But we said that if you were successful you would accept.'

'I know, but if we are both honest about this, we weren't that confident that I would get it.'

'Well, *you* might have thought that.'

Tom held her hand. 'That's what I love about you. You have always believed in me.'

'I always will.'

He pressed his fingers to his eyes as if trying to erase the tiredness. 'The competition was tough. There were four of us, two with more experience than me and a young guy who had a lot to say for himself. One for the future, I guess. I thought my interview went well, but it was still a surprise when they called me back in. They knew my background and that you were a deputy headteacher down here.'

'That's understandable. This is a very senior post and they have to be sure.'

Tom looked steadily at Lily. 'It's a big decision, and we don't have to go. I could say no.'

She searched for the right words. 'I know, Tom, but it has to be for the best. I should be sorry to leave Ragley and to move on . . . probably without a job.'

'You could apply for a post in Durham.'

'I know.'

'Maybe give in your notice and start applying.'

'There aren't many deputy headships around these days, especially for women.'

Tom shook his head. 'I wasn't thinking of *deputy* headships. I meant you could apply for a headship. You would be perfect and John would give you an excellent reference.'

'Do you really think so?'

'I *know* so.' He leaned forward and stroked her cheek gently. 'It would be an adventure for both of us.'

'I love my job, but it would be wonderful to have my own school.'

'Well, we could buy a *Times Ed* and I bet there are a few Church of England headships being advertised right now.'

Lily pursed her lips. 'This is all a bit too fast for me.'

'Sorry, I don't want to pressure you.'

Lily finished drinking her tea and sat back. 'I understand.'

Tom looked at her expectantly. 'So . . . what should I tell them on Monday?'

'That you will accept the post.'

He put his arm around her shoulder and she rested her cheek against his chest. 'What about you?' he asked quietly.

There was a long pause. It had been a day of new promise and expectation, but there was a hint of sadness in her voice.

'On Monday . . . I'll hand in my resignation.'

Chapter Seventeen

A World Without Love

John Pruett had a broken heart. At least that's how it felt. A never-ending ache had begun towards the end of May when Lily had handed in her letter of resignation.

He stared at the cream notepaper and her neat handwriting and touched her signature gently with his fingertips. Then he folded the letter, put it back in the envelope and placed it carefully beneath the huge leatherbound school logbook in the bottom left-hand drawer of his desk. He sighed, locked the drawer, stood up and walked out of school. He needed fresh air and time to think.

It was Wednesday, 10 June and he had arrived very early at school. The countryside was waking and an eventful day lay ahead. It was important that he was well prepared for his meeting with Bernard Pickard from County Hall. The shrewd and calculating Area Education Adviser didn't miss a trick.

He leaned on the school wall and watched the rooks

circling the bell tower with ominous certainty. Behind him a disc of golden light had emerged in the eastern sky. It was a new dawn, but for John it felt like the end of days.

In Kirkby Steepleton Tom and Lily had left for work together. Freddie had borrowed Lily's car to drive to Easington, complete with a picnic basket prepared by Lily with loving care. Following various meetings with staff to discuss their futures, the sixth-form students were having a celebratory picnic on the school field. Their A-levels were over and it was time to relax.

When Tom drove into Ragley, the villagers were waking to a perfect summer's day. As they drove up the High Street Lily saw Vera pinning a large poster to the noticeboard outside the village hall. She smiled. The indomitable school secretary was always busy.

In the border outside The Royal Oak butterflies hovered over the buddleia bushes and cuckoo spit sparkled among the lavender leaves. Bees were buzzing in their search for pollen and, in the far distance, the moors were streaked with purple heather. For Tom the world felt clean and new, and the woman he loved was beside him. Lily looked at him. There was a new energy about her husband; it was clear he was excited by his new post of chief inspector. In contrast, the look on John Pruett's face when he had read her letter of resignation was one she would never forget.

It was as if his spirit had suddenly broken.

Tom parked beneath the avenue of horse chestnut trees outside school and Lily kissed him on the cheek then walked quickly up the drive and the entrance steps.

Joseph Evans had arrived to take morning assembly and Tom got out to speak to him.

'Good morning, Joseph, and how are you on this lovely morning?'

'Fine thank you, Tom.' He looked up at the school bathed in morning sunlight. 'However, we are about to discuss arrangements for a replacement for Lily, so it's a mixture of sadness and optimism.'

'Yes, my fault I'm afraid, with my new post up in Durham.'

Joseph gave him an enigmatic smile. 'It's a great loss to the school, but a new opportunity for both of you. I wish you luck. I'm sure you will do well keeping law and order up there.'

Tom suddenly looked serious. 'Thank you, Joseph, but life will be demanding. I think we live in different worlds. Every day I'm dealing with theft and violence and much I can't discuss.'

'I understand,' said Joseph quietly. 'A prudent man concealeth knowledge,' he recited. 'Book of Proverbs. So have faith.'

Tom realized that during the past years he had only ever exchanged brief pleasantries with this kind man. 'To be honest, Joseph, I find it difficult to have *faith*, particularly in my job.'

'God will guide you,' said Joseph.

Tom was quiet for a moment. 'The concept of *God* is hard to grasp . . . whereas my world is one I understand.'

'Perhaps that's the difference between us, Tom,' replied Joseph with a knowing look.

'What do you mean?'

'Simply that the one certainty in *my* life is God. All the rest is a mystery.'

They both smiled as they shook hands and departed, each with his own thoughts.

It was shortly before 8.30 a.m. when Bernard Pickard drove up the school drive, parked his smart, light blue Triumph 2000 in the car park and walked purposefully into school carrying a slim leather briefcase. A short, dapper man in a pinstripe suit with knife-edge creases, he exuded efficiency. After he had shaken hands with John and Joseph and refused the offer of a hot drink from Vera, the three men settled in the staff-room.

Bernard took a sheet of foolscap paper from his briefcase. 'Time is short, gentlemen, but our earlier meeting last week gave me the opportunity to ensure the advertisement for the post of deputy headteacher will appear in the *Times Educational Supplement* this Friday. Applications will close two weeks later on the 26th of this month and we can shortlist the following week.'

John Pruett appeared subdued, but responded appropriately. Joseph was a little more insistent. 'It's important we appoint a practising Christian, Mr Pickard,' he said. 'After all, we are a Church of England school.'

Bernard Pickard often thought he would have made a good politician. Never rule anything out. 'Of course it will be an important consideration,' he declared with superficial sincerity.

Joseph glanced at his wristwatch. 'It will be part of the essential criteria, Mr Pickard. And if you'll forgive me, I have a christening to prepare for.'

After he had left, Bernard Pickard stood up and collected his briefcase.

'Just another matter, Mr Pruett,' he said and lowered his voice. 'We need to get the best possible candidate following the success of Mrs Feather's work here and the Education Committee were saddened to hear of her departure. She has a fine reputation and we were hoping she would apply for one or two of the forthcoming vacant headships in the area. There are a few retirements in the pipeline.'

'Yes,' said John. 'I'm sure she would make an excellent headteacher. However, her husband's promotion is final and they will be moving to the north-east after the end of term.'

Bernard Pickard was a perceptive man. The depth of feeling that was apparent was almost moving. This man clearly thought a great deal of his deputy headteacher and Bernard wondered what lay beneath the surface.

It was morning break and Vera was serving hot drinks.

'I saw you putting up a poster this morning, Vera,' said Lily.

'It's a special evening for the Women's Institute. Lavinia de Coercy is giving a talk on "Baking with Be-Ro".'

'Lavinia de Coercy?'

'Yes, she is one of the Berkshire de Coercys and famous in the world of baking.'

This meant little to Lily, but she was aware that Vera was a disciple of the *Be-Ro Home Recipes* booklet, hence her enthusiasm.

'Sounds wonderful,' she said without conviction and hurried out to the playground to take a cup of tea to Anne.

*

Rose and Freddie were stretched out in the sunshine under the welcome shade of a beech tree. A-levels were over and they were feeling relaxed. Their examinations had gone well and both felt confident they had done their best. The picnic basket was empty now and, after sharing news with their friends, they had wandered off hand in hand to the far corner of the field.

'I love being with you,' said Freddie quietly. He stroked her cheek with his finger. 'And if all goes well we'll be together at Leeds University.'

Rose lay back, stretching in the luxurious warmth. She had let her hair hang loose and it lay in soft strands on the grass.

Freddie looked around. They were out of sight. He pressed against her and kissed her on the mouth. His attentions became urgent.

'No,' said Rose, 'not here.'

'Why not? We can't be seen.'

Rose sat up. 'You know why not. We've discussed this. It's not right.'

Freddie breathed deeply, leaned back against the tree and stared up at the canopy of leaves above his head.

She reached for his hand. 'I do love you, Freddie, but I want to wait until after we've finished university. If we still feel the same about each other then, we can be together as we both would wish.'

Freddie nodded. 'You really are a remarkable woman.' For a moment he thought of Lily. *She can't have been as virtuous as Rose*, he thought.

'You may have my heart, Freddie. Other things . . . well, they must wait for another day. I have to be certain.'

276

In spite of his frustration, Rose went up in his estimation.

'I understand.' He shook his head. 'You're not like those unmarried Land Girls in the war.'

'Land Girls?'

'They gave their babies to their own mothers.'

Rose stared at him, surprised at the sudden shift in the conversation. 'You mustn't say that, Freddie.'

'Why not?'

'Well – that was wartime. They didn't know how long they would live.'

Freddie sighed. 'But surely it was wrong.'

Rose became forceful. 'You and I would have done the same. Think about it, Freddie. It was a selfless thing these women did to keep their baby within the family instead of giving them away to an orphanage.'

Freddie closed his eyes as memories flooded in.

'And how dreadful it must have been for the mother to pretend to be the child's sister. What courage they must have had.'

'I suppose so,' he muttered.

Rose took his hand. 'We're so lucky that we live in a time of peace.'

Freddie was impressed at the gravitas of her words.

Rose looked at him curiously. 'By the way, you never did tell me where you went at Easter. You said you didn't go camping.'

Freddie stood up and pressed his fingers to his forehead.

'What is it, Freddie?'

'I want to tell you but I can't.'

He saw the concern in her eyes and guilt consumed him.

Suddenly there was the shrill sound of two blasts on a whistle. It was time for a meeting in the school hall and a final address to the sixth form by the headmaster.

'We need to talk,' said Rose quietly.

'Let's go for a drive this evening,' said Freddie.

They set off towards the school building side by side, but they weren't holding hands.

Back in Ragley School, Sally Nobbs was in the lunch queue. Her teaching practice was going well and, of course, Vera had become a good friend.

She sat down at a table with some of the younger children in Anne's class.

'It's sunny today, Miss,' said a red-faced Margery Flathers. 'My mummy put some sun cream on my face and my arms.'

'Well, that's very sensible,' said Sally as the children attacked their toad-in-the-hole with gusto.

Tobias Fawnswater looked up from spearing a sausage. 'If I was in charge I would put sun cream on the sun. Then there wouldn't be a problem.'

Sally liked Toby and his forthright views.

Clint Ramsbottom entered the conversation after rubbing away two candles of snot with his sleeve. Sally tried to eliminate the vision and continued to eat.

'Miss?'

'Yes, Clint?'

'Do cows 'ave a langwidge?'

'I bet they do,' said Tobias. 'There will be different sorts of moos, just like we have different words.'

Sally thought there was more to Toby than met the eye.

Jane Grantham had finished her meal. 'My grandad says little girls are made of sugar and spice and everything nice.'

'No they're not,' exclaimed Toby. 'They're made of bones and blood.'

Sally stared at the remains of her meal. She was beginning to feel a little nauseous.

Toby put down his knife and fork. 'I like my belly button,' he declared.

Sally felt she had to ask. 'Why?' she said quietly.

'It stops my food falling out.'

Sally gave up on her meal, wondering if this was going to be her life for the next forty years.

During afternoon school there was no let-up in John Pruett's classroom. The children were waiting with ink pens poised and English exercise books open at the next clean page.

'I want you to write three or four sentences about each of the following on the blackboard.' He had written:

(a) The ascent of Everest
(b) Westminster Abbey
(c) William Shakespeare

As he sat there, he could hear Lily's voice encouraging her children as they played rounders on the school field. He walked to the window and stared out. The children who could see his face wondered why he looked so sad.

*

It was just before closing in the General Stores and Mrs Ollerenshaw had called in to collect her box of groceries.

'My Janet is disappointed about Mrs Feather leaving. She was so looking forward to going into her class.'

'Yes,' said Prudence, 'she's been a wonderful servant to the school, but she has to follow her husband to his new job up north.'

'That's the way it has always been. Perhaps one day it will be the other way round.'

'Let's hope so,' said Prudence with only a hint of conviction.

'I wonder who the new teacher will be.'

'No doubt we'll find out in good time.'

'Whoever it is, I can't imagine she will be as good as Mrs Feather. She's always been wonderful at sorting out problems.'

Prudence said nothing as Mrs Ollerenshaw collected the box and hurried out of the shop. She merely glanced up at Jeremy Bear and felt sure he knew what she was thinking.

It was shortly before seven o'clock when Freddie dropped off Lily at the Ragley village hall.

'Enjoy your evening,' she said. 'Vera has invited me back to the vicarage after the talk, so you can pick me up from there. Don't make it too late.'

'Fine,' said Freddie and drove up the Morton road to the McConnells' house.

The village hall was full and Vera, as Events Secretary of the Ragley & Morton WI, stood up to introduce the speaker and the subject for the evening – 'Baking with Be-Ro'.

Lavinia de Coercy was an experienced speaker and held her audience in rapt attention. Far from being animated, her face was serene. There was a tranquillity about her person, an aura of peace. Small and frail, she looked as if a strong gust of wind would blow her away. However, there was an inner core of strength to this lady.

As she held up a bag of flour in triumph she said, 'I know what I'm getting with Be-Ro. It's always the full weight and doesn't include the packaging. So I suggest you start with the one-pound bag. Eventually, work your way up to the three-pound and six-pound bags as you become more of a home baker and encourage your daughters to do the same.'

Prudence Golightly on the back row gave a satisfied smile. She had ordered a delivery of extra bags of flour.

Lavinia was working up to her big finish. After praising the advantages of Be-Ro 'Ruff Puff' pastry within the gospel of economical home baking, she declared, 'Remember the rules, ladies: handle your flour lightly, keep it cool and *do* use a hot oven.'

The evening ended with huge applause and a surfeit of perfect scones.

It was after nine o'clock when Vera and Lily walked back to the vicarage.

'A successful evening, Vera. You must be pleased.'

Vera smiled. 'I agree – and time for a nightcap, I believe.'

As they crunched across the gravel courtyard Vera paused. 'Joseph will be in, so I'll ask you now. How is Freddie?'

'The same,' said Lily. 'I'm still his sister as far as he is concerned.'

'And what about you and the future?'

'Tom is clearly looking forward to his new job and, as for me, I presume I'll apply for a new post when we're up in Durham.'

There was a long pause. 'I'll miss you, Lily.'

'And you have been a very dear friend.'

They walked into the vicarage together, each with her own thoughts and with many words unspoken.

For Rose it was an evening she would never forget. Freddie had collected her from her home and they had driven up the A64, through Malton and on to the pretty village of Thornton-le-Dale.

They had parked near the village green and sat in the evening sunshine outside one of the pubs. As they sipped on local beer, they could hear the calming sound of a stream, the Thornton Beck, as it meandered through the streets. It was a picture-postcard setting.

'This is a beautiful place,' said Rose with a gentle smile.

She knew there was something on Freddie's mind and hoped he would share his concerns.

'I can't keep it to myself any longer,' he said suddenly.

Rose put down her glass. She could barely say the words. 'Is there someone else?'

Freddie was shocked. 'No, it's not that, not ever. How could you even think such a thing?'

There was a moment of relief. 'So what's troubling you?'

He drank deeply from his pint glass. 'There's a secret I need to share.'

Rose stretched out and held his hand. She could feel his pain. 'Just tell me.'

'It's about Lily.'

'Your sister?'

Freddie shook his head. 'No, Rose, she's not my sister.'

'What do you mean?'

'Lily . . . well . . . she's my mother.'

Rose remained silent, trying to comprehend. She squeezed his hand.

'It came out at New Year. I found a photograph of someone who looked just like me. It was a picture from the end of the war. He was a German prisoner of war. Lily was in the Land Army. She said they fell in love.' He looked steadily into Rose's eyes. 'I'm their child.'

'I see,' said Rose quietly.

'Lily's mother, Florence, said she had brought shame on the family. She was forced to pretend to be my sister and I was brought up believing Florence was my mother. Lily has carried this lie with her all my life and Tom supported her.'

Rose gathered her thoughts. This was so unexpected. 'I'm sure they had their reasons, Freddie.'

'But I hate the deception and at first I hated her.'

'Freddie, remember when Mr Morris quoted Martin Luther King: *Hate cannot drive out hate, only love can do that.*'

Freddie nodded. 'I remember . . . but I still see her as my sister, nothing else.'

'But think how lucky you are. At least you've been brought up in a loving home.'

'So during the Easter break I went to Germany to find my father. His name is Rudolph Krüger.'

For the next hour a liquid stream of tender words eased his pain like a gentle caress. It was after nine o'clock, when the summer sun was beginning to set and the sky was turning from pink to purple, that they set off back to Ragley.

'I'm glad you shared this with me, Freddie.'

His eyes were fixed on the road ahead. 'So am I.'

John Pruett had settled down to his evening meal and was reflecting on the day. He had been impressed with the unconventional Sally Nobbs. It occurred to him that she would add a great deal to any school.

He sighed deeply and stared at his plate. It was his favourite salad, with a sliver of ham and a large slice of Wensleydale cheese.

For the Ragley headteacher it had been a life of cheese and chalk ... but mainly chalk. For as long as he could remember, hope and disappointment had been constant companions.

It was much later that he poured himself a gin and tonic, switched on the radio and sat down in his armchair. As he sipped his drink he thought of Lily and of a life without her. He gave a sad smile as the Peter and Gordon hit record 'A World Without Love' was introduced. The disc jockey explained that Paul McCartney had written it at the age of sixteen. Then in 1963, when the Beatle had moved in with his new girlfriend, Jane Asher, her brother, Peter, had asked if he could use the song.

When the sun finally sank in the west at the end of a long day, John had at last accepted that the love of his life was leaving and his world would never be the same again.

It was nearly midnight when he went upstairs to bed. Before closing the curtains he stared up at the cold stars and the crescent moon. Around him there was doubt in every shadow. That night in his dreams there was only a cracked mirror and a love that could never be.

Chapter Eighteen

Fond Farewells

It was Friday, 3 July and as Lily drove to school a pink dawn had crested the horizon and announced a perfect summer day. Beyond the hedgerows the branches of the sycamores stirred with a breathless promise and a morning mist hung over the fields of golden barley. Lily felt relaxed, but, of course, she had no awareness of the events that were about to unfold.

When she parked her car in the school car park a blackbird was trying to crack open the shell of a snail to discover what was hidden within. Secrets are often revealed at the most unexpected moments, and a time of arrivals and farewells was in store.

In the staff-room John Pruett and Joseph Evans were in animated conversation when Vera popped her head round the door.

'Excuse me. That was Mr Pickard on the telephone. He said he would call in at lunchtime.'

'Thank you, Vera,' said John. It was a brisk response,

almost curt, but Vera knew why. The shortlist for the post of deputy headteacher had proved unsatisfactory and tensions were running high.

'It would appear no practising Christian applied,' said Joseph mournfully.

John Pruett kept his thoughts to himself. First and foremost, he wanted a good teacher. 'Let's see what Mr Pickard has to say.'

Joseph nodded. 'I'll be back at lunchtime.' He paused in the doorway. 'I presume you approached Mrs Grainger?'

'Yes, she didn't apply because she doesn't want the extra responsibility.'

'A pity,' said Joseph and hurried out.

When Vera returned to the school office, Sally Nobbs was waiting for her.

'Yes, Sally, what can I do to help?'

Sally smiled. 'Actually it's the other way round. I know you will be busy tomorrow morning preparing for the village fair and I wondered if I could assist.'

Vera recognized a kindred spirit. 'Yes, please, thank you so much. Help is always welcome in the WI marquee, so if you come along to the cricket field it would be most helpful.'

'Fine, I'll be there.'

'Wonderful,' said Vera, 'and I know it's the final day of your teaching practice today, so do enjoy it. The children will be sad to see you go.'

'As *I* shall when I say goodbye.'

'What are your plans for the future?'

'Hopefully, a teaching post in Leeds. I've got a few interviews.'

'Well, I wish you luck and do keep an eye on vacancies here at Ragley in the coming years. You never know what turns up.'

'I shall and, talking of turning up, I've been told my teaching practice tutor, Miss Puddifoot, will be in shortly.' Sally looked a little anxious. 'So I'm hoping for a trouble-free morning.'

She hurried off to prepare the classroom while Vera reflected on her first meeting with the effervescent young student and recalled her mother's advice to *never judge a book by its cover*.

Sally's English lesson was going well. The children had been asked to write about where they were going for their summer holidays when Miss Puddifoot walked in.

A stick-thin woman of severe appearance, in spite of the hot weather she was wearing a tweed suit and sensible lace-up shoes. After a brief handshake with Lily, who was sitting in the book corner hearing Shane Ramsbottom read, she gave a curt nod towards Sally and sat down at the teacher's desk. Sally's teaching-practice file was open with her lesson notes neatly displayed. The pernickety tutor flicked through the pages, her lips pursed. Everything was in order. Then she scrutinized the children, heads bowed, all engrossed in the task, and she appeared satisfied.

She opened her duplicate notebook, inserted the carbon sheet between two pages and began to prepare what was commonly known to the students as their 'crit' –a tutor report on their lesson. She wrote, 'Miss Nobbs has prepared an effective writing lesson, discipline is good and the children are attentive.'

Then she stood up and walked to the first group of children, who were writing in their English exercise books. Dictionaries had been placed in the centre of each group and the children were checking spellings and writing them in their vocabulary notebooks. It was clearly a well-organized lesson, the children were all working hard and Sally was moving from one group to another supporting individuals according to their needs. Miss Puddifoot relaxed with the awareness of an effective student at work.

However, in a primary classroom the unexpected is always just around the corner.

Duggie Smith looked up at the stranger. "Scuse me, Miss, but are you a teacher?'

Miss Puddifoot was slightly taken aback by the direct approach of this bristle-haired boy. 'Yes, I am.'

Next to Duggie, Henry Tonks showed sudden interest. 'That's good,' he said. 'Can you 'elp me wi' a spellin', please?'

Miss Puddifoot was impressed the little boy knew his manners. 'Of course. What is your name?'

'Ah'm 'Enry, Miss. What's yours?'

Sally heard the exchange and glanced up anxiously.

'I'm Miss Puddifoot.'

Henry looked perplexed. 'Puddlefoot?'

Miss Puddifoot sighed. It was close enough and she had been called worse. Henry had opened his word book, pencil poised. 'So what word do you require?'

'Well, Miss . . . 'ow d'you spell *fuck*?'

'Pardon?' Miss Puddifoot thought she had clearly misheard.

'Ah said . . . 'ow d'you spell *fuck*?'

'Pardon?' She had definitely not misheard and stepped back in horror.

Henry assumed this strange lady was as deaf as his grandma and he always had to shout when speaking to her. 'AH SAID . . . 'OW D'YOU SPELL *FUCK*?'

'Dear me,' said Miss Puddifoot, her cheeks flushing rapidly.

Lily was about to leap up from the book corner when Sally took over, crouching next to the stocky son of a local farmer. She spoke quietly. 'Tell me, Henry, why do you want that word?'

'It's where we're goin' on our 'olidays, Miss.'

'But what has that word got to do with it?'

'Well, m'mam an' dad are tekkin' me on a boat.'

'A boat? But why do you want *that* word?'

'Well, Miss, ah know 'ow t'spell *Nor* but ah don't know 'ow t'spell *fuck*.'

Sally wrote *Norfolk* in Henry's word book while a relieved Miss Puddifoot returned to the teacher's desk and added in her notebook: 'Questions were handled with calm professionalism.'

She tore out the duplicate page, attached it to Sally's lesson plan with a paperclip . . . and smiled.

At morning break Anne was on duty and Vera carried two cups of tea to the playground. For the Ragley School secretary time was both a thief and a benefactor. It had taken away her youth but given back a wealth of experience. She was about to put it to good use.

The sun was shining and Vera and Anne leaned against the school wall and watched the children at play.

'They don't change, do they?' observed Vera. 'We get older and they stay the same.'

Anne gave a sigh. 'Very true, Vera. This is the second generation of Ragley children I've seen through the school. Those I first taught are teenagers now.'

'Ragley is lucky to have you.'

They sipped their tea and enjoyed the warmth under the dappled shade of the horse chestnut trees.

'I did have a thought,' said Vera. 'A favour, in fact.'

'Yes?'

'Well, with Lily leaving we need some *continuity* and, as you know, no appointment has been made so far for the post of deputy.'

'I presumed John would ask Miss Flint to take over Lily's class in the interim while another advertisement is placed.'

'That's right, but Mr Pickard may simply bring in a teacher from another school to give them experience in a deputy headship. That's the unknown, whereas you would be perfect for the post.'

Anne gave a wry smile. 'You know why I didn't apply, Vera. I enjoy my teaching too much and don't want the extra responsibility.'

'I do understand, but I have a solution.'

'Really?'

'Yes, I love this school and we need some stability during the coming months. It would help Mr Pruett if you would be willing to consider being *acting* deputy head in the interim. That way you are not committed, the school benefits and you retain choice in whatever you decide.'

'I see,' said Anne thoughtfully. Vera was a hard person to refuse. 'And what does John think about all of this?'

'It is *his* idea, of course,' said Vera. 'I am just explaining it.'

'I'll think about it.'

'If you've finished your tea, I'll return your cup,' said Vera.

'Thanks.'

'And if you could decide *before lunchtime* it would help,' added Vera with determination. 'Mr Pickard is coming in from County Hall and I could tell John that you would be willing to help out in our hour of need.'

She hurried back into school with a clatter of teacups.

At the end of the afternoon it was a tearful farewell for Sally Nobbs. She said goodbye to the children and had brought in a bunch of flowers for Lily.

'Good luck, Sally,' said Lily, 'and do keep in touch.'

'Thank you, Lily . . . for *everything*.'

It was early evening when Anne Grainger arrived at the vicarage. Vera was watering bright red geraniums and blue trailing lobelia in the window boxes.

'Hello, Anne, what a lovely surprise.' She gestured towards a pair of chairs overlooking her bountiful garden.

Anne smiled. 'I've spoken with John and I'm to be acting deputy next term.'

'I'm so pleased.' She gave Anne a hug. 'Congratulations.'

'Well, let's see how it goes. You were right, of course. I

needed to put the school first and, according to John, Mr Pickard was happy with the outcome.'

Vera smiled at a job well done. 'I've just made some fruit scones ready for tomorrow. Shall we sample a couple?'

Anne didn't need asking twice.

On Saturday afternoon alongside the Ragley cricket field the summer fair was in full swing. Bunting was fluttering above the huge marquee where Sally and Vera were serving cream teas. Behind the white picket fence, the Ragley and Morton Brass Band was playing 'Land of Hope and Glory'. Children were sitting on a semicircle of straw bales in the sunshine to watch Captain Fantastic's Punch and Judy Show and Deke Ramsbottom was supervising the Bowling for a Pig competition.

Meanwhile, Deirdre Coe was berating her brother, Stan, for drinking too much beer with his cronies. Eventually she wandered off, glowering at Ruby Smith, who was sitting on the grass with her children and wearing a pretty straw hat decorated with roses.

In front of the cricket pavilion Tom and Freddie were supping warm beer, looking relaxed in their white shirts and cricket flannels. A charity cricket match had been organized by Tommy Piercy, featuring a Ragley village team against a Select XI comprising players from some of the neighbouring villages. Freddie had volunteered to be a member of the Select XI, while Tom, after some persuading, had also agreed to play. Aloysius Pratt and Albert Jenkins had been installed as umpires and the match was played in a friendly spirit, with the exception of Freddie, who always played to win. When the Ragley team batted, he bowled at a ferocious speed until at the end of their innings they returned to the pavilion and sat on the steps to enjoy ham sandwiches and lukewarm tea.

Rose walked over to join Tom and Freddie. 'Good luck when you're batting,' she said with a smile.

Freddie was attentive as always. 'Shall I get you a drink?'

'No thanks, we've got some.' She pointed to the far side of the ground, where Joy Popplewell was sitting on a bench, drinking wine and smoking a cigarette. 'I'm with Joy.'

It was when Rose passed the copse of trees near the cinder track that led to the High Street that she saw a man she had never seen before. She stopped in surprise. The resemblance to Freddie was uncanny and the more she watched him the more she became certain.

He was standing in the shade of a weeping willow tree, intent on the cricket. Tall, with blond hair and a square jaw, he looked like an older version of Freddie and, in that moment, she knew who it must be.

Rudolph Krüger had finally decided to respond to Lily's letter and meet their son. He had travelled from Hamburg to Harwich, then on to London, from where he caught a train to York and checked into a city-centre hotel. There he hired a car and drove to Kirkby Steepleton, but there was no one at Laurel Cottage.

Ragley village seemed to be the next obvious destination and he had parked on the High Street and followed the crowds to the cricket field. He spotted Freddie immediately, sitting outside the pavilion talking to Tom Feather.

The tall policeman was familiar to him after their conversation all those years ago. Rudolph looked around him. It was almost on this very spot that he and Tom had first met. Freddie had been six years old and now he was a man.

He scanned the crowds. There was no sign of Lily.

Lily and Vera were taking a break, sitting on deckchairs on the far side of the marquee in the shade and away from the crowds.

'A perfect day, Lily,' said Vera, sipping on a glass of her home-made elderflower and lemon juice.

On the far side of the ground the tinkling sounds of Winston Eckersley's Gasparini street organ could be heard as the Ragley cricketers headed back out on to the field. The crowd clapped and Freddie and Tom, the two opening batsmen for the Select XI, walked out to the cricket square.

Lily smiled. 'Yes, Vera, and good to see Tom and Freddie on the same side.'

'Just like father and son together,' said Vera.

Lily gave a wistful look. 'Almost,' she said quietly.

After a while Vera went back into the WI tent and Lily was sitting alone watching Freddie hit another boundary. Tom was not a natural cricketer, but he had a good eye and was hitting the occasional single and leaving the scoring to Freddie.

Rose waved as she approached. 'Hello, Mrs Feather.'

'Oh, hello. Enjoying the game?'

'Yes thanks,' but Rose appeared distracted.

'What is it, Rose?'

'I've just seen a man standing over there.' She pointed to the copse of trees.

'Yes?'

'He looks just like Freddie . . . only older.'

Lily composed herself quickly. 'That's interesting. Perhaps I'll spot him too.'

Lily got up and set off slowly around the cricket field and into the shadows, where she saw Rudi.

It was as if the world had stood still. The man she had loved so long ago had reappeared like the echo of a memory. Life had settled again like pearls on a string . . . until the string had broken when Freddie had gone to search for his father. It had been a time of secrets and lies. Now the reason was standing before her. She breathed deeply and walked slowly towards him.

'It is you,' she said. There were flecks of grey in his blond hair, shorter now, in a severe cut. Nevertheless, he was still a tall, good-looking man and he was a calm presence beside her.

'You asked me to come,' he said simply.

'It's still a surprise.'

Rudi looked at the cricket field where Freddie was receiving applause after another excellent stroke. 'He's grown into a fine man.'

'Freddie would like to see you. He was disappointed when you weren't there in Hamburg.'

'I was sad I missed him.' He looked into Lily's eyes and his feelings stirred with the memory. 'I was in Frankfurt on business.'

'He would like to get to know you. It's been difficult since he found out about you . . . we need to make it right for him.'

'I understand, Lily,' he said softly. 'That's why I'm here.'

There was another burst of applause from the crowd. Tom was walking back to the pavilion waving his bat in acknowledgement after being caught on the boundary. They watched Freddie shake his hand and Rudi saw the bond between them.

'They look good together,' he remarked.

'Tom has been his friend since he was a boy. There is trust between them.'

'And you?'

Lily's eyes clouded over. 'Not so. Some memories can never be erased.'

'True.'

Lily looked around her. It was important to grasp this opportunity. 'You must come back to the cottage later this evening – say, nine o'clock. Can you do that?'

'Of course, and I have a car.'

Their conversation was brief and she watched him walk away. She thought of that time twenty years ago when she had loved this sensitive German who happened to be a prisoner of war. The memories flooded back – and the pain that went with them of losing her child to her mother.

Then there was Tom, the love of her life. She remembered his reaction when he first discovered her secret – another time, another cricket match when Rudi had watched Freddie playing on this very field.

And now he was here. She knew that Rudi was a good man. He would do the right thing for his son.

'Well done both of you,' said Lily.

Freddie and Tom had changed out of their cricket

whites and back into casual clothes. Rose was holding Freddie's hand and they looked relaxed together.

'Wasn't he brilliant?' asked Tom.

'So were you,' said Freddie. 'I didn't know you could play so well.'

'Beginner's luck,' said Tom. 'Although I did play at school.'

Lily decided to make an announcement. 'I should like to have a celebratory meal back at the cottage and, of course, you too, Rose.'

'Thanks, Mrs Feather, I don't think we had any plans.' Rose looked up at Freddie, who nodded.

'Fine,' said Lily. 'So have a drink with the team and I'll see you later.'

'I'll come with you, Lily,' said Tom. He rubbed his aching back. 'I think I need a lie-down after all that running.'

Back at the cottage, Lily was anxious about Tom's reaction to her news.

'Rudi is here,' she said.

'What? Here in the village?'

She nodded. 'Rose saw him in the crowd and told me she had seen someone who looked like Freddie. I spoke with Rudi and invited him round for drinks later this evening.'

Tom nodded but said nothing.

'Was I right to do that?' she asked anxiously.

'Yes, of course, but you must tell Freddie before he arrives. He usually dumps his cricket boots in the garden shed. So talk to him there in private. I'll keep Rose busy in the kitchen.'

*

An hour later Freddie was in the shed scraping the mud from the spikes on the soles of his boots.

'Can I speak with you, Freddie?'

He looked up and smiled at Lily, something he had not done for such a long time. In that moment she knew that she had the strength to tell him.

'He's here, Freddie.'

'Who is?'

'Rudi.'

Freddie put down his boots and stepped back. 'Rudi . . . he's *here*?'

'He got my letter and wanted to come. Now seemed to be the right time.'

Freddie stiffened with tension. This was unexpected.

Lily spoke calmly. 'Rudi was at the cricket match looking for us. Rose saw him in the crowd and came to tell me that she had seen someone who looked just like you. I knew immediately who it must be.'

Freddie gave a deep sigh. 'Lily – she knows.'

Lily remained silent.

'I told Rose. I didn't want to at first, but it helped.'

Lily recognized the depth of feeling Freddie had for this young woman. 'She's a lovely girl. I'm glad that you did.'

'So . . . will I meet him?'

'Yes, tonight.'

Freddie nodded slowly.

Lily was concerned. 'Is that OK?'

'Yes. Thank you.' He took a deep breath. 'I know this can't be easy for you and I'm grateful.' He took Lily's arm. 'Let's go in,' he said.

*

Lily and Rose were on their own preparing food together while Tom and Freddie were setting the table. The kitchen door was closed.

'Thank you, Rose,' said Lily.

Rose smiled. 'I enjoy helping.'

Lily shook her head. 'No, I mean thank you for being there for Freddie.'

The two women looked at each other and Rose knew instantly that Freddie must have told Lily that he had shared his story with her.

'I do understand.' She paused and looked directly at Lily. 'Freddie told me in confidence and I'm glad that he did. I hope you don't mind.'

'I am grateful, Rose. It has been hard for him.'

'And for you, Mrs Feather. I told Freddie what an amazing person you are. You had so much courage. I'm not sure I would have been as strong as you. But I am so pleased that you are all here . . . together. I wouldn't have met him otherwise.'

Rose's words were comfort for a troubled soul and Lily dabbed away the tears in her eyes.

Then she put her handkerchief back into her apron pocket and returned to slicing spring onions. 'Rose,' she said quietly, 'I'm so glad you found each other.'

Rudi knocked on the door of Laurel Cottage for the second time that day. He breathed deeply, but he knew what must be done.

The door opened quickly and Freddie stood there. This tall, strong young man was the image of his younger self.

Freddie smiled. 'You came.'

'I had to come. I am sorry that it has taken me so long.'

'Come in.' Freddie showed him into the front room where Lily was waiting.

It was a strange experience. Freddie looked at his mother and father and imagined them as a young couple. For the first time, he felt the pain they must have suffered.

'Welcome, Rudi,' said Lily. 'Let me get you a drink while you and Freddie get to know one another.'

It was awkward at first. There were so many questions in Freddie's mind. Lily served glasses of beer and Freddie sat with Rudi on the bench seat by the bay window. Lily and Tom gave them the space they needed and soon father and son relaxed in each other's company.

'So, tell me about West Germany,' said Freddie.

'It's growing, rebuilding, changing ... I hope for the better,' said Rudi as he sipped his beer thoughtfully. He looked closely at his son, a mirror of his younger self.

'I do engineering work now and manage projects.'

'I went to Hamburg,' said Freddie. 'I wanted to meet you.'

Rudi nodded and put his hand on Freddie's shoulder. 'I know and I'm sorry I missed you.' He smiled. 'My neighbour, Mrs Freund, said you spoke German well.'

Freddie flushed with pleasure. 'It's one of my A-levels.'

'Lily says you are a hard worker.'

'I try,' said Freddie simply.

'And you are a talented sportsman.'

Freddie shrugged. 'Maybe. What about you?'

Rudi was quiet for a moment. 'I could have been ... but the war got in the way.'

The conversation ebbed and flowed and the evening went quickly as Rudi shared his story. Tom nodded in quiet acknowledgement as he watched Freddie warm to this man and his generosity of spirit.

Freddie gradually came to understand that his father had loved Lily and she had loved him. He also knew that Rudi was happy that she had found real love with Tom and that his son would be safe.

Time passed with laughter and tears and, as they said their goodbyes, Rudi shook Freddie's hand.

'Rose is a lovely girl, Freddie. You are a lucky man. Don't let her go.'

Freddie understood the gravitas of his words.

It was Rudi who made the first move. He stepped forward and hugged Freddie. 'Thank you for seeing me, Freddie,' he said quietly. He walked down the drive and suddenly turned back. 'Visit me,' he said. 'Would you do that?'

Rose was standing beside Freddie and answered for him. 'We shall,' she said, 'I promise.'

Lily and Tom joined them and they all waved Rudi off as he went back to his hotel. Lily knew that it would be some time, if ever, before she saw him again.

'Let's leave them on their own,' said Tom nodding towards Rose and Freddie. 'It's been quite a night.'

Rose and Freddie wandered out into the garden. Around them was only the sibilant whisper of the leaves on the trees. The sun had set now and the vast sky was changing from red to purple. Stars were shining like celestial fireflies and the sky was scattered with stardust.

Rose broke the silence. 'Freddie, what a selfless thing he

did to walk away. He knew that you would have a far better chance in life here with Florence and Lily in post-war Britain.'

Freddie stared up into the night sky as a shooting star split the firmament with a spear of white light. 'I think you're right. It's beginning to make sense to me now.'

Rose stretched up and kissed him on the cheek. 'What a story, Freddie. It's amazing. Aren't you lucky?'

For the first time in many months Freddie began to believe that perhaps he was.

The young couple stood hand in hand beneath the endless sky while, under a blizzard of stars, Freddie reflected on an evening of fond farewells.

Chapter Nineteen

The Importance of Being Lily

It was Wednesday, 22 July and the breathless promise of a new day hung heavy as the world awoke. The air was humid and warm, and a dank mist lay on the sleeping earth.

It had been a stifling night and Lily had found it hard to sleep as the heat built up like a furnace. When she sat up in bed there was an empty pillow beside her. Tom was spending a week in Durham meeting his new colleagues and receiving a briefing from the chief constable. He was due back on Friday. The following week they had planned a short holiday in a rented cottage in Masham in the Yorkshire Dales. It would give them some private time together before moving to the north-east. Her time at Ragley was rushing to a close and the end of the school year was only two days away.

It was Freddie who drove Lily to school. He pulled up by the village green.

'I'll collect you after school, then take you back again for your governors' meeting.'

Lily checked her bag to make sure she had everything she needed for the school day. 'Are you still going to the cinema with Rose?'

'Yes, it's the new Beatles film, *A Hard Day's Night*. We're going to the first house, so I'll take Rose home and then pick you up. Is that OK?'

'Perfect. If the governors' meeting finishes early, I'll use the time to do some more packing.'

'See you later,' said Freddie with a smile, because, of course, he knew something that Lily didn't.

It was morning break and in the staff-room Vera was looking at her newspaper with a frown. Last week the Post Office Tower had been completed and the newspapers were full of photographs of this new London landmark. Vera was unimpressed. It lacked the classical charm of the palaces of Buckingham and Westminster.

Anne was on duty and John was sipping tea when Lily walked in.

'What's happening to your cottage?' John asked.

'It's been put up for sale and Millicent Merryweather has offered to check on it each day until it's sold.'

'It will be in safe hands with Millicent,' said Vera.

'So what are your plans?' asked John.

'A holiday, then a removal up to the new home in Durham.'

'Busy times,' he said. 'I should like to help.'

'Thank you, John.'

There was an awkward pause. Lily thought everyone was strangely quiet and wondered why.

At lunchtime Vera hurried across the road to the General Stores to buy two extra bottles of milk. An eventful afternoon was in store and she smiled in anticipation.

It was when she was crossing the road that she sensed a change in the wind and looked up. The weather vane on top of the village hall creaked ominously as it turned on its axis and pointed to the west. The air was hot and the breeze damp. In the far distance dark clouds were gathering. Vera shook her head. It looked threatening. A storm was coming – a big storm.

It was Vera's idea to get Lily out of the way and Anne had been assigned to keep her busy. She popped her head round Lily's classroom door. 'Would you mind taking a walk with me? Perhaps to the far end of the field out of earshot.'

Lily looked puzzled. 'Yes, if you wish.'

'It's about my new role of acting deputy – I need to pick your brains.'

'Ah, I see,' said Lily with a smile. 'Come on then.'

They wandered off into the distance and were still engrossed when the bell rang for afternoon school.

'Oh dear,' said Lily, 'we musn't be late,' and they hurried back across the field.

It was when Anne ushered her into the hall that realization dawned.

'What's this?' asked an astonished Lily.

'It's a celebration assembly,' replied Anne.

Lily was speechless.

Anne smiled. 'It's for you, Lily. We didn't want leaving Ragley to be a time of sadness. We wanted to celebrate everything that you have done for the school and for us.'

'Oh, Anne,' said Lily as she took in the scene before her. 'What a wonderful surprise. I can't believe it.'

All the children were sitting cross-legged on the floor in rows, while the chairs at the back were filled with parents and villagers. Anne took her seat next to Valerie Flint and school governor Albert Jenkins. On the other side, Vera was flanked by Ruby and Sally Nobbs.

John Pruett gestured for Lily to sit down. He began the proceedings in a sonorous voice. 'Good afternoon, everybody. Thank you for gathering here today. I know this is unexpected for Mrs Feather, but we didn't want to leave it until the last day of term to say goodbye.'

He turned to Lily. 'Everyone in this hall would like to thank you and we've selected a representative few who would like to say some words. First of all, I should like to welcome back our excellent student teacher, Miss Nobbs.'

Sally stood up and smiled at Lily. 'I'm here simply to say thank you on behalf of all the students who have benefited from experiencing a teaching practice at this wonderful school. For my part, I shall always be grateful to Mrs Feather for being my mentor and I shall carry with me all of her teachings.' She smiled at Lily. 'And I've just been appointed to a teaching post in Leeds.'

There was spontaneous applause, then John stood up again. 'Nothing would have kept David and Malcolm Robinson away today. They were in my class when Mrs Feather arrived back in nineteen fifty-two.' He smiled at the Ragley bin men. 'It's been a long time since I caught them sliding down the coke pile outside the boiler house.'

There was laughter as Big Dave and Little Malcolm stood up. As usual, it was Big Dave who spoke first. 'We jus' wanted t'say a big thank you t'Mrs Feather. Back when ah were ten an' Malc' were nine y'might recall we were famous in t'village 'cause we found that butterfly bomb. An' it were thanks t'Mrs Feather an' Mr Pruett that it were med safe.' He looked down at Malcolm. 'An' Malc' 'as summat t'say.'

He nudged Little Malcolm, who went bright red. Public speaking was not his forte. 'It were jus' that Mrs Feather, 'xcept she were Miss Briggs then, taught me t'speak in long sentences an' ah've never f'got.'

He sat down quickly. Lily and John Pruett clapped and everyone joined in.

Big Dave gave Little Malcolm a nudge and whispered, 'Well done, Malc'. Yurra star.'

'And now the chair of the PTA,' said John.

The tall, unassuming Mrs Ollerenshaw stood up. 'Simply to say a big thank you on behalf of all the parents, past and present, whose children have benefited from being in your class. Mrs Feather spent much of her time solving our problems and we shall always be grateful.' There were murmurs of agreement from the other parents.

John looked across the hall to Vera, who gave an imperceptible nod of the head. 'Before I ask the chair of governors to speak, I think Miss Evans would like a word.'

As always, Vera spoke with confidence and clarity. 'Mrs Feather is well aware of our special friendship as colleagues here in Ragley School. She has always been the essence of professionalism and there is no higher praise than that. Her sincerity, gentleness and kindness will always be remembered.'

It had been difficult for Vera to control her emotions. She sat down quickly, removed a lace handkerchief from the sleeve of her cardigan and dabbed her eyes.

Joseph Evans stood up, visibly moved by his sister's words. However, he was used to gathering himself and speaking to a congregation. 'We were indeed fortunate to appoint Mrs Feather eleven school years ago. She has been an asset to Ragley and has brought so much to our school and village community. On behalf of everyone here – parents, children, staff and governors – it gives me great pleasure to present Mrs Feather with a token of our appreciation.'

Vera brought to the front of the hall a large box, beautifully wrapped in lilac tissue paper and tied with lavender bows.

Lily sat in her seat and unwrapped it with trembling hands. She looked up and spotted Freddie and hoped he hadn't been forced to be here. Even so, she was glad that he was now that Tom was away.

The box was heavy and the children watched open-mouthed in excited anticipation. Inside was a magnificent clock and Lily held it up for all to see. The inscription read: *'For Lily Feather with love and sincere thanks from everyone at Ragley School.'*

She held it in her arms and stood up. It was time to respond.

'First of all, thank you for the care and time that you

have all taken to organize this amazing afternoon. I didn't know anything about it.' She laughed and looked down at the younger pupils. 'Boys and girls, how did you keep it a secret?'

The children called out and pointed. 'It was Mrs Grainger.'

Lily smiled at Anne and saw her nodding tearfully. She knew the school would be in good hands and hoped Anne would remain as deputy headteacher. Ragley needed her now more than ever.

'I cannot begin to tell you how much this all means to me. Not only this beautiful clock, which will sit on my mantelpiece in my new home, but the kindness you have shown me. I shall treasure this gift for the rest of my life and when I look at it I shall think of you.'

She scanned the sea of faces. 'I am so grateful to have had this time in Ragley School. All my pupils are so special to me and I will never forget you. Thank you to the parents and governors, who have been so kind and supportive, and, of course, the wonderful staff.' She nodded towards Vera and Ruby. 'You will always be in my thoughts . . .' She paused and looked at John. '. . . and Mr Pruett, a wonderful headteacher and a kind man. Where would we be without you?'

John was visibly moved. *Perhaps she does care about me; maybe not as I had hoped . . . but she does care.*

'Thank you, Mrs Feather,' he said quietly, 'thank you.'

When Lily sat down, John Pruett took a deep breath. All eyes turned towards him. It was the hardest place to be. 'I recall my first meeting with Mrs Feather all those years ago. She arrived *exactly* on time.' He gave a wry smile, although his heart was full of sadness. 'We did not know then what a wonderful teacher would be joining the staff at Ragley School . . . we know now. Her skill and her love of learning have been there for all to see. Pupils past and present have benefited from her professionalism.' He looked at Lily. 'Good luck for the future. Ragley's loss will be Durham's gain.'

He was close to tears as he sat down and the applause seemed to last for ever.

Freddie had watched and heard everything. He could barely explain his emotions. Tears pricked his eyes when he heard the many tributes.

Rose was right, he thought. Lily is a remarkable woman with so much strength. People love her, and rightly so. He knew that over the years he had taken her for granted. He would put things right. From this moment on he would be different. He would be kind, a better person . . . one that she deserved and wanted him to be.

That evening the governors' meeting was low-key. Joseph was in the chair and Vera acted as secretary, with John, Lily and Albert Jenkins in attendance.

After the meeting closed Lily walked out to the entrance hall followed by John. 'I'll lock up when I leave,' she said. 'Freddie is collecting me.'

There was a moment of disappointment for John. 'Well, don't be long. This weather could break any time.'

'Shall I wait with you?' asked Vera.

'No thanks, Vera. I thought I would pack a few boxes while I'm waiting.'

Vera smiled. 'To be perfectly honest, Lily, I'm quite keen to get back to watch the Royal International Horse Show.'

Vera tidied the staff-room and left with Joseph to drive back to the vicarage.

Albert paused in the entrance hall. 'Lily, remember the words of Abraham Lincoln,' he said with a smile.

Lily looked at this kindly man with curiosity. 'Knowing you, Albert, they will be words of wisdom.'

Albert smiled. 'Perhaps,' he said. He paused as he plucked one of his favourite sayings from his vast store of knowledge. 'In the end, it's not the years in your life that count. *It's the life in your years.*'

Very true, thought Lily and she thought of her work at Ragley School and the faces of the pupils. So many children ... so many memories. 'Special times, Albert,' she said quietly. 'I've been fortunate teaching here. I shall miss you all.'

'Never forget,' said Albert with a wry smile and recalling the works of Oscar Wilde, *'the importance of being Lily.'*

Above their heads the Victorian rafters creaked as the wind gathered strength. Albert glanced up at the windows. Darkness was falling earlier than usual and rain clouds were gathering. 'Are you sure I can't give you a lift?'

'Thank you, but Freddie is picking me up.' She looked at the hall clock. 'He should be here in half an hour. I said I would pack a few of my belongings, so I'll be fine.'

A few miles away the landlord of the Pig & Ferret grabbed Stan Coe by his collar. 'That's enough, Stan, time t'go 'ome.'

'Gerroff!' shouted Stan.

The Ragley pig farmer had been drinking steadily and

was now three sheets to the wind; in other words, he was rolling drunk.

'An' y'shouldn't be drivin'.'

Stan took no notice. He had always believed he was a better driver with a few pints inside him. He staggered out to his Land Rover, lit up a cigarette and drove unsteadily out of the car park.

Lily had packed most of her personal books in two cardboard boxes and stacked them beside her desk for taking home the next day. She looked around her classroom – everything was in its place. She was proud of her organization: the neat, carpeted book corner, paintings and writing on the display boards, and newly washed bristle brushes in a large jug next to the sink. It was time to collect her coat from the staff-room and wait in the entrance hall for Freddie to arrive.

She had just put on her coat when it happened.

There was a sudden flash of lightning and the lights went out. Plunged into darkness, she banged her knee on the coffee table and stood still, waiting for her eyes to adjust. A few seconds later there was a deep rumble of thunder that seemed to shake the building.

She remembered that John kept a large torch in a cupboard under the staff-room window and she felt her way around the room. It was there and she switched it on with relief. A yellow circle of light washed across the walls and she walked out to the entrance hall.

Fuse box, she thought, but then remembered it was in the caretaker's store and that would be locked. John would have the spare key in his desk.

It made sense to walk outside to the porch, lock the door and shine the torch so that Freddie could see where she was. That was when she heard the rain begin to fall. Heaven's army was on the march and it was almost overhead.

Stan Coe slowed as he drove down the Morton road and peered through his windscreen. Sheets of rain swamped the road ahead and he stopped next to the village green. Suddenly the lights of The Royal Oak and the adjoining cottages flickered and, a moment later, the lights of the school went out completely.

He pulled up and stared out into the inky darkness.

Lily held the torch and opened the entrance door. Above her, huge droplets shattered on the roof of the porch in an explosion of spray. The air seemed full of pressure and electricity, while lightning forked down from a sky the colour of Whitby jet. Giant thunderheads rolled over the earth with a shuddering boom as Lily locked the door behind her. They were immediately followed by white forked lightning and a ragged bolt of unbearable voltage lit up the school.

It was in that second of sharp, intense light that Stan Coe saw Lily, alone and vulnerable. Realization dawned in his blurred thoughts. A long-awaited moment had arrived.

Up the Morton road, Freddie and Rose were outside the McConnells' house.

'Thanks for a lovely evening, Freddie. I loved the film.'

'See you tomorrow,' he said.

There was a flash of lightning and Rose, startled, clung to Freddie's coat. He kissed her softly. 'I have to go – I promised Lily I would pick her up from school.'

There was a crash of thunder.

'Drive safely,' called Rose as she went inside.

Freddie hurried out to the car as the rain began to hammer down. He turned left at the village green past The Royal Oak and noticed a Land Rover was parked outside the school entrance. He pulled up and stared up at the school. There were no lights. Then he saw the beam of a torch under the porch and presumed it must be Lily. She must have locked the door and was waiting for him.

He eased the car into first gear and drove slowly up the drive. It was then that the torchlight went out and there was another flash of lightning.

Lily screamed and dropped the torch as a large figure loomed out of the darkness and mounted the steps. She was grabbed by her shoulders and pushed back against the wall. A fleshy hand pressed against her mouth.

'That bloke of yours saved you las' time . . . well, there's no one 'ere to 'elp y'now.'

Lily recognized the voice.

'It's time you 'ad a real man.' A groping hand began to fumble at her clothes. His breathing was heavy with anticipation. 'Ah've waited a long time f'this. Come t'Stanley.'

The foul smell of stale beer, cigarette smoke and sweat was overwhelming.

*

In the moment that lightning lit up the school, Freddie saw the silhouette of Lily with Stan towering over her.

He leaped out of the car and ran up the path. Without hesitation, he mounted the steps and grabbed Stan with savage strength. Stan fell backwards and Freddie held him by the scruff of the neck. With a ferocity and a strength Lily had never seen before, Freddie banged Stan against the wall again and again.

Stan's fear was palpable. Urine began to trickle down his leg and puddle at his feet. His eyes blinked with terror like the shutters of his soul.

'My God,' said Freddie as he looked down at Stan in disgust. He lifted him higher so that his feet almost dangled in mid-air.

'Remember this, Stan Coe. If you ever go near Lily again, I will find you and next time I will not be so generous.' With that he punched him in the solar plexus and dropped him to the floor.

'No more,' pleaded Stan, 'no more.'

Freddie stepped back. 'Now move before I change my mind.'

Stan clambered up unsteadily, coughing violently, and staggered back to his car.

Freddie knelt down beside Lily. He put his arms around her. 'It's okay,' he said softly. 'You're safe now.'

Lily stopped shaking. 'Please don't say anything to anyone, Freddie. Please don't.'

'We have to, Lily. Scum like that need to be dealt with.'

'But it may not be dealt with. It will be his word against mine.'

'And mine,' said Freddie.

'But that's what it's like, Freddie. You're still young. They wouldn't listen to you – and think what would happen if Tom found out. He would kill him and then where would we be?'

Freddie knew she was telling the truth.

Things had to change.

The world had to change.

He prayed that one day it would.

Back in Laurel Cottage Freddie helped Lily into the lounge. 'Let me take your coat. You sit down and I'll get you a drink.'

Lily began to relax. 'Thanks, a cup of tea would be fine.'

'No, I want you to have a small brandy first to steady your nerves.'

Lily simply nodded, aware that there had been a subtle change in their roles, with Freddie in control.

As she sipped her brandy Freddie sat down next to her. 'I'm glad I came to school this afternoon.'

Lily looked up in surprise.

'It made me aware of many things I didn't know. You really are an amazing person.'

'That's kind, Freddie.'

'But that's the trouble . . . I haven't been.'

There had been a time when the trust they once shared had been swept away like wheat before a scythe.

He paused as he sought the right words. Then he held her hand. 'You're a special person, Lily, to the school, to the village . . . and to me.'

Chapter Twenty

Changing Times

In the thin light of the pre-dawn, Lily woke to her last day as a teacher at Ragley School. As the morning sunlight lit up the distant hills with golden fire, she knew this was the day of endings. It was Friday, 24 July, the final day of the school year . . . time to say goodbye. The air seemed heavy, promising another day of summer heat, and she chose her lightest summer dress.

During the drive to school she recalled a journey long ago when she had cycled to Ragley and Stan Coe had forced her off the road. Scratched and bruised, she had been rescued by Tom Feather, then the local police sergeant. That's when it began and for the second time in her life she had fallen in love. Now she was following Tom to the north-east and a new life.

Beyond the hedgerows the fields of barley swayed in the gentle breeze. The cycle of life and the rhythm of the seasons had been the heartbeat of her world. She had enjoyed her days in the Yorkshire sun, but they were over now. Ragley School would go on without her. She smiled, but with a hint of sadness.

When she arrived in the car park she paused and looked up at the school that had become her life. The echoes of silent music were around her as she recalled happy times. So many experiences, so many memories.

Her reverie was broken when a familiar voice called out, 'G'mornin', Mrs Feather.'

It was Ruby Smith. 'Good morning, Ruby, and how are you?'

'Fine, thank you. Hope you enjoy y'las' day.'

'Have you any plans for the holiday?'

'Well, 'part from me an' Mrs Trott givin' t'school a good clean, Ronnie reckons we can afford t'go t'Scarborough in a caravan . . . but then again, pigs might fly.'

'Well, I hope it works out for you, Ruby.'

'So do I. M'kiddies need a 'oliday.'

On the far side of the village green Deirdre Coe walked by on her way to the Post Office and gave Lily and Ruby a withering glance. Ruby shook her head. 'She's a reight flibbertigibbet is that one. Never a kind word.'

'Oh dear,' said Lily.

'An' that brother o' 'ers is a proper barmpot an', come t'think of it, 'e's not been seen since 'e got drunk in t'Pig an' Ferret t'other night. It were all round t'village . . . prob'ly sleepin' it off.'

Lily remained silent.

'Anyway, mus' get on,' said Ruby. 'No rest for t'wicked.'

Her chestnut curls waved in the gentle breeze and her cheeks were red with the effort of sweeping the entrance steps, but Ruby's unflagging enthusiasm had always impressed Lily. As she walked away with her yard broom, Lily wondered what would become of this hard-working lady.

It was a busy morning in Lily's class and she was pleased with the children. She pondered on the fact that all of them were to experience change and wondered how they would cope with a new teacher.

At morning break Lily volunteered to do playground duty, mainly because she wanted to watch the children at play in the sunshine. She leaned against the school wall, while her heart felt like the fluttering of butterflies. It was a strange sensation as the world she knew so well was coming to a close.

Suddenly Henry Tonks was at her side. 'Miss, ah'm lookin' forward to this afternoon. Colin's brought his Scalextric.'

John Pruett had agreed to a games afternoon and the children had brought in their toys, dolls and comic books.

'It should be fun,' agreed Lily.

Henry looked thoughtful. 'Ah move up after the 'oliday, Miss, an' Colin said y'get *caned* in Mr Pruett's class.'

Lily sighed. She wasn't in favour of corporal punishment and had never used it, yet behaviour had always been excellent in her classes. 'Well, only if you're naughty – and you have always been a good boy, so don't worry.'

'Thanks, Miss, an' ah'm sorry y'leavin'. Ah've enjoyed being in your class.'

'That's kind of you to say so, Henry.'

He nodded phlegmatically. 'Thing is, Miss, it's like our cows.'

'Your cows?'

'Yes, Miss, they all grow up an' 'ave t'move on.'

Lily smiled. From the mouths of babes ... even if the analogy wasn't ideal. 'Very true, Henry.'

He ran off to join Shane Ramsbottom, who, unbeknown to Lily and out of sight, was demonstrating to an admiring crowd how far he could spit up the wall of the cycle shed.

Chris Wojciechowski was chasing Trevor Poskitt when he stopped suddenly. 'Miss, I'm eight now.'

'That's wonderful,' said Lily, smiling at this eager little boy.

'It's great, Miss.'

'Is it?'

'Yes, Miss – it's the oldest I've ever been.' He stared up at Lily. "Ow old are you, Miss?'

Lily considered a suitable reply. 'I'm in my thirties.'

It was clear he found this difficult to compute. 'Flippin' 'eck, Miss, you *are* old!'

Trevor Poskitt shouted out. 'You can't catch me!' and Chris ran off to continue his game of tag while Lily reflected on the innocence of youth.

It was just before lunchtime that Lily had an idea. She would buy a bunch of flowers for Vera. She popped her head around John Pruett's classroom door. 'I'm just going out of school for a few minutes.'

John was writing on the blackboard. He looked across at her and gave a cautious smile.

Lily looked around her as she stepped briskly down the school drive. It was an evocative moment. She had laid a footprint on this village and touched lives. Her memories would echo down the years, but on this her final day, time seemed to slip away like sand through her fingertips.

She walked across the village green and crossed the road. Next door to the Post Office, Muriel Tonks and Diane Wigglesworth were chattering like magpies outside the Hair Salon and gave Lily a friendly wave.

She stopped outside Nora's Coffee Shop and remembered that first day when she had stepped off William Featherstone's Reliance bus. The sign above the door had read 'DORIS CLUTTERBUCK'S TEA ROOMS'. Times change. Now teenagers were drinking their frothy coffees and listening to pop records. Post-war austerity was in the past and the number-one record, 'A Hard Day's Night', could be heard through the open doorway.

Timothy Pratt was outside his Hardware Emporium arranging a display of garden chairs with his usual precision and he gave a nervous smile as Lily passed by. In the doorway of the Pharmacy Herbert Grinchley was on duty watching everyone as they walked past. He missed nothing and added Lily's bright summer dress to his list of topics to be relayed to those villagers eager for gossip. Tommy Piercy, in his butcher's shop and always the gentleman, raised his straw boater when he saw her through the window.

The bell above the door of the General Stores tinkled brightly as Lily walked in. The shop was empty and Prudence stepped up behind the counter.

'What a lovely surprise, Lily. Jeremy was hoping to see you before you left.'

Lily looked up at the bear. 'He's certainly enjoying the summer weather,' she said.

Jeremy was wearing colourful striped beach shorts and a pair of sunglasses.

Prudence smiled. 'Now what can I get you, Lily?'

'A large bunch of flowers please.'

A dozen bunches were neatly displayed in vases near the window but out of direct sunlight.

Lily considered the selection. 'Roses, please, Prudence.'

Prudence glanced up. 'Jeremy says it's an excellent choice.'

'Thank you, Jeremy,' acknowledged Lily.

As Prudence went to wrap the flowers she murmured, 'Jeremy bought me roses once,' and Lily knew she wasn't talking about the bear.

Back in school, Vera was tidying her desk when Lily walked into the office. She handed over the flowers. 'A small token of my appreciation, Vera.'

'What a very kind thought,' said Vera. 'Thank you so much.' She gave Lily a hug. 'I'll put them in water for now. I told Mr Pruett I would stay on for the afternoon games.'

Lily paused in the doorway. 'I'll never forget your support, Vera.'

'That's what friends are for,' said Vera with a smile.

And there are secrets we take to our graves, thought Vera as the door closed. The room was silent and dust motes hovered in a shaft of sunlight. She scanned the row of school photographs on the office wall. For the past decade Lily had featured sitting next to John Pruett and now Vera wondered what the future might bring for him.

It proved to be a relaxing afternoon for the staff as they wandered from one group of children to another and discussed the various toys that had arrived. Susan Derwood and Janet Ollerenshaw were playing with a Sindy doll.

Tobias Fawnswater was listening to Clint Ramsbottom's chest with his Dr Kildare stethoscope and assuming a serious expression. Colin Appleyard and Norman Barraclough had pushed some tables together and set up Colin's Scalextric set and an enthusiastic crowd had gathered to cheer them on. Meanwhile, the Walmsley twins were sitting in the corner of the hall reading their *Fireball XL5* annual.

Finally, when the bell rang for the end of school, the children ran out of the school gate excited at the thought of six weeks of freedom, climbing trees, playing hide-and-seek and holidays at the seaside. From her classroom Lily heard their distant shouts as she sat at her desk and emptied the last of her belongings into her shoulder bag. She hated goodbyes. More than anything, she wanted peace, to be alone, away from the noise and clamour around her. She walked into the staff-room and filled the kettle.

It was a subdued Anne Grainger who joined her there. The room was quiet. Vera had said farewell to Lily and had left school, while John Pruett was busy with his logbook in the office.

'Good luck, Lily. Keep in touch.'

'Of course, Anne. I'll miss our orchestra and choir.'

'And they will miss you and your lovely voice.'

Lily grinned. 'Remember when you were a student here?'

'Seems a long time ago. I've learned a lot since then.'

'I'm so pleased you will be doing the deputy's job.'

'Well, let's see how it goes,' Anne answered cautiously.

'You'll be fine.'

'How did *you* feel when Tom got the job in Durham?'

'*Mixed* to be honest . . . but it was such a good opportunity for him.'

Anne sighed. 'Do we always have to follow our men?'

'Not always. I think Tom would have followed me to a new teaching post.'

'Really? I'm not sure *my* husband would have done the same.'

Deep down, Lily knew Anne was right. John Grainger was too set in his ways.

'Cup of tea?' she asked.

Anne gave a wan smile. 'Yes, please.'

When Vera walked down the cobbled drive to the school gate clutching her flowers, she spotted Lily's car parked next to the village green. Freddie was leaning against the bonnet and looking towards the Morton road. He was thinking of Rose.

'Oh, hello, Miss Evans.'

'Freddie, good to see you. Are you waiting for Lily?'

'Yes, and Tom said he would come here straight from work. We're going for a bite to eat in The Oak.'

'A lovely idea. I'm sure Lily will enjoy that. It will give her a chance to relax after an emotional day. We're all so sad to see her go.'

'Yes, I understand,' he said quietly.

'I do hope you achieve the A-level results you are hoping for.'

Freddie smiled. 'Yes, fingers crossed.'

'I hear that Leeds University is your first choice.'

Freddie nodded. 'The course looks ideal, so I'm hopeful.'

'I'm sure you will do well there.'

As he pushed his long wavy hair out of his eyes it occurred to Vera that he had changed from a boy into a handsome young man.

'And good luck in your new home in Durham. Exciting times.'

'Yes, looking forward to it.' He glanced at the school entrance but there was no sign of Lily.

Vera wanted to pass on a final message before Lily arrived. 'Freddie, do be proud of your achievements. Work hard, be true to yourself and don't shirk from honest toil. Time is precious.'

'Thank you, Miss Evans, I'll do my best.'

Vera looked steadily at the young man before her. 'Remember, these are changing times. You have one life – make the most of it . . . in all respects.'

As she walked away, Freddie wondered about this perceptive lady and the life she had chosen. She had been Lily's friend for many years, always in the background as he had moved through his teenage years, but this was probably the first meaningful conversation he had experienced with her. However, the message was clear: *one life, one chance* – and he was determined to grasp the opportunities before him.

John Pruett was sitting at his desk when Lily walked in. The school logbook was open and he was finding it difficult to write of Lily's departure.

He stood up and Lily saw the pain on his face.

'I came to say thank you, John, for your kindness over the years.'

John struggled for words. 'We shall all miss you, Lily.'
I shall miss you, he thought.

'Goodbye, John. I'll write to let you know how things go.'

'I'm sure you will do well.'

'Thank you for all your help in the past, especially when I first arrived here. There was much to learn.'

'I think it was *I* who learned from you.'

'You've been a wonderful colleague.' She stretched out her hand.

'Thank you, Lily.' He took a step closer. *I wanted to be more than that.*

They shook hands, then Lily turned and left.

John sat down again. On the wall the office clock ticked on. He looked at the time. It was five thirty and Lily had gone. He took a handkerchief from his pocket but he was too late to prevent a teardrop landing on the page.

A word became smudged and would remain so for ever.

Tom had driven into Ragley from Northallerton. He parked his car outside The Royal Oak and walked across the green to join Freddie at the school gate.

'Hi, Tom,' said Freddie.

Tom nodded towards the school. 'So Lily is still in there?'

'Saying goodbye, I guess.'

'John Pruett will take it hard. Lily has transformed the place. He'll miss her.'

They both glanced up. Above the pantile rooftops a flock of swifts were screaming noisily as they swooped up the Morton road towards St Mary's Church and beyond. It was then that Lily appeared, walking down the cobbled drive. She paused at the gate and looked back at the bell tower. It was a view she knew so well. Then she hurried over to Tom and Freddie.

'What a lovely surprise.'

'We thought we would come to meet you,' said Tom.

Freddie smiled. 'And go to The Oak for something to eat and a celebratory drink. Rose said she would join us there.'

A few minutes later Tom and Lily walked into The Royal Oak with Freddie and Rose following behind. They sat down at the table in the bay window.

Tom looked at the specials board. 'It's fish, chips and mushy peas.'

'Well it *is* Friday,' said Lily.

'A feast on a summer's evening,' said Freddie with a grin.

'Fine with me,' said Rose.

'And me,' said Freddie.

Lily looked up at Tom and Freddie. 'You know how to treat a lady,' she said with a smile.

Freddie followed Tom to the bar, where Sheila shouted the food order to Don and began pulling two pints of Chestnut.

'We'll miss you,' said Sheila with an appreciative look at the two tall men before her. 'Thanks for keepin' t'peace, Inspector . . . me an' Don are grateful t'you an' Sergeant Dew'irst.'

'And two glasses of white wine, please,' said Freddie.

Sheila glanced at Rose. 'You've gorra lovely girlfriend there. Look after 'er.'

'I will,' said Freddie.

*

328

In the hush of the cool, silent church Vera was content in her work decorating the pulpit with a display of flowers. They were the flowers Lily had given to her and a poignant reminder of their time together in this beautiful building.

She heard footsteps behind her. It was Joseph.

'God loveth a cheerful giver,' he said.

Vera put the finishing touches to the arrangement. 'There are so many beautiful flowers, Joseph. It seems a shame not to share them.'

A beam of light shone down on Vera from one of the arched windows. 'You have a great gift,' said Joseph quietly.

'We *all* have gifts, Joseph, and *yours* are very special.'

'That's kind, Vera.' He knew why she was here. 'You always come here when you need to find peace.'

Vera stood back from the pulpit and considered her creation. Satisfied, she turned towards Joseph. 'It's been a day of light and shade. I've said goodbye to a dear friend, but life goes on.' She sighed with a heavy heart.

Joseph looked with deep affection at his sister. Her eyes were soft with recent tears. He put his arm around her shoulder and they walked out of the church and into the vicarage.

'I noticed the chocolate cake you made, Vera,' he said hopefully.

'Yes, shall we have a slice?'

'Perfect,' said Joseph. 'Let's sit in the garden – it's a beautiful evening.'

Vera looked at her brother. 'And a hot drink, Joseph.' She knew what would surprise him. 'Perhaps a cup of coffee?'

'Coffee?' Joseph was both delighted and astonished.

'We could get out of the sideboard that delightful Queen Anne coffee set you gave me last Christmas.'

Joseph smiled. 'A wonderful idea, Vera.' He had known the delicate rose yellow crockery would appeal to Vera and thought that everything comes to he who waits.

Later, they sat together in their flower garden enjoying the breath of roses along with coffee and cake and watched the sun gradually sink behind the distant hills.

In The Royal Oak they had finished their meal. Lily felt relaxed and enjoyed speaking with Rose.

'So have you any holiday plans?'

'Yes,' said Rose. 'We're driving to Brittany. Dad's rented a gîte near Concarneau for a couple of weeks. So I'll be able to practise my French.'

'That sounds wonderful,' said Lily.

'Then it's back for my results and, hopefully, on to university.'

'We shall have moved by then, although I expect I shall drive down with Freddie to collect his results.'

'I shall hope to see you then.'

Lily looked at this positive young woman with her life in front of her and wondered about the choices she would make. Rash decisions didn't appear to be part of her persona.

As the evening wore on, singing could be heard from the taproom. Deke Ramsbottom was entertaining the drinkers with a rendition of 'Do Not Forsake Me, O My Darling', the ballad from *High Noon*, while Ronnie Smith was on his fourth pint of Tetley's and reading the *Sporting Life*.

Gradually darkness fell, until out of the bay window there was only a sliver of orange light on the far horizon. Lily looked out at the Hambleton hills as they shimmered in the summer heat haze and the sky seemed on fire with backlit clouds. The cycle of life in Ragley village was moving on. Tom was sharing his news with Rose about their new home in the north-east and Freddie was talking about saving up for a car while he was at university. On a full grant this was possible and Timothy Pratt had given him a neatly typed and very supportive reference.

Tom and Freddie had got up to go to the bar to order another round of drinks.

Rose appeared animated. 'I'm sure it will be exciting for you,' she said. 'Just think of all the new places that you can visit. I've never been to Durham Cathedral.'

'Well you must come and stay and we can visit it together.'

'I should love to do that.'

'We were talking about Durham, Freddie,' said Rose as he and Tom arrived with the drinks. 'I would love to look round the cathedral. Why don't we plan to do that in the summer holidays before we go to university?'

'Great idea,' said Freddie. 'Let's just hope we get the results we need.'

Lily sensed his urgency and there was no doubt about the depth of feeling he had for this young woman.

'You will be fine,' said Tom. 'If ever two young people deserved to get to their first choice of university, it's you two. You couldn't have worked any harder.'

'That's true,' agreed Lily. 'Whatever the outcome, I am

proud of you. It's a time of new beginnings, for you . . . and for all of us.' She looked up at Tom.

He smiled at her. 'Yes, a fresh start in a new home. I'm looking forward to it.'

'So am I,' said Freddie. He paused and looked directly at Lily. 'A new start for us all and a time to move on.'

Lily glanced up at him and heard his words. At last she felt she had found a precious tranquillity and her soul was singing.

Freddie leaned across the table and took her hand. 'Durham will be a place where no one knows you as my sister – they will only ever know you as *my mother.*'

Rose and Tom smiled at each other, knowing the import of these few words.

Lily's face was radiant with a joy that she had longed for. Suddenly, life was a blank sheet of paper, the future was a new story and the words had yet to be written.

'Freddie . . . my son,' she said quietly.

And in a heartbeat Lily's son was hers once more.

Epilogue

Lily Feather became a successful headteacher in Durham and Tom proved to be one of the north-east's finest chief inspectors. They remained there for the rest of their lives.

Freddie Briggs and Rose McConnell both gained first-class degrees at Leeds University and married in 1968. They had two children, Thomas Rudolph Briggs and Lily Rose Mary Briggs. After Freddie had completed his doctorate they moved to London, where Freddie taught German studies and Rose became a teacher of English in a comprehensive school. They visited Hamburg every year to spend a week with Rudi.

Sam Grundy went on to play rugby at a high level. He had a long string of girlfriends and three marriages, but no one ever loved him as Joy Popplewell had done. Joy met a boat builder from Auckland while at university in London. They moved to New Zealand and lived a happy life with their three children.

Vera Evans continued to run Ragley School in her

efficient style, while Ruby Smith worked hard, loved her children and despaired of the unemployed Ronnie.

After Lily's departure Anne Grainger became deputy headteacher and the local supply teacher, Valerie Flint, agreed to teach Class 2 until a permanent appointment could be made.

Sally Nobbs returned to teach at Ragley School a few years later. By then she had married a reformed beatnik named Colin Pringle.

John Pruett was never the same after Lily left. The light of his life had gone out. However, his love for his work never diminished. He remained at Ragley School until his retirement in 1977 when he was replaced by a young Jack Sheffield.

'If you loved *Changing Times*, why
not see where it all began?'

TEACHER, TEACHER!
Jack Sheffield

It's 1977 and Jack Sheffield is appointed headmaster
of a small village primary school in North Yorkshire.
So begins Jack's eventful journey through the school
year and his attempts to overcome the many
problems that face him as a young and
inexperienced headmaster.

The many colourful chapters include Ruby the
20-stone caretaker with an acute spelling problem,
a secretary who worships Margaret Thatcher, a villager
who grows giant carrots, a barmaid/parent who requests
sex lessons, and a five-year-old boy whose language
is colourful in the extreme. And then there's also
beautiful, bright Beth Henderson, who is irresistibly
attractive to the young headmaster . . .

PLEASE SIR!
Jack Sheffield

It's 1981, the time of Adam and the Ants, Rubik's Cube, the Sony Walkman and the Falklands War, as headteacher Jack Sheffield returns to Ragley-on-the-Forest School for another rollercoaster year.

Vera, the ever-efficient school secretary, has to grapple with a new-fangled computer – and enjoys a royal occasion – while Ruby the caretaker rediscovers romance with a Butlin's Redcoat. And for Jack, wedding bells are in the air. But the unexpected is just round the corner . . .

EDUCATING JACK
Jack Sheffield

As September 1982 arrives, Jack Sheffield returns to
Ragley-on-the-Forest village school for his sixth year
as headteacher. It's the time of *E.T.* and Greenham
Common, Prince William's birth, *Fame* leg warmers and
the puzzling introduction of the new 20p piece. Nora
Pratt celebrates twenty-five years in her coffee shop,
Ronnie Smith finally tries to get a job, and little Krystal
Entwhistle causes concern in the school's Nativity play.

Meanwhile, for Jack, the biggest
surprise of his life is in store . . .

SCHOOL'S OUT!
Jack Sheffield

As the new school year begins, Jack Sheffield prepares
for an even more eventful year than usual.
A new teacher is appointed, and before
long tongues start to wag.

Meanwhile, five-year-old Madonna Fazackerly
makes her mark in an unexpected way, life
changes dramatically for Ruby the caretaker and,
in the village coffee shop, Dorothy Humpleby
plans a dirty weekend.

It's the era of the new CD player, the McDonald's
McNugget, the threat of a miners' strike and a final
farewell to the halfpenny piece.

Jack has to manage a year of triumph and tragedy . . .

SILENT NIGHT
Jack Sheffield

1984 – the time of the miners' strike, Trivial Pursuit, Band Aid, Cabbage Patch dolls, and a final goodbye to the pound note as Jack returns for a new school year.

Christmas is an important time for the children of Ragley-on-the-Forest school . . . They are to sing a carol in a church in York, and are actually going to be on television! Keeping his excited children, not to mention their parents, under control during these momentous events taxes Jack and his staff to the limit. But little Rosie Sparrow's singing brings some special Christmas magic, and the lives of several people are transformed as a result.

STAR TEACHER
Jack Sheffield

It's 1985, and as Jack returns for another year
as headteacher at Ragley-on-the-Forest village school,
some changes are in store.

It's the year of Halley's Comet, *Dynasty* shoulder
pads, Roland Rat and Microsoft Windows. And at
Ragley-on-the-Forest, Heathcliffe Earnshaw decides
to enter the village scarecrow competition, Ruby the
caretaker finds romance, and retirement
looms for Vera the secretary.

Meanwhile, Jack has to battle with some
rising stars of the teaching profession to
save his job and his school . . .